WHEN BLOOD CALLS

WHEN PLEASURE RULES

"Rich with moral dilemmas, steamy sex and a timeless political feud between vampires and werewolves, there's something for all paranormal fans here. . . . Sexy, dark and intense."
—*RT Book Reviews*

"Right from the get-go, Lissa and Rand's story grabs you and won't let go. . . . *When Pleasure Rules* is a super-fun, action-packed, and let's not forget sizzling story."
—Night Owl Romance

"*When Pleasure Rules* lives up to the standard set by *When Blood Calls*. The tension is high, the action is intense, and the romance is scorching."
—Bitten by Books

WHEN WICKED CRAVES

BY J. K. BECK

When Blood Calls
When Pleasure Rules
When Wicked Craves
Shadow Keepers: Midnight (eBook)
When Passion Lies

WHEN PASSION LIES

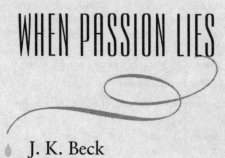

J. K. Beck

A SHADOW KEEPERS NOVEL

BANTAM BOOKS
NEW YORK

A Bantam Books Mass Market Original

Copyright © 2012 by Julie Kenner

Excerpt from *When Darkness Hungers* by J. K. Beck copyright © 2012 by Julie Kenner

"Shadow Keepers: Midnight" by J. K. Beck copyright © 2011 by Julie Kenner

Published in the United States by Bantam Books, an imprint of The Random House Publishing Group, a division of Random House, Inc., New York.

BANTAM BOOKS and the rooster colophon are registered trademarks of Random House, Inc.

ISBN 978-0-345-52563-5
eBook ISBN 978-0-345-52564-2

This book contains an excerpt from the forthcoming novel *When Darkness Hungers* by J. K. Beck. This excerpt has been set for this edition only and may not reflect the final content of the forthcoming edition.

"Shadow Keepers: Midnight" by J. K. Beck was originally published as an eBook original by Bantam Books, an imprint of The Random House Publishing Group, a division of Random House, Inc., in 2011.

Cover art: Craig White

Printed in the United States of America

www.bantamdell.com

9 8 7 6 5 4 3 2 1

Bantam Books mass market edition: June 2012

To Shauna, an amazing editor. Thanks.

CHAPTER 1

France, 1720

The abandoned farmhouse stood in a clearing fifteen miles outside Marseilles. Inside, Caris and Tiberius waited for word from Richard, the hours passing so slowly that Caris feared she would pull her hair out in frustration.

"Something has happened to him," she said to her lover's back. "We were wrong about him. The sickness has taken him." The thought ripped through her. It had been her suggestion to send one of Tiberius's most trusted men into the port city where the plague was cutting through the population like wildfire. They'd believed that Richard was immune to the Black Death, as he'd already survived the plague twice, though many friends had died at his side. Vampires who'd become ill and then faded into dust as if they'd been staked.

Her worry kept her in motion, and she paced the small structure, moving in and out of the shafts of moonlight streaming down through the dilapidated roof.

At the window, Tiberius turned to face her. As always, she was struck by the unchanging beauty of his face. Not feminine, but rugged and strong, with dark eyes that saw everything and broad shoulders onto which he'd invited the weight of the world. Tonight, that weight was heavy indeed.

"He'll be here," Tiberius said. He held out his hand to

her, and she went to him, letting his arms engulf her, pressing her cheek against his chest. Even after more than two hundred years, it was his touch that calmed her best. His lips soothed her fears, and his body made her feel alive, even though life had slipped from her veins so long ago.

"And what if he couldn't find it? We have to kill it." The world had been tormented long enough by the vile creatures. The shadowers believed this to be the last surviving hybrid, and it needed to die. The horror had to end.

"We will find it. And *I* will kill it. That is not in question." He tilted her chin up and looked into her eyes. "The only question for tonight is where that happy occasion will occur. Richard will bring us news of our destination."

She nodded, grim. Humans might not understand the horrible illness that befell them century after century, but the shadowers did. Vampires like her and Tiberius. Werewolves. Jinns and para-daemons and all the other creatures that humans feared and prayed were only myths and nightmares.

They weren't. They were real.

And the hybrids? Though rare, a mix of vampire and werewolf was truly a creature plucked from nightmares. Feared and reviled even among the shadow creatures themselves, a hybrid brought destruction with its touch and desolation with its breath. The Black Death. The plague. Whatever you called it, it always ended the same. Festering wounds. A hacking cough. And slow, torturous death that filled entire towns with doors marked in bold red X's, silent reminders that the plague had come to those within.

Caris pressed her hand to Tiberius's back. "Do you think this one changed form on purpose?" she asked. "Do you think it wanted to destroy Marseilles?"

Tiberius stroked her hair. "I don't know. But I fear the answer is yes."

"This time, I will fight at your side." Whenever he stepped out in battle, she felt as if the birds ceased chirping and the tides stopped their eternal pull.

"No."

"Am I not strong? Am I not capable? Even when I was human, you said that I had uncommon strength for a woman." They'd met after she'd set out to rescue her brother Antonio from the clutches of a particularly vile werewolf, not realizing that Tiberius had already sworn allegiance to her family and had set out to do the same. He'd found her disguised as a boy, battling a singularly nasty clutch of humans.

His lips curved into a proud smile. "Whether human or vampire, you are exceptional."

"Then why do you refuse me? Did you not train me as a warrior? Have I not already fought at your side many times?"

"We've spoken of this before, Caris. I made a mistake. You are my heart and my soul. You understand me more than any woman ever has or ever could. And I cannot lose you." He clutched her hands tightly on these last words, his eyes boring so deeply into hers that she couldn't help but see the fear—and the regret.

Less than fifty years prior they'd fought side by side in an abandoned palazzo. She'd been unaware that a moldering tapestry at her back hid a secret passage, and when a werewolf burst through with a stake, it was almost the end of her. Fortunately, he missed her heart, but she'd fallen, blood gushing from her, her strength leaving her.

For the first time, she'd seen Tiberius's daemon, the depraved creature that every vampire fought to keep buried lest he be compelled to do little more than rend and kill. She saw it—and it was a terrifying thing indeed. He moved with speed born of millennia, and he was on the werewolf in a second, his fist breaking through the weren's rib cage, his hand thrusting the still-beating heart high.

She could remember the scent of him as he knelt over her, covered in the werewolf's blood. A harsh, angry scent mixed with a terror she'd never before experienced, nor ever again. *His terror.* Not of the wolf, but of losing her.

He'd ripped his own flesh open and she'd drunk, and only once he was sure she was healed did his daemon fade into the background and his eyes clear, so it was only Tiberius she saw, and not the daemon within.

After that, she no longer fought at his side. The odd battle, yes, if they were taken by surprise. But she did not set out on missions. He had his *kyne* for that. Men. Brothers, in loyalty if not in blood.

She was his woman, his lover, his friend, and his confidant. She was his political advisor and strategist. His right hand in everything except that one part of his life. It should have been enough for her. She should have willingly accepted it.

But she couldn't. Her own daemon cried out for a fight, and it was the battles that kept it down, easily subdued. Without that, it paced and gnawed and begged for release.

Without that, she was missing a huge part of their life

together. She would stand for it no more. He might not yet have accepted it, but this time, Caris would fight at his side.

As if to punctuate her resolve, the door behind her blew open with a gust of wind. She whipped around, sword drawn, and saw a black cat leap through the doorway and then transform into Richard, who stood before them with a bloody wound at his shoulder.

"Speak," Tiberius said as she moved to his side. "Did you see the hybrid?"

"I did not, but I met many weren in town. They are well, but they flee anyway. The hybrid's power comes from a curse and they believe their survival is tainted." Not much was understood about how a hybrid was created, and what little was known was a mixture of fact and myth. It was said to have started with a feud between two warring brothers who murdered a third brother to steal his power. Having done so, the two became the founders of the shadow world—the first vampire and the first werewolf. But the blood of the third seeped into the ground, and from within the earth he cursed them never to find peace.

As a physical manifestation of that curse, any creature that was a weren-vampire mix had blood that burned through flesh. Moreover, upon changing into a wolf, the hybrid sent an illness out into the world from which only either vampires or werewolves were spared—but which species survived depended entirely on the underlying nature of the hybrid in question.

It was that peculiar immunity that was the truly dastardly part of the curse. Vampires were immune to the sickness wrought by an original werewolf bitten and turned by a vampire. And werewolves were immune to the sickness wrought by an original vampire bitten and changed by a weren. But how either was changed in the first place was a mystery. Because as far as the shadowers knew, the vampiric transition was fatal to a werewolf, and no vampire could survive the transition forced upon it by the bite of a werewolf.

"So no news of the hybrid?" Caris asked.

"On that account, fate smiled," Richard said. "I met a weren who stayed hidden as the hybrid passed by. He overheard the beast muttering. The hybrid travels this night to Cluny."

Tiberius nodded, taking in the information. "Your shoulder?"

"Courtesy of Faro Lihter," Richard said. "Apparently he was offended that I wasn't already dead."

"And the vampires?" Caris asked.

"All dead. Except for me. I know not why, but if there is a God, I thank him." He shifted, focusing hard on Tiberius. "Lihter was praising the beast that did it, saying it was clear now which of the ancient brothers had true strength. He said he couldn't wait for the day when all vampires were dust and the order of the world could be restored." He glanced ruefully at his shoulder. "That's when I got distracted from my mission. I'm happy to say he looks worse."

"Good man," Tiberius said.

"There's more," Richard said. "After Cluny, the hybrid intends to continue to London. And, Tiberius, I believe it is mad. It didn't wait for a full moon at Marseilles. It will not wait in London."

Beside Caris, Tiberius tensed, his hand going automatically to his blade. London was the center of the vampire community, and had been since the founding of Londinium by the Romans. The vampire population there was the highest in all of Europe, and every vampiric representative to the Alliance table made his home there.

Caris squeezed Tiberius's hand. "This is your chance. You already hold the governorship to three territories. Defeat this creature before it can infect London, and the people will demand that you sit at the Alliance table. You know Tomas will not lift even a finger." The current vampire representative to the Alliance was a self-important slug who would flee in terror rather than fight to save his people, and then blame his cowardice on others. The faster Tiberius could unseat him, the better.

She could tell from his eyes that Tiberius had already thought of that.

"Go," he said to Richard. "Take Caris with you. Feed if you must to regain your strength, but go with all speed to London. Tell them of the news. And tell them that I will stop the beast before it reaches the city."

"I shall not go," Caris said.

"You shall," Tiberius insisted.

"No." She crossed her arms and stared him down. "I'll not be tucked away in London while you fight for your life, for all our lives. I will fight at your side, Tiberius, and you cannot stop me."

He took a step toward her, his face as harsh as she had ever seen it. "I believe that I can."

It was a fair point. "Perhaps. But it would take time. You tell me that you will not fall prey to its illness, and so I must assume that you will fight by stealth. If you are safe, then I am, too. Presumably it doesn't know its mutterings were overheard. We have the element of surprise."

"The task falls upon *my* head," Tiberius said.

"It does," she agreed. "And when you perform it, I will be at your side. Even if I have to abandon Richard and double back to assist you."

He wasn't happy, that much was obvious. And he stood for two full minutes before finally turning to Richard. "Go," he said.

Richard wasted no time. He nodded to Tiberius and Caris, then disappeared into the night, presumably to feed before rushing home.

"Then you have accepted that I will fight at your side?"

A muscle at his jaw twitched. "Accept, no? But I am resigned to the reality of the situation."

She smiled brightly. "That is sufficient for now."

"Are you well fed? We must transform ourselves if we wish to get to Cluny with all speed."

She was, and they shifted into spine-tailed swifts, sleek birds with incredible speed. Even so, Cluny was far. By the time they reached the city, they had less than an hour to both locate and kill the creature before they had to find shelter from the sunrise.

"Where?" she asked. "And how will we know it?" It was a fair question. If the hybrid transformed, they would recognize it by the humanoid shape moving on all fours, with elongated limbs and a wolven snout. They'd also know it because they would both be dead, a casualty of its mere existence.

"The scent of both weren and vampire should be upon it," Tiberius said. "That, and the smell of death still clinging to it from Marseilles."

"Shall we split up?"

He shook his head. "I am resigned to having you here, but you will stay at my side. We must make a stop first, but then we'll head to the abbey. Perhaps he seeks redemption for what he is about to do."

It was a solid guess. Cluny didn't stand on a direct route to London. So if the hybrid had come here, it was probably for a reason. And Cluny was most famous for its abbey.

They stopped first at a small house near the abbey where the monks gave shelter to travelers. They entered in stealth, found a crossbow and a blade beneath the bed of a sleeping soldier, and left in silence. That was the unfortunate part of transforming to travel. Their weapons could not transform with them.

"The abbey is huge. How will we find him?"

"He will be in the central tower," Tiberius said, his voice as firm as his jaw. "He will wish to feel small so that when he moves on to kill, he can prove that he is powerful after all."

She took his hand and pulled him to a halt, then pressed a soft kiss upon his cheek. He'd told her of the horrors of his youth and she knew that had left him with an understanding of the madness that could stem from both power and servitude. Sometimes the depth of that understanding scared her. Sometimes it mystified her.

But when they entered the central tower, some of what he'd spoken of became clear to her. The room was enormous, the ceiling reaching higher than any she'd ever seen, as if it were trying to reach God himself. Even with all her power—even with immortality looking back at her—she felt as small and weak as a child.

"Come," Tiberius said, pulling her into an archway. "We wish to see him before he sees us."

They'd barely eased into the shadow of an archway when the telltale sound of footfalls echoed. She tensed, uncertain whether it would be the hybrid or a monk moving about the abbey before matins.

She knew the answer soon enough, smelling the creature even before seeing it.

Without having a stake dipped in silver, they had to move quickly. A wooden arrow through the heart would kill a vampire, but not a hybrid. Their plan was for Caris to shoot it through the heart even as Tiberius raced forward to lop off its head. If her aim was true, the heart-shot would at least prevent it from changing—though Tiberius would still be forced to deal with the tainted blood and the hybrid's incredible strength.

It was moving closer . . . closer . . .

She readied the crossbow, felt Tiberius stiffen beside her. "Steady," he whispered, his voice pitched so low only she could hear it. "Do not fire unless you are sure of the shot."

Waiting was a painful thing, like a serpent coiled tightly around her chest. And when the hybrid finally came into her range, it was even closer than she'd anticipated. She adjusted her aim, said a silent prayer, and let the arrow fly. It was as if she'd launched Tiberius as well. He flew from the archway, his blade swinging.

And then everything happened so fast that it seemed to her addled mind to move in slowed time. The arrow penetrated and the hybrid howled, a pained, horrible sound that echoed through the massive tower. Tiberius leaped, but they hadn't counted on the hybrid doing the same thing. Its legs were powerful, and it bounded up and over Tiberius. Though the upward thrust of his sword caught the beast's thigh as it leapfrogged over the vampire, that wound did little damage to the already injured beast.

It landed in front of Caris and she backed away, wishing for her knife, trying desperately to load another arrow despite knowing that it would do no good. It was too close, and vile blood was pumping out, making its clothes smoke and disintegrate. Though she dodged to the left, she knew it was futile, and she readied herself for the pain of melting, burning flesh.

But it didn't come. Instead she felt the pain of a kick to the ribs as Tiberius shoved her out of the way, taking the blow instead. He yelled in agony as the hybrid's blood burned the shirt off his back, cutting into the already deep scars left from his years in the mines and the gladiator ring.

As she rolled to safety and looked up, she saw him execute a perfect spin, leading with the blade, his face a grimace of pain and determination. And then the hybrid's head was on the ground, its body dropping to the floor. Tiberius stood over it, like Perseus with the head of the Gorgon.

"It is done," he said, and then collapsed beside it.

She hurried to him, pulling him out of the way of the expanding pool of blood, then helped him roll over so she could get him out of the burning, smoldering clothes and soothe his back with holy water from the altar.

"My love," he said, as he clutched her hand in his. "It is dead. The last hybrid is dead, and we will survive."

CHAPTER 2

◗ *Present Day*

"So we have a problem on the para-daemon front." Tiberius was speaking to the human who sat in his office, but he wasn't looking at the man. Instead, he was gazing out his window at the traffic on Piccadilly Circus. An apt metaphor for humanity, he thought. No matter how much they rushed, no matter how hard they worked, the end came just the same. For most, anyway. He'd been human once, too. But that was a long time ago.

The human cleared his throat. "If by problem you mean there's no way on God's green earth that Drescher Bovil is giving you the time of day, much less his vote for Alliance chairman, then yes, sir, you have a problem."

Tiberius pressed his lips together, fighting the impulse to smile before he turned around. He admired humans as a group—their art, their literature, their science. As if in each creation they were thumbing their collective noses at death and grasping for some elusive brand of immortality. There was a strength in humanity that he admired—that he remembered even after more than two thousand years.

Yes, as a group, humans were most remarkable. Individually, though, he had to admit that many humans irritated him.

Thankfully, the one seated in his office had proved an exception.

As far as he knew, Severin Tucker had produced no art or literature that would resonate past his lifetime. He'd made no impassioned speech, had fought bravely in no wars.

But unlike other humans Tiberius had encountered since the arrival of the industrial age, Tucker didn't immediately bend over and kiss Tiberius's ass, agreeing with his every word and cowering in fear if he so much as yawned.

It was a welcome change.

That, however, wasn't a fact he intended to share, and when Tiberius turned to face Tucker, the human saw only Tiberius's practiced calm. The facade of a ruler, the poise of an ancient. Tucker saw a leader, not a friend; Tiberius made sure of that. "If there's a problem, we need to deal with it. And as the Alliance members will vote on the new chairman in exactly ten days, we need to deal with it soon."

"We?" Tucker asked. He was sprawled in a chair, his legs extended in front of him, an electronic notepad glowing in his hand. "Not going there, sir. When I took this assignment, we talked about the rules. Information only. No pushing for change. I'm willing to poke around in their heads and make them tell me what they'd normally keep secret, but I'm not going to actually change what they're thinking. I thought we were clear."

Tiberius studied the man's face. "You would defy my direct order?"

Tucker pushed himself up in the chair, straightening his relaxed posture. His throat moved as he swallowed, but to his credit no fear showed on his face. "Yeah. About that, yeah, I would."

"Good."

"Oh." Tucker's brow furrowed. "Well, all right, then."

"Now tell me what else you've learned. Is Bovil going to make a claim for the chairmanship himself?"

"Afraid not. He's throwing his weight behind Lihter." Tucker shrugged. "You already know that Lihter's not susceptible to my particular talent," Tucker added, referring to Faro Lihter, the new Therian representative to the Alliance. The Therians included all shape-shifters, but their leader tended to be a werewolf, and the newest representative was a particularly unpleasant one who had easily wrested the alpha position away from the wounded previous leader, Gunnolf.

Once, Tiberius would have bemoaned Gunnolf's fall from power, not to mention the horrific injury that had caused it. There'd been a time when they'd worked together, Tiberius even managing to forget the beast's weren nature and overcome his inherent distrust of the species.

But now . . .

Now he held not even an ounce of charity for the crippled weren. The beast with whom Caris now shared a bed.

Caris.

The pen he'd been holding snapped in his hand, and he forced her from his thoughts. Now wasn't the time to think of the choice he'd made or the love he'd lost.

"You're right, of course," Tiberius said. "Lihter will undoubtedly challenge me."

"Right. Absolutely. But you survived Sergius's rampage. What started out as a bloodbath turned into political gold for you."

It was a cavalier way to discuss the political ramifications of Gunnolf's injury and the horrific deaths of the previous para-daemon and jinn Alliance representatives, but the bottom line was that Tucker was right. Tiberius had remained standing after the slaughter, and that gave him the appearance of strength and stability, useful assets for a leader. Assets he intended to exploit.

His craving for power had pulsed through him since the day he'd been yanked from his mother's arms and sent to mine the quarries. And that ambition had been burned even deeper when he'd been pulled into the ring and made to fight his friends—to kill them in order to ensure his own survival.

He'd been human then, but his ambition hadn't faded with the change. If anything, it had grown stronger. Before, he'd been merely a man, and a weak one at that. Now he was immortal. He had strength and time and patience. As a human, he would have needed several lifetimes to climb up from the muck into which he'd been thrust.

As an immortal, he had all the time he needed.

He was close now. So close he could count the remaining obstacles on one hand. And one of them was named Drescher Bovil. That problem would have to be handled, quickly and with little fanfare. But not, as Tucker had pointed out, by the human.

The intercom on his desk buzzed, mercifully interrupting his thoughts. "Lucius Dragos is here, sir," Mrs. Todd, his secretary, announced.

Tiberius nodded to Tucker that they were done, then told Mrs. Todd to let him in. The two men—one vampire, one human—nodded to each other as they passed in the doorway. Neither smiled.

"He's Ryan Doyle's lapdog," Luke said, the words coming out before the door had shut entirely behind

Tucker. Undoubtedly, Tucker would repeat that assessment to Doyle, a para-daemon with whom Luke had repeated run-ins. Undoubtedly, that's what Luke wanted him to do.

"Until I cut him loose," Tiberius said, "Tucker is *my* lapdog. So far he's proven to be both skilled and loyal."

"He's been useful?"

"He's been quite effective in areas where we cannot," Tiberius said. As vampires, Luke and Tiberius had the ability to compel the human mind. But they held no such sway over other shadow creatures.

"I'm sure he has been," Luke said as Tiberius watched his face. To anyone other than Tiberius it would have revealed nothing. But Tiberius had brought Luke through the Holding, the ritual to control the daemon that lived in all vampires. He'd trained him. Hell, he'd tamed him. And he relied daily on both Luke's strength and his integrity.

"You don't approve," Tiberius said.

"No."

"Does it matter so much? Cheating wraiths and jinns and para-daemons? Ryan Doyle is a para-daemon. Don't tell me you wouldn't mess with his mind any chance you got."

"Doyle is an ass," Luke said. "And he's not the issue. The Alliance serves a purpose, Tiberius, and it has served it well since the aftermath of the Great Schism," he added, referring to the dark period in history after shadowers had brought about the fall of that great human civilization Rome. History called them barbarians, but it had been marauding, warring shadowers who had ushered in the Dark Ages as they'd fought among themselves, vampire against weren, and all the others falling in line, raising their swords, bathing in blood. It took many years before the Alliance was restored.

"If the Alliance is to remain on its course," Luke continued, "the unity it provides must be true, not the result of manipulation."

"You think I don't agree." Tiberius allowed himself the smallest of smiles. "I thought you knew me better than that."

A hint of relief flickered in Luke's eyes. "You're using Tucker for intelligence," he said. "Not manipulation."

"Tucker is my eyes and ears," Tiberius confirmed. "He has not and will not manipulate anyone to act contrary to themselves." He picked a crystal decanter off the credenza and poured two glasses of scotch. "I'm not interested in manipulating free will. But I have no problem with him suggesting that they open their mouths and reveal their allegiances, their weaknesses, their concerns." He passed a glass to Luke. "Does that violate your code?"

"No." The answer was simple and direct, and held a world of relief.

"When one aspires to live within the bubble that is politics, one must accept the value of espionage. Eavesdropping is a lever. I'm using Tucker to help me move the world."

"And what have you learned?"

"I'm well positioned," Tiberius said. "But not well enough."

Luke nodded, and Tiberius knew that his friend understood. The shadow world was one of hierarchies, ruled by power and longevity and, yes, ruthlessness. The fae community might have power, but they tended to keep to themselves, as did the earthens—trolls and dragons and similar creatures that were unable to move easily within the human world. As a result, political power fell most directly on the jinns, the para-daemons, the vampires, and the Therians. Tiberius needed to ensure that as many of those influential creatures were behind him as possible.

"The jinn are with me," Tiberius continued. "But Drescher Bovil presents a problem."

"The para-daemon. He seeks the chairmanship?"

"Worse. He's throwing his support to Lihter."

"That is worse," Luke agreed. "Ten days is a long time. He could persuade the others to shift their loyalty. Word on the street is Lihter's going to do whatever he can to scrape his way to the top of the food chain."

"Yes. It's a problem that must be dealt with." He turned away from Luke and moved to stand in front of the Monet he'd acquired at the turn of the twentieth century. He'd met the artist, admired his ability to look at the world and see each element so clearly and then ensure that all the pieces worked together to create one stunning, organic whole. It was a skill that served as well in politics and battle as it did in art, and one that Tiberius strived to emulate.

The painting hung over a squat oak bookcase, the ancient wood polished and oiled until it was as smooth as glass. Volumes from Kant, Descartes, Aristotle, and others filled the shelves. On top, lying open, was a copy of Sun Tzu's *The Art of War*.

Tiberius lay his hand gently upon the page. "A victorious warrior wins first, before engaging in war."

"There's no guarantee Bovil's replacement will throw his weight toward you," Luke said, his comment revealing that he understood the direction of Tiberius's thoughts.

"Nothing is ever certain," Tiberius agreed. "But still we try to stack the odds in our favor."

"And Lihter?"

"I'd love to take the bastard out," Tiberius admitted. "But it's not feasible."

"Agreed," Luke said. "You'd be the first suspect in any attempt on Lihter's life. And that's a complication we don't need. Not with the election so close." Luke stood, his expression harsh. "Do you wish me to handle the matter?"

"No." Tiberius crossed to his desk, pressed the intercom, and instructed Mrs. Todd to contact Bael Slater, another vampire among the *kyne*.

"Mrs. Todd?" Luke asked after she clicked off. "What happened to Aretha?"

"We had a misunderstanding," Tiberius said. "She thought that because I welcomed her into my bed, I also welcomed her into my life."

He had blamed himself for the young vampire's misinterpretation of the situation. He'd sought companionship and she'd provided it. When he declined a repeat performance the next evening, she was upset. That being the polite term for trashing a Picasso and threatening to stake him with the edge of the frame.

He'd decided to avoid future misunderstandings by removing temptation. Mrs. Todd had been turned by her son at the age of eighty-seven. She was efficient, prompt, and not in the least bit attractive to him. Or attracted to him, for that matter.

It was the perfect scenario.

"Slater's going to take care of the para-daemon issue,"

Luke said, returning to the business at hand. "But I can't believe you summoned me simply as a sounding board."

"There's something I need you to take care of."

"Whatever you need."

"Since the weren continue to remain my primary weakness, I need to know what my enemy is up to, before and after the chairmanship is determined."

"You want to know what's going on in Lihter's head?"

"Exactly."

"Tucker?"

"Unfortunately, no. I hoped that Tucker would be able to help, but Lihter isn't susceptible to the human's particular skill. We tried. We failed."

"And that leaves you with a lack of intelligence about what's going on in the weren camp."

"Maybe not. There's a man. A werewolf. He's already provided me with enough tidbits of information to prove that he has the potential to be an extremely valuable resource."

"You want me to meet with him," Luke said. "Simple enough. When and where?"

"Zermatt," Tiberius said, referring to the cozy Swiss town that by tradition was neutral territory in both the human and shadow worlds. "Tonight. And you won't be going alone. You'll be accompanying me."

As expected, Luke looked surprised. "It's been a few hundred years since you felt the need to supervise my missions."

"There are circumstances. He says that he has valuable information about Lihter, and he's agreed to be an ongoing source. But in exchange for a favor."

Luke's brow lifted. "An informant with a knack for

negotiating. Sounds like you're going to have your hands full."

"His daughter's been kidnapped. He has reason to believe Lihter took her."

"Why would Lihter want her?"

"He says he doesn't know. Obviously I don't believe him, but until we meet in person, until he trusts that I'll get her back, I doubt he'll tell me."

"So who is he?"

"His name's Cyrus Reinholt. For years, he lived in Paris. He had his own home, but with unencumbered access to the château," Tiberius added, referring to the ancient, sprawling mansion that the werens used as their central location.

"Past tense?"

"He is currently in hiding."

"From Lihter," Luke said, nodding. "If Lihter's taken his daughter, that suggests that Reinholt has something Lihter wants. Any idea what that is?"

"Not yet. Again, I expect the situation will become significantly more clear after we meet."

Luke nodded. "Considering he's hiding, I doubt his information is going to be useful."

"A valid concern," Tiberius admitted. "But I expect he'll have at least some information I can use. And possibly access to other sources."

"You do have another way in, you know."

Tiberius heard the hint of hesitation in Luke's voice, and his head snapped up. "No," he said firmly. "I don't."

"Dammit, Tiberius. You can use her. Hell, you should use her."

Her. Caris.

Within him, the daemon twisted and turned. He'd had millennia to learn how to keep his daemon suppressed. How to control it rather than have it control him. And yet from the moment he'd met Caris, that control was never complete. Every time she'd been in danger, that knowledge had not only ripped him to shreds but had threatened to release the daemon with the same vibrant fury that battered his will whenever he remembered the dark days of abuse at the slave-master Claudius's hand.

And now that Caris herself was weren, just as Claudius had been . . .

He clenched his fists, battling the beast back down. Love and hate. Didn't the poets say they were like Janus? Two sides, but ultimately the same? Certainly in him they were the same at the core—both brought forth the most primitive of emotions, and he could think of neither Caris nor Claudius without falling victim to the thrashing of his daemon.

"No," he said slowly, forcing himself to be calm. To keep control as he'd learned so well to do. "Absolutely not. I won't use her."

"She betrayed you to be with Gunnolf," Luke said. "She can't be happy now that he's out and Lihter's in. If you bring the right pressure to bear, she could be an asset."

"She will have no part of this," Tiberius said, keeping the emotion from his voice even as he kept the memories out of his head. The truth was she hadn't betrayed him—not as Luke believed, anyway. But now was not the time to tell Luke the truth about Caris's secrets. As far as Tiberius was concerned, that time would never come.

"She probably wants Lihter removed as much as we

do," Luke continued. "No matter what she's done, no matter what's between you two, she is still a vampire."

"*No,*" Tiberius said, his voice carrying the weight of finality. "She's taken to a werewolf's bed. Her loyalties lie elsewhere."

A muscle in Luke's jaw twitched, then he nodded, just the briefest dip of his head. "It's your call. I won't mention her again."

"Good," he said, and he meant it. He appreciated Luke's silence, but knew that it wouldn't help. Because no matter how much he wished her away, Caris stayed locked in his thoughts, and he fought the memory of her every single day, mourning what they'd once shared, and knowing that it was lost forever.

And when one was immortal, forever lasted a very long time.

CHAPTER 3

The Alpine bar was dark, so dark that it was hard to see the faces of the men and women huddled around tall tables or leaning against the centuries-old bar, looking for a drink or a good time or both.

Caris stood in deepest shadows, back in the far corner, beyond the dartboard and the karaoke stage where a Teutonic male croaked out the Beatles' "Help!" in broken English.

He spread his arms wide, gyrated his hips, and mangled the chorus. Caris cringed, and in a moment of rare charity hoped that he hadn't come to get laid, because no woman in the bar looked drunk enough to take him home. And that said a lot, since most of the people in the small bar smelled of sex and lust and pure, animal heat. So much so, in fact, that the power of their passion seemed to cling to her, making her skin burn and her hunger build.

But she hadn't come for sex. She'd come for something entirely different.

Caris had come to kill.

Slowly, she scoured the faces of the men in the bar, looking for the one from the picture, the darkness no hindrance to her preternatural vision. He was supposed to be in Zermatt this night, though she didn't know where. But Zermatt was a small town, and she was thorough, the image of his face from the dossier now burned into her mind.

Until she'd received that information from the investigator she'd hired, she'd never even seen his face. During her captivity he'd taken care to hide his features and mask his scent. When she'd first seen his picture, she was surprised by how tame he looked.

She knew better. According to the dossier, the weren's name was Cyrus Reinholt. By all accounts he was an average werewolf, but before he'd been bitten, he'd been a scientist in Germany. She remembered the injections, the studious way her captor had recorded her reactions. *Please. Let her have finally found the right one.*

For nineteen years, she'd followed so many leads, only to find that she'd been stalking the wrong prey.

This time, though . . .

By the gods, this time she had to be right. One more false lead and she feared she would snap. Orion had told her over and over she should simply quit. Pack it in. Throw in the towel and all those other cutesy sayings for giving up, because killing the one who'd done this to her wouldn't change anything. But she couldn't. She *wouldn't.* That would mean that *he* would have won. That he'd taken her perfect life and ripped it into tiny pieces. That he'd turned her into something new. Something reviled. Something toxic.

And that was unacceptable. There was a price for pain.

Tonight, he'd learn just how heavy a price her pain had borne.

One by one, she examined the faces in the bar, ignoring the two blond male vampires hunched in a corner. She wasn't interested in other vamps. Not tonight.

She let her eyes pass over the females, focusing only on the men. The breadth of their chests. The cut of their shoulders. Searching for a man with a bulky frame and the same dark hair and thin mustache reflected on the dossier picture.

He wasn't there.

Goddamn it all, he wasn't there.

With a series of curses burning her tongue, she whirled around. Maybe he was in another bar. Maybe he was hiking the damn Matterhorn. Maybe the universe was playing one big nasty trick on her.

Didn't matter, she thought as a man slipped in front of her, heading for the bar. She knew he'd come to Zermatt. Ultimately she'd find him. Ultimately, she'd—

Tiberius?

It wasn't him, of course. Not the man she'd once loved with every breath in her body. The man who'd ripped her heart to shreds.

The man in front of her wasn't Tiberius. But the midnight-black hair and infinite eyes had caught her attention as surely as Tiberius's had that first night when she'd glimpsed him in her father's house, a stranger offering his services as a warrior. The resemblance was striking, and for the briefest of moments, her throat tightened and her pulse burned, violent anger warring with the deepest of desire.

"Buy you a drink?" the man in front of her asked, and when he spoke the illusion faded. His was the voice of a man who picked up women in bars. Definitely not Tiberius.

She paused, looked him slowly up and down, then continued toward the door.

He fell in step beside her despite the brush-off. Apparently, he was either stubborn or stupid.

"You're alone," he said.

"Your powers of perception are mind-boggling." She kept on walking.

"A woman like you shouldn't be alone."

She stopped, then slowly turned to face him. "And what kind of woman is that?"

"A beautiful one."

"Trust me," she said. "It's a deadly beauty."

"I know." He was looking at her hard, and she could smell the truth on him. He knew what she was, and damned if that didn't excite him. The prospect of blood teased her daemon, the dark malevolence that lived deep inside every vampire, and her hunger grew.

The wolf stirred, too. The secret beast inside her. *He'd* made her this way, and she'd come to kill in payment for his dirty little tricks. For turning her into walking death. An outsider in her own damn world.

For making her a hybrid.

Can't go there, Caris. Don't even think it.

"I want what you can give." He looked at her with eyes wide and wild, like a junkie staring into a candy jar filled with meth.

"Death?"

"The rush." His chest rose and fell with his breath, the scent of desire wafting off him. He licked his lips and took a step toward her. "I know what you are," he said, then tilted his head to the side. "Feed."

Something raw and angry welled inside her. "You have no idea what I am," she said. "You don't have a goddamned clue."

"You're a vampire."

The word hit her with the force of a slap, and she stepped closer, so close she could feel the heat of his excitement rising from his bone-pale skin. "I'm not," she said. "Not anymore."

She looked into those dark eyes and saw the fear growing, a fear that fed and fueled her, that primed her and begged her to take, take, *take*. To get revenge. Against the man she hunted, yes. But more against the man who'd loved her until the day he'd banished her. She wanted to give Tiberius the big Fuck You. And right now . . . right now it was this guy standing in front of her. This guy, waiting for her to take his blood, his life . . .

She fought it down, fought it back.

Not now. Not when she was on the hunt.

"Go," she said, pressing her palm against his chest and pushing him away from her. "Find yourself a less dangerous game to play."

He went, hurrying back into the shadows of the bar to find another playmate.

She shook her head, sorting her thoughts, making a plan. She'd hit the next bar, then the one after that if she had to. She'd find her quarry. She'd come to this town with a purpose, and she didn't intend to be distracted. Not even by the goddamned memories of Tiberius.

It took her a while to navigate through the crowd, people crushed together, their hot breath warming the air, the scent of sweating bodies beneath thick sweaters teasing her senses. She paused for a drink at the bar and searched the crowd for her quarry. He wasn't there, but humanity pressed all around her, and the scent of it both taunted and saddened her. She'd been human once, too, but Tiberius had changed all that. He'd promised her forever and she'd believed him.

She'd been a fool.

She burst through the door, and the cold air stung her cheeks and cooled her thoughts. She started down the street toward the next pub, snow crunching beneath her feet.

A scream ripped through the night as if echoing her own need to rend and tear. She told herself to ignore it—not her problem. But the smell of fear permeated the air. Whatever was happening, it was close. And, dammit all, she was already heading in that direction.

She found them in the alley behind the bar—the two vamps and the idiot patron with Tiberius's eyes. One of the vamps leaned lazily against the rough-hewn wooden wall while the other held the human in a mockery of a lover's embrace, his teeth sunk deep into the male's flesh.

She started to turn away—she wasn't with the Preternatural Enforcement Coalition. It wasn't her job to arrest vamps who ran around feeding on humans, even dumbass ones who'd been begging for trouble. Especially not dumbass ones who reminded her of Tiberius. And wasn't there some sort of sweet justice in seeing the life sucked out of him?

She watched for a second, breathing in the scent of fear, the aroma of death. She watched, and then she cursed.

Goddamn it all.

Three long strides and she was right in front of them. "Funny," she said, speaking to the one with his fangs buried in flesh. "He doesn't look like a licensed faunt."

"Not your business, little girl," the one with his mouth free said. "Not unless you're interested in sharing."

She faced him, her hand going to her hip, pushing the leather of her coat back, revealing the knife she habitually wore there. "I don't think we've been introduced," she said. "I'm Caris."

"Caris?"

She actually saw him swallow, and she had to bite back a smile. Apparently her reputation was worth something even up here on the Matterhorn.

"You should go if you want to live."

She didn't have to repeat herself. The one who'd been holding up the wall cut and ran. The other dropped the human, wiped the blood off his lips with the back of his hand, then backed out of the alley, his eyes fixed on her as if she might jump him for spite.

Any other night, and she might have done just that.

The human slumped to the ground, his cheek pressed against a slush of dirty snow. She could hear his pulse, weak but steady. She walked away, leaving him to the cold, but she pulled out her cellphone and had information connect her to the pub. She told the bartender who answered that there was a man in his alley bleeding from the neck. Just her little charitable contribution for the day.

She paused to look up and down the Bahnhofstrasse. She lifted her chin, sniffing the cold air out of habit. She expected nothing—so far her luck hadn't exactly been stellar—and was surprised to catch a scent. Musky. Animal.

Weren.

Not necessarily the one she hunted; couldn't get her hopes up yet. But she turned left, following the scent up the hill, through twisting streets and finally out of the village and up a hiking path into the mountains. She slowed her step, wary. Was she walking into a trap? Or had Reinholt come into the trees to change? To romp and hunt?

To her left, she saw a sign pointing toward a picnic area. The scent was stronger now, even despite the snow that was beginning to fall in earnest, and she increased her pace, realizing she was gaining on him. Behind the blanket of clouds the moon hung heavy in the sky—not full, but waxing gibbous—and the animal within was relishing the hunt. She could feel the wolf growing inside her. Could feel it begging to come out, especially now that she was on edge, sweet revenge almost upon her.

Unlike a regular weren, she didn't change at moonrise on the night of a full moon. The vampire part of her fought that. But it was an advantage of only a few hours. Still, those hours had helped keep her secret when she was living with the pack. Once they changed, they could care less about her, and she could sneak off to a specially sealed cell and lock herself in.

Right now, though, the moon was days from full, and she had control over the wolf. It had been a long time since the wolf had burst out when there wasn't a full moon.

But trapped though it was, it was still clamoring for release. So was her daemon. Primed from the blood and charged from the memories, it wanted nothing more than the kill.

She moved in silence, following the path around a copse of trees and then stopping short as she entered the small clearing—he was there, standing beside a snow-covered picnic table. And he hadn't yet realized she was behind him.

Her hand went to her knife. She had a gun, too. A

discreet revolver tucked in at the small of her back. Five silver bullets. They'd kill a werewolf dead enough, but this was one kill Caris wanted to make with her hands, not with a gun. And definitely not with her fangs—the thought of her mouth closing over this pile of flesh made her ill. In her fantasies, she'd considered slicing herself and letting the acid blood he'd given her burn through his body. There was poetic justice there, but she still didn't want it.

No, for this kill, she wanted a blade. One quick motion across his throat—face-to-face so she could see his expression and watch as he understood that the time had come to pay for his sins. Risky, she knew. If Reinholt saw her face before he died, a percipient daemon could pull out that image. But the weather was getting harsher, and she already knew that Switzerland had no percipient daemon on staff. It would be hours before the body was found. Time was her ally. And what she wanted was worth the risk.

She stepped forward, no longer caring about stealth. She wanted a fight. Craved it, in fact. Her daemon wanted to play. And as long as the weren ended up dead, she was more than happy to let her daemon get out and stretch its legs.

But right then, Reinholt turned, and a flicker of joy passed through her as she saw the recognition—and the fear—in his eyes.

She tensed but didn't lunge. Didn't move forward, didn't attack, and for a split second she wondered at her hesitation. This was the weren she'd been looking for. The son of a bitch who'd destroyed her life, her love.

Inside, the daemon growled, wanting blood. Her body itched to leap, the wolf within wanting to rip, to destroy.

Still, though, she didn't move, and as the blood boiling in her head calmed, she realized why. It wasn't the kill she wanted—not right away. It was answers.

"Why?"

The question came out as a whisper, but she knew he heard it. Even so, he didn't answer.

"Tell me what I want to know, and maybe I'll let you live." It was a lie she didn't regret telling.

"Let me live?" He reached into his coat and pulled out a gun. Not something she usually feared, but this was the one man in all the world who would know what type of bullet would hurt her. Wooden bullets coated in silver. A weapon designed to kill either a vampire or a werewolf. Or both.

"*You.*" He held the gun steady. His finger moved on the trigger, and in that same instant, she launched herself sideways. The bullet sang out, burning through the leather sleeve of her coat, slicing into the flesh of her arm and raising a line of crimson that bubbled and burned through the leather of her jacket.

He'd hurt her, but he hadn't killed her. He'd fucked up there big-time.

She fell back into the snow and rolled, and when she came up, she had her own gun in her hands.

In the back of her mind, she registered approaching footfalls, moving faster than a human, but she couldn't worry about that now. He was going to get off another round, and this was about survival. She fired one shot at his head, and he stumbled backward, a neat little hole in his skull. She stood, aimed, and put another through his heart, knocking him to the ground.

The man she'd come to kill was dead, but somehow she didn't feel any better.

She drew herself up, ignoring the pain in her arm and the putrid scent of acid eating through leather. Someone was coming. She needed to go.

And then she heard her name, and her heart quivered in her chest.

"Caris!" he said again.

She turned, not wanting to, but compelled to see his face. Because she knew that voice. Knew that man. And when she looked at him, it took her breath away.

"Dammit, Caris, what the hell have you done?"

She forced herself to smile, an outward picture of calm control even though inside she was shaking. "Hello, Tiberius," she said. "It's been a very, very long time."

CHAPTER 4

Tiberius had heard the shots fired as he transformed from mist back into his corporeal form. He hadn't bothered waiting for Luke but had rushed through the clearing to the small picnic area that Reinholt had picked as their rendezvous point.

He'd arrived in mere seconds, but even in that short time, he'd known it would be bad. How could it not be? A shoot-out. His informant likely dead or injured.

And yet never once did he fathom it would be as horrible as the reality that faced him. *Caris.* Standing right in front of his informant, a gun in her hand, a wound on her arm. And Reinholt had a hole in his head.

Now she was smiling at him, trying to act as if nothing was unusual. The hell with that.

"Goddamm it, Caris. What have you done?"

"What I had to."

"No," he snapped, unable to keep the anger out of his voice. "You will not evade my questions. I want answers, and I want them now." Behind him, Luke burst through the trees.

Caris smirked. "Hold that thought," she said as she ripped her jacket off then held it to her chest so that it partially covered her arm. At first, Tiberius wasn't sure why she'd done that. Then he realized she was hiding her injury, and the portion of her jacket that had been burned away from the acid that had flowed from the wound.

He tensed. He'd known for years what she was, but seeing the truth of it again so unexpectedly rattled him. He schooled his features into a mask of calm, but Caris knew him well. She would have seen his reaction. All he could hope for was that Luke did not.

As if acknowledging his thoughts, Caris smiled broadly. "Lucius. Welcome to the party." She shot a quick glance at Tiberius. "Well. This little reunion has been fun, but I think I'll be on my way now."

She moved to step aside, but Tiberius sped forward and took her arm. She froze, then met his eyes. With a single, deliberate movement, she jerked her arm from his grip, and there was something so cold in that gesture, so final, that he felt the ice inside him crack.

"Caris, the gunshots. The human police will arrive soon, as will the PEC. We need to go."

"Exactly what I intended to do," she said. "You're the one who stopped me."

"I had my reasons."

She glared at him with a defiant expression he knew only too well. "I'm waiting."

"Cyrus Reinholt was my informant," he said. "You've caused me more than a little inconvenience."

"So sorry to put you out."

Despite everything, he couldn't help but smile. She'd always been good with a comeback, and it was comforting to know some things hadn't changed.

A sharp snap rang out from beyond the line of trees, as if someone had stepped on a twig. Tiberius glanced at Luke, who nodded quickly, then slipped away to check it out. Tiberius turned back to Caris. "As I was saying, you killed my informant. Are you working for Lihter?" He didn't believe it, but he had to ask.

Her laugh seemed genuine. "Not hardly."

"Why, then? I want to know why Reinholt's dead."

Her eyes were cold, emerald ice. "There are a lot of things I want, Tiberius. Right now, the most pressing one is to go home."

"We'll go to London."

"*London* and *home* don't go together anymore. Or had you forgotten?"

He hadn't, of course. He remembered that every single day. "I'll have my answers, Caris. One way or the other."

Her brow lifted.

"We have limited time until someone discovers us," he added. "We should leave now."

"What will you do, Tiberius? Throw me over your shoulder? I'm stronger now. I've been training, working in the field." She smiled sweetly, then glanced pointedly up at the moon, less than a week from being full. "In fact, I think it's fair to say that right now, I'm strong enough that I could probably even take you."

He didn't flinch, even though he knew she was probably right. He might have the strength of two thousand years to draw upon, but she now had the strength of two species, and that was powerful indeed.

"Or are you threatening to hurt me some other way? Maybe you intend to share my secrets?"

He met her eyes, gave her the tiniest shake of his head, well aware that with his vampiric senses, Luke could still hear them even though he was no longer standing nearby. And even Luke, his oldest friend in the world, didn't know the truth about what she was.

"But you couldn't mean that, could you? After all, you made a promise to protect me once. Or had you forgotten? All things considered, I'd certainly believe it if you had."

"There were others I owed protection to as well," he said, speaking carefully. "And I have never failed to shield you from harm."

"Didn't you? Despite all those years of shielding me—despite refusing to let me work alongside the *kyne*—despite working so very hard to keep me safe and protected, you hurt me worse than anyone else ever has."

He couldn't speak. Everything she said was true, and yet he'd had no choice. If faced with the decision again, he would do nothing different. Though it had killed him to do so, he'd saved thousands of lives when he'd sent her away after she'd returned to London as a hybrid. All of the vampires at his court. Hell, he'd saved every creature in London, human and shadower.

He was a leader, a protector. And that meant he had to make the impossible choices.

The truly hard choice would have been to kill her. But that was something he'd been unable to do.

"You're right, of course," he said, and his agreement seemed to surprise her. "But I will not relent. And it makes no difference to me if answers come easily or with great difficulty."

"No difference? I don't believe you."

There was subtle lightening of her tone, and he matched it. This was a truce they were negotiating, and that at least was familiar territory. "You're right, again. I'd much prefer the easy route."

It took a moment, but she nodded. "Very well. London? I'd hate to deny you the home court advantage. And as at the moment I have no home, it seems the most logical choice."

The words surprised him. Tiberius knew that Lihter had banished Gunnolf from Paris, but Tiberius had assumed Caris had traveled with the former weren leader to Scotland.

Now, however, was not the time for questions. "London," he agreed.

"Fine. I'll meet you there. Before dawn." She looked at him, her expression unreadable. "You have my word." And then she was gone, racing into the trees with incredible speed, then rising out of the canopy of leaves as a solid black raven.

Tiberius stood for a moment watching the sky. Then he heard movement behind him. He turned to see Luke emerging from the trees.

"You heard?"

Luke nodded. "But I feel I should have been issued a codebook before that conversation."

"There is a lot of history between us."

"Do you think it was wise to let her travel on her own?"

"Did you see the speed at which she left us? I'm not sure I had a choice." More, he hadn't wanted her around as he considered how to deal with the fallout from Reinholt's death. He'd spoken truthfully when he said that she'd seriously inconvenienced him.

"She's grown stronger in the last two decades," Luke said. "You're not surprised, are you? She has quite the reputation now."

Tiberius nodded. He knew about Caris's fieldwork, knew that her name incited fear. "She's become a bit like you," he said to Luke. It was the one thing she'd always wanted, to fight at his side. And at first she had. But then he'd almost lost her, and after that, he'd prohibited it. How could he risk her in battle when to lose her would have destroyed him?

And then he'd been the one to destroy her. The world was full of ironies.

"Will she come?" Luke asked.

Tiberius nodded. "She will."

Luke looked dubious, but Tiberius was certain. Despite her speed and strength, he wouldn't have let her go if he hadn't been certain. But he knew her well, despite everything. She wouldn't want Tiberius or his men seeking her out. More important, when Caris gave her word, she didn't break it.

"We should go," Luke said.

Tiberius shook his head. "I'll go. I need you to stay. Unless Caris merely stumbled upon him and decided to kill a perfect stranger, it's safe to assume that Reinholt must have told someone of his plans to meet me."

"Which means that your name will come up when the locals investigate."

"And if I'm not here—or my representative—there will be even more questions. Go back to town, but return here after the body's discovered. Learn what you can, tell them that Reinholt was going to provide me information about Lihter."

"Throw the spotlight on the weren."

Tiberius half smiled. "I see no reason not to make his life as difficult as possible. But say nothing about the kidnapping." At that, he frowned. Reinholt was supposed to have relayed more details about that. Now the girl was at Lihter's mercy, and the task of rescuing her had gotten that much harder.

"It's possible that the blame you're throwing toward Lihter isn't the stuff of fiction," Luke said.

"You think Caris is lying? That she really was sent by Lihter?"

"We can't discount the possibility."

"I can," Tiberius said. As much as he now despised Gunnolf, the previous weren leader, that weren had a core of morality. Lihter, though, had always been dangerous. Caris would never align herself with him.

He could tell from Luke's expression that his lieutenant didn't share his certainty.

"Keep your eyes and ears open," Tiberius said. "I want to know if they have any reason to suspect Caris." He clapped his friend on the shoulder. "I'll see you in London."

"Good luck," Luke said, which was not his usual parting comment. Under the circumstances, though, Tiberius appreciated it. More, he had a feeling he'd need it.

♦

Gabriel Casavetes looked down as the American tourist beneath him—Sally? Jenny?—moaned and writhed and dug her fingernails into his back.

"Harder, baby. I'm so close."

He dutifully pumped harder, trying to erase everything in his head, trying to just simply *enjoy* it. She was young, she was beautiful, she was responsive.

And all he was doing was going through the motions.

Beneath him, she arched up, her muscles contracting and pumping him as she screamed and cried and basically shook the whole damn room with her orgasm. Then she collapsed back down, her arm over her eyes, her breathing wet and heavy. "Oh, yeah, that was amazing." The arm shifted and she looked at him. "It was amazing, wasn't it?"

"The earth moved," he said. He rolled off her and headed for the bathroom.

"Oh, come back. Baby wants to snuggle."

He hesitated, glad his back was to her, because the hesitation gave him the chance to roll his eyes and wonder what the hell he'd been thinking inviting her up to his room. It was not because he was tempted to return and snuggle.

He continued, shutting the bathroom door behind him. With any luck, he'd come out in a minute and find she'd gotten the hint, gotten dressed, and gotten gone.

Instead, he pulled the door open and got an eyeful of naked tourist, the coverlet tossed aside, curled up on his dark green sheets. She patted the spot beside her. "Round two."

"Tempting," he said, wondering what was on the television.

"Get your cute little Swiss ass over here."

"Actually, I'm from Texas."

Her brow lifted at that, and her surprise knocked his estimation of her down a notch, which put it deep in negative numbers. He said y'all for Christ's sake. Did she really think he'd been raised in the shadow of the Matterhorn?

If she was embarrassed, though, she covered well. She sat up, ample breasts bobbing. "Well, that makes us neighbors. I'm from Phoenix!"

"I think you forgot about New Mexico," he said, but she just brushed it away, basic geography apparently beneath her.

Note to self, he thought, no more talking to women while drinking.

Then again, he'd moved to this iceberg of a town to get away. Because he wanted a dull life, an easy existence. And this woman was both dull and easy.

What was that saying? Be careful what you wish for?

"Do you hear that?" she said, as a sharp ping filled the room. He said a silent thank-you to whoever was calling him, then snatched his cellphone from the bedside table. The caller ID showed Everil, and Gabriel didn't think he'd ever been happier to hear from his smarmy excuse for a partner. "I'm here. What's up?"

"Humans caught one," Everil said, his high, nasal voice grating on Gabriel's already worn nerves. "An actual, bona fide homicide."

The little fae sounded excited by the prospect. Gabriel didn't share his enthusiasm.

"I assume there's a reason you're telling me this?"

"Humans caught it, but it's our jurisdiction. Victim's a werewolf. Looks like he's been dead a couple of hours. Apparently someone heard shots, but didn't report it. Didn't realize what they'd heard, I guess, until some teenagers decided to go out for a late-night hike and make-out session. They found the body, and then our earwitness came forward when they saw the cops." He was talking a mile a minute, obviously thrilled as shit to be in the middle of an actual homicide investigation. "I'm heading to the scene now. Koller's gonna do his liaison thing and work it out with the human big shots at the Polizei," he added, referring to Benjamin Koller, the subdirector of Division 12's violent crimes unit.

"Remember what we talked about. Make sure the scene is preserved. These guys don't have a lot of experience with homicide. I don't want someone's rookie mistake destroying evidence."

"You got it, partner," he said, then trilled, "Damn, but this is exciting."

Gabriel snapped the phone shut with a shake of his head. *Exciting* wouldn't be his choice of words. But as he looked at the woman on the bed, he had to admit that *fortuitous* and *convenient* fit quite well.

♦

Moonlight spilled from the sky, the snow on the mountains magnifying it and painting the scene in shades of gray and white. It was a breathtakingly beautiful sight.

Gabriel barely noticed.

He found the scene easily enough. Even without Everil's overly detailed directions, the path to the picnic area was obvious enough, having been well trampled by the authorities, both human and shadower. With a frown, he hurried forward, afraid the clods had mucked up the crime scene. He was pleased to discover that the area around the victim had been cordoned off with crime-scene tape. Gabriel would have preferred a wider perimeter, but it was too late now. That's what happened when homicide came to paradise—mistakes were made and evidence was lost.

He approached the scene, breathing in deep. Half hellhound on his mother's side, his sense of smell was as well attuned as any shadow creature's. But if the perp had left a distinctive scent, it had been masked by all the activity. More than that, unless he was familiar with the suspect's smell, catching a scent would hardly matter.

He paused outside the tape and peered down at the victim. Male. Thin. Reasonably tall. Appeared to be in his late forties, though if he was weren he could just as easily be in his late four hundreds. The same biology that altered and then repaired their cellular structure every month also healed their cells as they aged. A neat trick, actually.

A single bullet hole had penetrated the victim's skull, and another had breached his chest. Now the snow around his head and torso was stained red, giving the odd impression of a fallen angel with crimson wings and halo.

He saw Everil to one side, talking with a tall man who smelled human. Gabriel lifted his hand, signaling to his partner, who scurried over, his face prissy and his manner self-important.

"I've got everything under control."

"Then why are the humans still here?"

It was hard to imagine Everil's already pinched face squeezing any tighter, but somehow the fae managed it. "There are procedures. They take time."

"Time we don't have," Gabriel said. "The images only last so long."

Everil blinked, his expression blank. Gabriel bit back a curse and tried to draw from his rapidly depleting supply of patience. He hadn't asked to be partnered with Everil, he begged a new assignment every chance he had, and yet they were still stuck together like glue.

"A percipient daemon," Gabriel said. "Get the images. Solve the crime. Ring any bells?"

Two blinks of those oversized black eyes. "We have no percipient daemon on staff."

One. Two. Three. Gabriel didn't bother counting to ten. "Then you request a loan from another division. Never mind," he snapped. "I'll handle it."

"You do that," Everil said with an officious nod. As if summoning a percipient was all his idea.

He scurried away and Gabriel pulled out his phone. It took him all of three seconds to contact Koller and have him put the request in motion. With luck, the percipient would quickly conjure a wormhole and arrive within ten minutes. He knew of two currently working for the PEC: Armand Ylexi, who was stationed in Berlin, and Ryan Doyle, from Division 6 in L.A.

By the time he ended the call, Everil was back, this time accompanied by a tall vampire with a scar cutting across his right cheek.

"Says he came to Zermatt for a meeting with the victim," Everil said. "Hasn't told me his name yet, though."

"Lucius Dragos," Gabriel said. Everil's eyes went wide, and he took a step back. Dragos, Gabriel was happy to see, looked amused. "If you had a meeting planned, I'm guessing you can identify our victim? Save us a little time?"

"I've never met the man in person, but he'd arranged a meeting with Tiberius at this spot," Dragos said.

"So where's Tiberius?"

"If you know who I am, you also know that I often stand in Tiberius's stead."

"Fair enough. Who's the guy?"

"Cyrus Reinholt."

Gabriel shook his head. "Should I know him?"

"Are you weren?"

"Half human, half hellhound," Gabriel said. Beside him, Everil's pinched face had pulled into a frown.

"No reason you'd know him, then. He's weren, obviously. This was a preliminary meeting. He'd contacted Tiberius about acting as a possible intelligence resource."

"He offered to spy on Lihter?" Gabriel said. "Why?"

"That was one of the questions I intended to ask him."

Gabriel nodded, then turned toward Everil. "This puts Lihter at the top of our suspect list." Dragos was on the list, too, of course. At least until his story was confirmed. But Gabriel didn't intend to mention that. "We'll see if the percipient can give us anything else to work with."

"You've summoned a percipient?" Dragos asked. His expression shifted then, so slightly that Gabriel doubted anyone but himself noticed. But Dragos wasn't happy with the idea of a percipient arriving. In fact, if Gabriel had to pin it, he'd say Dragos looked irritated. And that was interesting.

"Should be here any minute," Gabriel said, keeping his eyes on Dragos's face.

A pause, then, "Good thinking."

"But?"

Now Dragos's smile came easy. "Unless you want to deal with the inevitable consequences of the human Swiss police witnessing the arrival of a percipient daemon by wormhole, I suggest you clear away the humans."

"We're working on that," Gabriel said, shooting a sideways glance at Everil, who was in fact supposed to be working on that. "The PEC can take exclusive jurisdiction pursuant to our agreement with the Swiss Polizei. But it takes time. Unfortunately, we don't have any vampires on staff. No one with any sort of persuasive abilities, actually, so there's no easy way to convince the humans they have somewhere else they need to be."

Dragos nodded, obviously only half listening as he surveyed the scene.

"But you're a vampire . . ."

Dragos turned, surprised. "I am."

"You're here. You're a vampire. And," Gabriel added, taking a step toward him. "I'm sure you must want your informant's killer caught as much as we at Division 12 do."

Dragos didn't hesitate. He was either innocent or very, very good. Considering what he knew of the vampire, Gabriel wasn't about to discount either possibility. "I'm happy to help," he said. "By the way, who did you summon?"

"Whoever's closest," Gabriel said. "Probably Ylexi. Shouldn't take any time to arrive from Berlin."

"No, it shouldn't," Dragos said, and the hint of irritation that Gabriel had seen earlier faded.

Beside them, Everil shifted nervously from one foot to the other. "Gabriel, I don't—"

"It's homicide," Gabriel said, cutting him off. "And technically, I outrank you." He turned back to Dragos. "Do it."

And just like that, Dragos did.

Gabriel watched him disappear into the crowd. He

watched the forensics team examining the body. The staff protecting the scene. A hive of activity, just as it was supposed to be, and he was back in and hip deep whether he wanted to be or not.

What a goddamned, fucked-up mess.

CHAPTER 5

She was running, the forest thick around her. She was in the heart of it now, where witches built gingerbread houses and ate small children for breakfast.

Trouble.

It was brewing all around her. Thick and heavy.

She needed to run faster, look harder.

But she didn't. She couldn't.

The dream had its claws well into her now.

This was her personal mission, and she couldn't fail. She had to find the traitor. Had to prove that she could once again be an asset in the field. That she could be kyne by action if not by bond.

He would be angry, of course. Tiberius. Her mate. Her friend. Her love.

For years, he'd refused to send her into the field, and that one small point was creating a hard knot of dissension between them. He'd relented only once—when they'd hunted the hybrid in France—but she'd almost been bathed in the beast's acid. In the end, they'd prevailed and Tiberius was hailed as a hero, raised up to sit at the Alliance table, and she had been praised as his mate and advisor.

But never again had he let her hunt.

Her daemon itched for the release of battle. This day, she would prove herself worthy.

Around her, the forest hummed with life. The wind

whispered through the leaves, its music her anthem. In-digenous animals watched with glowing eyes, her witnesses to the traitor's inevitable apprehension. He'd been clever enough to elude her for a time, but she'd found him. Was closing in on him. The bent branches and footprints lightly dusted with snow testified that the gap between them was closing.

Her smile was thin and determined. You're mine. You're all mine.

A sharp crack sounded to her left, and she froze, momentarily confused. Her quarry was in front and to her right—of that she was certain. So what had she heard?

An animal?

She sniffed the air, drawing in the sharp green scent of pine needles and the pungent smell of decaying undergrowth. There was something else, too. A heavy musk hanging in the air. A feral smell that she didn't recognize.

Trap.

The word ricocheted through her, torn from some deep-buried instinct. But it came too late: The arrow pierced her shoulder while she was still corporeal, and suddenly her ability to change was gone. Hematite. The damned arrow tip was hematite.

Within her, the daemon roared, brought to the surface by the heady combination of anger and fear.

She let it rise, using its strength to speed her actions, and trusting that it wouldn't rise so far and so fast that it punched through, leaving the daemon in charge rather than Caris herself.

Moving as fast as she was thinking, she reached back to remove the arrow, but the angle was no good. Instead of freeing the thing, she merely broke off the shaft. The metal tip was still inside her, and there was no way it was coming out.

She forced herself to remain calm, to keep her focus so she could keep her head. If they'd wanted her dead, a wooden arrow to her heart would have been the way to go. So that meant she had the advantage. Her attacker wanted her alive; she didn't hold the same compunction. Whoever put an arrow in her was a dead man.

Too bad she didn't have an enemy to fight.

Above her, a flock of birds took off with a flurry of wings and caws. Time she did the same.

She ran. The hematite in her shoulder slowed her some, sapping her strength, but not so much that she couldn't fight through it. She'd make it.

By the time Caris heard the soft whoosh of the net being released from its anchor in the trees, it was too late. The hematite threads were already snugged tight around her, tripping her. Binding her.

She struggled, her daemon snarling as she tried to rip apart the web that had captured her, but it was no use. Her strength was fading in the presence of so much hematite, and her captor was approaching. Tall and dressed in fatigues. Face hidden by a mask. The body shapeless under the loose-fitting clothes.

In front of her, he raised his weapon—a tranquilizer gun. Fear ripped through her, an emotion she hadn't felt with such force in centuries. She didn't much like feeling it now, and she bit the inside of her cheek to keep from begging. Begging would do no good, and she wasn't about to show weakness.

He fired, and there was nowhere to go. The dart penetrated her chest, just above her breast, and the world began to spin.

Her attacker stepped closer, and she saw cold calcula-
tion in his gray-hued eyes. She breathed in through her
nose, testing the air, trying to catch the scent of him, but
he'd masked more than his face, and she smelled only
the heady scent of the earth.

"Blaine?" she whispered, forcing the traitor's name
out as reality dissolved beneath her.

"No," a man's voice replied. "Now sleep."

◆

Caris shook herself, forcing her mind to clear. Tiberius
was the last person she'd expected to see on that moun-
taintop, and his proximity had thrown her off her game.
Pain mixed with a desperate longing. Emotions going
where they had no business going. She should be over
him. She should hate him as much as she'd once hated
herself. More, even.

So why the hell did he still make her blood burn?

Stop thinking about it.

Good advice, and she was trying. Except it wasn't
working. Her mind was all over the place. The moun-
taintop. Tiberius.

The past.

She clenched her fists, once again trying to force her
thoughts not to go back to those weeks when she'd been
changed.

Not to go back to when Tiberius had banished her.
When he'd looked at her with such horror in his eyes.
She'd hated him for not having the strength to kill her,
even while she wanted to rail on him for not having the
balls to step up and help.

He'd picked politics—his people—over her, and the wound had cut deep. It still did.

She shivered.

Her word. Why the hell had she given Tiberius her word?

She should have told him no way, screw you, just forget about it.

But she hadn't, and now she was pacing the Tower Bridge's pedestrian walkway, watching the Thames flow by beneath her. The mansion was a few kilometers to the south and sunrise was fast approaching.

She should go. But somehow she couldn't get her feet moving in that direction.

Everything was so confused where Tiberius was concerned. For so long she'd told herself she hated him. That he'd betrayed her and their love, and that he'd destroyed everything.

But seeing him again . . .

She hugged herself, shaking her head to clear her thoughts, frustrated that her skin still tingled at the sound of his voice, and her throat still caught when she said his name.

Seeing him again so unexpectedly had driven the truth home, and hard. She *didn't* hate him. Not really. That emotion had been reserved for herself, at least at first. Because of what she was. What she'd done.

She closed her eyes, clenching her fists against the pain and the regret and the guilt.

How quickly life could turn around. For centuries, she and Tiberius had been united. But then her hubris had gotten in the way. She'd gone out to prove that he was wrong and that she was a warrior. That she could capture a fugitive traitor. She'd been a fool. And that one choice had destroyed them both.

Reinholt had captured her—not because she was Tiberius's woman, or because she was Caris, or because she was anyone in particular at all. He'd needed a female. He'd needed a vampire. And she'd been in the wrong place at the wrong time.

He'd caught her and he'd tortured her and he'd changed her.

"*Stop it,*" Caris said out loud, leaning against the railing of the bridge, wishing the wind would whip the memories from her mind.

But they stayed, and there was no forcing them back now.

She'd escaped from Reinholt—*how* was a painful blur—but she'd managed. She'd raced through the forest in a daze, hiding when she felt the wolf bursting free, transforming to mist when she could. When she reached London, she'd gone straight to Tiberius, and she'd seen the relief in his eyes as she rushed into their bedroom.

The air between them had been charged, and she could feel his need, his desire. She'd pushed him away, though. She felt the wolf beneath her skin, begging for release, and she feared that losing herself to passion would bring it out—and that would be the death of Tiberius.

Even more than that, though, she'd feared that if he knew the truth he wouldn't want her. The weren were vile to him. They'd abused him, body and soul, and while she didn't want him to look upon her like that, she knew that she couldn't lie with him without telling him the truth.

She'd feared he would be unable to meet her eyes. She'd feared he would storm from the room, and that it would be hours—possibly even days—before he would come to her and tell her that it didn't matter. That he loved her and always would.

She'd feared all that . . . but she hadn't feared what had actually happened.

"It is in you, then?" he asked, after she'd forced herself to tell him the truth. "The wolf?"

She'd nodded. "I can feel it, pulling at me."

She thought of his past at the hands of the vile werewolf Claudius. "I'm still me," she'd urged. "I'm still Caris."

She'd reached for his hand, but their fingers had only brushed as he'd moved away, rising to stand.

"And you changed? The wolf came out?"

She nodded. "At the full moon. My captor—he kept me in a basement. There was no one around. I infected no one, I swear."

"And since the full moon? Has the change come upon you?"

She hesitated. It had, and she'd raced into a cavern, hoping like hell that no one would come along. Hoping she would get lost in the winding tunnels, unable to escape and rush to a nearby town. She'd been lucky. She truly didn't know if she would ever be that lucky again.

He was watching her, his expression harsh. "Caris. Have you learned how to control it?" She thought she heard a hint of hope in his voice, but it was buried, deep beneath a harsh stoicism. She tried to ignore it, but she couldn't. His overcalm voice made her afraid, so very afraid, and with fear came the wolf.

"I haven't," she admitted. "But I can learn. I can feel control inside me, but it's edging just out of reach. Please, Tiberius, I need—"

"What?" His word was sharp.

"Help."

He looked at her then, his eyes so full of love that she'd felt safer than she'd ever been in her life. Only after an eternity did he speak. "Come," he said. "I know what to do."

He didn't take her hand, but he led her back to his office. Giorgio Dane was there, a newly inducted *kyne*. A young man who'd fought at Tiberius's side in a recent battle with Gunnolf and his men.

Giorgio looked up, confused as they burst in. Caris was just as confused. "What—" she began as Tiberius circled behind his desk and pulled open a drawer. And then, because he moved so fast and because she had her guard down and because she never would have expected it of the man she loved, he managed to pull out a gun and fire a tranq dart into her before she even had time to react.

"I'm sorry," he said, as a shocked Giorgio leaped to his feet. "I can't risk you changing. Not here. Not with hundreds of vampires in the mansion. Giorgio will take you to Belgium. To the safe house."

She'd tried to speak, but the words wouldn't come.

"I love you," he'd said, and the world went black.

Now she clenched her hands around the Tower Bridge railing, then shut her eyes tight, warding off memories of the nightmare that followed.

In front of her, the horizon was beginning to glow. No time for memories now. No time to be that Caris. The girl who'd had no control.

That girl was gone. She was strong now. She'd learned control. She'd harnessed the power of the two species inside her, and she knew how to keep them both where they belonged.

She was a warrior, and she had been for two decades.

And a warrior could face Tiberius without getting nervous.

A warrior could . . . and so could she.

CHAPTER 6

Tiberius paced the length of his London office, wondering why the hell she hadn't arrived yet.

He'd gone down the mountain to Zurich as mist, then had one of the staff para-daemons at Division 12 transport him back to London by wormhole. The whole trip had taken under two hours. Presumably Caris was arriving by a less direct route.

Still, he was beginning to fear that his trust in her had been misplaced. That she was trying to pay him back by pissing him off.

So far it was working.

The truly frustrating thing was that it wasn't her tardiness that had him on edge, but the anticipation of seeing her again. Dammit all, it had been almost two decades. He should have worked the woman from his blood by now.

Never.

The familiar scene came from the back of his mind, and he recognized it immediately. He was speaking to her. *"You are my heart and soul, Caris,"* he'd said. *"And you will be forever."* Her laughter had covered him, as refreshing as a bubbling brook. *"You'll take that back one day,"* she teased. *"Push me aside. Toss me away."* He'd pulled her tightly into his embrace, then kissed her hard. *"Never,"* he whispered, after his lips had sealed the promise.

He'd meant it, too. Hell, he meant it still.

Would it be hard to see her when she walked through his door? Absolutely, but like all pain, there would be pleasure, too, and he'd be lying if he said the anticipation wasn't killing him.

He might lie to another about that, but with his own heart he could only be honest.

Seeing her in Zermatt had hurt. Seeing her in his home would hurt more. But he'd survived unbearable pain, and he could survive this. He had to. He needed to find out what she was up to. Needed to understand why she gave a rat's ass about Reinholt. Was it personal? Or, God forbid, was she working for Lihter?

His hand rested on a heavy bookshelf that sat next to the window, and he realized that he'd opened a small cherrywood box while he'd been lost in thought. He held a miniature frame in his hand, the glass fogged after so many years, the photograph now aged and faded.

Even so, her eyes shone through, bright and intelligent.

His chest tightened, this time with regret. She'd been his mate, his confidant. The one person he'd trusted above all others. The one person who'd never left his side as he'd risen in the Alliance. Who'd understood his ambition and supported it. Supported *him*.

She was also the one person who knew the painful truth about his past. About the youth who'd been battered and abused at the hand of the weren.

There was no woman who could take her place in his life. He'd ripped his own heart out when he'd banished her, but even in that small mercy, he'd failed. He should have killed her. How could he do otherwise after what had happened to Giorgio?

Forcing his hand to remain steady, he lifted the picture, once again looking into her eyes—eyes that now seemed both sad and reproachful.

His hand clenched, tighter and tighter until the glass cracked under the pressure, and he hurled the frame across the room, then watched as the glass shattered against the wall.

He dropped his hand.

He didn't feel any better.

Disgusted with himself, he crossed the room, glass cracking beneath his shoes as he reached the mess and bent over to pluck the photograph from the array of shards.

On the far side of the room, the door clicked open, and Mrs. Todd poked her head in. "I heard a—oh." She frowned at the mess surrounding him. "Is everything—"

"It's fine."

"Oh." She cleared her throat. "There's a hand broom and dustpan inside your closet. I'll just go get . . ." She trailed off, then busied herself with tidying the floor. Tiberius watched, feeling more the fool with each whisk of the broom.

"Was there something else?" he asked.

She tilted her head up from where she was crouched on the floor. "There's someone here to see you."

"Mrs. Todd, do you recall me mentioning that I was expecting someone?"

"Of course, sir."

"Then perhaps you could have announced their presence earlier?"

"Oh. Right. Of course, sir."

He forced his temper under control. He was on edge at the moment, and he knew it. It would do no one any good if he took it out on Mrs. Todd. "Who is it?" His voice sounded thick with anticipation, and he could only hope that his secretary hadn't noticed.

Caris, she would say. And he would calmly nod and tell her to let the woman in.

"It's Mr. Dragos, sir."

An odd mixture of relief and disappointment washed over him. "Fine. Send him in."

Luke eased inside and took a seat on the couch. "I've got one hour for a briefing, and then I need to be at the airport. I've got my plane waiting, and I want to get home."

"I don't blame you." Tiberius leaned against his desk. "So what's the news from Zermatt?"

"They brought in a percipient," Luke said. "Ylexi, from Berlin," he added. "The delay in discovering the body worked in our favor. He saw nothing."

Tiberius nodded, relieved. "Good." He needed his own answers as to why she'd killed Reinholt. Answers that would be hard to come by if she was the focus of a criminal investigation. Not to mention that having her executed for murder didn't sit well with him for a lot of reasons.

"Any other evidence at the scene that might lead back to her?"

"Nothing. It looks like we're good."

"Excellent."

Luke started to rise.

"Just one more thing."

Luke sat again.

"Give Koller a call from the airport. I want Division 12 pulled off the case. We're putting an Alliance task force on it. If Koller has an issue with that, he can call me directly."

Luke was watching Tiberius carefully. "I understand the need to deal with her first, to understand what she did and why. But where's the benefit in a task force?"

"We got lucky with the percipient. Lucky with the evidence on scene. But a potential Alliance informant was assassinated, and that justifies an Alliance task force. Division 12 doesn't need to be playing in this sandbox."

Luke's eyes narrowed only slightly. "Why are you protecting her?"

"I assure you I'm protecting my own interests as well." It was a testament to their friendship that Tiberius answered at all. As a lieutenant, Luke's question crossed the line to insolent. As a friend, it was fair.

Luke stood and headed for the door. "I'll call if I get any flak. Otherwise, call when you need me."

"Give Sara my best," Tiberius added, referring to Luke's wife. At her name, Luke's eyes lit up, his warrior's countenance softening with a smile.

Tiberius had to smile, too, as he watched his friend leave. Once, he'd seen that look on his own face—the knowledge of a love so pure it could never be shattered.

It had been, though. Misfortune and circumstance had conspired against them, and at the end of the day, he'd hurt her. And in turn, she'd hurt him.

And both of those events were something he'd once thought impossible, especially since he'd been honor bound to help her even before they'd met, an obligation placed on him when an old man had saved him from dying in the streets.

Tiberius had been human then, a prince ripped from his mother. A future king sold into slavery so that his cousin would inherit the throne instead of him.

Tiberius had remembered none of that, though. He knew only pain and abuse and hours in a ring, made to fight his friends. Made to kill.

It had been the only life he knew, the years before he'd been pulled away from his mother at the tender age of four nothing but a vague memory, replaced by pain and torment and the horrific knowledge that he had no self. That he was the property of the man who owned him, a vile creature named Claudius.

They'd expected him to die quickly, but he'd surprised them. He'd been forced to work first in the mines, then removed to the ring as he gained age and strength. He killed his first man at the age of eleven, and that kill had earned him his life.

His master had decided to train him, and for years he had lived in the training ring, beaten when he did poorly, beaten less brutally when he didn't. He learned Claudius's secret when he was fifteen—the master was a werewolf, and a damn brutal one at that.

In truth, Tiberius wasn't surprised or shocked. By then, all emotion had been stripped from him. He knew only that Claudius was a monster. The new revelation that he was a werewolf didn't really change anything. The beatings grew bolder, more fierce, more excruciating as Tiberius grew older, as if Claudius and the trainers feared Tiberius's growing strength, and yet so wanted the coin that his presence could command in the ring that they simply wouldn't kill him.

When freedom finally came, it was wrapped in its own kind of nightmare. Claudius came to him in the night—this time not to beat him, but to use him. And *that* Tiberius would not abide. He fought, not caring that Claudius's guards would surely gut him. He lost his mind in the melee, knowing only that he could not allow Claudius to take that one, final part of him. To rape him. To taint him. If he did, Tiberius knew his humanity would be lost, and he would become as much the monster as his master.

He threw himself into a frenzy, battling and fighting and hitting and kicking. No practiced moves there, just a wild beast chained too long in a cage. And when he exploded out, it was with rare fury.

How he made it out of the compound he didn't know. Even more, how he was not discovered as he lay passed out in a ditch was as much a mystery as it was a miracle. But escape he did, though not into the warm arms of safety. He'd escaped one fate only to die of starvation and thirst, and though he wandered down a sand-covered road for three days, he saw no travelers who could offer him comfort.

He lay down on the ground and prepared to die. And the next thing he saw was those eyes—*Caris's eyes,* though he had no way of knowing that yet.

The old man who knelt in front of him was her ancestor, and though Tiberius at first believed him to be a mirage, the old man proved to be quite human. His name was Horatius, and he tended to Tiberius's wounds as best he could, but Tiberius hadn't been restored. Instead, he lay dying, his head in the old man's lap, his story on his parched lips. He told Horatius everything, including his lust for revenge, and how it had kept him alive well past another man's breaking point.

When he was finished, he believed that his time on this earth was done. But blood still coursed through his veins and his lungs still drew breath, though ragged and painful.

Horatius had stood then, and he'd looked into the sun as if praying. Tiberius never learned what he'd asked, but the old man hunched over and hoisted Tiberius gently into his cart. As Tiberius slipped in and out of consciousness, they made the long trek to the village where Horatius left Tiberius in the care of the one creature on all the earth who could save him—Magnus, a vampire.

The vampire did not change him right away, but he fed Tiberius his blood and restored him to health even as Horatius watched. And that very night, Tiberius swore an oath to protect Horatius and his family, for he owed the old man a debt that could never truly be repaid.

Throughout the years, Magnus continued to feed him blood, strengthening him. And at the end of five years, he told Tiberius what he'd learned about Tiberius's heritage. About his royal blood, and about the cousin who had betrayed him. He offered Tiberius a choice— Magnus could either help Tiberius return to the life from which he'd been banished, or he could grant Tiberius the gift of immortality.

Tiberius had accepted the latter without hesitation. The human world had almost destroyed him. He had no desire to return. Within the shadow world, however, he wanted power. And revenge.

"Kill Claudius," Magnus said calmly. "I have no objection to that plan. But do not build your future on vengeance. The blood of leaders flows in your veins, but you are stepping into a new world where such things do not matter. It is your character and not your blood that will see you rise. Lead them, Tiberius. You have suffered much, and that is your gift to the masses. You can lead because you understand what it is like to have no voice. It is your privilege and your duty. Lead the vampires, and then lead the world."

And so Magnus had changed him. And exactly one year later, he'd walked off into the desert, and Tiberius had never heard from him again.

Magnus had saved him, fueled his purpose, given him the strength to find his destiny. Horatius had shared his own strength, had shown him common kindness, and had ultimately led Tiberius into love's embrace.

How ironic that it was ultimately the clash of duty and love that had lost him that which he'd valued most in all the world. *Caris.*

A sharp knock sounded at his door, fast and urgent, snapping him out of his thoughts.

"Come in!"

The door burst open and Mrs. Todd bustled in. "Are you all right, sir? I've been knocking and knocking."

"I'm fine. What is it?"

"It's Caris, sir. The guard just buzzed from the gate. She's entered the grounds."

For hours he'd been waiting, and yet now that she was here the thought of seeing her again weighed heavily on him. It pained his heart to look upon her. To remember what they once had—and the reasons why she was no longer part of his life.

But that was the man in him talking.

The politician needed to know why she'd killed Cyrus Reinholt.

And the man?

The man curled his hand around the photograph, and counted the seconds until he saw her again.

CHAPTER 7

The mansion looked the same as it always had. Sprawling. Stodgy. English.

It was massive, containing both residential and office wings, not to mention the ballrooms for entertaining and the recreation and workout facilities. A self-contained little paradise populated by more than three hundred vampires including guests and permanent staff.

There'd been a time when Caris had walked the halls freely. When she'd been the one eyeing strangers and wondering if they might be bringing mayhem into their world.

She didn't want to spread mayhem. She just wanted the hell out of this place that once upon a time she couldn't have imagined leaving.

"This is our home now," Tiberius had said back when they'd walked in triumph through the doors after his victorious return to London following the death of the hybrid. Tomas had conceded his position, and Tiberius and Caris had moved in.

She'd been the one to help decorate the public rooms. She'd tossed out Tomas's moldering settees, replacing them with beautifully carved tables and chairs, pricey at the time, now priceless. *Important things happen within these walls,* the decor announced, and they did. They truly did.

Back then, she'd had a hand in those decisions. She'd

strode through the double doors that led to Tiberius's office with impunity, always welcomed by his smile, always drawn to his side. He'd asked her opinion, sought her counsel, and trusted her above all others.

But that was a long time ago.

Now Caris had an escort. Now the vampires she passed in the hall sneered and whispered and called her a traitor.

Before, happy memories had enveloped her, triggered by little more than the scent of the hallways. Now those memories of happy times were subsumed under a dark haze. He'd shot her. He'd knocked her out.

And he'd sent her away from this place that she'd once loved so very much.

She forced her steps to stay even as she walked beside her guard, concentrating on picking her feet up and putting them down. Trying to keep her mind empty of everything except the physical necessity of moving down the hall.

It wasn't working.

The things she wanted to forget were pressing up against her. Memories were writhing like black clouds. Circling her. Haunting her.

And as she walked, those dark memories swallowed her, as deep and black as the oily, roiling sea of pain she'd swum through as she clawed her way back to consciousness so many years ago.

She'd been shaking. A nightmare swirling inside her head, and she'd awakened in a terrorized state, confused, freaked, her daemon roiling and the wolf snapping for release. She'd fought desperately to pull it in—tried to prevent the change, but she couldn't. The wolf wanted to come out, and even all her vampiric strength couldn't hold it back.

It came. She changed. Her body shifted, pulled, ripped itself out of her control, muscles stretching, bones elongating. Pain so vivid it seemed alive.

Beside her, Giorgio screamed, and her eyes flew open. She realized too late what it meant that he was there—and she couldn't have done anything about it even if she'd realized in time. The change had her, and she was too new to have gained any control in the weren state.

She breathed, and the plague burst out upon him.

He knew it, too. He grabbed her arm, tugged her toward the containment chamber, then thrust them both inside. As she writhed and snarled on the ground, trying to force the wolf to retreat, he tapped a code into the keypad, locking them in. He took a step toward her, but already he was unstable. She watched through a lycan haze as his skin festered and his nose bled. As his mouth turned black.

By the time the wolf was in retreat and she was Caris again, he was delirious. And by the time Tiberius arrived at the safe house and peered through the containment room window, Giorgio was dust.

Caris looked up, her chest tight with self-loathing and regret, only to meet Tiberius's horrified eyes.

"I didn't—When I woke up. I couldn't—" Her throat was thick, her mind unable to process what she'd done. What she'd become.

"He had a family," Tiberius said, his measured words filtering through the intercom. She knew him well enough to know that he was holding in an explosion.

"I—I can learn. I can control it." She felt the tears stream down her face. "I just need time."

Their eyes met and held, and it seemed as if all the time in the world passed between them. Then he shook his head. "You fought the last hybrid at my side, Caris. You know exactly why we had to kill it."

"Please." She wasn't sure what she was begging for, because right then she believed he was right. She looked at the pile of dust that had been Giorgio, and she knew that, yes, she deserved to die.

But this was Tiberius, the man who was supposed to protect her. To save her even when she couldn't be saved. He was the man who was supposed to love her even when she didn't love herself.

And yet he stood there and told her that she could destroy the world.

"Do you know what this room is?" he asked.

She did, of course. She'd helped supervise the team that had designed it. One of the sad facts of political life in the shadow world was the occasional need to keep a captive. And when captives had the ability to transform to mist, airtight rooms were often required. More than that, rooms sometimes needed extra features. Such as the capability to incinerate. To completely destroy an enemy so no trace was left. Not even dust.

Giorgio had dragged them into that room and locked them in.

Now Tiberius stood on the outside with the power to either activate the incinerator or open the door.

"I know," she said.

"I love you," he said, his voice breaking. "But there are no second chances," he said. "Not for something like this. You can't go back. I can't risk it. I took an oath to protect my people, Caris. You know that."

She clenched her hands, her eyes going to the pile of dust as she readied herself for the pain of the fire. The death she deserved. "I know."

He pressed his hand to the glass, and she saw her own torment reflected in his eyes. She wanted to hate him for what he was about to do, but she couldn't. All she could be was numb.

"I'm sorry," he said.

She closed her eyes as he punched in the code. But there was no fire. No pain.

And when she opened her eyes, he was gone.

She stood cautiously. The door to the chamber was open.

She understood then that his words hadn't been a condemnation, but a warning. *Learn control,* he'd been saying. *Or he'd kill her himself.*

◆

"Caris? Miss Caris?"

The words pulled her from the unwelcome memories, and Caris peered down at the gray-haired vampire with bulbous eyes and a grandmotherly smile. She was standing beside a door, gesturing at Caris.

"Tiberius will see you now," she said, as she pushed open the door.

Right. Of course.

Caris lifted her chin and reminded herself that she was in control now. She was strong. Powerful. And she was here because she wanted to be, not because she'd been summoned.

She was a warrior.

Hell, she was *Caris*.

Right.

With a quick nod, Caris swept past the receptionist without another word, then stepped over the threshold into another world entirely. Unlike the antechamber's antique warmth, this room was cold and crisp. Chrome and glass surfaces, gleaming electronics. And the scent of brutal sterility.

The only hint of the Tiberius she'd known lay on the walls—rich, vibrant Impressionist paintings that gave much-needed color to the austere surroundings.

He'd been facing the window when she entered, and he hadn't yet turned around. Which, frankly, ticked her off.

She cleared her throat, but the sound came out weak rather than annoyed.

She saw the way his shoulders stiffened before he turned slowly to face her, and she forced herself to look at him. At the midnight-black hair that had once felt so soft beneath her fingers. At the patrician jaw she used to trace with her lips. And at those onyx eyes, his gaze so solid and stoic. Eyes that revealed nothing to anyone else, but had, once upon a time, told her everything she'd ever wanted to know.

She met those eyes now, cold and inscrutable, and she realized she was standing with her jaw clenched as tightly as her fists. Deliberately, she tried to relax.

"Thanks for finally opening up the inner sanctum," she said, painting her words thick with sarcasm. "I was beginning to think you'd forgotten that you'd invited me."

"Invited? Were you under the impression you could politely decline?"

She tensed, then bit back her instinctive response, which was a rather colorful curse word and an assault against his parentage. Now really wasn't the time to get into it with him. "Politely?" she repeated innocently. "I thought you knew me better."

His smile was quick and genuine and the ice between them melted just a little. "Thank you for coming."

"Oh." She shifted her weight, his conciliatory tone disarming her. "You're welcome. I guess I should apologize for killing your snitch. It wasn't about you."

"Even so, it has caused me quite a bit of inconvenience."

"Yeah, you said. I'm all broken up about that."

Tiberius moved away from the window, circling his desk until he was standing in front of it. He leaned back against it and regarded her. He looked both casual and commanding, something she'd always admired about him, and something that she knew served him well in the world of shadow politics. One minute he could be chatting someone up like his best buddy, the next minute he could lop off his head.

She looked around the room and then moved to one of the low leather chairs. She sank into it, and then with her eyes on Tiberius, casually kicked her feet up onto the glass coffee table. "So, you got me here. Whatever shall we talk about?"

"I have a few suggestions. For example, you tell me you're not working for Lihter, and yet the same day I'm scheduled to meet with a werewolf willing to reveal secrets of Lihter's inner circle, that werewolf is killed. And at the hand of a woman highly placed in weren circles."

"Dammit, Tiberius, I didn't kill him for Lihter. I don't give a rat's ass about Lihter. I killed him because—"

No. She closed her mouth. No, she wasn't going there. "Why?"

"You know what? Forget it. I've already told you it has nothing to do with you. And you gave up the right to ask me that when you banished me." She cringed, wishing she hadn't said quite so much. Because that was the crux of it, wasn't it? He'd washed his hands of her when he'd walked away from the safe house, and his indifference had been like a knife in her heart.

"I never forgot," he said.

"Didn't you? Sure felt like it from my end."

"You went to the weren." His words were flat, harsh. "You joined them."

Anger curled within her. "Dammit, Tiberius, I didn't go to Claudius. I went to *Gunnolf.* I went to a *weren.* One who could teach me how to control the new and exciting tricks and tribulations of my body." She leaned forward. "And what the hell was I supposed to do? You made it perfectly clear I was no longer one of your people. I guess that made me one of his." She leaned closer, getting right in his face. "*Weren.*"

A tic in his cheek was the only sign that his composure had been compromised. "Exactly," he finally said. "You've sided with the weren. And therein lies the rub. Because Reinholt had offered himself up as a spy."

"Oh, for Christ's sake. Do you really believe I'd step in as Lihter's go-to girl? Do you really know me so little?"

"No," he said. "I don't believe it."

"Oh." The swiftness and certainty of his response surprised her. "Well, you're right." She stood and moved toward the window that he'd abandoned earlier. Outside, she could see a faint purple glow at the horizon. Dawn was coming. She frowned. In the back of her mind, she'd known they wouldn't have time to finish their talk before the morning, but it was only now, standing in his office, that the full ramifications of that reality hit her. Today she'd have to stay in the guest wing. The thought made her shiver with a mixture of nostalgia and, yes, anticipation. Despite everything, she'd missed it here.

He moved to her side, and she had to focus to concentrate on his words rather than on the awareness of his proximity and the air that hung thick between them. "I may not believe that you're working with Lihter, but Reinholt is still dead, and my ability to obtain intelligence about the weren community has been severely compromised."

"Life is full of inconveniences."

He paused, and she had a feeling he was debating something. "I need your help, Caris."

"I asked you for help once," she said. "In this very room, in fact."

"Caris . . ."

"You turned me down flat. Kicked me out. Chose your precious politics over me and left me to find my own damn help." She saw him flinch. Saw regret color his eyes. "What?" she snapped, unable to keep the rising anger suppressed, the hurt that was flooding back now that he was standing right in front of her. "Are you going to tell me you made the wrong decision? That you regret it all and would do it differently if you could?"

"No." The word was soft, but it stung like a slap. "I would do nothing differently. You returned to a city of vampires with no ability to control the change. *My* vampires. My people. My responsibility. Do I regret the choice I made? No. Do I regret that my choice hurt you? I will regret that to the end of my days."

The air between them grew thick. She wanted to rail at him, to scream that he damn well better regret it. That he hadn't just hurt her, he'd destroyed her and everything she'd believed was true about the two of them. About the world.

But she couldn't. Speak of it, and she feared she'd melt, and though she might be willing to tell him that he'd kicked the shit out of her heart, she wasn't about to show him.

"It's dawn," she said.

"That means we have the entire day ahead of us to discuss this matter."

"Give me a room and we'll talk later."

At first she wasn't sure he was going to answer. Then he nodded, the movement strangely formal. "Of course," he said. "And we will talk, Caris. There are things I need to find out, and you're the one who will help me discover them."

CHAPTER 8

Gabriel Casavetes didn't like the cold—he never had. Ask almost anyone why that was, and the answer was always the same: Hellhounds like to be warm. Their native habitat was pretty damn hot, after all.

Maybe so, but Gabriel had never been to hell. Not a mythological hell, nor any otherworldly dimension that passed for that particular ill-documented but well-pondered place.

Closest Gabriel had been was El Paso. Come to think of it, maybe he'd set foot in hell after all.

Now here he was, smoking and stamping his feet to stay warm while he waited for Everil to come out of the third tavern they'd been in since sundown.

They'd both spent last night on the mountain, talking with the percipient—who'd seen nothing—and hovering near the forensic guys, urging them to make conclusions based on footprints and trace evidence. But the snow had filled in the footprints, and they hadn't found any decent trace.

Which left Gabriel in the irritating position of being an investigator without a lot to investigate.

"So what's our next step?" Everil had asked, and Gabriel had to admit that they were going to have to rely on the long-standing tradition of legwork.

"Wonderful! Wonderful!" Everil had been so giddy he'd practically clapped, and the tiny wings he kept hidden under a jacket fluttered unseen but made an odd scraping noise that Gabriel found incredibly distracting. "So what first?"

"Sleep," Gabriel had said, and despite Everil's disappointment, Gabriel had insisted. He wasn't any use to anyone, much less the dead, if he couldn't think, so he had caught a few hours of rest and then woke up with a plan.

He'd thought about heading out on his own, but he couldn't get his partner's excited, albeit prissy, face out of his head. So he'd called Everil and outlined their course of action.

Zermatt wasn't a town with murders, not of the human or shadower variety. And yet last night a weren snitch had ended up dead and an Alliance big shot had come to town. That suggested that Big Stuff was afoot. And in Gabriel's experience, Big Stuff tended to not be homegrown.

"So you think the killer came in from out of town."

"I think it's highly likely."

"Zermatt gets a lot of tourists," Everil said, and unfortunately, the little guy was right.

"Hopefully this tourist made himself known. We have two possibilities. Either our killer knew about the rendezvous point, or the killer simply knew Reinholt was going to be in town."

Everil nodded seriously. So seriously, in fact, that Gabriel was a bit surprised he didn't whip out a pad and start taking notes. "So which scenario are we hoping for?"

"The second," Gabriel said. And then, because he was suddenly possessed by the spirit of his third-grade teacher, he added, "Do you know why?"

Everil's forehead furrowed, his slightly pointed ears wriggling. "Because then the killer would have to look for him?"

"Got it in one."

And since Zermatt was, for better or worse, a heavy tourist establishment, the taverns seemed like the best bet for starting their inquiries. They'd gone to the first two together, but with this third one, Everil had wanted to go in alone to test out his newly honed investigative mojo.

And that was how Gabriel had found himself standing still in the cold outside the oddly named Lone Star Tavern, wondering what the hell was going on in there.

He took another drag on his cigarette and considered going inside. He decided against it, though. Let Everil try his luck. The junior detective was certainly eager enough.

Gabriel stood for another ninety-seven seconds, then dropped his cigarette, crushed the butt into the snow with the toe of his boot, and marched toward the tavern entrance. Everil deserved a chance, sure, but Gabriel was freezing his ass off.

Like all the bars on the Bahnhofstrasse, the tavern was dark and woody, managing to be both atmospheric and inviting. Give the human tourists a sense of being somewhere different, a glimspe of something more than just the urge to drink and ski and fuck that had lured them to this tiny tourist town in the first place.

From behind the bar, Tex looked up, then waved Gabriel over. "Usual?" the expatriate asked in his broken German.

For form—because he so rarely got to do it in this sleepy town—Gabriel flashed his badge.

"Well, look at that," Tex said, switching to his native English. "Little Gabe's all grown up. How come you never told me you were a cop? And both of us from the same great state."

"You running anything illegal through the pub?"

"Shit, no."

"Then you didn't need to know, did you?"

From Tex's expression, he was less than thrilled with that explanation, but he knew better than to push it. "You're not the only one playing cop in here tonight."

"Didn't think I was." He slid onto one of the stools, then tapped the counter. When his usual appeared, he took a long swallow, then glanced around, looking for Everil. "Where'd he go?"

"Thought he went to the john, but I'm thinking now he slipped out the back. Probably wanted to see the scene of the crime."

Gabriel cocked his head. "What crime?"

"Some guy got stabbed back there last night. I was gonna call the cops, honest, but he begged me not to."

Gabriel was only half listening. While unusual in Zermatt, human crimes weren't his jurisdiction. "Stabbed?"

"Punctured, really. Two jabs in his neck. Like some idiot got him with a barbecue fork."

That caught Gabriel's attention. And explained Everil's disappearance. "The other cop who was in here, did you tell him about this?"

Tex squinted at Gabriel. "You're both cops. Why don't you ask him?"

"He's my partner, and I will. Why don't you tell me now?"

"Partner, huh?" Tex shrugged. "He's an odd one. Freaky aura." Tex was as human as they came, and

Gabriel doubted he could see an aura if one reached out and slapped him.

"That a fact? And what's my aura like?"

Tex snorted. "Gabe, if I told you how weird the shit floating around you is, we probably wouldn't be friends anymore."

"Are we friends now?"

"I keep hoping."

Gabriel took another sip to hide his smile. He'd worked hard not to make any friends in Zermatt, but if he had, Tex would've been high on the list.

"So you told Everil about the attack in the alley. What else?"

"Not much. Just the vic's name, is all."

"You know the vic?"

"Sure. Jenson Graham. Tourist, but he comes here at least twice a year. Big skier."

"Medics take him to the hospital?"

"Yeah, he was bleeding pretty bad."

"Any idea who stabbed him?" Gabriel asked, hoping to get lucky.

"That I couldn't say. Although if I had to guess, I'd go with the chick's boyfriend."

"What chick?"

"Although come to think of it, she didn't much look like she was with a guy."

"Tell me," Gabriel said, propping his elbows on the bar.

"Not much to tell. Jenson was hitting on her, you know."

"What did she look like?"

"Short dark hair. Green eyes. Attitude. I saw her.

Didn't pay much attention." A pause. "Okay, that's not exactly true. Girl was hot. But it was a busy night."

"Anything else?"

Tex shrugged. "Don't really know what you're look-ing for."

Unfortunately, neither did Gabriel. "You seen her around before?"

"Can't say that I have. Her, I woulda remembered."

"She pay with a credit card?"

Tex considered. "Cash. And just the one drink."

"Anybody else new come through last night?"

"Hell, yeah. We're as tourist friendly as they come, Gabe. You know that."

Gabriel did know it. But he'd been hoping that he was on a lucky streak. "Thanks." He slid off the bar stool.

"That's it?" Tex sounded disappointed, as if he'd ex-pected Gabriel to rough him up for information and was bummed that he hadn't. *Humans.*

Gabriel slid the half-empty drink away from him. "Put it on my tab." He was gone before Tex could point out that he didn't have a tab.

Everil wasn't hard to find. He was on his hands and knees in the alley and looked up as Gabriel approached. "There was a stabbing here," he said, his black eyes wide. "A human did it, though. Tex in there said the kid was attacked with a barbecue fork."

Gabriel waited a few seconds for the punch line, and when it didn't come, he realized his partner was serious. "Ah, Ev? I think the attacker was probably a vampire. Two pointy teeth." He made fangs from his fingers to demonstrate.

Everil's eyes got even wider. "Oh! Right!" He stood,

then lifted his nose to the air, sniffing. "Yeah," he said. "I shoulda picked up on it before. Vampire. Definitely vampire."

"I didn't realize the fae had such a keen sense of smell."

Everil stood up straighter, then puffed his chest out. "Hello? Half weren."

"Yeah?" Gabriel peered closely at his partner, but he didn't see the signs. Must've been a recessive gene. "I talked to Tex. Medics took the vic away. Let's go check the hospital. Even if they didn't admit him, they should have an address."

As it turned out, he was still there, sitting in a crowded emergency center awaiting discharge.

Gabriel flashed his badge, the one that said he worked for Interpol, and a nurse took them into a private room. Graham shifted, antsy. "So, should I be calling my embassy? I mean, I didn't do anything wrong. I'm the victim, right?"

"As far as we know," Gabriel said. "We're interested in who did this to you."

"Oh. Right. It was a fight, you know. Some guys. Locals. We've, you know, had run-ins before."

"Locals?" Gabriel met Everil's eyes. He doubted locals blew Reinholt away.

"Yeah. I—we don't get along. I guess I finally rubbed them the wrong way and they decided to, you know. Mess me up a little."

"Names?"

Graham told them, and Everil typed them into his PDA. A few seconds later, he nodded. "Got 'em. They're locals, all right."

He passed the PDA to Gabriel, who skimmed the file.

Vampires, yeah, but your basic troublemakers. Not the kind likely to go after something big, and Gabriel's current operating theory was that this murder was related to something big.

"So they're locals," Gabriel said. "Tell me about the girl. You ever seen her before?"

"Girl?"

"The one you were hitting on in the bar. Green eyes. Short dark hair. A looker."

"Oh. Her. Right." Graham shifted in his seat again. "She in trouble?"

"Might be. You might be, too, if you don't tell me what I want to know."

Again with the shifting. "Ah, hell. Okay, look. She was a bitch, right? I mean, yeah, I, uh, hit on her. But she turned me down cold. But then when I was in the alley and these guys got all danger zone with me, she's the one who got them the hell out of there." He shrugged. "So, you know, I guess I owe her."

"And the men in the alley, they just decided that the neck seemed like the best place to stab you?"

More shifting, and he didn't quite meet Gabriel's eyes. "Weird, huh?"

Gabriel raised his brows. He'd seen this before. Humans who liked to get down and dirty with the vampire crowd. "So she saved you from a vampire. Was she talking to any other vamps? Talking to anyone else in the bar?"

"What?" The tourist's eyes were wide and overly innocent, as if he was trying just a little too hard. "Vampire? I mean, wow. That's crazy. You guys are—"

"We're not your average cops is who we are. And unless you want to be high priority on my office's radar—

and you don't—you tell me everything you can about the girl."

"You're not going to, you know . . ." He trailed off, then made a knife motion across his throat.

"Not today." It wasn't common for humans to know about shadowers, but it wasn't unheard of. As long as Graham stayed out of dark alleys with hungry vampires, he'd be fine.

"There's not much to tell. I mean, she's a vamp, too. I could tell. Once you learn about 'em, you can pick them out. She sure as hell didn't want me to know, though. I called her a vamp and she about bit my head off." He shrugged. "It wasn't my head I wanted her to bite, but she wasn't interested."

"What was she interested in?" Gabriel asked.

"Don't know. Probably a dude. She was scoping the place out."

And there was the meat of it. "She find anyone?"

"Beats me. She told me to scram. I scrammed."

Gabriel stood. "Okay, Mr. Graham. I think that about wraps it up." He got the guy's address and phone number, just in case, and told him he could leave as soon as the hospital released him. "Just one more thing," he added, before he and Everil headed out. "Did you happen to get her name?"

"I didn't," Graham said. "But she told it to the vamps who had me pinned. I swear they just about peed their pants."

"Is that a fact? So what was it?"

"Caris. She just said that it was Caris."

"*Caris!*" Everil said when they were under the emergency center's awning. "You were right. This is big."

Gabriel frowned. Everil wasn't exaggerating.

"She's Gunnolf's woman," Everil continued. "And she used to be with Tiberius."

"I know," Gabriel said, barely managing to speak without a groan. "We're walking straight into a political shitstorm."

Everil nodded enthusiastically.

"Calm down, partner," Gabriel said. "We play this one close to the vest. We go making accusations or applying for an arrest warrant before we've built a case, and we could both experience some serious consequences."

"Right. Consequences. Right."

"There's gonna be eyes on this case. Dragos was there for a meeting, Reinholt was set up to be a weren snitch. And Caris is in groin-deep with the werens."

Everil shook his head. "Not anymore. She was Gunnolf's woman. I don't think she's tight with Lihter."

"Probably not," Gabriel conceded. "But from my perspective, it's anyone's guess who she's cozied up to now. And Lihter could just as easily be pulling her strings as anyone."

He caught himself, realized he was already putting theories together.

Shit. He hadn't transferred to Zermatt so he could get pulled into a Big Fucking Case. The last one he'd handled had ended when an innocent girl fried.

And that was something he didn't relish repeating.

But want it or not, he was stuck. He hadn't found the case. The case had found him.

CHAPTER 9

The next time he came to Memphis, Bael Slater hoped it was the American version. Pyramids were fine and dandy, but the dry desert air irritated him, and when you got right down to it, what was the point of Memphis if you couldn't see Graceland?

Right now, of course, the point was to find Drescher Bovil. Find. Kill. Get the hell back home.

Normally he'd take a bit more time with an assignment, but Tiberius had stressed the urgency of the matter. The Alliance vote was coming soon, and the new para-daemon rep needed time to get in the job, get settled, and make the right decision about whom to vote for.

But all of that meant that the old para-daemon rep needed to be removed from the equation.

Fortunately, Bovil wasn't particularly popular even with his own kind, and it didn't take too much effort for Slater to learn where he was tonight—tucked away in a five-star hotel with a steady parade of human hookers. At the moment, Bael was crouched in the hallway outside Bovil's hotel room. The guard beside the door was lolling forward in his chair, most likely because Slater had broken his neck. He'd already taken care of the security cameras, so that wasn't a problem. And while he would have liked to slip into the room as mist beneath the door, the room had been reinforced with hematite.

Apparently Bovil used this particular love nest a lot.

Bad, in that it made Slater's mission that much more difficult.

Good, in that those precautions would make it harder to place blame on the vampire community.

According to his source, Slater's men checked each girl for weapons, recorders, cellphones, the works in the lobby. Once they were cleared, they were given a five-digit code and told to memorize it. The code worked the keypad lock on the door. And there was no other way in. Slater had searched the guard just in case, but he'd found no key card, no traditional key, and no number scrawled conveniently on his body.

The girls were the only way in.

So now he waited.

The elevator dinged, and Slater stood at attention beside the slumped guard. The doors opened and a petite blond human stepped out. She licked her lips, squared her shoulders, and walked straight toward him.

"Code?" he demanded.

She glanced down at the guard in the chair, her face a question mark.

"He's on break," Slater said. "We rotate. Code?"

"Five, two, five, three, one."

Slater nodded, as if satisfied. "Fine. Stand for inspection."

"But I—"

"Stand for inspection."

She stood straight, eyes wide, and he punched in the code. The lock clicked, he pushed open the door, and ushered her inside with a sweep of his arm.

He'd chatted up the front desk clerk earlier and learned the layout of the suites. He'd expected that Bovil would be in one of the two back bedrooms and that the foyer and living area would be empty. He'd been right.

He took a guess, nodded toward the bedroom on the right, and told the girl to go on in. Then he positioned himself at attention in front of the door, just for show. He waited until he could hear moans and the creaking of bedsprings. Then he crossed to the bedroom door, pushed it open, and evaluated the scene: Bovil on top of the hooker, pumping his brains out, his back—not to mention his ass—right in Slater's field of vision.

Damn, but he was making this easy.

He reached into his jacket pocket and pulled out the ice pick he'd stowed there.

Two quick steps and he was at the bed. One more economical move and he had his arm around the para-daemon's throat. With his other hand, he pressed the end of the ice pick against Bovil's right ear.

"I've got a message," he said as Bovil thrashed, though he wasn't certain Bovil could hear him over the girl's screams. And then it didn't matter, because he knew damn well that Bovil couldn't hear him once the ice pick penetrated his ear, not to mention his brain.

The para-daemon went limp and Slater dropped the body. "Shoddy security, dude. You really should be ashamed."

In the bed, the girl trembled. "Trust me," Slater said. "He wouldn't have been nice to you." He pulled a wad of bills from his pocket. "Consider this a tip. Keep your mouth quiet, and I think it's fair to say you earned it. Got it?"

She nodded, fear clinging to her like dime-store perfume.

"Go," he said, and she was out the door before his voice faded.

"Nice girl," he murmured as he pulled out his knife and removed Bovil's head, just to be safe. You couldn't be too careful with para-daemons. He'd learned that one the hard way.

A ringing phone interrupted his attempt to clean his knife on the bedspread. He looked around and found it on the floor beside the bed, the caller ID reading Private.

He answered, his voice deliberately low and raspy.

"What?"

"Sir," a breathless voice said. "Sir, you were right. All those rumors. They're true. Something's up with Lihter. He's working on something big."

The speaker paused, and Slater debated only a moment before deciding to press his luck. He scratched at the mouthpiece, hopefully simulating static. "Tell me."

Too much. The caller knew.

He heard a gasp, then a click.

And that, Slater thought, was his cue to leave.

♦

"Sir, they've arrived."

Faro Lihter turned as Dr. Honas Behar hurried toward him, sweat glistening on his forehead. He wiped it with the sleeve of his crisp lab coat, then grimaced.

Lihter smiled. "Nervous, Doctor?"

"These creatures aren't even supposed to exist anymore. To have the chance to study one . . ." He trailed off, and Lihter had the distinct impression he was literally buzzing with pleasure. "But, sir, the chamber. I haven't had the opportunity to test it."

"Do you think I'd bring you to a lab and not have it be sufficient for your purposes? Do you think I'd spend years building this complex without ensuring that everything is perfect?"

"No, no. I didn't mean to insult. I only—"

Lihter held his hand up. "She comes."

Behar fell silent as Lihter cocked his head, listening to the sound of his team's footfalls on the long stretch of stairs that led down from the surface to the thick metal door. He savored the moment.

"Do you know how many years I've waited for this moment?"

"I . . . No, I don't."

"I was there, in Marseilles, right in the middle of the very last outbreak of the plague."

"You were there?"

"I walked through the destruction with my head held high. I was a god walking through the valley of the shadow of death, and I knew then what I would do. Capture the hybrid. Use the hybrid. And repopulate the world the way that it should be." He met Behar's eyes. "The way we will."

"Sir!" He could see his own passion reflected in the doctor's eyes, and he smiled.

"Unfortunately, my plan has taken longer than I'd hoped. Tiberius put a bit of a kink in it when he killed the last hybrid in Cluny."

"The last?" Behar's eyes darted toward the door. "But—"

"The last," Lihter confirmed. "At the time, anyway. That will be our first question for our guest. How she came to be. A new hybrid in a world without hybrids. A creature created from something that cannot be made.

It's a mystery, and one that neither I nor my team have been able to solve."

Behar was a relatively new addition to the team—he'd joined only a decade ago. But for centuries now, Lihter had been gathering like-minded werens around him, setting them to various tasks aimed at only one goal: the creation of a new hybrid.

It wasn't easy work. Lihter had spent years researching ancient texts, trying to learn how a hybrid was made. He'd found only one clue, a transcript of a story handed down within a family. A vampire warrior in the third century who'd come upon a woman who begged the warrior to kill her.

As the warrior recounted the story, he'd refused at first. But then the woman had threatened to bring out the wolf right there in the middle of the Roman forum. And so he said he would do it. But first she had to answer one simple question: *How?* How had she come to be?

But the woman didn't know. She'd been a vampire, and one night she met a werewolf prowling deep within a forest. They'd fought, and she'd somehow lost her senses. She remembered torture and pain. And when she came back fully to herself, she knew that she'd fallen under the curse, and that what she'd once believed was only rumor was alive within her. She had no explanation as to how, and assumed it must have come about by dark magic.

She could tell the warrior nothing more, and he had honored his promise. Right then, right there, he drove a stake through her heart, then lopped off her head.

At the time he'd discovered the document, Lihter wished the warrior had asked for a few more details.

And hoping that maybe the warrior had in fact learned the secret but had recounted the truth elsewhere, he began a systematic search for every document authored by the vampire warrior.

The process was long and tedious, but he knew he would succeed. Lihter had both confidence and patience, and he'd begun building this facility even before he had the first clue about how to create a hybrid.

His confidence and preparation had paid off. About eleven months ago, his research had taken a most extraordinary turn. He'd been perusing the collection of a small library in Peru when he had run across one particularly interesting tidbit: He was not the only one following the trail of hybrids.

There was another.

Another researcher was reviewing the same books. Another scholar was following the same leads.

Lihter had shifted his plan. He stopped searching for the warrior and instead began to look for the researcher.

That hadn't taken long. The researcher had taken some pains to hide his identity, but not many. After only a few inquiries and bribes, Lihter was able to obtain a name: Cyrus Reinholt.

And as luck would have it, Reinholt happened to be a werewolf. A werewolf who lived in Paris and was a frequent guest at the château.

Truly the stars were aligning in Lihter's favor.

His plan had been simple. Fabricate a security breach and bring all of the werens with château access in front of a Truth Teller. But apparently Reinholt got wind of the plan and ran.

It had been most inconvenient. At least until Lihter

had learned that Reinholt had a daughter. And children meant leverage.

He'd arranged to kidnap the bitch. A straightforward, simple arrangement that had turned out to be not so simple after all. Because during the course of the abduction, she'd been injured, and her blood had destroyed one of his men.

Acid blood.

The hallmark of a hybrid.

Everything had fallen into place—Reinholt had found the answer in the research, and he'd made a hybrid of his own daughter. A horrible thing for a father to do, really, and Lihter felt no guilt about taking her away from such a worthless excuse of a parent.

But the girl was his now. His years of researching had been fascinating, to be sure. And he would still very much love to have Reinholt's secrets at his disposal.

None of that, however, was critical anymore.

The girl was his weapon.

And he intended to use her well.

And soon.

The thunder of footsteps stopped outside the heavy steel door, and he heard the steady *beep beep* of the twelve-digit security code being entered. Beside him, Behar stiffened, anticipation coloring his face like a mask. Lihter felt the same way. The day the girl had been apprehended in Frankfurt, Lihter himself had been in Paris, addressing the day-to-day tasks that occupied him as the Therian representative to the Alliance table— and ensuring that he wasn't directly tied to the girl's disappearance.

Now they were in the small Liechtenstein laboratory that he'd so carefully—and secretly—constructed over the years. He hadn't even seen the girl yet. His unexpected prize. His glorious reward.

The moment would be unforgettable.

The door opened, and four of his most trusted men came in, each carrying one corner of the hassock on which the girl lay, unconscious.

"You used enough tranquilizer?" Lihter asked. "Her resistance will be as abnormally high as her strength."

"Could knock out five circus elephants with the dose we pumped into her."

She lay on the hassock, her arms at her side, her eyes closed. Her hand was scarred where it had been cut, but was already starting to heal. Except for the ten hematite straps that crisscrossed her body and the IV tube feeding into the back of her hand, she could have been simply sleeping peacefully.

"Beautiful," Lihter said, then caressed her face. She was young, only about eighteen, and in repose she looked as innocent as she was deadly.

"Remove the straps and the IV and put her in the room," he said. He glanced at Behar. "How long will it take for the drug to wear off?"

"Without a better understanding of her physiology, I can't be certain, but I'm guessing four or five hours."

Lihter nodded, then glanced at Rico, his right-hand man. "Run a complete diagnostic on the system. Make sure all vents are opening and sealing properly."

"Will do," Rico said. The console phone, the hard line, began to ring. Lihter gestured for him to answer it, then waited impatiently for Rico to finish.

"Sir."

"I also want you to confirm all monitoring equipment is calibrated. We'll run the first test as soon as she wakes."

"Of course, but, sir, our cellphone encryption's been compromised."

Lihter's brows rose. "Has it?"

Rico nodded toward the landline. "That's the word from your guy in the Alliance."

A frustrating reality, but hardly crippling. "Make sure everyone on the team knows not to use cellular communications. Hard lines only. They disobey, they die. This operation is too important to compromise."

"Yes, sir. Absolutely."

Lihter nodded in dismissal, then moved toward the airtight chamber, with its two-foot-thick Plexiglas walls. A simple folding chair sat in front of it, and he took a seat. He didn't care how long he had to wait. He would be the first thing she saw when she awoke.

And once she did, he would tell the girl all about the wonderful plans he had in store for her.

CHAPTER 10

Caris's scent lingered in Tiberius's office, putting him on edge, getting into his thoughts. His blood.

With considerable effort, he turned his focus to tracking down the kidnapped girl. He'd made a promise to Reinholt to help his daughter, and it was a promise Tiberius intended to keep.

He dug into the work and slowly Caris faded from his mind, replaced with notes about contacts, leads, anyone who might have known Reinholt or the girl.

One of the few solid pieces of information that Reinholt had provided was that the girl was a vampire, a fact that had raised Tiberius's brow.

"I know," Reinholt had said when they'd talked over the phone. "It is most unusual. But you see, it is for this reason I come to you. Unlike many of my kind, I do not distrust the vampires. And," he added, "I do not believe that you will allow one of your kind to be taken by Lihter. Not if you can do anything to help it. Please, sir. Please help my Naomi."

"How is it that you are a weren and she is not?"

He hesitated, then drew in a breath. "Her mother, she was human. We fell in love, we had a child."

"And the child was not weren?"

"It . . . it . . . doesn't always transfer. She was human, beautiful and vibrant."

"And then she was turned."

This time the pause was so long Tiberius feared the connection had been lost. "Yes."

"And what good would the girl be to Lihter?"

"I—I— Please, please you must find her. He . . . he took her to get to me. Because I went away. But I didn't know. I didn't know what he wanted."

"What do you mean?"

He could hear Reinholt breathing softly. "I heard rumors that Lihter had engaged a Truth Teller. Everyone with access to the château would be tested. For loyalty. I ran."

"You've been selling Lihter's secrets?"

"No! No! I've been nothing but loyal. I mind my own business. But there are things that I have in my head. Things I don't want to share."

"And you thought a Truth Teller would reveal those things?"

"Undoubtedly. And so I left. I never thought Lihter would care. I was under no suspicion. I didn't run, but neither did I advertise where I went. And when he left messages for me to return to Paris, I ignored them."

"And so he took Naomi to get your attention."

"Yes. Yes, please, you must help me."

Tiberius held the phone, silently considering the weren's words. He believed that Reinholt was afraid for his daughter. He believed that Reinholt had left to avoid the Truth Teller. But that wasn't the full story. There were things left unsaid and truths twisted, and it was in the silence that the real story lay. "Why have you not told me everything?"

Reinholt gasped. "I—please. There are . . . things you should know. And when we meet, I will tell you everything. I swear upon my life that you will know the truth, but please, please do not make me speak of it now. Not when there may be other ears."

Tiberius hesitated. The fear in Reinholt's voice was so real he could almost catch the scent of it even across the telephone line. But was it fear for his daughter, or fear of Lihter, the werewolf against whom Reinholt was prepared to turn?

"We will meet," Tiberius said. "In case you are right about other ears, we shall set the time and place later. I'll be in touch. Meanwhile, tell me what you can about your daughter's disappearance. Perhaps by the time we meet I'll have news."

"Then you will help me?" His voice shook with relief.

"I will help your daughter."

"Thank you, thank you."

"Where was she taken?"

"Frankfurt. She was on her way to Austria to visit me. I have—I *had*—a safe house there. She called me from the Zeil," he said, referring to Frankfurt's main shopping district. "She told me she intended to shop before catching her train—my Naomi loves to shop."

"What makes you think that Lihter took her?"

"Again, that part must be told in person. But rest assured that I am certain."

It had been an unsatisfactory answer, but though Tiberius tried to pry more information free, Reinholt refused to talk. Tiberius didn't go so far as to refuse to help—he believed the girl was truly in danger—but now he wished that he had threatened. He might know more. Because right now he was starting from nothing except Frankfurt, the knowledge that the girl was a power shopper, and a photo that Reinholt had forwarded by text message.

Damn.

He circulated the photo to his contacts in Frankfurt but decided against formally calling in the PEC to search for the missing girl. Reinholt had been prepared to provide information of a political nature. Best to consider this an Alliance matter, and a vampire matter at that. The PEC agents were undoubtedly competent, but there were some things that were so politically charged that they were best investigated in-house.

He frowned, thinking of Caris. He'd ordered Luke to initiate a task force primarily to protect her. But the truth was he'd have done the same thing no matter who Reinholt's assassin had been.

Caris. He'd let his thoughts shift back to her, and now she dominated his mind once again. *Dammit.*

His phone buzzed, a welcome interruption, and Mrs. Todd's voice filled the room. "It's Mr. Slater, sir. He said it's important."

"Done," Bael Slater said as soon as Tiberius took the call.

"I had no doubt. You could have waited to inform me in person."

"There's more. I intercepted a call. Bovil's cellphone was ringing, and it seemed rude not to answer—"

"Tell me."

"Apparently Lihter's on the para-daemons' radar, too. Couldn't tell who was speaking, and the damn ID and GPS were blocked, but the message was clear enough. He's learned that Lihter's planning something. Something big."

"That fits," Tiberius said. Reinholt must have gotten wind as well, and was willing to trade Lihter's plans for his daughter's safety. "Could you get any details?"

"I tried. Call went dead. I have to assume I did a less-than-stellar job of impersonating Bovil."

Tiberius asked Slater a few more questions, then ended the call, his mind full of strategy and theory. The urgency had just ramped up.

He stood, telling himself that he was going to Caris now because time was of the essence. Lihter was up to something. The election was in less than ten days. And the girl could be in grave danger.

All valid reasons, but none surpassed the basic, under-lying truth: He simply wanted to see her again, and he'd held back for as long as he could.

When he found Caris, she was standing at the window beside the blue room's massive oak desk, looking out at the sky through the protective glass. He paused, watching. She wore a black leather jacket and simple jeans, except that there was nothing simple about the way they hugged her curves. Curves that he had once known inti-mately and could still recall the feel of.

He slipped his hands into the pockets of his own slacks, warding off the memories—of her, of his past. He realized with a start that he was seeing the woman, not the weren, not the hybrid.

He stood silently, knowing he should walk forward, say something, announce his presence to the room. But although he hated to admit it even to himself, he didn't want this moment to shatter. So instead, he simply watched. Her pale hand, pressed against the glass. Her raven hair gleaming.

She stood perfectly still except for her chest, rising and falling. He wondered vaguely if she had to breathe now, then cursed the question, which only reminded him that more separated them than the expanse of room. So much more.

"If you have something to say, then say it." She spoke to the window, not bothering to turn around. "Otherwise, I'm anxious to get out of here."

"I told you, I need your help with something. I need your access to the weren world."

"Is that a fact? And you just expect me to help you for nothing? I thought you knew me better." She turned. A muscle twitched in her cheek, but she held steady, the moment ripe between them, and for that instant he could almost—almost—forget.

She looked away, and the moment shattered.

"For nothing?" he said. "I'd say not. You killed my informant, Caris. You owe me."

This time when she turned back, her eyes were blazing. "You know what, Tiberius? Fuck you. Oh, wait. I don't do that anymore. And that means I also don't owe you anything. Not help, not explanations, not anything."

"I'm afraid I disagree on that point."

She stood firm. "Yeah, I thought you might. So I've been thinking about that. You want my help? Fine. But you have to do something for me."

His brow lifted. "I think you may be confused about who owes whom."

"I assure you I'm not."

"What do you want, Caris?" Better to just satisfy her whim and get on with it.

"I want you to appoint Gunnolf the governor of the Scottish territory. Transfer your authority to him."

It took great effort for him not to laugh out loud. "That's never going to happen."

"Then I guess we've reached an impasse."

For the moment at least, he had to agree. Time to try a different tack. "The Alliance is taking over the murder investigation, Caris."

She looked up, her expression alarmed.

"In light of Reinholt's controversial political positions, I've arranged for a task force to be created and jurisdiction to be transferred from Division 12 to the Alliance."

"You son of a bitch. How can you—"

"A task force that will not—I repeat *not*—find any connection to you. A task force that, frankly, will ultimately stall out."

She stared at him, her face blank, her thoughts hidden behind a well-schooled facade. The corner of her eye crinkled, as if something unpleasant was buzzing nearby. "Why would you do that?" Her voice was low, measured. And it was dangerous.

"You know why."

She shook her head. "No."

"I made a promise, and I will see it through."

"I release you from your promise."

"Your father tried that once. I turned him down as well. The promise wasn't made to you, and I will honor my word to Horatius."

"I don't want you looking over my shoulder. I don't want you in my life. You gave up that right when you banished me."

He stiffened, his words measured. "To be in your life, yes. To protect it, never."

"You swore to protect my family from harm. Not from the consequences of our own actions."

"I will have you safe."

He knew her well enough to recognize the fury in her eyes. She took a step toward him. "You won't have me at all."

"I don't recall you being this infuriating when we were together."

A tiny smile played at her mouth, and the tension between them lessened. "I'm a work in progress," she said. "Dynamic."

"You are indeed."

"And I still don't owe you anything, and you sure as hell owe me nothing."

"You know that's not true."

"This conversation is over."

"What did Reinholt know of Lihter's plans?"

She took a step toward him, putting her hips into it as well as her smile. She looked sexy as hell and just as dangerous. "You can stop this interrogation now. Get used to the idea of not always getting what you want."

She started to stalk past him, and he reached out and grabbed her arm. "Sorry. That's not something I'll ever get used to."

She jerked away and looked up at him, eyes blazing, that fierceness he'd once admired now directed at him. "Why the hell should I help you? I'm out of here at sunset. In the meantime, get out of my room."

"Stay. Caris, it's important."

She bristled, but held her ground. She was only inches

away, and even after so many years, the scent of her was achingly familiar. Everything, that is, except the wolf.

The wolf.

Always, it was the goddamned wolf.

He took a step backward. And then he looked away.

As if sensing weakness, she moved closer. "Gee. Thanks so much for the invitation. Your hospitality is overwhelming. How can I possibly refuse?" She casually pulled her phone out of her jacket pocket and held it up. "I should probably call Gunnolf. I told him I was coming. By now, he's probably wondering if you slit my throat." She said the words blandly, and the lack of humor chilled him.

He looked hard at her, the casual mention of Gunnolf erasing any lingering wisps of the woman he'd once loved and leaving only the warrior standing before him. *Good.* He didn't want the woman in his head. Not now. Not anymore. "You wish for Gunnolf to have all of Scotland? It won't happen. But the Highlands . . . If you help me—if we succeed—that I will consider."

That he hadn't soundly dismissed her suggestion that he abdicate all of Scotland was testament to his concern about Lihter's activities and his need for solid intelligence. And, yes, to his desire to have Caris at his side again, even if only for a mission.

He had banished her because of politics. Because he was a ruler who had an obligation to protect his people no matter what the cost. He'd let her live because of love. And still, he'd lost her.

But now it was politics that could pull them together again. He'd be a fool not to exploit the opportunity.

Then again, perhaps he was a fool because he hoped to do that very thing.

Caris stepped sideways, her posture like a predator circling its prey. "Consider? It's all about the politics, isn't it? But with you, it always was. I should know that better than anyone."

"You admired my commitment once. You even shared my ambition."

"I'm a different woman now," she countered. "I thought we'd already established that."

"Different, but not foolish. You want something, I want something. Tit for tat."

The tiniest smile touched her lips as one eyebrow lifted. "Tit for tat?" she repeated, her eyes dipping toward his crotch, the movement so quick he doubted she even realized she'd done it, and he forced himself not to react. The connection between them was still there, and he wasn't the only one who felt it.

But under the circumstances, he wasn't sure if that was good, or very bad.

She turned away. "The Highlands?"

"The offer is on the table."

"And how do I earn such a precious reward?"

"Reinholt. I need to know what he'd learned of Lihter. What he came to Zermatt to tell me."

"Gee, is that all?"

"Actually, no. His daughter has been kidnapped. By Lihter. I made a promise to find her. You will help me."

"And all you're offering is the Highlands?"

Tiberius said nothing.

"You're operating under a misconception if you think I can just waltz into Paris and come away with the goods on Lihter. The weren don't trust me. Even those who remain loyal to Gunnolf. To them I was just a vampire. Just Gunnolf's whore." Her voice was thick with outrage as she said the last, and for the first time he was struck by the possibility that her transition from his world to Gunnolf's had not been as clean as he had let himself believe.

She shook herself, as if tossing off memories. "I'm not the help you need."

"Perhaps not," he said. "But right now, you are the only help I have."

CHAPTER 11

As soon as the door closed behind him, Caris realized that she could breathe again. Before, her body had seemed frozen. Tight. As if she were in someone else's skin, unable to move the way she wanted to.

Now that tightness had vanished, but instead of the Caris she knew, the woman left standing in the room was broken somehow.

She'd told him she'd think about it, but she knew she'd accept. She told herself she didn't want to. That she was only agreeing because of the girl. But that wasn't true. Damn her, she was stepping in because she wanted to. Because she wanted to be near Tiberius, even if only on a mission.

She'd returned wanting to hate him—she *did* hate him. But she thought after coming here she'd hate him even more.

But she didn't. She'd seen regret in his eyes. Just a hint, just a flicker, but it had ripped through her like a shard of glass. And that single look had said more to her than all the words they'd bandied about.

The Tiberius she'd once known would never have shown weakness to an enemy. And yet even after everything that had passed between them, he'd shown it to her.

She closed her eyes, willing her thoughts to calm. She was here, she was working with him. There was no changing that.

He was no longer her lover. There was no changing that, either.

But she'd been wrong about one thing. All these years she'd assumed he was no longer protecting her. That the promise he'd made to her ancestor Horatius meant nothing to him anymore—not after what she'd done to Giorgio.

He'd banished her, and that had cut like a knife. But when he'd let her live, she'd assumed it had been the last concession to his promise. She believed that he'd washed his hands of her, of his promise, of all the De Soranzo family.

But that wasn't true at all. He'd created this task force to protect her. Even after everything, he was looking out for her.

She reached out to steady herself, not liking the way that reality was shifting beneath her feet. She'd shaped and polished her hate over the years, but now she was finding it cracked, its layers beginning to peel away.

That wasn't a reality she wanted to examine. Because hating Tiberius was easy. If that hate chipped away, she wasn't sure if she could stand the pain.

She curled her fingers around her phone, craving Gunnolf's voice. Hard to believe she'd come to rely so much on his friendship. When she'd first gone to him, she'd half expected that he would kill her. She was a vampire, after all. At least as far as he was concerned. She was Tiberius's mate, and Tiberius hadn't made life easy for the werens, or Gunnolf in particular.

But he'd granted her a private audience, something she'd hoped for but hadn't really been expecting.

"If this is a trap, lass, you'll no walk out of here alive." He'd looked at her harshly, his eyes narrowed, his hair a fiery mane. She remembered that she hadn't been scared. Why should she be? She'd already been made a hybrid; she'd already killed a man. She'd already lost Tiberius. Nothing could be worse than that.

"It's not a trap," she said. "And trust me when I say that between the two of us, you would not come out the victor."

"Is that a fact?"

"It is. And once you hear my story, you'll understand why."

To his credit, he'd sat and listened as she'd talked, speaking of her plan to prove to Tiberius that she could be an asset in the field. Telling him of how she had tracked the traitor—and how her plan had gone so completely wrong.

When she finished, he stood and walked slowly around her.

"You don't believe me?"

"There is the scent of the wolf on you. What you say may be true."

She crossed her arms and cocked her head. "Want me to prove it to you? Trust me, it's a lot easier to let the wolf out than to keep it in. Even when it's not a full moon, the effort just about kills me."

"And if you succumb, you kill many others."

"Not you," she said.

"No, not me. Nor my kind." He was silent for a moment, watching her. "You say that he banished you."

She tensed, her hands tight at her side as she fought both anger and the wolf. "He did."

He met her eyes. "Were you one of mine, I would have done the same. And he was a great fool to let you live."

She looked back at him, just as hard. "He was," she

agreed. "And I think I hate him for it." That was the crux of it. Of her anger with Tiberius. He let her live because he loved her or because he owed her. But that life came with horrible memories of Giorgio. Memories she didn't want and couldn't escape.

She might hate Tiberius, but she hated herself more.

For a moment he said nothing, and she feared he was going to send her away. But then he nodded and stood. "I will help you. But not here."

He told her where to meet him—a secluded cave, far from the city. It was a location he used when his own kind were punished, and it was already complete with chains and shackles and other devices to ensure that she would not escape. She'd hesitated at first—how easy it would have been for him to assassinate her.

Of course that was why she'd complied, because a part of her wanted death.

She'd craved an end to a life in which she no longer belonged, either to the world or to Tiberius, and so she'd allowed him to shackle her, and then she'd let go with what she'd been holding in for so long. The wolf. The beast. It burst from her, hard and fast and oh, so painful.

She could remember nothing of that change, but when she'd regained her senses, Gunnolf was smiling down at her, mopping her forehead with a damp rag.

"No one must know," he said. "You cannot kill my kind, but you can scare them. More than that, though, there are some among my people who would provoke you."

"Provoke me? To what end?"

"To this end," he said, indicating the room. "To making you change. To making you dangerous."

"And to killing the vampires." She nodded slowly, understanding. "And you?"

"I would not hesitate to kill a vampire if he stood in my way, personally or politically. But I would not risk human lives to do it. And I would not use an innocent as a weapon."

She thought of Giorgio. "I'm not innocent."

"Perhaps. But in this matter, you are." He looked at her hard. "You don't see that. Perhaps you never will. But I can make the pain lessen. And I can teach you to control the change."

He grinned. "You say that Tiberius wouldn't let you go into battle with him? I say you'll be my strongest warrior. You will come live with me. And after a month on the field you'll have control. And the guilt you feel will have faded to regret."

"But you just said we can't tell your people the truth. What possible explanation could we have for me moving into the château?"

"Not the château, lass. My bed. I think my people would see the intelligence benefits of having Tiberius's former woman at my side."

She'd shaken her head slowly. "I— No. You've been very kind, but I don't—"

His hearty laugh had cut off her stammering words. "Nor I, lass. There is another who holds my heart."

"But then why?"

"She has no love of France, no need of Alliance politics. My Moira stays in the Highlands. It is where she belongs. And for now, I belong here."

"But you've been in France for centuries."

His shoulders rose and fell. "A blink of an eye for creatures such as ourselves. We will find each other again, Moira and I. Until then, I do my duty for my people."

Caris remembered his words now, and they butted uncomfortably against Tiberius's choice. He'd done his duty for his people, too, sacrificing her in much the way Gunnolf had sacrificed Moira. Moira, however, had made the decision with him.

It hadn't been easy slipping into life at the weren palace. Except for Gunnolf, the weren had never fully accepted her. She'd almost refused his offer, but when he'd pointed out that the scent of the weren was upon her, she'd known she really didn't have a choice. She was a vampire with a weren scent, and she needed a reason for that anomaly other than the truth. And so the fiction of her relationship with Gunnolf was born.

No, the relationship wasn't a fiction. He'd become one of her closest friends. But there was nothing else between them.

That, however, was a truth they both guarded carefully, because as long as it was believed that she was Gunnolf's woman, she carried an extra layer of protection. Moreover, by taking on that role, she was protecting Moira as well. Any enemy who sought to get to Gunnolf by going after the woman he loved would go after Caris. His true love stayed safe and secluded in the Highlands.

It was a perfect arrangement except when she thought of Tiberius. He didn't know the truth, and they knew that it wasn't safe to tell him. She was a creature that could destroy the vampires with nothing more than a burst of rage, and Tiberius knew it. She had tried to make herself believe that he wouldn't kill her—that if he'd meant to kill her he would have done so, not merely kicked her out.

But she couldn't be sure. He'd chosen his people over her, and he knew the harm she could bring. He could change his mind. Decide that her death was the only way to ensure their safety. As Gunnolf's woman, her death would surely instigate a war. Gunnolf was her protection and her friend. A line of defense against a man she'd once loved.

A man, if she was honest with herself, whom she loved still.

"You're a fool," she whispered.

She clutched her phone tight in her hand. She wanted to call Gunnolf now.

She wanted his low voice to remind her that Tiberius had banished her. That any softness she saw in him now wasn't meant for her.

She wanted him to say all those things, yet she didn't dial the phone. Because deep down, she was afraid he'd only be silent. That he'd make her come to her own decisions. And that she wouldn't like what she saw when she peered deep into what was really going on in her heart and her head.

Besides, if she talked to him she'd tell him about her ploy to gain him the Scottish territory. And that was something she wanted to hold close to her chest. If she wasn't able to obtain it, he'd never know. But if she was, it would be a happy surprise for a man who'd once saved her.

"Screw it," she whispered, then tossed her phone onto the desk. She neither had nor wanted a degree in psychology. She wasn't the type to analyze or ponder or pick apart motives. She was the type who *acted,* and that—*that* was what had her all screwed up in her head. Because right now, she wasn't *acting*. Right now, she was *waiting*. And it pissed her off that there was nothing she could do to change that status quo.

And to make it worse, she was waiting in the blue room. Was it intentional, she wondered? Had Tiberius asked Mrs. Todd to put her here, in the guest chambers to which they'd retreated so many times when the burden of work had taken a backseat to the flames of desire? They'd escape from his office, taking solace in this room. She'd pull him down on the bed and cover his mouth with hers, and abandon the world for the desperate necessity of finding each other.

She remembered it all. Every touch, every kiss, every stroke. And it had been right here.

But that was almost twenty years ago, and the room had changed, the furnishings she'd acquired switched out for more practical pieces. Even the walls were a deeper blue, and the bright Mondrian canvases to which she'd been so partial had been replaced by more somber Wyeths, giving the room an almost sleepy atmosphere where once it had been so vibrant it practically hummed.

She wondered how quickly he'd changed things after he'd banished her, because that had certainly happened with head-spinning speed. Reinholt had kept her for more than a month, and he would have undoubtedly kept her longer or killed her had she not escaped.

She pressed her fingers to her temples and silently cursed. She seriously needed to get out of this room. She didn't want to think, she wanted to hit. To pound out her frustrations. She punched the air once, twice, and decided it was time to burn off some of the shit that was stirring inside her. She headed toward the door. Hopefully Tiberius's stint at redecorating hadn't run to eliminating or moving the gym.

More important, she thought as she eased up next to the door, she hoped he hadn't put a guard outside her room.

She paused, her fingertips grazing the wood as she listened for movement outside. She heard it, and bit back a curse. He really *had* assigned a guard. Wasn't that just the most fucked up—

The scent.

Slowly, quietly, she stepped closer, her chin tilted up, her nostrils flaring as she breathed in.

She knew it—knew him.

Tiberius was there, beyond the door.

Carefully, she moved closer, her blood pounding in her veins, some emotion she didn't want to name sweeping over her. Desire? Surely not. Anger? Maybe.

Curiosity?

Slowly, she pressed her hand to the wood. *She could feel it—raw emotion.* Pain and anger, but also longing. And, yes, that hint of regret. For a moment, her throat tightened, and she realized she was watching the door handle, waiting for it to turn, cursing herself because she wanted it to.

And then cursing him when it didn't.

Quickly, she yanked her hand away, hating that she'd revealed even the smallest weakness to him, and not caring at all that her weakness had been his as well.

He'd find a way to turn it around on her. He always did, after all.

Frustrated, she headed back toward the desk. No way

she was leaving the room now, not with him right outside the door.

She was just about to give in to temptation and call
Gunnolf when her phone rang. She snatched it up, saw
that it was Orion, and answered.

"I just heard," he said. "Where are you?"

"Heard?"

"About . . ." He hesitated, and that was all she needed
to know. He'd heard about Reinholt's murder.

"Don't say it."

"Am I an idiot?" he retorted.

She had to smile. Richard Erasmus Orion III was her
nephew, cousin, something like that. Whatever he was,
it was a billion times removed. Point was, he was family.
The only family she had left, for that matter.

After he'd been plucked from the human world by
Nikko Leviathin and recruited to work as the medical
examiner for the Los Angeles PEC, she'd seen an opportunity. She'd done some snooping and learned that his
medical background was laced with a significant amount
of research and development. There was nothing noble
about her reintroduction to her family; she'd sought him
out for purely selfish means, interested only in what he
could do for her.

After four days with him—four days of cautious
getting-to-know-you, four days of looking into her long-
dead brother's eyes, four days of fearing that she was
making a horrible mistake—she told him the truth. She
told him about the man who'd captured her. Who'd tortured her. Who'd changed her.

And she told him about what she'd become.

Instead of shunning her, betraying her to the PEC, or
reporting her as a hybrid—he actually *helped* her.

She would never have imagined it, but next to Gunnolf, her closest friend and confidant in these long dark years since she left Tiberius had become Orion. A human. And one working in the PEC, at that.

"I can't talk right now," she said.

"Where are you? And are you all right?"

"I'm with Tiberius."

The silence hung long and heavy. Finally, Orion cleared his throat. "And so I ask again: Are you all right?"

She wanted to come up with a profound response. Something that illustrated just how *not* all right she was. But the words wouldn't come. "Sure," she said simply, and knew that she hadn't fooled him when he swore softly under his breath.

"Like hell. What can I do?"

"Same as always—nothing you can do."

"Caris—"

"I swear. I'm okay." She forced a cheeriness into her voice. "I've actually got a job."

"Huh?"

She laughed. "Turns out Tiberius needs my help. Seems he's out one informant and he wants my insight into the weren community. Lihter's up to something. And there's a kidnapped girl."

"You're actually going to work with him?" Orion sounded positively shocked.

"I am indeed."

"Why?"

She told him about her bid to get Gunnolf the Highlands, and he laughed appreciatively.

"Not a bad maneuver. But why are you really doing it?"

"What do you mean?" She cursed silently, knowing exactly what he meant.

"You've told me a lot about Gunnolf. And if you think I believe he cares about lording over the Highlands now that he's got Moira back, you're crazy. A nice perk if you get it, sure. But it's not a big enough deal that you'd go out of your way to barter for it."

Okay, he really did know her too well.

"So what's going on?"

She shrugged, even though he couldn't see her. "Lihter screwed Gunnolf. I want the chance to screw him back. I want it bad. And if I have to work with Tiberius, then so be it." That was true, but she had to admit to herself that there was more to it.

For almost twenty years, the château in Paris had been home, but she was no longer welcome there, not with Gunnolf gone. And the only other home she'd ever known had been at Tiberius's side, and for centuries that home had been within these very walls.

She'd been terrified to come back. Afraid the anger would sneak up on her. But it wasn't anger, it was melancholy. This place had been her home, and despite the pain, despite the memories, it felt good to be back.

Right now, she had nowhere else to go. And if staying here meant that she could help Tiberius screw Lihter, then so much the better.

She didn't share any of that with Orion, though she would bet that the perceptive human already knew.

"Listen," he said, as if to prove the point. "Anything you need, you know that, right? You can call me anytime. Don't worry about the time difference or anything."

"You're a prince among humans."

"Nah. That's just what family's for."

"I know," she said. "And I appreciate it."

"Listen to you, all sentimental."

"Sentimental my ass," she said, this time with a hint of warning in her voice, but it only made him laugh.

"At least it's a hot ass," he said with a growl.

"I'm your cousin, you perv."

"Aunt, I think, and I'm pretty sure we've passed the level of consanguinity that makes that sort of thing illegal."

"In that case, the answer's just plain no. And don't taunt me or the pissy mood will come back."

"Go work it off," he said. "Beat up some unsuspecting flunky or something."

"You really do know me too well," she said before they hung up.

She realized as she tossed the phone onto the bed that she meant it, and that the smile on her lips was genuine. Orion and Gunnolf—a human and a werewolf. The last time she stood in this room she never would have believed that the two people she depended on most in the world were so very unlike herself.

At least things were never dull.

And, yeah, she needed a workout.

She headed back to the door, hesitating as she approached.

Was Tiberius still out there?

She pressed her hand against the door, but felt nothing but the warm wood against her palm. She closed her eyes, feeling suddenly hollow.

He'd left, and damned if he hadn't taken part of her soul with him.

CHAPTER 12

Caris thrust her fists out hard, punching the bag in a quick one-two sequence. She wasn't wearing gloves, and it felt good to get down and dirty. To pound out the memories.

To take out her frustrations on a goddamned punching bag.

She'd finally opened her door, expecting to see Tiberius at the end of the hallway, looking for her the way she was looking for him. He wasn't there, though.

She told herself she didn't care, and that she was happy he hadn't been nearby. She didn't want to see him, didn't want to talk to him. He made her feel vulnerable, and that was something she hadn't felt for years.

She didn't like it.

Hell, it had been in this very room where Tiberius had told her about Blaine. A traitor. A goddamned vampire bastard who'd turned into a snitch for the werens. Tiberius intended to send one of the *kyne* out after him. The men. The warriors.

She'd held her tongue, but she'd had a plan of her own. And the memory of that moment washed over her—the way Tiberius had held her close, their bodies naked in the pool. The way she'd pressed a palm to his face, memorizing his eyes and silently promising him that she would return. He'd made love to her, fast and hard, both of them desperate for each other. And then slow and sweet. He hadn't known what she was thinking, of course, but she'd relished the press of his body against hers, savoring the time until she went out into the world to kill for her lover.

Smash, bam!

She lashed out at the sand-filled bag again and again. Searching for exhaustion. Trying to shut down her mind. She didn't want those memories, not now. Not the way she'd felt in his arms, and sure as hell not the way she'd felt in the forest, Blaine in front of her and her chasing him.

Again and again, she lashed out, pounding harder and harder until she wasn't thinking about the bag or the gym.

Until it was just fists and memories, trying so hard to exhaust her body and get her mind to stop spinning, to stop twirling.

Trying to stop remembering.

But it was no use.

It was never any use.

The memories always came.

◆

She woke in a stone cell, her mind thick and fuzzy. She knew that time had passed, but she had no sense of it. Had she been captive for an hour? A year?

Putting all of her meager energy into the task, she struggled against the chains that bound her wrists and ankles to the wall, but it was no use.

"It's hematite, of course." Her masked captor's face appeared at the small, barred window in the metal door.

"Don't bother fighting. You'll only sap what little strength you have left." His words were matter-of-fact, as if he'd invited her over for tea rather than torture.

He pushed open the heavy door. It swung inward with a hollow groan. "If this goes well, I'll release you soon enough."

"When?" she growled.

As if in reflex, he glanced heavenward. "Soon enough."

A riffle of panic welled inside her, along with a hunger so intense that every cell in her body seemed wrung out and dry. She'd fed well before she'd left on the hunt, and the depth of her hunger gave her some idea as to how long it had been since she'd tasted blood. "You've kept me chained up here for weeks."

"Don't worry. You haven't yet worn out your welcome. Now be a good girl and don't move." He pulled out the tranq gun. "I don't want to have to do this more than once."

"Don't," she said. "You already have me chained up. Don't force me to sleep, too."

"Not to worry, my dear," he said as he fired. "There's no tranquilizer in here."

His words sent cold terror through her, and she concentrated all of her energy on ripping the chains from the stone. It was no use. The vampiric strength she'd once cherished and relied upon was gone. Starved of blood and bound by hematite, her body was even weaker than that of a human woman.

The dart pierced her skin, and she screamed, crying out in pain and anger. He'd spoken the truth—there was no tranquilizer in the dart. There was hematite. Somehow he'd converted the metal to liquid, and now it coursed through her, ripping her up from the inside, *making her dizzy, making her sick. Making the world swim with dark colors that shifted to fiery red as her daemon howled and roared, searching for a fight. Longing for a kill. But she was trapped, bound, and the enemy danced just out of reach.*

She tried to speak, tried to curse and yell and rant, but the hematite was fully in her system now, doing its work upon her body, upon her mind. The world fell away from her as the chilling numbness of defeat settled over her, and she slid down into the dark embrace of pain. It held her, fed her, kept her. Pulling her in, embracing and keeping her until—

Something changed.

Caris opened her eyes, feeling reality curl around her like a welcoming blanket. She was still bound, but the pain had lessened to a dull throbbing within her. For days, he'd been injecting her repeatedly until what little concept of time that had remained within her had vanished completely.

Was he coming back now? Or had the torment truly ended?

And if so, what did that mean? She no longer clung to the illusion that he would let her go. Nor did she hold on to the promise that Tiberius would come to save her. He'd looked—that much her heart knew for sure. But he'd failed.

He'd failed, and now she was alone. Alone and, dammit, scared.

The fear coiled through her, and she tensed, expecting the daemon within to rise. In the past, it had always struck out like a serpent when fear or anger burst within, latching onto those raw emotions and using them as footholds to climb to the surface of what made her Caris. To take over. To control and rage.

She'd fought it back once with Tiberius's help—called upon the numen and banished the daemon back within the depths of her soul. He'd given her the strength to fight again when it tried to escape its soul-bound prison, and for centuries she'd remained Caris, the evil inside her having no claim on her personality or her actions.

If it tried again now, she knew she didn't have the strength to fight.

Was that her captor's purpose? To weaken her so that the daemon could take over? To make her rogue?

If so, he'd won. She was wrung out. A shell of herself. Her emotions paper thin, capable of being cut down with nothing more substantial than a breeze.

She waited, dreading the inevitable. Knowing with absolute certainty that the daemon would rise—this time in full force and power. And the woman she'd fought so hard to remain would be lost forever, trapped inside silent walls, fists battering against a force beyond her control and a power she no longer had the strength to overcome.

♦

Her hair flew out wild around her. Her body glistened with sweat. And her arms and fists moved with a speed that defied sight, so fast she was a blur even to Tiberius's keen vision.

He watched, unable to turn his gaze away as Caris brutalized the punching bag, her face contorted, her lips moving as if she were talking to herself, urging herself on, narrating a kill in her mind.

She was a natural fighter. The way she moved, her speed and agility. In the early days he'd trained her, fought with her. And over and over again he'd been astounded by her uncommon skill.

He'd taken that from her, and selfishly, too. He'd been so afraid of losing her that he'd forced her to give up something that was clearly at her core. He'd let her train, yes. But not go out in the field as she'd wanted. He'd been too close to see the truth of how much she both wanted and needed the fight, and in the end, he'd lost her anyway. Now it was too late. The damage had already been done. He'd denied her what she'd needed, and Gunnolf had let her march into battle. Tiberius hated the weren all the more for it. And, yes, he hated himself as well.

She wore a sports bra and shorts that showed the curve of her rear, and her body was covered by a thin layer of sweat. How many times before had he found her like that, beating out her frustrations? He'd take her in his arms, and let her find a more pleasant way to work through her issues.

He couldn't do that now, though there was no denying the tightening in his body that proved he wanted to.

He pushed the thoughts aside, focusing only on her. On her fists. On the bag. Tiberius didn't know what she was brutalizing in her head, but from the furious intensity of her punches, he could hazard a guess. Someone had done this to her—some filthy, stinking weren had ripped her flesh, had violated her body. Some vile, anonymous lupine Therian had transformed Caris—and in doing so the son of a bitch had destroyed her.

And in her mind, Caris was taking him down.

Bam, pow, bam!

Caris battered the bag some more, and Tiberius watched jealously. He wanted a piece of the bastard, too. Wanted to pummel and break. Wanted to look into that weren's eyes and see the one who'd harmed her. And Claudius, the weren who'd tormented Tiberius all those long years ago. Wanted their faces to swim before his eyes, bloodied and battered as life drained out of them.

Stop.

Goddammit, stop. His past was rising up around him. Memories he'd kept pushed down for millennia were poking out, creeping into his thoughts like clinging vines, and every time he ripped one away another lashed out, winding around him and refusing to let go.

Her.

She'd pulled them out, her proximity making them swirl around him with an intensity he long ago conquered. Send her away, and he'd banish the memories as well. He had to.

If he was going to keep his head as they approached election day, he should send her away.

"Caris."

She didn't respond, just kept up her assault.

"Caris."

Still, nothing.

This time, he walked to her, then tapped gently on her shoulder. She spun—a wild thing—and lashed out at him. He caught her fist before contact, but the blow was stronger than he'd anticipated and he stumbled backward, taking her with him. She fell against him, and they both tumbled to the ground, his back to the mat, her body on his so he was bathed in the scent of her.

Again, memories washed over him, but this time they

weren't vile, though they were just as painful. Memories of this room. Of this mat. Hell, memories of this position, her throwing him down as they practiced, and him more than willing to be thrown because when they practiced fight techniques even the loser won.

He'd missed this—missed *her*. The Caris he used to love.

She stayed there a moment, her mouth open slightly in surprise, her chest rising and falling. Then she straightened, straddling him now, her legs on either side of his hips and her ass nestled firmly against his crotch. She shifted—the slightest of movements—and he bit back a groan. Her eyes narrowed knowingly and she moved again, a delicious sensual pressure. An erotic tease.

A reminder of what he'd once had—and what no longer existed.

"Get off."

Her brow lifted, her mouth quirking flirtatiously. "Off? I've gotten the better of the great Tiberius. Do you really think I'd give up the advantage so easily?" She wriggled devilishly, and his body—his body that knew her touch and feel and scent as intimately as his own—responded, his cock hardening, his blood burning.

No.

In a flash, he flipped her over, gaining the edge she'd claimed for himself. But he could see the knowledge in her eyes. She'd felt the effect she'd had on him, and even though he might have taken the advantage, they both knew that she'd won.

He rose off her, then stood as she lay back on the mat, propped up on her elbows. She looked back at him, soft and innocent. But he knew better. She was hard and wicked, and the softness he saw now was only an illusion.

Once upon a time, he'd seen the real unguarded woman beneath the facade, but Caris knew better than to show herself to her enemies. And Tiberius knew better than to count himself among her friends. Not anymore.

"Get up."

"I'm perfectly comfortable."

"Fine. Stay down there. But I came to tell you that you can go." He hadn't come to tell her that at all. But his reaction to her suggested that really was the best decision.

Her brow furrowed as she rose to her feet. "Go? As in—"

"Home. Back to him."

"What about your intelligence? What about the girl?"

"Not your problem."

She peered at him. "A few hours ago you were making it my problem."

"A fact about which you complained loudly. I'm doing you a favor. I'll find another source. As you said, you hardly have an in with Lihter."

"I have more of an in than you do."

He looked at her, standing there with sweat glistening off her, her hair pushed back from her face and her eyes blazing. Right then, he wanted nothing more than to touch her. It was an impulse he fought and would continue to fight. A battle that would be more easily won when she was gone. "Why are you arguing about this? You don't really want to stay."

"Ah, but I really want the Highlands."

"For your precious Gunnolf."

She smiled sweetly.

"Fine. Go, and the Highlands are yours."

He could tell from her expression that she hadn't been expecting that.

"Aren't you generous today? But I think I'm going to stay anyway."

He almost growled in frustration. "Dammit, Caris. Why?"

She shrugged. "Maybe I changed my mind. Maybe I'm a little pissed off at Lihter for everything he's done to Gunnolf. Maybe I want to help you find out what he's up to." She smiled, all sweet and innocent. "Or maybe I just can't stand to leave your side. It's so warm and cozy and welcoming here."

"Dammit, Caris. We are not playing this game."

"Good. Then we're agreed. I'm staying. I'm helping."

"No. Learn when to back out gracefully."

"Me? Perhaps you need to learn to graciously accept help when help is offered." She got up, then strode toward him, all strength and determination. "Maybe I don't have an in with Lihter, but I have spent almost twenty years with the werens. Or had you forgotten? No," she added, looking into his eyes. "I see that you haven't." Her nose wrinkled. "Is that anger I smell? Loathing? Do you hate me so much that you won't let me help you?" She cocked her head to the side. "Or maybe you're afraid I'll bring out the wolf and destroy your precious Paris."

"You wouldn't do that."

"How do you know?"

"Because I know you. Because you've learned how to control it."

"Then tell me, Tiberius. Why can't I stay? Why refuse my help?"

He had no intention of answering. He'd played politics long enough to know how to school his face to reveal only what he wanted. He could come up with pretty words that masked the truth. And yet he didn't.

Instead, he spoke the truth.

"Because it hurts, Caris. It pains me to look at you. To know that you've been in another man's arms, and that I was the one who drove you there."

She was looking at him, her mouth slightly open and her brow furrowed.

He turned away. "I looked at you. I looked at Giorgio. And the daemon—Caris, my daemon. It burned. It raged and it burned and it tore at me like it hadn't for over two thousand years."

"Because of me."

"Because of *me*," he corrected. "Because I let that happen to you. I was supposed to protect you, and yet I couldn't find you. I looked, and you were gone, and when you came back I saw just how much havoc my failure had wrought."

"And so you tossed me away?"

"I tossed you away so that I wouldn't lose myself. I'd failed you already. And I failed my people by letting you live. Hell, you were dangerous. And there wasn't any scenario in which you could stay."

"You told me to learn control. I did. But you never came after me." She spoke matter-of-factly, but he heard the recrimination.

"How could I? You were with Gunnolf."

She said nothing, then cocked her head. "Because my being with a weren disgusted you? Or because there was no way a Vampire Alliance rep could be with a woman who once cozied up to Gunnolf?"

"Both," he said. And then, before he could close his mouth and keep the truth in, he continued. "But what really hurt was that you found solace with Gunnolf. That he helped you, when all I did was hurt you. Hell," he added, "it's as much my fault as yours that Giorgio's dead."

She shook her head. "No. That was me."

"And I drugged you. You woke up scared. Betrayed." He closed his eyes. Gathered himself. "That weighs heavy upon me."

She managed a half smile. "You could try hitting the punching bag. I promise it helps."

He forced himself to relax, to lose the tension that the memories had strung through him. "Oh, Caris. That's why I want you to go. Because I look at you now, and I cannot escape the simple truth. What has passed between us can never be changed. And when you're near, the wounds open all over again."

He watched her as he spoke, watched her face, as unmoving as ice. And then he turned away, her stoicism cutting as much as her sharp tongue could.

"Did Reinholt turn against Gunnolf? Was that why you killed him?"

She shook her head. "No."

"Then why?"

She cocked her head. "It's just driving you crazy that I'm not telling you exactly what you want to know, isn't it?"

"It's rather irritating, yes."

She laughed at that, and the tension diffused just a little.

"Dammit, Tiberius," she said. "Can't we just chalk it up to PMS and be done with it?"

"It's not as satisfying an explanation as I was hoping for." He took a step toward her, saw the fire in her eyes flare when she chose to hold her ground and not back away. Between them the air crackled and sparked, the product of her desire to run battling against her determination to stay. He could feel it, the scent of her will thick upon her. It was heady. Intoxicating. And the memories it brought back were dangerous ones.

He clenched his hands into fists, fighting the urge to see if her skin was as soft as he remembered. "Tell me," he said. "Tell me what Reinholt was to you."

She took a breath, her shoulders rising even as her head dipped down, her eyes aimed at the floor. When she lifted it again, they were as hard as emeralds, her expression equally stony.

"What he was to me? He was *nothing* to me. Nothing and everything all rolled into one."

Tiberius shook his head, not understanding.

"Dammit, Tiberius. Don't you get it? He's the one who did this to me. He's the one who made me the way I am now."

He stepped back, her unexpected words hitting him with the same force with which she'd battered the punching bag.

"He caught me. He tortured me. He held me and starved me and tranqued me. He injected me with liquid hematite. Do you have any idea how much that hurts? Do you?" She'd moved closer to him as she spoke, and he saw the way her eyes glistened, tears threatening.

"He made me a hybrid. He *destroyed* me. My life. *Our* life. And now you have the gall to stand there and ask why I killed him." She jammed a hard finger into his chest. "Well, fuck you, Tiberius. Fuck. You."

"Caris," he whispered, and that was all it took. Her tears fell in earnest, and she started to turn away from him. He reached out, stopping her. "No."

She looked up at him, her eyes wet with tears, her face as soft and anguished as it had been when she'd begged him to help rescue her brother Antonio all those long years ago.

"He did this," she whispered. "And he—"

But then she was quiet because his mouth was on hers, kissing her, holding her. He wanted to absorb the pain, to erase the hurt, and damned if she wasn't letting him. Her mouth opening to his, her fingers clinging to him. Her familiar moans, the sweetness of her curves pressed against him. And then—

Nothing.

Hard hands against his chest, pushing him away. And there she was, her eyes wild, her head shaking. "No," she whispered. "No."

"Caris." He tried to fill the word with apology, but there was nothing that could erase the anguish he saw in her face.

"This isn't—*no*," she said again, this time more firmly. "Dammit, Tiberius, don't you get it? I hate you. You hurt me, and I fucking hate you."

"You don't," he said. "You want to—you have reason to—but you don't hate me."

"I do," she insisted. "I do. I really—"

But she didn't finish. She couldn't, because once again his mouth closed over hers, his palms against her face, his fingers in her hair.

She pounded on him, fists thrusting against his back,

but she didn't force her way out of the kiss. Despite all of her strength, she let him capture her.

He slid his hands down, clutching her back, pulling her toward him. Her mouth opened, her fists stilling as her hands flattened. She gasped beneath him, her mouth hot, her tongue demanding.

He had no illusions about what this meant, what she wanted, even what he wanted. All he knew was that right then, in that moment, he had to have her. Had to soothe her. Had to soothe himself.

Right then they both needed to lose themselves in each other. Recriminations could come later. Now there was nothing but need and desire and a fire so hot it could burn away pain and turn memories to ash.

For now, that would have to be enough.

CHAPTER 13

Her mind was in a whirl. She wanted to pound her fists against him. To kick and pummel and push him away.

But she didn't. She *couldn't*. Because his touch—oh, how she'd missed his touch.

This was *Tiberius,* the man whose hands had awakened her, whose body had belonged to her, whose mouth had teased her.

Whose decision had banished her.

No.

She broke away, thrusting her arms up and out, breaking his grip on her even as she backed up, breathing hard, her body primed to fight—primed to do a whole lot more than that.

"No," she said.

He stepped toward her. "It's all over you, you know. The scent of desire. Of sex."

She shook her head. "I don't want you anymore," she lied. "I have a lover, or haven't you heard?"

He reached out and grabbed her arms with incredible speed. She could have dodged, but she hadn't been expecting it, and she found herself pressed hard against his chest. "Don't mention him. Not now. Not in my house."

"My life, Tiberius. You're not calling the shots anymore." She was having trouble concentrating. His body was right there, and her skin was so aware, as if every cell had opened up and was singing. He was right, she was drenched with desire. She knew what she should do—she should walk away. Go back to her room. Take a cold shower. Do *something*.

But what she wanted to do was right there in front of her.

What she wanted was to show him what he was missing.

Roughly, she wrapped her hand around the back of his head. "You want to go a round? Is that what this is about?"

"That pretty much sums it up."

"Get all hot and sweaty for old times' sake?" She brushed her mouth over his, trailing her lips to his ear. She nipped at his earlobe. "Do you want to fuck me, Tiberius? Do you want to fuck me because you can't anymore?"

He didn't answer. Not in words, anyway. But in one quick motion he had her lips under his, his tongue hard and demanding.

She started to melt against him, but that wouldn't do. She had to stay in charge. Had to be the one calling the shots in this little game.

Deliberately, she kissed him back, nipping his lower lip so hard it drew blood. She tasted it, metallic and salty and male. More than that, she tasted the need in it.

There were no secrets in blood, and the extent of his desire filled her up. Whatever else might be between them, the longing was real, and she let herself go just a little, losing herself to pleasure in the arms of this man whose body she'd once known as well as her own.

No. Not losing herself.

She was in charge here. And as she slid her hand down

and stroked his cock, huge and hard under his jeans, she couldn't help but think how nice it was to be a woman with power.

"Out of these," she said, her fingers working the button, then the fly. She worked feverishly, getting him out of the pants even as he ripped the sports bra over her head, leaving her clad only in the tiny nylon shorts. Already damp with sweat, and now with desire as well.

"Caris," he said, his voice as rough as she'd ever heard it. He slipped his hand down between her thighs, stroking her. Sending pleasure ricocheting through her— *God, she was so ready,* and she had to fight and fight so she didn't come right then. But the proximity of that pleasure—it was like the wolf beneath her skin. Something dangerous just waiting to burst out.

She'd learned to control the wolf, but dammit, she didn't want to control this.

"More," she whispered, before she could stop herself, and then his hands were at her hips, and he was peeling her shorts off. Her flesh tingled, like lightning crackling up and down. His touch was memory and perfection.

And she'd missed it horribly.

A support beam extended from ceiling to floor, and he eased her up against it, his hands caressing her, teasing her, making her want more than she should want—not now, not with him.

And yet with who else? This was Tiberius, the man who'd first brought her body to life.

Dear God, she wanted him to do that to her again.

As if her thoughts were wishes, he was on his knees, his hands cupping her rear, his mouth closing hard over her nipple.

He suckled, and she arched back, moaning, desperate

for more, for the sweet pain of intense pleasure that his touch could bring.

His tongue laved her, teasing and flicking at her rockhard nipple, as her body quivered under his ministrations. Slowly, sensually, one hand slid up her thigh. His finger found her, hot and slick, and he stroked her clit in sweet, sensual motions, bringing her closer and closer, then easing off until she was a melting pile of frustration, her hips gyrating with need.

He trailed kisses down her belly. His tongue edged out his finger for the prize, and he gently spread her legs more, then traced the tip of his tongue over her swollen clit.

The tremor that rocked her body was so tight, so fast and hard, that she had to hold on to the support beam so that she wouldn't fall.

But he didn't take her over—he didn't make her come. That was just a preview of coming attractions.

He murmured something she couldn't understand, then worked his way up her body, bringing washes of pleasure in his wake. He stood, then slanted his mouth over hers, her taste still lingering on his lips. He pulled her close, the motion rough, pressing their bodies tight so that she felt every inch of him, including the hard length of his cock.

She reached down, her hand encircling it, stroking gently, then harder as he moaned. She kissed him deeply, shifting her legs so that the length of him was pressed between her thighs, her hips shifting, teasing and tormenting him as the friction of skin against soft, male velvet drove him absolutely mad.

It felt good to make him crazy.

"Still with me?" she asked.

He made a low, guttural sound. "Don't tell me that's all you've got."

Her laugh escaped involuntarily, and she covered by kissing him again. She told herself she wouldn't think about how it made her feel, the memories it brought back.

This was Tiberius. And with Tiberius there was the good, and there was the bad. And that was just the way it was. This wasn't make-up sex. This was fuck-you sex.

And she was damn well going to enjoy it.

His hands were on her shoulders, his body tight as the pressure of his passion built. "Enough standing," he growled, and he pushed her back, hard, onto the mat.

She fell, sprawling, and found herself looking up at him. He was right there, his face in front of hers, his dark eyes gleaming with dangerous possibilities.

"Kiss me," she demanded, but instead of finding her lips, his mouth closed again over her nipple. Pleasure warred with pain, ripping through her, making her wriggle and writhe as she struggled for an elusive more. As she fought not to plead with him to never stop touching her.

With lips and fingers he explored every inch of her, stroking sweet spots, nibbling in soft areas. Generally driving her wild.

His fingers danced against her, dipping between her legs, teasing her and making her buck, making her crave that final showdown, and at the same time making her never want it to come so that this little slice of heaven could go on and on.

He knew her body so well. For hundreds of years, she'd been his, her body his instrument, and it was clear he hadn't forgotten. He played her, making shocks reverberate through her body, so intense that she had no choice but to cling to him and ride it out.

And then his lips were on hers again, warm and demanding. Battering. Taking. Claiming.

Claiming.

This was supposed to be her party, and yet somehow the tables had gotten turned.

That was something she could remedy immediately.

"Tiberius," she whispered, her voice dreamy. And then, before he could even ask what she wanted, she hooked an arm and a leg around him and flipped him over.

She straddled him, laughing, the slow sensuality replaced by a hard and fast demand.

She didn't mind. From the look on his face, neither did he.

Between her legs, his erection twitched, hard and ready. She reached down and stroked him, then guided him to her. He was velvet steel beneath her fingers, and she wanted him. Had to have him.

And so with the whisper of a single word—*Tiberius*— she impaled herself on him, arched her back, and reveled in the pleasure of this man's touch.

♦

Tiberius thought he would lose his mind.

He held on to her as she rode him, their bodies rocking together. Hard and hot. Demanding and intense.

He'd understood what she was doing—sex, nothing more. But he'd also seen the softness beneath. He saw it now in the passion on her face.

He felt it in the stroke of her fingers.

Even her wild bucks and thrusts were a coming to-gether, not just of sex, but of *them*.

She'd gone to Gunnolf's bed, but she was back in his arms. *His*. He lost himself in her smooth skin, her responsive body. He closed his eyes, her soft moans taking him close to the edge.

She'd brought him to the hilt and he was deep in her core, their bodies so close, so joined, that he wasn't sure where he stopped and she began.

All he knew was that he wanted to stay lost inside her. That he wanted this feeling to last. Wanted the wild bursts of bodies crashing together, but also wanted the soft strokes of slow lovemaking, touches and caresses and skin against skin.

"Harder," he demanded, and she willingly complied. "Kiss me," he insisted, and there she complied, too, bending over so that her breasts brushed his bare chest, and then closing her mouth over his, pulling him up until they were both sitting, both connected, joined like some ancient statue.

"I want more," she whispered when she broke the kiss. "I want everything."

She eased off him, and he moaned in protest, since her leaving definitely didn't fit his definition of everything. But then she pushed him to his back again. She was still straddling him, but she moved higher, then guided his hand so that his finger slipped inside her. "Yes," she whispered. "Touch me."

He obeyed willingly, teasing and tickling and feeling and then, when she pulled away and eased closer, tasting as she lowered herself gloriously over him.

He feasted on her, reveling in every tiny twitch of pleasure until finally the twitches added up to an explosion and she moaned in true passion and collapsed beside him. He rolled over and traced his fingers over her bare, beautiful skin, but she pushed them away. "Not yet. I'm not done with you."

She crawled down, all the way to his feet, then stroked her hands along his legs as she worked her way up to his hard-as-steel cock.

"Sweet," she said, then gave it a tentative little lick that just about sent him over the edge.

Slowly, methodically, she tasted every inch of him, so expertly that he stayed on the brink. When she finished that, she flashed a wicked grin, then took his entire cock in her mouth.

He groaned, involuntarily thrusting up to meet her, his body tensing and tightening as she sucked and pulled.

"No more," he begged. "I want you, Caris. I want to be inside you."

She eased off him, met his eyes, and said in a tone of voice that alone was sufficient to thrust him over the edge, "Me, too."

Her words were like a drug, and he flipped her over, his hands exploring every ready inch of her. He traced his fingers between her thighs, slid them over soft skin, and whispered everything he was going to do in her ear.

Her body shivered and quaked, and he stroked and played her, making her even wetter, even more open for him.

And then, when neither of them could stand it any longer, he leaned over her, took his weight on his arms, and thrust deep inside her.

Her hands cupped his rear, and she pulled him toward her, lifting her hips in silent demand that he go faster, harder. She tilted her head back and moaned. "Harder. Tiberius, deeper."

He did. Hell, he couldn't stop. It was as if she was a drug, and he was completely addicted.

He'd missed her. The heat of her body, the sound of her voice. Just having her beside him.

And this. Oh, by the gods, he'd missed this.

He felt her tighten around him, little spasms building to something bigger, and he thrust harder. Beneath him, she bucked as their bodies pistoned together, and then, when he thought he couldn't hold on anymore, she exploded beneath him, and her orgasm drove him over as well, his body trembling from the pure pleasure of losing himself inside her.

They lay side by side, his fingers idly stroking the curve of her hip.

Silence lay heavy yet comfortable between them, but after a moment, she broke it.

"That was wonderful," she said.

"It was, wasn't it?"

She rolled over in his arms, then faced him, her expression serious. "It was . . . nostalgic."

He lifted a brow. "Was it?"

"Old times' sake."

"I'm pretty sure some of those tricks were new."

"Tiberius—it felt great, but I don't think—"

"You think it was a mistake."

She hesitated. "I think we shouldn't do it again."

It was a diplomatic answer, and he forced himself not to analyze it too closely. She was right, after all. They probably shouldn't do that again.

"It's just that you're right," she said. "The past can't

be changed. There's history between us that I don't know if we can ever truly get around. But . . ."

There was a hesitancy in her voice that made him look up. "Yes?"

"It's just that there's enough real stuff between us without you believing things that are wrong."

"Such as?"

"I never shared Gunnolf's bed."

"I heard differently." Tiberius spoke cautiously, wondering what the punch line was.

"You were meant to," she said. "Not just you. Everyone. We thought it was better if everyone believed . . ." She trailed off. "But he was—*he is*—a friend."

Tiberius heard the accusation behind the confession— Gunnolf had been there for her when he had not.

And right then, that truth somehow hurt even more than when he'd believed she'd run straight into another man's arms.

CHAPTER 14

"Seals?" Lihter asked.

"Check."

"Air-quality evaluators?"

"Check."

"Shackles?"

"Checked and double-checked."

Lihter looked sideways at the doctor, who managed a half shrug. "If what we've heard about hybrids is true, she's going to prove exceptionally strong."

The doctor was right, of course. But they had her strapped to the metal gurney with hematite wrist and ankle binders, along with mesh hematite straps over her chest, waist, and thighs. "She's secure," he said. "Doctor, are you ready?"

"I am," Behar said, and Lihter heard his own excitement in the doctor's voice. He was still giddy from the discovery that Reinholt's daughter was a hybrid. It was as if fate had smiled upon him, a silent gift to prove that he was on the right path. The universe giving him a vigorous nod of approval.

"Then let's begin."

Behar adjusted some dials on the control panel in front of him, then used a joystick to maneuver a mask over the girl's mouth and nose. Made of malleable plastic, the mask was connected to a sterile tube that wound its way into another sealed chamber.

Behind them, Rico and the rest of the support team gathered, all looking through the six-inch-thick glass wall. Lihter and Behar stood right before that wall, separated only by the length of the control table that Behar now operated. "Charging," the doctor said. "Power almost full—and *now*."

The doctor threw the switch and electricity coursed through hidden wires into the metal table onto which the girl was strapped. She was naked, and her body began to sizzle wherever flesh touched metal. She tensed and lurched, but there was nowhere to go, so the truth was it wasn't much of a show. Not for the first minute or so.

The tranquilizer had been on the verge of wearing off, and now the electricity did the last of the work, bringing the girl fully into consciousness—and pain.

Lihter watched, unable to help his smile as she screamed and jerked and thrashed on the charged table, electricity pouring through her, her skin so fried it was actually smoking.

"Change," he whispered. "Dammit, bitch, *change*."

She couldn't possibly have heard him—not through the glass, not through the pain—but she turned her face toward him. Eyes wild, blinded with agony. And still he couldn't shake the feeling that she was looking right at him. That she was purposefully defying him.

Bitch.

He lunged for the controls and increased the electricity, sending the needle shooting into the red zone.

"Sir! You'll fry her. If she dies—"

"Quiet!" he snapped, holding the dial. Watching. Watching . . .

Then things got interesting.

The body might look like that of a human girl, but it was so very far from that. Naomi Reinholt was a vampire. She was also a werewolf.

Naomi Reinholt was a hybrid—and the moment she changed into the wolf, great things were supposed to happen. Great, terrible things.

And then it started. The body shifting. The bones elongating. Skin puckering as coarse fur poked through.

Behind the mask, the girl screamed and screamed, until suddenly it wasn't the girl screaming, but a wolf. A trapped, impotent wolf strapped down because Lihter had willed it so. Because *he* was the one with dominion over the girl. Because he was the one who had trapped the hybrid and would tame her. Would take the curse that brought havoc when vampire and weren met, and turn it to his advantage.

He dialed the electricity back. Behar was right. He couldn't risk damaging his weapon.

"Test it! Quick. Test the air!"

Behar was already on it, of course. Behind them, Rico and the other men pressed in closer, their eyes on the girl. On the first hybrid any of them had ever seen.

On the weapon Lihter would harness to bring forth his new world.

He turned to Behar, silently willing him to move faster. He needed the news. Needed to hear aloud how she had spewed infection from her body. How she was a walking bomb that could erase humans, vampires, and the rest from the world. Only werens would remain. Werens and a select few who were immune or saved. Slaves in a perfect new society.

"It's not there," Behar said, his voice tight, confused. "Nothing. The air handlers are finding nothing."

"What?" Lihter turned to him, shocked. "What do you mean, nothing?"

"The air is clean. There's no infection. No plague."

"But she's a hybrid," Lihter said. "Her blood is fucking acid."

"Perhaps this is something her father discovered in his research? Have you located the father?" Behar asked.

"Not yet," Lihter admitted. "But I've put feelers out to all my sources." Fortunately, he had a number of snitches within the various PEC divisions. Reinholt may have gone into hiding, but he couldn't hide forever, especially since he was undoubtedly searching for his daughter.

At the moment, though, the machinations of the investigation meant nothing to him. All he cared about was the girl. And she wasn't working out as he'd expected at all.

"I don't understand this." Behar frantically twisted knobs, double-checked readouts. "Maybe her father cured her. Maybe—"

"Goddamn motherfucking—" He cut himself off, took a long, deep breath. "Are you certain?"

"The instruments, they all—"

"Fuck the instruments. Are. You. Certain?"

"I'm certain," Behar said.

Lihter drew in a breath, then another.

He forced calm upon himself.

He'd waited centuries for this moment. He could wait a little while longer.

"Very well," he said. "When the girl's back to herself, she and I are going to have to have a little conversation. I need answers, and I have a feeling she's the one to give them to me."

♦

"I understand perfectly what you're saying, but it's absolutely not acceptable." Benjamin Koller spoke firmly into the phone, his fingers tapping his desk, his eyes on Gabriel. The subdirector of the Division 12 violent crimes unit might look calm, but Gabriel knew him well enough to know that Koller was incredibly pissed off.

Gabriel, on the other hand, didn't give a shit. He'd thought he was wiping his hands of homicide when he'd transferred to Division Freeze Your Ass Off. And if the Alliance wanted the case, then that was fine. He'd tell the Alliance investigator what he'd learned so far, then Gabriel could go home, get some sleep, and spend the rest of the week investigating allegations that teenage trolls "redecorated" the slopes during the night, making the ski runs unsafe for humans.

He shifted uncomfortably in front of Koller's desk. That was what he wanted, dammit. To let this case go. To dump the problem of Alliance reps and dead snitches and a murderous vampire bitch off on someone else.

Hell, yeah.

But if that was what he wanted, why couldn't he get the victim's face out of his head?

Not your problem anymore, Gabriel.

Koller tapped a button on his phone, shifting the call to the speaker.

"—not me that's pulling jurisdiction, Koller. The Alliance is keeping Reinholt's death quiet and shifting the matter to a task force." The gravelly voice belonged to Morag Crill, the Alliance representative for the earthens, and governor of the Swiss territory.

The man was a troll, literally, and although Gabriel told himself that he had no issues with the outcome, he still couldn't believe that Crill was bending Division 12 over and taking it up the—

"We're perfectly capable of handling the investigation," Koller said, his voice reasonable even though his expression was not. He looked ready to blow. And when a para-daemon blew, everyone in the vicinity needed to look out. "Agent Casavetes has handled numerous homicides. He's exceptionally competent."

Gabriel grimaced. Maybe he'd been competent once. But he'd moved here so he didn't have to be anymore. Beside him, Everil shifted, apparently ticked that his competence hadn't been duly noted as well.

"Capable's not the issue," Crill said. "Turns out Reinholt's a political hot button. And the Alliance likes its finger on those buttons, not a PEC section chief's."

"And which representative initiated the task force?" Koller asked, even though he undoubtedly knew the answer just as well as Gabriel did: Tiberius.

"It's done, Benjamin," Crill said. "Let it go." The call ended with a click, and Gabriel watched as Koller growled, then yanked up the handset before slamming it back down. The phone shattered.

"I'll file my report," Gabriel said, telling himself he was relieved. "And I'll requisition you a new phone."

He started to push out of his chair.

"Fuck that," Koller said, stopping him. "A high-profile murder took place in my town on my watch. No way am I letting go of this case."

Gabriel sagged back. "Sir . . ."

Koller's fuzzy eyebrows lifted. "You want to say no? Have me assign another agent?"

"No, sir!" Everil said. "This is a Division 12 matter. It should stay in Division 12."

Gabriel might not be singing a happy tune at the thought of working with his oh-so-charming partner, but on this one, he had to agree.

A man was dead, and as much as Gabriel didn't want to get sucked back into homicide, he was damn certain that this would be a political butt fuck if the Alliance took over. Either they'd shove Caris off to an executioner without pulling any more evidence than what Gabriel had already found, or else she would walk, protected from charges of murder by virtue of whom she'd slept with.

He didn't know which way it would go down, but either was equally unacceptable.

He'd moved to Zermatt to avoid homicide, not to pretend that it didn't exist. And he sure as hell hadn't moved here so he could watch politicos trample all over a case.

He'd look the other way for a lot of things. But not this. Goddamn it all, not this.

"We're in," he said. "We've already got some solid leads."

Koller nodded. "Off the books. The Alliance gets no wind of our investigation until we have sufficient evidence for trial. They want to create a task force, fine. Our investigation will run parallel. By law we have dual jurisdiction. I'm exercising that jurisdiction in secret." He looked at both of them. "Gentlemen, get to work."

◆

Caris stood in the shower and let the water pound down from above, wishing it could wash the thoughts from her head. The desire.

And the regret.

What had she been thinking?

Then again, that wasn't an entirely fair question. She knew exactly what she'd been thinking. She'd been thinking about Tiberius. About his touch. About his hands.

She'd been thinking that despite all the anger that still boiled up within her, that she wanted to touch him. *No.* It was *because* of that anger. He could banish her, but she couldn't do the same to him. But she could use him. She could take what she wanted, draw pleasure from his touch, battle down the daemon by battling herself in his arms.

Angry sex. How cliché was that?

But dammit, it had seemed like a great idea at the time. And it hadn't stayed angry. No, instead it had turned . . . confusing.

Now came the little lies. Not to Tiberius, but to herself. Whispers that said she did it only to get off. That it was just a fuck, and nothing more.

Lies that said she didn't care, that all he was to her was pain and the past.

Lies that whispered as they swirled around her, saying that she could handle it. That she'd been cold, using him. That she'd felt nothing at all. Only lust. And certainly no hint of the love that had once overwhelmed her heart every time she'd looked at him.

She'd opened a door by sleeping with him, and that had been a very big mistake. Time to slam it shut. Tight and fast.

Because if she didn't, he'd stab her through the heart again. And this time, she didn't think she could survive.

She frowned at her thoughts. If she was so concerned

about slamming doors, why the hell had she told him about Gunnolf? There was one for the psychology books.

With a groan, she rolled her head. She doubted the hot water could wash away the thoughts surging through her mind, but with any luck, it would work the kinks out of her neck.

Of course, the last time she'd showered here had been under similar circumstances. Only they hadn't done it on the gym floor but on the bed. And she hadn't been alone in the shower, he'd been right there, touching her, caressing her, stroking every inch of her.

Enough already.

Frustrated, she turned off the water then stepped out of the shower and grabbed a fluffy white towel. She dried off, then wrapped it around her body like a sarong before opening the double doors that led into the suite to let in some cool air. She was about to turn back around and head for the sauna when she froze. *He was standing in the doorway, a dark form shrouded in shadows.*

Her hand clutched at the towel, the reaction instinctive. "I didn't realize you'd come in," she said. "I didn't catch your scent."

"You weren't meant to," Tiberius said. He glanced up, and she followed his gaze, noting the odd, concave vents that lined the office ceiling. "Olfactory filtration. I often allow ambassadors to use this suite. The vents allow me and my men to approach with stealth. We've accidentally overheard some very interesting conversations that way."

"Handy," she said.

"There's very little I don't think of." He took one step

forward, moving into the light. He'd showered as well, and he looked vibrant and commanding in black slacks and a white starched shirt.

"Yes," she agreed. "You're very thorough."

"Very," he said. "I've come to talk shop. I've got a bit of intel we're going to pursue."

"Are we?" Her voice sounded overly tight, as did his. Then again, how could it sound natural when they were having to squeeze the words out around the giant elephant standing in the middle of the room? The one both of them were thinking about but neither wanted to mention.

Well, maybe he was right. Better to write off what happened between them as a mistake. A blast for old times' sake. A huge lapse in judgment.

Now was the time for professionalism. Now was the time to be cool.

From the way his eyes were targeted on the spot where her hand clutched the towel at her breast, though, she had a feeling he hadn't yet stepped into line with the professionalism plan. Well, fine. He could learn the hard way.

"Well?" she said as she turned her back to him. "The intel?" She headed into the bathroom and dropped the towel in a swift, deliberate movement, fully aware that he could see everything, and at all angles, in the mirrors that covered every wall.

He said nothing, and she smiled. Petty, maybe, but it felt good to torture him. She was suffering, after all. And they were right about misery loving company.

She looked over her shoulder. "Tiberius? Did you fall asleep back there?"

He stepped forward, then leaned against the bathroom door, watching her boldly. If he was tormented at all, he really wasn't showing it. "Sorry. I was just enjoying the view."

She turned away, wanting to hide her scowl—but of course the scowl was broadcast right there for him to see, live and in person on four mirrors along with a series of reflections disappearing back into infinity.

"The intel," she said. She clipped on her bra, facing him as she did. Cool and casual despite the air between them, thick with the scent of desire. His, and yes, hers, too. She'd caught it—hell, she couldn't avoid it. But they were both ignoring it.

Casually, she bent to get her jeans. Just another day at the office . . .

"Lihter's involved with something big. Something that has the para-daemons scrambling."

She froze. "That's the chatter?"

"That's the word from Slater."

"Slater?" She heard the pleasure in her voice and took it down a notch. She'd always liked Bael, but now wasn't the time. "What's he got?"

"He intercepted a phone call meant for Bovil. His snitch was calling to give Bovil the scoop, but he cut the call short before Slater could get the details."

"So that's where you start," Caris said. "Find the snitch and politely ask him to share his secrets. What did he learn, and how did he learn it."

"That's the plan," Tiberius said. He moved to sit on the bed, facing into the bathroom, where she was running a comb through her hair. The situation was so familiar it made her heart ache, and she turned away, then went to the sink and splashed some water on her face. If she was smart, she'd tell him to get out of her room.

Instead, she turned around and faced him. Just business, though. She could handle just business.

"Have you got a lead on the caller?"

"Not yet," Tiberius said. "Slater's on it. Someone close to Bovil. No one else would have his cell number."

"And Reinholt? You need to talk to his friends. See if you can figure out what he knew about Lihter's operation."

"I'm putting Luke on that. And I have a number of agents pulling background."

"Why not let me take that? I already know a bit about his background."

"Pass what you can to Luke—"

She shot him a harsh look.

"—Cull anything that relates to you being a hybrid."

"Wouldn't it be easier for me to just take point?"

He smiled. "Probably. But I thought that you and I could take a little shopping trip. To Frankfurt."

"Frankfurt?" she repeated.

"That's where Naomi was when she was kidnapped. Reinholt's daughter," he added, to clarify. "Lihter must have known she'd be there. Chances are he left a clue."

"And Frankfurt has a high weren population," she said.

"Lots of werewolves who remain loyal to Gunnolf," he agreed. "Or so I've been told."

"You want me to use my contacts. See if there's any buzz about Lihter."

"I do indeed."

She nodded slowly. "I can do all that on my own. Move in, move out, report back."

"You could," he agreed. "But I want you to do it at my side."

"You don't trust me?"

He walked forward and grabbed her arms, the contact ricocheting through her. "I trust you." He spoke gently, and she watched the way his lips formed the words, hating herself for thinking about those lips doing more than simply speaking.

"I do trust you," he repeated. "I want you at my side."

"Oh." Her head was spinning from his words as much as from the feel of his hands on her bare skin. The heat seemed to bubble up between them, a heat that had nothing to do with the steam that still lingered in the room.

No.

She shook free of his grasp and hurried into her shirt, grateful for the time it covered her face, even if she could only claim a few seconds as her own.

"I don't think that's a very good idea," she said when she'd slipped her head through the top of the T-shirt. She didn't look at him, though. And even she wasn't sure if she meant traveling to Frankfurt with him or something entirely different.

"Probably not," he said. "But that's the way we're going to play it." He looked hard at her. "Are you going to fight me on this?"

She squared her shoulders. "This isn't—this doesn't change anything. About what I said in the gym, I mean." That had been a mistake. She was certain of it. But unless he was on board, she feared it was a mistake she would repeat.

He nodded, slowly and thoughtfully, and she felt an unwelcome ribbon of disappointment curl in her stomach. "I understand," he said. He moved to the doorway.

He stopped at the threshold and looked back at her. "Caris—"

"Yes?"

A pause, so long she thought she would drown in it.

"Get your things together," he said. "And meet me in the hangar. We leave in one hour."

And then he was gone, and she was left staring after him.

It wasn't what he'd intended to say, she was certain of that. But that was okay. She was here. She was working with him. And although it hadn't disappeared, the pain in her heart had lifted just a little.

CHAPTER 15

◗ Luke slid his cellphone back onto the bedside table and pulled Sara close. The windows were closed and the blinds drawn against the last bit of California sun. Outside, the Pacific surf pounded, and he could hear the pulse of the waves in the otherwise quiet house.

Sara sighed and kissed his chest, then lifted her head to look at him. "Let me guess," she said. "You've got to run off on some wildly exotic mission."

He chuckled. "I'm not sure how exotic, but yes, I have things to do."

"But Tiberius just sent you home." There was both question and accusation in her tone. "We should just sneak off like Petra and Nick did."

Luke laughed. "They didn't sneak," he said. Petra and Nick had gone on a tour of the world, traveling in crowded planes and trains, rubbing shoulders with the masses. Formerly cursed to not be able to touch, Petra was now having the time of her life, at least according to Nick's emails. "Nick planned it all out, and Tiberius knows exactly where he is if something comes up."

Sara made a face. "I just had the bad luck to fall in love with the one of Tiberius's men who gets all the calls."

"Unfortunate for you," he said, pulling her into a kiss, one that she returned with equal enthusiasm.

"At least he sent you home for a little while." Her

smile was small, but genuine. "You've been through so much lately." She pressed a hand to his cheek. "I miss you."

He covered her hand with his. "The Alliance will soon pick a new chairman, and these tasks will be over." He'd been quite busy lately following up on intelligence reports, meeting with various lieutenants to the other representatives, attempting to gauge if their leaders were being honest with Tiberius about the way they intended to vote. It was the business of politics. And while he was much more comfortable with a blade than with diplomacy, he had to admit that he was finding this foray into the political arena invigorating. And he was certain that Sara appreciated the fact that his missions lately tended toward the gathering of information, not political assassinations.

"And then it's back to business as usual," she said, as if reading his thoughts.

"It is," he said. He felt the familiar tightening in his gut. Sara knew better than anyone his role in the Alliance. He often stepped in where the system failed. Taking out killers that, for whatever reason, the PEC was unable to prosecute. And, yes, taking out some that the PEC never even got wind of, dangerous shadowers with political ambitions. If Tiberius ordered it, Luke did the job.

As a prosecutor, Sara stood firmly on the side of the system, and the scent of vigilantism that covered his work hadn't sat well with her. Not at first. Not when they'd fallen in love.

She accepted what he did because she loved him, and because she'd realized that the world isn't painted in black and white. She understood now. But that didn't mean she liked it.

He waited for her to slip out of bed and pull on a robe, a signal that the conversation disturbed her. She didn't, though. Instead, she slid closer to him, then pressed her cheek against his chest. He relaxed, his body losing the tension he hadn't even realized had built during the moment. She was his heart, his soul. And yet he still feared that this was the issue that would crack the love that bonded them together. Today, at least, that fear was unfounded.

"So what do you need to do?"

"Slater intercepted a call. The para-daemons got wind of something big that Lihter's up to."

"What?"

"That's what we're hoping to find out. Tiberius assumes it's the same thing that Reinholt was going to tell him about."

"But Reinholt's dead."

"With any luck, I'll find some indication at his house or learn something relevant when I talk to his friends."

She sat up to face him better, holding the sheet over her bare breasts. A good idea, as otherwise he'd be too distracted to hold an intelligent conversation. "Sounds like a long shot."

"It is. But it's necessary. Caris killed Reinholt. We have to figure out what he knew somehow, and this new information from Slater makes it more urgent."

"I assume Slater's going to talk with the para-daemons?"

"You assume right. And Tiberius and Caris are going to try to track down the kidnapped girl. They know she was taken from Frankfurt."

"He's working with Caris?" She sounded alarmed. "She was with Gunnolf for twenty years, wasn't she?"

"She was," Luke said. He had his own doubts about whether Tiberius was thinking with that brilliantly analytical mind . . . or with certain other parts of his body. "He assures me he has the situation well in hand."

Sara smirked. "Does he?" She stood and slipped on her robe before pushing the button to open the electric blinds. They slid open silently, revealing a stunning view of the ocean painted in purple and orange as the sun disappeared beneath the horizon. "So, how can I help?"

"We don't want PEC involvement. Not yet."

"I get that. Dead political snitch equals political matter. But this matter is pulling my husband away again. I'd like to speed up the process. Can I?"

He thought about it, then nodded. "You can. Tiberius is sending me a copy of a report the investigator provided to Caris. But it lists only one address in Paris, and identifies neither relatives nor friends."

"You want me to do a run on the guy."

"If you wouldn't mind. Addresses. Family. Marriages or bonds." Some shadowers followed the tradition of marrying their mate, others merely bonded. But even informal bonds should show up on a background check. "He told Tiberius his wife was human. I doubt there's anything there, but you can poke around in the human system, too."

She crawled back onto the bed, her robe falling open as she straddled him. Then she bent down and whispered in his ear, "That all depends. What do I get in return?"

He stroked her bare back, pulling her down to him as

he did. "Don't worry," he murmured as he brushed a soft kiss over her lips. "I'm sure we can think of something."

◊

The intercom light flashed, and Lindy Kruger gratefully removed her headphones. She'd spent the last hour listening to chatter flagged by the computer, going slowly through it to determine if the cellphone conversations about bombs and explosions were kids talking about video games, couples discussing the latest movies, or terrorists planning the next attack.

So far, she'd run across nothing scary. Good for the world, but it made her job significantly less exciting.

She pressed the button to operate the com. "What's up?"

"Got someone here to see you. Says he's with Homeland Security."

"Is he?" That was unusual. Lindy was stationed at the American Embassy in Egypt as a CIA analyst. A lot of Company agents passed through her doors, but the Homeland Security guys tended to stay back home in the States. "What's his name?"

"Bael Slater."

Lindy grinned. Maybe her job was about to take a turn toward interesting after all. Because while Lindy might officially work for the CIA, she had an unofficial job, too. One only the director and the president knew about. Lindy Kruger worked with vampires and werewolves and all sorts of freaky creatures that she used to believe didn't really exist.

They did. She'd met a slew of them. And it was wholly ironic that what had landed her this particularly fabulous side of her job was her bad-girl days as a hacker. The CIA had learned about her antics and recruited her. Rehabilitated her, too. Or so the story went.

"Send him in," she said, hoping she didn't sound too eager.

He was through the door in a minute. A hulking vampire with a body big enough to be the star defensive dude on an NFL football team, and eyes that could convince a woman to peel off her clothes, even without using those vampire compulsion tricks.

His grin was dangerous, and the tiniest tilt of his head was her invitation to slide into his arms for a kiss.

She pulled back with a sigh. "Tell me you're here for fun and not business."

He flashed an easy grin. "Sorry, kid. Maybe next time."

"Just my luck. Whatcha need?"

"I'm trying to track someone down."

She nodded. "Since you're here, I'm guessing he talked on a cellphone?"

"I answered the call. He didn't realize, and he started talking. Said Lihter's into something bad. I need to know who was at the other end of that call."

"That's all he said? 'Bad'?"

"Pretty much."

"Jesus, Slater. My system doesn't even flag 'bad.'"

"It flags Lihter."

He was right about that. She'd inserted a subprogram to pull all chatter relating to the key players in the shadow world.

"Tell me that's enough to do a search," he said.

"If you don't have another keyword, it'll be slow, but yeah. I can do it."

"I have the time of the conversation."

"That'll help. We can narrow the parameters."

"And once we find the call, you can search the voice prints?"

"Sure," she said. "But you'll only get a match if your caller is already in the system."

From his expression, it was obvious he'd already thought of that. "The guy had Bovil's cellphone number. He was highly placed."

Lindy's eyes went wide. "You answered Drescher Bovil's cellphone?"

Slater's expression was hard. "It seemed unlikely he'd be answering it himself. Lindy, this stays between us."

"Of course." She had no illusions about the kind of work Slater did. And although she was technically supposed to be neutral, her position intended to help all the shadowers and not just the vamps, she'd always thought that Bovil was something of a worm.

She glanced at the wall of computers and high-tech recording equipment. "I'm going to need to program the search. Then we let the system do its thing."

"How long will that take?"

She bobbed her head, thinking. "Since you know the approximate time, we may get lucky. An hour? Maybe two?"

He grinned, slow and wolfish, then ran his finger down her arm.

Lindy shivered.

"Is that so?" he asked. "In that case, maybe we should lock the door."

♦

"Here," Everil said, pointing out the window of the tiny Volkswagen they'd rented. "That's the cutoff to the château."

Gabriel peered down the dusty road, pretty sure no one had taken a car down there in centuries. "You sure?"

"I've been here before," Everil said.

Gabriel shot him a sideways glance. "'Cause you're part weren?"

Everil sniffed. "On a case, actually. Had to interrogate some werens," he added, then sat up straighter in that smarmy, self-affected way that he had. "Although to answer your broader question, yes. Many local werens come to the château. It's been used as a gathering hall for centuries and its library is unsurpassed."

"Is that a fact?" Gabriel made the turn and kept the car slow. The road was rough. Nothing like the concrete and steel infrastructure of Paris and the French highway systems. This was backwoods all the way.

But his whiny little excuse for a partner was right, and in only a few miles they reached the Château du Lupe, a centuries-old mansion behind an overgrown lawn and a thick growth of trees that stretched for four acres in each direction. A rusty iron fence surrounded the property, the barbs that topped each fence post discouraging visitors.

The gloomy atmosphere did its job well, and for years, humans had avoided the château, none even so much as turning into the long cobblestone driveway. In the nearby Parisian suburbs, the humans whispered among themselves that it was haunted. That demons walked there, and that any person entering would find himself ripped apart, thrust into a hellish nightmare that would make a Clive Barker movie look like the Disney Channel.

Gabriel knew it was a reputation that the werewolves who occupied the château had worked long to foster. The rumors and whispers kept the humans away, giving the creatures within much-needed privacy. On occasion, someone unfamiliar with the château's reputation would drive too close to the fence and catch a glimpse of one of the weren—in full wolf form—rutting in the forest that surrounded the ancient mansion.

But those incidents never came to anything. If the surprised human reported to a friend or a local bartender that a feral creature was loose outside Paris, he was patted kindly on the head and told that Paris had all sorts of ghosts and goblins. If the human reported the incident to the police, he was assured that an investigation would proceed immediately, and the matter was promptly forgotten once the human moved on.

All of which probably explained why it took so long for anyone to answer the intercom when Gabriel buzzed for entry at the gatehouse.

"This is private property," a voice finally responded, crackling through the weather-beaten speaker.

"Gabriel Casavetes and Everil Torq. Division 12. We need to talk to Faro Lihter."

The pause lasted long enough that Gabriel began to think no one was coming at all. Then the gate swung slowly open. Gabriel shot a glance toward Everil, who was sitting stiffly and looking straight ahead.

"All right then," he said, and tapped the gas.

The driveway wound through trees and landscaped

shrubbery, finally depositing them at a porte cochere extending from the front door over the driveway.

A uniformed weren marched toward them as Gabriel stepped out of the car. "Identification?"

Gabriel flashed his badge and Everil did the same.

The weren squinted at the badges, then looked up at Everil. "Torq?"

Everil bristled, then shifted nervously. Gabriel resisted the urge to nudge him hard in the ribs. A cop never showed nerves. First lesson of investigating. The cop was always in charge.

"I've heard that name," the weren continued.

"I—I've been here on a case before."

That seemed to satisfy the officer. He headed toward the door. "After me."

They were escorted through the lush mansion to a sitting room straight from the Victorian era, with velvet-upholstered furniture and a cozy fire. A young woman in a traditional maid's outfit wheeled in a cart of tea. It was all Gabriel could do not to lift his eyebrows and snort.

Behind her, another woman stepped in, this one in a linen pantsuit. "How can I help you?"

"We need to see Lihter," Everil said. "We were very specific about having questions for him."

Gabriel shot his partner the kind of look that was designed to kill but never managed to do the job. "My partner's a little overeager. We're investigating a murder. The victim is a werewolf. We're hoping to get some background."

Of course they were hoping for more than that, but Gabriel never showed his hand to a suspect. And Lihter was most definitely a suspect in this investigation. Better to concentrate on the victim, gather intel, and come back if necessary.

Gabriel had gone over that plan of attack with Everil when they were first partnered, again on the plane to Paris, and finally in the line to pick up their rental car. Hopefully he'd pounded the plan into the fae's thick head. And he hoped Everil wouldn't make some other misstep and fuck up the investigation.

"Of course," the woman said. She took a seat. "I'm the house mistress here. Delia Schnell. I should be able to help you."

Everil leaned forward, as if he was trying to memorize her face. "How long have you worked here at the mansion?"

"I came with Mr. Lihter. When he moved in, so did I."

That seemed to satisfy Everil, and he leaned back, his expression smug. Gabriel didn't have a clue what that was about, and he wasn't sure he cared. He just wanted to get to the heart of the matter. "Did you know Cyrus Reinholt?"

"Not well," she said. "He was a frequent guest at the château, though."

"If he came often, why didn't you know him?"

"To be honest, I only recognized him after we were informed of his death. The château is notified of all weren deaths worldwide, of course."

"Naturally."

"Part of my responsibility is to forward information regarding weren deaths to Mr. Lihter. As I didn't recognize the name, I looked him up in our system and learned that he actually spent quite a bit of time here."

"Were his visits during Lihter's tenure? Or before, with Gunnolf?"

"Both," she said. "His visits were never long, and he never socialized. I'm sorry, but I don't think anyone here would be able to give you much information about the man."

"Well, I appreciate your time." He stood as if to go, ignoring the surprised expression on his partner's face. He took a step toward the door, then paused. "Oh, just one more thing. I heard a vampire used to live here at the château."

Her face pinched, as if he'd just said something nasty. "You heard correctly."

"She around?"

"And how does she relate to Mr. Reinholt's death?"

"We think she—"

"We don't know that she does," Gabriel said loudly over his overeager partner. "But I've heard a few rumors that suggest Reinholt got along better with vamps than with the average weren. Thought if anyone at the mansion had chatted him up it would be her."

Beside him, Everil shifted in his chair.

"I see." Delia conjured a smile, but shook her head. "I'm sorry, but I'm afraid she no longer resides here. She left when Gunnolf did."

"So she's not in tight with Lihter?"

He wouldn't have thought it possible, but the face pinched even tighter. "No. She most definitely is not."

He nodded. "Right. Well, thank you for your time."

"Of course." She walked them to the door and handed them off to the uniformed valet, who watched with an eagle eye as they piled back into the tiny car and headed off down the drive.

Gabriel waited until they were back on the main road, then glanced at Everil. "So what did we learn?"

"Not a thing," he said, sounding particularly snippy. "Maybe if we'd told her the theory that Caris was working for Lihter . . ."

"Yes, I'm sure that would have opened her right up. Look, Ev, the trick in investigating is to pull the information out one strand at a time. You try to snatch the whole blanket, and everything will just get ripped to shreds."

Everil scowled. "But we don't have anything to work with."

"The hell we don't. We know that there's no way that Lihter would have sent Caris to take care of Reinholt."

Everil nodded thoughtfully. "Yeah, yeah. So, if she was working for someone, it must've been Gunnolf."

"He certainly tops the list," Gabriel said.

"But why would Gunnolf want Reinholt dead?"

"No idea. But we're going to have to tug that line."

"So we're going to Scotland?"

Gabriel nodded slowly. "I think we may have to. How are we doing on the rest of it?" He'd put Everil in charge of tracking down Caris's contacts. Vamps or werens she tended to hang with. Confidants she'd made over the years. He wanted to talk to them all. You never knew where a key bit of information would come from.

"Got some more on that just a few hours ago. I was going to type it up at the hotel and forward it to you."

Gabriel turned to his partner. "I think the conversational approach will do us just as well."

"Right. Sure." Everil cleared his throat. "Well, you already know she cozied up to Tiberius for a butt load of centuries. Then she up and betrays him and heads over to Gunnolf's camp."

"Why?"

"Huh?"

"Why'd she betray him?"

"Uh." Everil's mouth hung open. "I—"

"Calm down, it's not a pop quiz. But it might be relevant. Make some inquiries. Let's see if we can't figure it out. It may have been twenty years ago, but considering the life spans we're dealing with, that's hardly ancient history."

"Right. Got it. Uh, there is one other guy. Human."

"She hangs out with a human?"

"Apparently he's in her family tree. Name's Orion."

Gabriel frowned, trying to remember why that name sounded familiar. "Richard Erasmus Orion? The medical examiner for Division 6?"

"That's the guy. You know him?"

"Our paths have crossed." He liked Orion. The human was thorough and smart. "Good work. We may have to pay Mr. Orion a visit. Could be he knows something about our suspect's defection to the weren camp."

"You think he'd tell us?"

"Won't know until we ask."

After that, they rode in silence a few miles, until the chirp of Gabriel's cellphone filled the car. Gabriel didn't recognize the number, but he picked it up, hopeful that one of the weren at the château had heard about their visit and was calling with under-the-table information.

That wasn't the case. Instead, the caller was Peter Dietz, a former PEC agent turned private investigator whom Gabriel knew from his Texas days.

"Gabe, buddy! I heard you're in town."

"Shit, man. You heard wrong. I'm in Paris."

Peter chuckled. "That's what I mean. Paris is my playground these days. I'm supposed to be in Zurich tomorrow. I just called your office to track you down. See if you wanted to come to the big city. They told me you're down here in my neck of the woods. You staying the night?"

"Looks that way."

"Tell me where you're staying. I'll buy you a drink."

"Buy me two," Gabriel said with a grin, "and you've got a deal."

CHAPTER 16

Even at night, the area bustled with shoppers and tourists hurrying along, paying no attention to the two vampires who moved through the crowd, looking at everything and hoping that some idea would leap out at them.

"This is ridiculous," Caris finally said. Window-shopping for fabulous leather jackets was all good and well, but it was hardly helping them locate the girl. "What do you expect to find? *Help me* written in blood and signed with an *N*?"

"I was hoping to retrace the girl's steps. It might give us insight into who took her. And where." He looked her up and down. "You're a woman."

"Thanks for noticing."

"Where would *you* go?"

"Here?" She looked around the street, a bit baffled. Caris had never considered herself a girlie-girl. Even when she'd been human, she'd been more interested in having her brothers teach her how to fight and ride than in doing needlework and brushing her hair.

Despite that, she had to acknowledge that there was something decidedly decadent about the Zeil, and it made her want to whip out cash and buy all the fabulous clothes that filled the glass storefronts. She'd once heard the area referred to as the Fifth Avenue of Germany, and there was no denying the accuracy of that assessment.

"I'm not sure," she admitted. "It's all so over-whelming."

"Naomi had a train to catch, and she was a vampire. That meant she was here at night, with a limited amount of time to shop before she had to get to the station."

"He said she loved to shop, too, right? So she was probably one of those power shoppers. The women you see on Fifth Avenue and Rodeo Drive."

"A fair assumption."

"So she'd want one-stop shopping." She turned and pointed to the ten-story glass structure that loomed a block away. "The Zeilgalerie."

It wasn't a sure bet, but it was a good one, and they hurried that way, then entered the unique shopping mall. Like the Guggenheim museum, there were no stairs, just a sloping ramp so you could walk and shop and walk and shop. It was chrome and glass and shiny, and Caris could see how someone with a shopping fetish could get lost in there for hours. Even so . . .

She turned to Tiberius. "We're still floundering. She would have been into fashion. We've got a picture. Should we divide up and start talking to salesclerks?"

He nodded, but it was a distracted gesture. He was looking up the slope. "I can see three ATM machines just from here."

"Except she didn't use them," Caris said. They'd already run her credit and debit cards. None had been used in Frankfurt. None had been used for weeks, actually.

"No, but look at the placement of the machines."

She did and immediately saw what he was talking about. "The angle of the ATMs. Their cameras must cover at least three or four storefronts."

"And look," he added, pointing to the ceiling where the mall's own security cameras swept the halls.

"Tedious, but we might get lucky. Why don't I contact the banks and you contact mall security? With any luck, one of us will see her."

"I think we can do it more efficiently. Considering the placement of the machines and cameras, I'd be surprised if the mall didn't require the various banks to feed their surveillance footage through mall security."

"So we should be able to check both in the security office."

"All we need to do is convince one of the security guards to give us access," she said, then smiled. "Fortunately, you can be very persuasive."

They found the security office in the basement. A bald officer sat behind a barren desk, and he scowled up at them as they approached.

"We'd like to see your security footage," Tiberius said in flawless German.

The officer snorted. "I'm sure you would."

Caris waited for Tiberius to compel the officer, but he didn't. Instead he very calmly and politely asked to see the security chief.

"We're searching for a missing girl," he said, when the chief arrived. A rotund man with beady eyes and sweat stains marring his underarms.

"Are you with the police?"

"No," Tiberius answered. "But it's important."

The chief glanced sideways at the officer. "Come back with a cop. Until then—"

"We're not going to do that," Tiberius said, catching the chief's eye. "You see, we're in a bit of a rush."

"A rush. I see." The chief nodded. "If you're in a hurry, then of course. We'll help any way we can."

Tiberius's smile was thin, and just slightly triumphant. "You're very kind."

"Huh?" At the table, the officer was looking between the two of them as if he was witnessing a tennis match. "Sir, the rules. We can't just let—"

Tiberius shifted his piercing gaze to the officer. "You can, and you have. And I assure you, we appreciate the assistance."

"Right. Well, sure. Anything we can do."

Tiberius pointed toward the door. "Shall we?"

He and Caris followed the security chief inside, then settled into chairs by the monitoring system as he scrambled to cue up the machine to the proper days. As a rule, she tried not to influence humans. Especially now that she'd become close to Orion it just seemed rude somehow. But she had to admit that when you really needed it, the trick came in pretty damn handy.

Unfortunately, after skimming through hours of footage, she was beginning to think that as handy as influencing humans might be in general, today it wasn't paying off.

And then she saw the girl. "Stop!" She leaned forward, her finger touching the monitor. The camera had caught Naomi emerging from a lingerie store, and although someone was crossing in front of her, the glimpse of her face was enough to let Caris know they'd found the right girl.

"Take it forward one frame at a time," Tiberius ordered the human. He complied, and they watched as Naomi exited the store and turned to the right, heading down the sloping mall walkway.

She exited the frame.

"Shit," Caris said.

"What's the next camera that would pick her up?" Tiberius asked.

The security chief fiddled with some knobs, and the monitor snapped to a different view. The time code was the same, and after four seconds clicked by, Naomi strolled into the frame.

This time, they saw two men behind her. They followed her out of frame, and they were still following her when the next camera picked her up.

"Weren?"

Caris shook her head. "I don't know them, and I can't tell from here."

On screen, Naomi stopped at the elevator to the parking levels. The two men stood behind her, their faces entirely expressionless. Caris felt herself tense. They were going to take the girl, she was certain of it, and there wasn't a damn thing Caris could do about it. It had already happened. All they could do was find her . . . and hopefully help her.

Beside her, Tiberius turned to the security chief. "You've been extremely helpful. Now, if you could just pull up the footage from the parking garage . . ."

◆

Luke paused outside of the secluded Austrian cottage, nostrils flaring as he tested the scent of the surrounding air. He caught lingering traces of both werewolf and vampire, but there was no one around now. Not shadower, not human.

He'd already checked out Reinholt's Paris house, only

to find it both empty and sterile. So sterile, in fact, that he'd concluded that it was nothing more than a prop. A local address for the curious.

Fortunately, Sara had been able to ferret this Austrian address out of the PEC's maze of databases. "It's not in his actual file," she said. "I found it in a cross-reference. Some sort of disturbance there once, about eighteen years ago. But that's it. I can't even be certain Reinholt ever owned it, much less that he still does."

She'd added that property tax records were no help, either. For some reason, the cottage wasn't recorded. For all intents and purposes, it didn't exist. The only proof that it was real and solid was some vague testimony in the decades-old case and the fact that Luke was standing on the front porch.

That rather dubious history was the very thing that made Luke believe he was exactly where he needed to be.

The door was locked, but that wasn't much of a barrier. He kicked it down, only to find himself in another spartan living area. He canvased the room, searching for anything that might reveal some clue about who Reinholt was and what he was up to. But there was nothing.

Just rugs and furniture and the scent of abandonment. Reinholt hadn't been in this cottage for weeks.

Still, Luke moved through the place methodically, checking every drawer, skimming every scrap of paper. He tapped on walls, searching for hidden safes, and pulled back rugs looking for trapdoors.

He didn't actually expect to find one, though, which was why he was surprised when he opened the pantry door and felt a draft.

The kitchen was in the center of the house, with no walls with outside exposure, so a draft made no sense. He stepped into the pantry and pressed on the shelving, his motions slow and careful. He had a number of secret passages built into his Beverly Hills home, and he knew a bit about how to hide a spring latch. But despite his expertise, it took him a good five minutes to figure out how to make the back wall of shelves swing open. Whoever built the place had been both smart and careful.

The open door let in a wash of cool air, and Luke found himself looking down onto a set of stairs that descended into black. Not an obstacle for his preternatural sight, though, and Luke took the stairs carefully, slowly, watching for traps, senses primed for attack or sabotage.

There was nothing.

He reached the concrete basement floor quickly and found a switch for the lights. He turned it on, and two neat rows of overhead lights illuminated the room, barren except for one thick metal door on the far wall.

He crossed to it, then peered through the small barred window. As in the rest of the house, there was no one in the room beyond. That room, however, wasn't empty.

Luke tried the door and found that the latch turned easily enough. He pulled the door open and stepped in, then immediately felt his strength begin to fade. *Hematite*. The concrete in the floor was mixed with hematite.

Not only that, but a set of wrist and ankle chains was bolted to the wall. He crossed to them, a quick inspection confirming that the chains and shackles were also hematite.

He knew of vampires who bound themselves in hematite. His friend Sergius, in fact, would lock himself up when he felt his daemon begin to rage out of control.

But the only reason a weren would need such a room would be to hold a vampire captive.

Luke frowned, thinking of the other interesting tidbit of information that Sara had provided—Reinholt had told Tiberius that his mate was a human. And yet Sara had found a reference to a bonding ceremony between him and a vampire. The ceremony had taken place about twenty-five years ago. Sara had tried to track Reinholt's other addresses by finding the female vampire's addresses.

A good idea, and Luke appreciated the effort. But it hadn't panned out. In fact, as far as Sara could tell, the female vampire had pretty much disappeared. Innocent, maybe. But as Luke looked around the hematite-laden room, he couldn't help but think that the vampire's disappearance raised a very interesting question: What the hell had Reinholt been up to?

♦

"Sweet digs," Peter said, looking around the interior of *Le Bar* in the Four Seasons George V hotel in Paris. "Division 12 must have a better expense account than I do."

"Ha!" Everil said.

"I'm staying here," Gabriel admitted. "He's staying down the road a piece."

"Is that a fact?"

"One of the perks of a West Texas upbringing," Gabriel said. "Black gold. Texas tea." And while he'd been known on occasion to be generous with his overflowing bank account, that hadn't kicked in where Everil's lodging was concerned.

Peter leaned back in the red upholstered chair, then lifted his scotch and took a good, long slug. "I'm glad I caught you. I've been meaning to check in. See how you were doing."

"You heard about all that?"

Peter lifted a shoulder. "Not the deets. Just that something went bad with one of your cases."

"What went bad?" Everil asked.

"You wanna talk about it?" Peter continued, ignoring Everil.

"Hell, no," Gabriel said, as Everil's bulbous eyes narrowed in concentration.

It was one of those homicide-gone-wrong stories that always seemed to be attached to another story about a cop changing the way he worked or giving up the badge altogether. Gabriel hadn't given up the badge—or maybe he had. He'd sure as hell been trying to skate when he'd requested the transfer to Zermatt.

Homicide gone wrong. Yeah, that pretty much summed it up.

Not that the homicide part itself had gone wrong. No, the victim—one Arturo Hernandez—had ended up as dead as dead can be, a silver bullet put right through his werecat heart, and his head whacked off with a silver dagger just to be on the safe side. It was the investigation that had gone wrong.

So very wrong . . . even though by the numbers it went completely right. Killer found. Killer prosecuted. Killer sentenced to death.

Yeah, it looked great on Lieutenant Gabriel Casavetes's record. Got him the attention of the brass—and

186 ♦ J. K. Beck

why not? Arturo was a big deal in the local weren community, and around the Mexican border, the Therians—especially the werecats—were king. Arturo's death had shaken El Paso to the core, and when Gabriel had hauled Jillian Taylor into the interview room he'd been a goddamned fucking hero.

He'd walked out of there with a pile of evidence seven miles high that proved without any reasonable doubt that she killed the motherfucker.

And he'd been so goddamned proud of himself for dotting those i's and crossing those t's.

What a crock of shit.

She'd killed him all right. But she'd had damn good reason. A lifetime of reasons. Of abuse. And torture. But Gabriel hadn't gone down those roads. He'd followed the victim, lined him up with the suspect, and set the merry-go-round turning.

An easy conviction, and Jillian had been beheaded for her crimes. She'd died . . . and as the abuse and torture started to come to light, part of Gabriel had died, too.

He'd done his job to the letter, and by doing that, he'd fucked up royally.

"Hey, hey, Gabriel," Peter said. "I didn't mean to send you traipsing down memory lane."

Gabriel waved it off. "No. I'm good. How about you? Any war stories?"

Peter took another sip of scotch as he considered. "Hell, I wish. It's the same old, same old."

"You here on a case?"

"Skip trace. Nothing worth writing home about." He finished off the scotch. "Although, now that you've got me thinking, I do have one story. Ties into your neck of the woods, that's what made me think of it."

"All right," Gabriel said, finishing his gin and gesturing to the waitress to bring another round. "Entertain me."

"This crazy chick. Looker, but wants me to do these totally fucked-up background checks."

"On who?"

"No rhyme or reason as far as I can see. Other than that they're werewolves. Every last one of them. I must've done dozens for her. Most recent one was a hell of a thing. She gives me these parameters—where the guy was in a certain year, if he has a certain type of educational or job experience. And if they're a go, then I find them for her. Give her an address, the whole nine, right?"

"Sure." The back of Gabriel's neck was tingling. He reached back to rub it, but the odd sensation didn't fade. "So what happened?"

"Turns out the guy's gone into hiding," Peter said.

"No way!" That from Everil, who was leaning forward, sipping on his Sprite.

"Makes it hard for me, right? I mean, I don't get paid until I find the guy. And let me tell you, I must have jumped through more hoops than they got in a circus, but I fricking did it. I found him. He might be in hiding, but I found out where he was going to be. Just a couple of nights ago, too. Zermatt. The fine town of."

The tingling had turned into a complete prescient sensation. The details were too similar. It had to be Caris.

And if it was, it meant that Gabriel was about the luckiest son of a bitch in the world.

"How long have we been friends, Peter?"

His buddy's brow furrowed as he mentally calculated. "Dunno. Long time."

"Have I ever asked you for a favor?"

"Odds are good you have."

"I haven't," Gabriel said. "Trust me on that one. But I'm asking you for one now."

Peter shifted, getting interested. "All right . . . What do you need?"

"I need to ask you a question. Off the record. The girl you're doing the werewolf hunt for—is it Caris?"

"Aw, fucking a, man," Peter said. "You know I can't answer that question."

"It's no problem," Gabriel said with the smallest of smiles. "You already did."

CHAPTER 12

◊ "Sir," Rico called, the word barely registering with Lihter, who was pacing, frustrated, trying to find a way around the inevitable. A way to fix this goddamned, fucked-up mess.

How the *fuck* could she not be toxic?

How the *hell* could her blood be acid and yet her pores not leak the plague?

The bitch was still unconscious—apparently the level of electricity had done a number on her—so he couldn't even ask her his questions.

He needed Reinholt. He needed her father, dammit, and even though he'd put feelers out to all his PEC contacts before he'd gotten the bright idea to snatch the girl, he still hadn't heard a goddamned thing.

"Sir." This time it got through.

Lihter turned and railed on his lieutenant. *"What?"*

Rico held up the phone. "Division 12, sir. Your contact."

Lihter almost didn't take the call. The fae from Division 12 was a disgrace to the weren population. A half weren with not even one characteristic to show for it. No ability to shift. No strength. No brawn. And the creature was damned annoying, too.

But he was determined to earn his way into the château, and Lihter was equally determined to use him as long as the little cretin allowed himself to be used.

"Everett, isn't it?"

"Everil, sir," came the high, nasal response. "You circulated a request recently. You were trying to locate Cyrus Reinholt. I—I have news."

Lihter tilted his head back and looked up at the heavens. He'd long ago stopped believing in any god but himself, but the universe? Well, she could be a cruel bitch. Today, the bitch was smiling.

"Where is he?"

"Uh, well, actually, he's dead."

Lihter's blood ran cold. "You want to repeat that?"

"He's dead, sir. Homicide. In Zermatt. I'm stationed there. Remember? At least until you can get me transferred to Division 18 in Paris."

"Dead." The man who knew how to make a goddamned hybrid was *dead*. He picked up a chair and hurled it across the room, shattering it into thin metal splinters. "Who? Who the fuck did this?"

"That's why I'm calling. It's—well, we're still working on it. I didn't want to call earlier, because if we were wrong, but now it looks pretty certain, and—"

"*Who?*"

"Caris, sir. You know, from—"

"I know Caris," Lihter said, barely able to get the words out past his gritted teeth. "Tell me."

"Tell you? Tell you what, sir?"

"Tell me why the fuck you think she killed him. What evidence do you have?"

"Oh, well, a lot of reasons." And he started to rattle them off. She'd been in Zermatt. She'd been looking for someone. And for years, she'd been systematically searching for werewolves. She'd found dozens, but this one was apparently the only one she killed. "We're still gathering evidence."

"What about motive?"

"Um, well, no idea yet, sir." He cleared his throat. "Do you—do you want me to keep you in the loop?"

"I do," Lihter said, thinking how much he'd like to crush the life from the vampire bitch for fucking with his plans. "I'd like that very much."

♦

Café Chirac looked like your average Rive Gauche coffee shop, with dozens of students usually littering the small tables outside. Tonight a light rain was falling and those students were inside, where the atmosphere was damp and noisy and smoke-filled.

Caris pushed easily past the humans until she reached the last seat of the bar that surrounded the barista area. A skinny American student sat there, his foreignness obvious in the beret he wore just a little too jauntily, the clove cigarette he'd lit but hadn't smoked, and the way he scribbled in a journal, looking up every minute or so to soak in a bit more atmosphere.

"Move," Caris said.

He twisted in his seat, looked up at her, and smiled. "For you? I think I'd rather stay," the human said, his accent pure Brooklyn.

Tiberius stepped up behind him. "Move."

This time the guy turned, looked, and was out of there so fast he caused a breeze.

Caris scowled up at Tiberius. "I was handling it."

He chuckled. "We make a good team."

Caris didn't bother responding. She just slid into the

guy's vacated seat. After a moment, she saw one of the baristas—a tall twenty-something guy with a goatee—tap the svelte blonde beside him. She finished spooning foam onto a latte, then turned, saw Caris, and gave Goatee a nod. Then she slipped out from behind the bar and disappeared into the crowd. A moment later, a bit of wood paneling from the wall behind Caris opened, and Caris stepped inside, Tiberius at her heels.

The café, for all its legitimate front as an average establishment, also happened to be a backroom shadower bar, a dive of a place where the local shadow population came for drinks and smokes and the occasional fight. And since this was Paris, the locals tended to be werens. Which was probably why heads turned as the two vamps moved through the packed room. Either that or they were admiring Tiberius's good looks and winning smile.

"Do you see him?" Tiberius asked.

"Not yet," Caris said as she looked around, trying to catch a glimpse of the werewolf they'd seen on the mall security footage. After they'd seen Naomi get on the elevator, Tiberius had the security chief pull up the parking garage footage. Two werewolves had grabbed her, but Caris had recognized only one. Cody. A sniveling little weren who used to hang out at the château, willing to do anything for anybody.

She heard the beep of Tiberius's phone, and saw him step to one side to take the call as she continued to scour the room for Cody.

"Knew you was nothing more than an opportunistic bitch." The insult, in colorful French, came from a scrawny weren nursing a beer at a nearby table. She stopped, then turned to look him dead in the eye. He didn't flinch, but his two buddies—who obviously had higher IQs—each scooted their chairs back.

"You have something to say to my face?"

"Damn right, bitch." The weren stood, wobbling a little. "You're all warm and cozy with Gunnolf when he's riding high. But now that Lihter's taken over, you go running back to the fang gang. Always knew you were nothing but an opportunistic whore." He spat, and a glob of it landed on her cheek. Her body tightened, fury rising.

"If I was opportunistic," she said, "then why the fuck aren't I in Lihter's bed?"

" 'Cause he don't want filthy vampire whores. He ain't a traitor to our kind like Gunnolf." He took an unsteady step toward her. "You think it was Gunnolf's leg that brought him down? It weren't. It was *you*."

That was it. She lashed out, her punch hitting him in the gut, and when he doubled over to gasp for air, she brought her knee up and nailed him in the balls. He howled, started to fall, and she grabbed the back of his shirt, ready to toss the impudent bastard across the room—except another weren had stepped up and was blocking her way.

Dammit. Didn't people have any manners these days?

The new boy in the fight had brought toys, and he held his knife out toward her, his mouth cut into a leer. "I'll enjoy this, vampire. You should have known you weren't welcome here no more."

"Sorry," she said. "Didn't get the memo."

He lunged, and she swung around, keeping her hold on the first weren and using him as a battering ram to knock the second guy back. He went tumbling, crashing into a table and spilling pitchers of beer. The two weren sitting there pushed their chairs back and stood as her second attacker slid on the now-slick floor and fell on his worthless ass.

Her first nemesis picked that time to get all superior on her, and he came out of his cringe with a knife in his hand, his face still contorted in pain.

"Don't be stupid," she said. But he was. They always were.

He rushed her, and she moved with vampiric speed, disarming him even as she circled behind him.

His knife was now at his throat, and she pressed the blade firmly against his skin. "You sharpen this thing lately? Think I could gut you if I flick my wrist?"

He stiffened in her arms, but apparently he'd gained a few IQ points, because he was smart enough not to say anything. She pushed the knife tighter—just enough to leave a thin line of blood rising—and then yanked it away even as she shoved him forward. "Go," she said. "Now."

Again to the credit of his growing intellect, he did as he was told, hurrying out the door with his buddy, and pausing only long enough to shoot her a murderous glance from the doorway.

"Love you, too," she said, then wiggled her fingers good-bye. A few feet away, Tiberius stood casually leaning against the side of an empty booth, his phone back in his pocket.

"Thanks for the help," she said.

"Did you need help? You looked perfectly capable from where I stood."

She looked at him hard. "I always was."

She saw the old argument spark in his eyes, and silently cursed herself. Now really wasn't the time. She shrugged. "Where I come from it's just good manners to help a girl take down her enemy," she said lightly.

He nodded slowly, accepting her truce. "Shall we try again?" He did a slow turn around the pub, glancing at all the weren faces that were staring back at them with expressions that suggested they'd really rather be somewhere else. "Perhaps a signal? Like a safe word to tell me when you want me to jump in?"

"Good idea. How about bastard?"

He pressed a finger to his chin as if considering. "Catchy, but I'm not sure it captures the essence of me."

She laughed, then quickly turned away, not wanting him to see her face. Not wanting him to realize that even for a second she let him get in through the cracks.

Behind her, he moved forward, his steps firm and even on the wooden floor. "Our boy?" he asked, thankfully all business.

"Still haven't seen him."

She took a step, intending to go. This wasn't the only bar the locals hung out in. Then she stopped. Because there he was, sitting at the bar. A skinny, bespectacled weren. She pointed her finger at him, then cocked her head toward the hall that led to the back door and alley.

"Shit, Caris," he said.

"Don't whine, Cody. It's not flattering."

"What did I ever do to you?"

"I'm sure I can think of something." She moved closer. "We can do this inside or outside. Choose."

"They'll fucking kill me if I talk to you. You think I want everyone to think I'm loyal to Gunnolf? Or worse," he added, glancing up at Tiberius, "to *him*?"

She made a fist and punched him hard in the face, shattering his nose.

"Fuck!"

She grabbed his arm and tugged him away from the bar. "Now they'll know you don't like me," she said, then dragged him to the hall.

As soon as they reached the alley, Caris slammed Cody up against the brick wall. "Where is he?" she demanded. "Where's Lihter?"

"Well, gosh and golly, Caris. When he and I were having tea at the mansion the other day, he gave me a copy of his weekly agenda. Let me just check it for you."

She got right in his face, working hard to hold tight to control. The moon was waxing, and inside, the wolf was rising. And right then, she wanted to take it out on somebody. She really, really did. "Don't play stupid with me."

"Shit, I'm not. I don't know where he is. I swear!"

"Where did you take the girl?"

"What girl?"

"Frankfurt. Zeilgalerie. Ringing any bells?"

"That snatch was for *Lihter*? Holy shit."

"So where is she?"

"Honest, I don't know. I was just hired. Me and Jacob."

"Fine. Where's Jacob?"

Cody's eyes went wide. "He's dead. Holy fucking shit, she killed him."

Caris shot a questioning glance toward Tiberius. "Naomi killed your partner?"

"He wasn't my partner. We were both hired, you know? Never worked together before. Supposed to be a simple snatch and grab. Look what the bitch did to me!" He ripped up his shirt, and Caris saw the ugly scar on his abdomen, as if his flesh had been burned away.

She took a step back, fear mixing with the rising power of the wolf. *No.* It couldn't be . . .

"How did you get that?" she asked, her voice tight.

"Bitch's blood," he said. "It fucking burned."

Beside her, Tiberius stiffened. She did the same. This was bad. All of a sudden, this had gotten really, really bad.

"Why?" Caris asked.

"How the fuck should I know? Some sort of daemon species I never met before. Maybe she was taking some funky-ass drugs. All I know is that she slit her own wrist and burned Jacob's face away, then managed to get him through the heart with a silver stake. Got a chunk out of me, too, before I managed to tranq her."

He didn't know what she was. But Caris knew. Holy shit, Caris knew exactly what Naomi was.

"Where is she now?"

"I—I dunno."

"Goddammit, Cody, you are really trying my patience!"

"I really don't!"

"Enough." Tiberius grabbed the weren and spun him around even as he dropped to a crouch. He had Cody splayed across his leg, and he was pressing down at shoulders and hips. "How much do you value your spine, weren?" he asked.

"Please, please," Cody squealed. "I was just the hired gun. What? You think Lihter calls me up to share the scoop? I didn't even know the bitch burned!"

"Who hired you?" Caris asked.

"I don't remember—I mean I do! Yes!" he said as Tiberius applied pressure. "His name's Duggin. I delivered the girl to him."

"Where?" Tiberius asked.

"Outside of Munich. He's got a house. I don't know what he did with her after. I swear I don't."

She looked at his face, then at Tiberius, who nodded. "Fine. Appreciate the intel."

Tiberius met her eyes, then snapped the weren's spine. He stood, and Cody's lifeless body fell to the ground.

"He didn't know what she was," Caris said.

"But it's too good a story not to spread. A woman with acid for blood? Someone would hear. And someone smarter than him would know."

"And there'd be panic," she said harshly. "Believe me. I get it. How could I not?" She met his eyes. "I'm the thing that frightens the world. Hell, I'm the thing that frightened even you."

"You're a weapon, Caris," Tiberius said. "Or you could be used as one."

She peered at him, not sure where he was going with this. "Yes, sure. I guess. A walking tool of biological warfare. But—"

"Slater called," Tiberius said. "He tracked down Bovil's lieutenant. The buzz on the street is that Lihter's acquired a weapon."

The words shot through her, their effect almost painful. "Naomi," she whispered. "He's going to loose the plague upon the world."

CHAPTER 18

A hybrid. The plague.

Dear God, how could this be true?

Inside her, the daemon and the wolf fought for power, both of them battled down by the will that was Caris— just Caris.

She stalked the alleyway, unconcerned that Tiberius was watching her. She had to focus. Had to tighten.

It had been years since she'd come this close to letting the wolf out when there wasn't a full moon—on a full moon, she didn't have any goddamned choice.

But Gunnolf had taught her. *Dammit*, she knew what to do.

She kicked a trash can and sent it flying.

Fight. Beat. Hit.

Battle it down.

But there wasn't anything to fight, and there wasn't anyone to hit. Not except Tiberius, and oh, God . . .

"Caris—" He was right in front of her.

"Don't," she said. "I have to— I have to—"

Go the other way. A place of peace. Calm them, don't feed your rage.

"I can't. I can't," she said to the voices in her head. She was walking in a circle, well aware that Tiberius was watching her. Well aware that she must seem like a freak, and he was going to run. That he'd leave her here. That he'd fucking abandon her one more time.

"*Caris,*" he said again, this time grabbing her shoulder. "What do you need?"

"I need to fight," she said. "*No.* No." That wasn't right. If she fought, it would only grow bigger. This time was different, the worry about more than herself. "No. I need to calm it."

"How? How can I help?"

"Help?"

That one single word stopped her feet.

"Yes. Help. What can I do?"

She looked at his face through the haze of her battle. Past the snapping wolf and the snarling daemon. There was no revulsion in his eyes. No recrimination. No fear.

There was just warmth. *For her.*

Inside, the daemon shifted, calming ever so slightly.

"I—I need to focus. Can you sit with me?"

She didn't wait for an answer. Of course he'd do what she needed. She dropped to the ground, then sat Lotus style on the hard asphalt. He sat across from her. He held out his hands, and she took them.

And then she closed her eyes and focused, moving her thoughts inward. Finding those parts of her she despised, but could never cut out—the wolf, the daemon. She spoke to them. Whispered to them. Told them to calm. Told them she was in charge.

And through it all, Tiberius held her hands and gave her his strength.

She didn't know how long it would take, but she knew it didn't matter. He'd help her through this.

And he'd stay with her until the end.

♦

As the rented limo sped toward the private airfield, Tiberius barked orders into his phone at Luke and Slater, both of whom he'd conferenced in. He had the privacy screen up so the driver couldn't hear, but he'd put the phone on speaker, and Caris was leaning forward, hanging on to every word.

She was back to herself again, the wolf battled down, her daemon under control. He'd been terrified when he'd seen her like that, his own daemon rising with the fear.

And not the fear of infection. No, his concern was purely for her. That after having kept such tight control for so many years, losing it so violently and quickly would mess with her head, her confidence.

That it might make her run from him and back to Gunnolf for the kind of help that Tiberius simply wasn't able to give.

He didn't want her to leave, he realized. He wasn't entirely sure what to do with that revelation, so for the time being he tucked it away and simply enjoyed the fact that her departure wasn't an issue. She wouldn't need to race off to Gunnolf. She'd battled it down herself. "Fighting," she'd said afterward. "Fighting is the only way to win. That's one of the reasons I did so much fieldwork for Gunnolf. Because the battles kept the wolf in check."

"You didn't fight in the alley."

"You've studied enough philosophy to know that not all fights are with fists."

He had to acknowledge the point.

She'd taken his hand then and squeezed it. "I couldn't have done it without your strength. Thank you."

"There is no need," he said. "But you're welcome."

She hadn't released his hand, and he hadn't wanted to tug it free. So he'd awkwardly used his left hand to call the car.

Once in the limo, he'd called Luke and Slater.

He'd spoken to them both only a few minutes before, when he and Caris were in the bar. At that time, Slater's news of Lihter's weapon had overshadowed Luke's report about Reinholt's house with the hematite shackles and the odd news about Reinholt's vampire mate. News of the weapon remained top priority.

"I want the *kyne*, I want Alliance security, and I want every division of the PEC searching for that son of a bitch. We've confirmed the rumor that he's acquired a weapon. It's armed, it's ready, and he could use it at any time. We don't have the luxury of time on this one. But we do need to work under the table. Reduce the chance of Lihter learning what we know. We move silently but fast, and maybe we'll get lucky."

"You got it," Luke said over the speaker. "We'll keep the werens out of the loop, at least for as long as possible."

"Good. And although we believe he's in Europe, we can't be certain. The search needs to be global."

"Understood," Slater said.

"What weapon has he acquired?" Luke asked.

Tiberius hesitated. "A hybrid."

He heard Slater whistle.

Tiberius glanced at Caris, who was sitting stiffly, her hands clenched at her side. "That information is for your ears only. Word gets out that a hybrid is out there, and there will be panic."

"Understood."

"Presumably he's developed some system to deliver

the toxin," Tiberius said. "Maybe he has captive humans he'll infect and release in populated places. Maybe he's figured out how to shove it into fucking aerosol cans. We don't know."

"He could release it at any time," Luke said.

"But he won't," Caris said. "Not yet."

"Why the hell not?" Luke asked.

"Because every story about hybrids makes one thing clear: The virus is at its most infectious during a full moon."

"So he's probably waiting," Slater said.

"It's a good bet," Caris said. "Although we can't count on it."

"Three days," Luke said. "There's a full moon in three days."

Caris met Tiberius's eyes. "Yeah," she said. "I know."

The limo entered the airfield and they ended the call. The plane was a private, Alliance-owned jet, and Tiberius had already called in a flight plan. It was just shy of 2 A.M. With a decent tailwind, they'd arrive in Munich about four, and would have a couple of hours of darkness in which to locate Duggin before they'd need to find shelter for the day.

It was times like this when Tiberius felt the weakness of his species. The damn sun. The trade-off for strength and transformative power. He'd lived with the reality for thousands of years. Today he realized what a burden it could be.

"What I find so unbelievable," he said as they settled into their seats on the small jet, "is that he turned his own daughter into a hybrid."

Caris shook her head slowly. "Maybe he didn't."

Tiberius watched her face. It was tight, as if she was

holding back an explosion. "What are you talking about?"

"I don't think he turned his daughter into a hybrid," she said. "I think he turned his wife."

"I'm not following," Tiberius said.

Caris ran her fingers through her hair. "Luke said the records of the wife disappeared, right? About— what?—twenty years ago? Eighteen?"

Tiberius had relayed this information to Caris as they waited for the limo. "Right. So?"

"That's about when I was captured and experimented on. And his experiment worked. That meant he was ready to turn theory into practice."

"You think he turned the wife eighteen years ago?"

"I do. When he had me—when he held me—he said he had to get it right. That I was helping him. That he did it for love." She shivered, as if something vile was crawling up her spine.

"So how did Naomi become a hybrid?" He had a feeling he knew her answer, and the thought reviled him.

"I think she was born that way."

Tiberius cocked his head. "I follow you," he admitted. "But there's one problem. Vampire women can't get pregnant."

"No," Caris said. "They can't." She held out her hand. "I have an idea about that, too. Pass me your phone."

He did, and she dialed, then pushed the button to put the phone on speaker. After a moment, a voice Tiberius recognized answered: Orion. A human in Caris's family tree. A descendant of Horatius. The last human descendant, actually.

"I'm with Tiberius," Caris said. "We need your help."

"Sure. Right. Hang on." A heavy bass sound echoed through the phone, along with garbled voices. A club of some sort. There was a pause, and shuffling, and then the background noise cleared up. "Sorry. I'm outside now. Quieter. What's up?"

"Reinholt," Caris said. "I have a theory. I need your help shaping it."

"Uh. Okay."

"Can I have children?"

Tiberius gaped at her. From the silence at the other end of the phone, he assumed Orion was doing the same.

"Can you—huh?"

"It's a simple question. Can I have a kid?"

"Oh. Well, wow. Is, uh, there something I should know?"

"*Orion.*"

"Right. Right. Well, I've tested your blood, Caris, but I've never done that kind of exam. But let's think about it. When you were vamped, you died. And that meant your eggs died, too."

"That's why vampires can't get pregnant."

"Exactly," he said.

"But vampire men can father a child," Tiberius said. "I know several who have impregnated human women. Their children are dhampires, possessed of strength, but without the immortality or the allergy to the sun."

"That's because guys work different than girls," Orion said. "A girl's born with all the eggs she's ever going to have. Guys make sperm all the time. So a guy gets vamped, and that batch of sperm dies. But when fresh blood flows through him, it's like his body's alive again, right? And a vamp who's recently fed can have a nice strong supply of healthy sperm."

"All right," said Tiberius. He looked at Caris. "Keep going."

"That's pretty much it. Girl vamps, no babies. Boy vamps, babies."

"My question was about me," Caris said.

"Well, you're an enigma, aren't you? You started out as a vamp, but then you got turned into a weren, too. And the thing about weren biology is that their cells repair themselves. That's how they can change back and forth without their bodies wearing out. And it's why they're essentially immortal. They're *not* immortal. But their lives are so long they might as well be."

"So you're saying my eggs might have regenerated."

"I'm saying it's possible. No way to tell for sure without taking a sample, but it wouldn't surprise me. So, why? You guys doing a little family planning? Because, honestly, you've got issues to work out before you take that kind of step."

"*Orion.*"

"Right. Sorry. Just going for a little levity." He cleared his throat. "So are we done?"

"Yeah," Caris said.

"No," Tiberius interrupted. "Orion, Caris isn't the only hybrid. Lihter's found another."

"Holy fuck."

"That is a fair assessment, yes. I need to know if you've made any progress on a cure. A vaccination. Anything. If Naomi changes—if the toxin gets out—it's going to be very bad."

"Nothing concrete," Orion said. From her seat, Caris was looking hard at Tiberius, her head tilted, her eyes narrowed. He looked away, focusing on Orion's words. "But I got ahold of some documents from the PEC in Spain. Really interesting stuff from back in the Dark Ages."

"Tell me."

"So the plague hits, right? And all these vamps are dying. Humans, too, right? And there's this one human—he's got it bad. Open sores, the whole shebang. And any minute he's expecting he'll drop dead."

"Since you're telling me this story, I assume he didn't."

"Right. He got turned. A vamp came along, all infected and oozing. And did the whole bite, suck routine. So our human dies, right?"

"Orion, is there a point to this story?" Caris asked.

"*Listen.* The human dies, and then he wakes up a few hours later *as a vampire*."

"And then what?" she asked. "He went poof?"

Like humans, vampires infected with the Black Death suffered from open sores and horrible discoloration. Unlike humans, they didn't leave stinking corpses when they died. They disintegrated into piles of dust.

"Not only did he *not* poof, but he's the one who wrote the account."

Tiberius sat a little straighter as Orion's words hit home. "You're saying that all the vamps are dying of the plague, but this newly changed one didn't?"

"Exactly."

Caris looked from the phone to Tiberius and shrugged. "So?"

Orion sighed, long and put upon. "He survived, Caris. For a period of time he was dead, and then he survived the plague. And what am I spending all my spare time doing?"

"Trying to find a way to cure me," she said, though her eyes were tight on Tiberius as she spoke. "Or a way to vaccinate or cure the world."

"Exactly."

"And this is like a clue."

"It's not *like* a clue. It *is* a clue. He died, and something about that process gave him the ability to fight off the virus when he woke up. It's awesome."

"You've done a good job, Orion," Tiberius said. "Keep working. You know how to reach me. Anytime, day or night."

"Got it," Orion said, then clicked off. And Tiberius was left facing Caris, who was looking at him with something akin to shock.

"You've been in contact with Orion?"

"He's in your family line. I take my obligation seriously."

"You've watched over humans in the family before without contacting them," she said. "You've been discussing his research with him? His research about me?"

"It's all part of looking out for you," he said. "But to answer your specific question, no. I haven't been discussing the research with him. I've been financing it for him."

♦

Tiberius's words curled around her, clinging to her like a warm blanket. She wanted to draw it close, to revel in it. And yet at the same time, that warmth—that protection—went against everything she'd believed for almost twenty years. It was an uncomfortable shift in reality.

But she couldn't deny the fact that she liked the way this new reality felt.

When she'd fought the change in the alley, she'd feared that he would be repulsed by her. By what she was. By the harsh reminder that weren blood now flowed through her, especially considering his past—how he had suffered at the hand of Claudius.

But there'd been no revulsion. Instead, he'd stepped up to help her. And when it was all over, the primary emotion on his face was pride.

It had humbled her.

"Did Gunnolf teach you that?" he'd asked in the alley.

"He did. He taught me a lot. I was lost, and he pulled me back in." As soon as the words were spoken, she wished she could take them back. Reminding him of the time she'd spent with his enemy seemed imprudent. And yet once again, he surprised her, telling her only that he was glad she'd had someone who could help her pull through.

He was full of surprises lately. Not the least of which was the bomb he'd just dropped about Orion's research.

"All this time?" she asked, needing to be certain that she understood. "You've been financing Orion's research for all these years?"

"Did you really think the PEC was paying for it?"

"I—I never thought about it."

"I did," he said. "I swore an oath to protect you, Caris. As a hybrid you're inherently in danger."

She licked her lips, that warm blanket starting to chill. "Of course. Your oath."

"No," he said, reaching for her hand. She looked down at their twined fingers, then back up into his eyes.

"The oath exists, yes. And I will not break it. But even if I owed you no bond, I would have done this for you."

"Why?" She had to force the word out through lips that seemed afraid to ask the question.

"You are the love of my life," he said, his words like a fist around her heart. "Love can be interrupted. It can be broken. It can even be betrayed. But it cannot be erased."

She didn't trust herself to speak. Instead she nodded. His words moved her, there was no denying it. But she still wasn't certain if she wanted to be moved. He'd cut her deeply when he'd banished her, and she'd nurtured that wound for years. It couldn't suddenly disappear. She wasn't even sure she wanted it to.

Slowly, she tugged her hand free.

He waited a beat, and then pulled his back as well.

She turned away, afraid her face would reveal too much. "How many do you think he tried before me?" she asked.

"Dozens, at least," he said without hesitating. As always, he understood her with uncanny awareness. "Perhaps even more. It is undeniable that making a hybrid is difficult. If there was ever a body of knowledge about how it is done, it's been long lost."

"Bastard."

"You've had your revenge," he said. "For yourself, and for them."

She nodded, remembering with pleasure the way Reinholt had fallen. The way he had stained the snow. She turned to face Tiberius. "I apologized in London for killing your snitch. I didn't really mean it. I wanted him dead, and I'm glad."

"I know," he said, and there was a hint of a smile at his lips. He pressed his palms together, then brought his fingers up under his chin. She'd seen him do that many times before, and she knew what it meant.

"You're considering something. What?"

"I want you to drink from me."

That was not what she'd been expecting. "Excuse me?"

"You heard me, Caris."

So she had. She thought of closing her mouth over his wrist. Of the intimacy of being connected like that. Of the taste of him, the scent.

She shook herself. "Why?"

"He kidnapped a hybrid. You're a hybrid."

"Ah, hello? Not really in a position to get kidnapped at the moment. Not to mention the fact that I think one hybrid is enough, even for an evil psycho bent on world destruction. And let's not forget the fact that no one knows I'm a hybrid, least of all Lihter."

"All good points," Tiberius said. "But I didn't get where I am today by not preparing for the worst."

"And where exactly is that?"

"You know perfectly well."

She leaned back. "Right. Politics."

"You're angry because you think I chose my political position over you."

"You said yourself that you did."

"So I did. But that wasn't all of it."

She shifted so that she could look at him more directly. "Tell me."

"I swore to protect my people, but Caris, you were one of those people, too. I failed you."

"No, you—"

"Please. Right or wrong, I felt as though I failed you. At the same time, I was angry—angry at you for running off by yourself. At your attacker, for changing you. At the world. I had to make a choice. And the only information I had to go on came from the past. From the hybrids we hunted. From the plagues that swept the earth."

"And so you banished me."

"And so I should have killed you." His mouth pulled into a small frown. "Do you see the irony? I banished you so that I could save my people. And yet I let you walk free. If you'd been so inclined, you could have walked right back to London and destroyed us all."

"I would never have done that."

"And I knew that. Even in my shock and anger, I knew that you didn't mean to kill Giorgio. That you were horrified by what happened. And that you would find someone who could teach you control."

He was right. He was absolutely right.

"And so I let you go. I gave you up to the world, and you found someone to help you. I'm grateful to Gunnolf, and yet I never hated him more than I did when he took you in."

She licked her lips. "That's quite a complicated mix of emotions."

"You sound surprised. Are you suggesting I'm shallow?"

She laughed. "Not at all." She tilted her head to look at him again, a new thought occurring to her. "All the time we were together, I was right there with you chasing the political ball."

"You were. I miss that."

"Yeah, well, we can't ever get that back. You wouldn't have a chance in hell of getting the vampire vote with a traitor who supposedly slept with Gunnolf at your side."

She could tell by his expression that she spoke the truth. A truth that left a nasty hole in her stomach. Because it *was* true. And he was a politician. A born leader. And that meant they were at a rock-solid impasse.

But she'd think about that later. Because thinking about it now would only drive her crazy.

"You were saying about politics?"

"Oh. Right. I was right there with you, and you told me the stories about your heritage and your royal blood. And I understand how you identify with the people you represent because of your years in the mine. But I just today realized the point."

"What do you mean?"

"Lihter," she said simply. "He's the reason the Alliance needs men like you. Men with a conscience and a code. Because without you holding the front line, he'll creep in deeper and deeper until sooner or later the Lihters have taken over and we're living in hell."

"The Dark Ages, actually. It was before your time, but you've just very accurately described what happened. It took many centuries and many determined men to pull us out of those horrid times. As you say, men in my position are the watchmen. The first line of defense."

She smiled. "It's very noble."

He met her eyes, held them, and she felt her breath hitch. "Drink," he said. "If the worst happens, I want to be able to find you."

"You realize you can just trace my cellphone," she quipped. "You vampires, always living in the past. Get with technology."

"I'll make a note of it."

"Can't you already find me? I've drunk of you before."

"I've tried," he said. "Maybe the hematite he injected in you did something. Maybe it's the weren part of you. But my ability to track you has been blocked."

"You tried?" She should probably stop being surprised, but she couldn't help it.

"Caris," he said gently. "I never stopped loving you."

She swallowed, his words warming her. They didn't, however, surprise her. And that warmed her as well. "If it's the hematite, it probably won't even work. And I'm still weren. So there's no point."

"We won't know until we try. Please," he said, and she heard real pain in his voice. "I cannot lose you. Not like that."

She looked into his eyes, and saw both regret and fear looking back at her. "All right," she said, and then lifted his wrist to her mouth.

She bit down, relishing the taste of his blood, drinking deep of his essence. He moaned, and used his free hand to pull her in close. They melted together, and she knew she'd taken enough. She should stop. But she didn't want to. Because there was truth in the blood. And in Tiberius's there was pain and regret.

But there was also love. Pure and simple and reaching out to embrace her.

CHAPTER 19

Lihter flipped the intercom switch on the console, allowing him and Naomi to have a lovely little chat.

"You realize you're making things very difficult for me?"

"Not . . . really . . . caring . . ."

The girl's voice was low and raspy, and Lihter had to strain to hear her. "Speak up, girl. This is a conversation, not a pity party."

"Fuck. You."

"What's that? You want some more of this?" He stood and walked along the console. He saw her eyes widen. Just like a little lab rat, she'd figured out where the juice came from.

"No," she said, and this time there was more punch to her voice. Good girl.

"So tell me about your father. He was a very bad man to turn you."

"Turn me?"

"You're a hybrid, are you not?"

"Yes. But—"

"But, exactly. Why do you not carry the infection?"

"I—I don't know."

He was alone in the lab, and for a moment he considered calling the doctor down. But this was an intimate moment. Just him and the girl. She could still be his weapon. He hadn't given up on her yet. And he was enjoying this quiet moment with her.

"You're saying your father didn't transform you into a hybrid?"

"Not me."

"Then how did you—"

"I was born this way."

He stood. "Born? Your mother?"

"Please—please let me go."

He put his hand on the switch. "Do you remember the electricity? Do you remember how it feels?"

She swallowed, her face slack. Her spirit was waning, which was a bit of a pity. But as she was useless to him now, he was quickly sliding beyond caring.

"Now tell me," he said. "Was your mother a hybrid?"

"I— She . . . Yes."

This was getting better and better. "And where is Mommy?"

"She died when I was born."

Lihter clenched his hand so tight he almost broke the joystick controller off the console. Why did his luck continue to be so miserable?

"And how did your mother become a hybrid?"

"My father—he . . . he turned her."

"Did he? And do you know how?"

"No." The word was a whisper. Even so, it cut right through him.

"Bitch!" he said. "You're not helping! Are you trying to die? Do you want me to kill you?"

Big tears rolled out of her eyes. "No. Please. All I know is he did experiments. They wanted a child, but she was a vampire, and so they experimented."

"He could have killed her."

"He used other girls. And—and I guess he finally figured out how it worked."

"He did," Lihter said. "Of course he did. And then you were born. A wonderful circle of life." He peered hard at her. "The names of these experiments?"

"I don't know. I swear, I don't know."

He believed her. But just to be on the safe side, he cranked up the voltage and asked again. Then again.

He stopped asking when she passed out.

A hybrid. Probably created about nineteen years ago, right before Naomi was conceived. A female.

A vampire originally. Captured and changed.

Dangerous.

And probably very pissed off.

He stood, his sudden realization thrusting him to his feet.

He pounded his finger on the intercom button and yelled for Rico and the doctor to get down there.

"Caris," he said when they arrived. "*Caris*. They say she killed Reinholt. *This* is why."

Behar looked at him blankly.

"Don't you see? It's so obvious. About twenty years ago she leaves Tiberius and cozies up to the weren. She's strong as shit, or so the stories go. And she's suspected of killing a man who experimented on female vamps in an effort to turn them into hybrids."

He looked at Behar. "Eh? Eh?"

Behar frowned slightly, obviously turning the information over in his head. "It sounds possible . . ."

"Possible? Like hell. It makes perfect sense."

"How are we supposed to get her?" Rico asked. "She's with Tiberius. And like you said, she's strong as shit."

"That's not a problem." Lihter put a hand on Rico's shoulder and leaned in close. "Let me tell you exactly what to do . . ."

♦

"The sun's going to be up soon," Caris said. Tiberius nodded. He knew well they were running out of time.

They were in a rented car, twining through dusty streets in the countryside outside of Munich toward the address they'd found for Duggin. But they were both tense, on edge, pushing forward against time. Afraid for the girl. Hell, afraid for the whole world.

"What if he doesn't know where Lihter is?" she asked.

"He'll know something," Tiberius said. "And we'll follow that lead and then the next and the next."

He looked at her, and he knew what she was thinking: Following leads could take too damn long.

"We'll have another lead soon." He'd ordered all of the PEC divisions on it, and analysts were combing through cellphone chatter for any and all keywords that might relate to Lihter. He was hopeful he'd have a hit soon. "We'll find him," he said. "And we'll stop him."

A few more twists and turns, and they reached their destination. He pulled over and killed the engine. "Here, this is the address."

The house in question was set back far from the street, a ramshackle stone house hidden behind tall shrubs and tucked in behind an iron security fence.

"Let's move," she said and slipped out of the car.

He followed quickly. With the night wearing away, they needed to either stay in the house—ideally because this place just happened to be Lihter's secret lair and they were kicking the crap out of him—or get back to the car and steer it to an underground parking garage. Either way, the clock was ticking.

Getting in was easy enough—they both changed to mist to get through the fence, then kept that form as they traveled down the vent hood into the kitchen.

Not the most elegant of entry points but it had the advantage of being quiet and effective.

"Nice kitchen," Caris said. "Stainless steel. Stone countertops. Roomy."

"Too dark," Tiberius countered, glancing sideways at her.

She grinned. "That's what Home Depot's for."

He stayed close to her as they checked out the rest of the house, passing through a huge living area that had two walls entirely of glass. A great view of the hills below, but hardly vampire friendly.

They continued into the back halls, then down the stairs into a basement. For a moment Tiberius was hopeful, but as far as they could tell it was completely empty.

And nowhere in the place did they catch a scent of human. Even the weren scent was so faint as to be almost undetectable.

"Perhaps I killed Cody too quickly," Tiberius said. "I think the little worm lied to us."

"His story checked out, though. This place is owned by a Mazin Duggin."

"Who unfortunately isn't home, and who left no convenient clues scribbled on napkins and sitting in plain sight."

"I hate it when the bad guys are uncooperative that way."

He held out his hand. "Shall we check the upstairs again?"

They were heading back upstairs when a slight vibration shook the house. Tiberius pressed his hand flat against the wall. Footsteps. He caught Caris's eye, saw her nod in acknowledgment. She'd felt it, too.

They continued up the stairs, stopping just outside the basement door. They waited, listening as the weren moved about inside. And then, when there was only silence, they slowly opened the door and stepped into the long hallway. They split up, moving in unspoken understanding, just as they had for centuries. Centuries when they'd been so close they would finish each other's sentences and read each other's thoughts.

He'd missed that. Hell, he'd missed her.

"Found him," Caris called.

He hurried toward her voice and found the two of them in a simple kitchen. Caris might be one hell of a fighter, but Duggin's attacks and parries proved to Tiberius that Lihter had gone the extra mile to train his men.

Even so, Duggin was no match for Caris. She dodged his blows, handily twisting his arm behind him, then locking it in place by jamming it against the kitchen counter, his body pressed back against his twisted limb. Any thought of moving was erased by the foot she kept pressed against his chest and the knife she held out toward him with her one free hand.

Her other hand held on to the island, ensuring her balance as she stayed in position.

He couldn't help but smile. She really was a remarkable woman.

"Lihter," she was saying as he approached. "Where is he?"

"What the fuck makes you think I know?" Duggin growled.

Tiberius punched the weren in the chest, shattering a few ribs. "I'm afraid that's the wrong answer."

"Fuck you," the weren retorted, which wasn't particularly polite, but under the circumstances was to be expected.

Tiberius punched him again, this time in the temple. The weren howled with pain.

"Where?" Tiberius demanded. He'd moved in front and Caris had shifted back. Tiberius had filled the gap, and now he held Caris's knife at the bastard's throat, his own body pressed so close to the stinking werewolf that Duggin had nowhere to go. He inched closer, and watched as the werewolf grimaced in pain as his wrist pressed harder against the granite countertop.

A shove, and the bone shattered. The weren's howl of pain filled the house, and Tiberius smiled, slow and easy. "Where's Lihter?" he said.

This time, Duggin spat in his face. And that, frankly, was the last straw.

Suddenly Tiberius was no longer seeing Duggin but Claudius. Not a weren in jeans and a T-shirt, but a monster in the garb of a nobleman. A vile bastard armed with a bronze rod and a whip. Lashing out. Cutting flesh. Slamming down. Shattering bones.

His body was breaking, burning. Pain came in red-hot waves of black and red, knocking him back, drawing him into the abyss. He lashed out against it. Pounding. Fighting.

"Tiberius!"

Bone shattered beneath his fist as he came back to

himself. The weren in front of him was Duggin again, Claudius lost to the mists of memories.

"He can't tell us anything if you kill him."

Duggin's face was almost unrecognizable. Swollen and broken and oozing with blood.

"Come on," she said, her hand on his shoulder. Gently, she eased him back. "Lay back a little."

He relaxed—and that was a mistake.

Duggin burst away from the granite, using the moment to snatch a wooden stake from the windowsill. He thrust it forward, catching Tiberius right in the chest—

Right in the heart.

Tiberius fell, the world turning gray around him. He could watch, but he couldn't move. He could only lay there, body dead, the stake protruding, and the world going on around him.

Caris screamed and leaped for Duggin, who had a knife in his other hand. He lashed out, slashing Caris across the palm as he did.

"Bitch!" Duggin cried out. "Your boyfriend's fucking dead!" And that was his second mistake, because even as Caris winced with pain, she leaped toward the weren and pressed her bloody hand against his face.

Acid.

Duggin's flesh sizzled and burned, and his anguished cry was like something out of hell.

Caris kept her hand pressed against him, unfazed by his cries. "Where?" she demanded. "Where is Lihter's headquarters?"

"In a mountain," he said. "That's all I know. I swear."

With her good hand, she grabbed his neck. Her bloody hand she moved to his crotch.

"No!" he cried out. "I don't know where. I swear! He

only told folks at the highest level. That's not me. For fuck's sake, that's not me."

"Where did you deliver the girl?"

"To the airport! I packed her in a crate and put her on a cargo flight. I just did what I was told to do. I swear. I swear!"

She released Duggin and took a step back. "See how easy it is to be cooperative?"

Duggin was actually nodding when Caris moved in for the kill, slipping a kitchen knife right into his heart, and then using that same blade to slice off his head.

That was all Tiberius saw before the coldness of death took him. Darkness, nothingness.

And then . . .

Caris's face above his, the stake that had been in his heart now in her hand.

"It's a damn good thing you're so old." She smiled. With more than two millennia behind him, Tiberius had physically changed. Unlike younger vamps, merely piercing his heart wouldn't kill him. Or, technically, it did kill him. The death, however, didn't last, and the deeper the thrust of the stake, the more complete the death and the longer it took to recover.

An elder vampire only truly died from a staking—only turned to dust—when the organ was fully penetrated, complete with an exit wound.

Duggin hadn't managed that.

Tiberius glanced at her hand. "Will it be okay?"

Without a word, she turned from him, then dug through the drawers in the kitchen until she found one filled with pot holders and towels. She folded a pot holder and pressed it over the wound, then twisted a towel around it like a bandage. Neither said a word as he stepped over to help her tie it into place.

For a moment, the material fizzled and bubbled, the polyester threads reacting to the acid in her blood. Then the reaction slowed as her body healed itself and the blood ceased to flow. She turned away from him, deliberately not meeting his eyes, and he wanted to lash out. To tear the goddamned countertop off. To pummel the weren who lay dead on the floor.

Most of all, he wanted to kill Cyrus Reinholt.

But Caris had already done that on her own.

Caris.

She'd already left the kitchen, and the image of her face—tortured, embarrassed, ashamed—seemed burned in his brain.

This wasn't the first time—she'd been like this for almost twenty years, so how many times had she been cut? How many times had she been forced to hide a wound?

He wanted to hold her and soothe her. Wanted to tell her it would be all right. That no matter what, she was still Caris at the core.

But he realized with profound sadness that someone else had already told her all those things. Gunnolf.

And if that pained him, he had no one to blame but himself.

♦

Caris was standing in front of the living room window when he found her. She kept her back to him, but she could see his reflection in the glass, and beyond that the pale gray that signaled the coming sunrise.

"Quite the fight," he said.

"It's what I've been doing for years. Fieldwork. Wet work." She met his eyes in the reflection. "And I'm good at it."

"You are," he said, his words surprising her. "You are. I was wrong to keep you from it."

"I—" She cut herself off, not sure what to say.

"You're a fighter, Caris. You always have been. It's one of the things I loved most about you, one of the things that attracted me to you. The way you refused to accept your father's failure to send troops after your brother. The way you were taking on those men in the tavern when I found you. For years you fought by my side, and I didn't want you anywhere else."

"And then you made me stop."

"I did. I was so terrified of losing you that I allowed myself to not see all of you. And then I lost you anyway." He paused. "I'm truly sorry."

She turned to face him. "Thank you for that."

"We should go."

She nodded at the window, and the streaks of pink that were now coloring the gray. "I don't think we can."

"This place could definitely use window treatments. Curtains, perhaps."

"Oh, please. Shutters. Or electrical blinds."

"Expensive proposition for all those windows. But we can afford it," he said.

"True." She headed out of the room. They couldn't leave now, but they did need to find a place that wouldn't be invaded by sunlight. She was halfway up the stairs when he tugged her to a halt. She turned to look back at him, and saw the amusement in his eyes.

"Like old times," he said.

"Except we never looked at inland property in the hills. Only on the beach."

"You like the water."

"I do," she said. "Do you remember—" She cut herself off with a shake of the head. Better not to go there.

"The house outside of Nice?"

"Yeah," she said. Apparently he was willing to go there. "The pool." They'd swum naked in the pool, not realizing that when the real estate agent had said she was leaving, she'd only meant for ten or so minutes.

"First time in a long time that I'd had the urge to kill a human."

"You convinced her to leave, though. You were most polite."

"I scared the poor woman to death," Tiberius said. "But we had the place to ourselves for an entire night."

Caris met his eyes. "We have this one, too."

"No pool. And no night."

"We can make do." She tugged on him again, urging him up the stairs and into the master bathroom. There was a huge walk-in shower with multiple showerheads along with a garden tub. "Sweet," she said, turning the water on in the tub and then getting the shower going as well.

She stepped back from him and eyed him mischievously as she peeled off her clothes.

"Nice bathroom," he said. "Love the fixtures. And all the other amenities."

"Ha," she said, then stepped into the shower. "Coming in?"

"Absolutely."

He slid in next to her and she grabbed the soap, lathering him up, sliding their bodies together. "And here we thought that being stuck in a house during the day would be a bad thing," she said.

Her lips parted in question, but she didn't know what to ask. There was hope hanging there. Hope and comfort and home. Because that's where she was now. She'd come home to his arms, but it was only an illusion, and if she hoped too much she'd only get hurt.

"I—" she began, but he cut her off, his mouth closing over hers, erasing her memories, her fears. Leaving only the blood-deep desire to lose herself. To let go and forget everything that was happening. Everything that had happened before. To simply be with this man again, this man she loved—yes, loved and always had. Always would.

Gently, she pulled away, and got a little feminine thrill of satisfaction down her spine when she saw the frustration in his face as she broke the kiss.

"Caris—"

"No," she whispered. "I like this. I want this. It feels wonderful. Your lips, your arms. It feels like we have a chance." She pressed a finger to his lips, just in case he was thinking about chiming in. "Not for it to be like it was before—I know we can never get there again. But just that we can work together again, be together again. You were my best friend for over five hundred years, and as much as I've hated you, I'd be lying if I didn't say I missed you."

"And I, you."

"But, Tiber— I know . . . I . . . I don't want you to think I expect more. I know what this is."

"And what is that?" he asked.

"Really hot sex."

He laughed, just as she'd wanted him to, and the moment of truth was defused. But it was out there, and that was good. Because Caris knew reality when she saw it, and in Tiberius's reality, he couldn't be with her. Not forever. Not anymore. Not when every vampire he ruled believed that she'd betrayed him to go into Gunnolf's arms.

But for now . . .

She looked at him, then kissed him, forcing her mind not to go places that it shouldn't. Not to wish for things she couldn't have and shouldn't want. Right now, she had him. His touch, his company. And that was enough. It had to be.

"Make me forget," she said, sliding his hands around her back and pressing against him. She felt his cock harden, knew that he wanted this as much as she did— and since they had all day she intended to draw it out for as long as possible.

Duggin might have been an asshole, but he had good taste in soap, and she lathered her hands with the enticing scent of vanilla, then stroked it over him, rubbing, teasing, as he did the same to her, making heat build, making want grow.

And after a while she abandoned that whole making-it-last thing and simply begged him.

He didn't hesitate, and as she pressed her palms to the cool tile, he slid behind her, their bodies fitting together, his hands on her breasts, his knee easing her legs apart. And then, sweet heaven, he was inside her, filling her, and she really didn't want it to end.

He slid one hand down her belly, his hand cupping her, playing with her and bringing her higher and higher until she couldn't stand it any longer and she shattered in his arms, then sagged down, relying on his strength to hold her up.

"Too fast," she murmured.

"Just the beginning," he countered.

The tub was full now, and she turned off the shower, then eased him out of the stall and down into the languid heat of the tub. She straddled him, her legs wide, her body wet and needy.

He was inside her, filling her, pulling her into a sensual haze filled with memories of the hundreds—thousands of times they'd done this before.

Dear God, how she'd missed him.

There'd been a time when they'd fought, and hard, to be together. She remembered making love to him like this, soft and sweet. She remembered her father rushing in—going so far as to kill Tiberius to keep them apart.

As with Duggin's attempt, it hadn't succeeded. How could it have when they were meant to be together? And finally, after nineteen years they were back again. Even if it couldn't last—at least she was in his arms again. At least she felt alive one more time.

"Caris," he murmured, and she realized she was thinking too much. She didn't want to think. Didn't want to do anything but feel. His hands on her, his cock inside her.

"Yes," she whispered. She splayed her hands across his back, feeling the scars of the past still etched into his skin.

She slid her hands down farther, spreading her legs wider, feeling the water pulse in waves around them as she rode him, deeper and deeper, over and over, until she was climbing a wall of pleasure and he was reaching down to tug her over the top. Close, so close—and all she had to do was grasp and then—*yes.*

Dear God, yes.

Her body shook with the force of the orgasm, and he rode through it with her, drawing it out, making her crazy, taking her to the place where pleasure merged with pain.

And then her body went limp in his arms. He pulled her close, stroking her, kissing her, holding her, pulling her down until she was enveloped in warm water and the strength of his arms.

The world was unraveling around them. A madman on the loose, a hybrid poised to infect the world. But right then she wasn't scared.

Right then, they were together.

And together, they could do anything.

CHAPTER 20

Tiberius couldn't remember ever wanting her more. The taste of her. The touch of her. The scent of her.

He'd been starving for almost two decades, and now he wanted to lose himself in the feast of her.

She'd been his life, his heart. And then she'd been ripped away. Worse, he'd been the one doing the ripping.

And yet here she was, soft against him, her lips brushing his, her hands in his hair, and he couldn't quite believe that he'd gotten so lucky.

Maybe there would be hell to pay in the end, but right now he didn't care. He hadn't been with the woman he loved in almost twenty years.

Love.

He'd told himself he didn't still love her—not that way. How could he after everything?

But he did. And nothing mattered but the woman who was touching him. And if he couldn't have love now, then the living memory in his arms was the next best thing.

"Caris," he whispered, relieved when she pressed her hands to his face and kissed him with gusto.

"There you are," she said. "I thought—"

"Second thoughts?"

"Never." A small smile tugged at the corner of her mouth.

"Good."

They dried off and moved to the bed, still wrapped in Duggin's thick towels. He was sitting with his back against the upholstered headboard, and she slid onto his lap, straddling him. He had to fight back a groan. "Cheater," she said with a laugh, her eyes as knowing as they'd always been. "Go ahead and let it out. I promise I won't tell." He'd always teased that she could read his mind, especially when they were in bed. Nice to know it looked as if she still could.

"Let it out?" he said in an equally teasing tone. "So soon?" He took her hand, sliding it down between their bodies until her palm cupped his crotch. That time he did groan, as much from the way his body hardened as from the way her lips parted erotically, as if she was imagining tasting him.

He hoped it wouldn't be only his imagination for long.

She leaned back, her eyes searching his face. He wanted to hold her gaze, to get lost in it. To somehow tell her with his eyes what this meant to him—more than Really Hot Sex. It was what he'd wanted for years but couldn't have. Not then. Not even now.

As far as his people were concerned, after all, she was a traitor. And they wouldn't respect a leader who cozied up to the woman who'd betrayed him.

But for the moment? For the moment, she was his. And he was hers, as well.

He pulled her close, kissing her hard, mouth open, demanding. He wanted to lose himself in the taste of her. Wanted nothing but her mouth against his, her skin against his.

He slid his hands under her towel, relishing the silkiness of her skin against his palms, delighting in her soft moans when the towel fell off her, leaving her before him with only hot, damp skin.

He closed his mouth over her nipple, one hand splayed across her back as she arched against him, giving herself fully to his mouth. He remembered the taste of her—like sweet wine, like ambrosia, like *Caris*. He teased her nipple with his tongue, feeling it harden, feeling her stiffen, catching the scent of desire rise up around both of them as she shifted and squirmed in his lap, as if his ministrations at her breast were a direct line to her clit.

He kept the one hand on her back, but let the other slip down, feeling her soft and wet and slippery and beckoning for him to slide inside, to explore every inch of her.

He did, teasing her clit as she sighed and moaned and made all the soft noises he'd remembered so well, not stopping even when she told him it was too much, begging him to wait. He didn't—he couldn't. Not when he could feel her tightening around him, not when her body was going tense with pleasure, and certainly not when she lost it, going over the edge and trembling in his arms.

"There you go," he whispered.

"Been there already," she murmured. "Or had you forgotten?"

His body tightened. "I assure you I haven't."

"This time, I wanted to go there with you."

"You will," he promised.

She pulled him close, kissing him again, taking the lead now as she laid him out and straddled him. She brushed her lips against his, feather soft. Then harder, more demanding. She explored him with lips and fin-

234

gers, sliding down his body, tasting him, making him groan, making him even harder.

She cupped him and stroked him, making him desperate. And when she closed her mouth over him, he thought he would explode right then.

He didn't. She was expert at teasing and taunting. At building and anticipating. And when she finally worked her way back up his body to kiss him again, he was beyond ready for her. He flipped her over, his own hands exploring her now. Finding all her soft places. Her waist, her thighs.

He kissed her chin, stroked her shoulder. "I'm going to make love to you. I'm going to make you tremble under my hand. I'm going to make you come."

"Yes," she whispered, and he could feel the desire rolling off her in waves, the scent of her arousal driving him wild.

"I want to forget, Caris. I want to forget that we can't have more than this. That what we once had can never be again. I want to wash it from my mind, at least for a little bit. And I want to do that by losing myself in you. Would you do me that one little favor?"

She swallowed, then managed a small, flirty smile. "Sure, I guess," she teased. "If it's important to you."

"It is," he said. And then he lay down beside her, gathered her close, and lost himself inside the only woman he'd ever loved.

◆

Caris stretched, practically purring as Tiberius's arms wrapped tightly around her. For at least a little while, the world had slipped away.

Hard to believe that not so very long ago she couldn't even have imagined this moment. A huge wall had dropped between them almost twenty years ago, and she'd known that it would stay there forever. It was still there, in fact. But sometimes people found a way over the wall. Hurt faded, anger dimmed. And understanding dawned.

She'd wanted so badly for him to come after her, but never once had she returned to him. She'd left that burden on him, despite telling him for centuries that she was capable of carrying the heavy weight and fighting the hard fights. She'd bowed out of that one, content to stay with Gunnolf, warm and protected, and lick her wounds and beat out her frustrations in the field.

And though he hadn't come to her and wrapped his arms around her and whisked her away to paradise, neither had he turned his back on her as she'd believed. Just the opposite. He was still protecting her, still honoring that promise he'd made to Horatius. Looking for a cure. Watching her back.

Except he hadn't done those things because he was under an obligation to her. He'd done them because he loved her.

He loved her. He always had. And, she realized now, he always would.

But love didn't always win, and as long as he was an Alliance rep or got elected to chairman, she couldn't be at his side. Politics was sacrifice, and if there was one regret she had from loving him, it was that where Tiberius was concerned, the people would always come first.

Beside her, he shifted, his hand stroking lazily down her arm. "You're thinking deep thoughts," he said.

"I am," she confessed.

"Tell me."

"I'm jealous," she said.

He shifted to sit up. "Are you? Of whom?"

"Everybody," she said. "Because they have you, and I cannot."

He cupped her cheek, his eyes deadly serious. "You have me," he said. "You always have."

He leaned close to brush his lips over hers, but before things could get interesting again, his phone rang. She flashed a half grin. "The burden of being so damn important."

"It's a dirty job," he agreed, then answered the call. "It's Luke," he said, then switched the phone to speaker.

"The cellular surveillance paid off. Lindy in the Egyptian office intercepted an encrypted conversation between Lihter and one of his lieutenants. A fellow named Rico. Apparently, they're moving the girl."

Caris sat up. "When?"

"Seven in the morning," Luke said. "In Zurich. But that's not all. Lihter's not handling the actual transfer. Apparently he's heading off to Sri Lanka to meet with a biologist about a delivery system for airborne toxins. He's chartered a plane out of Vienna. We know where he's going to be and when."

"This is incredible," Caris said after they'd hung up. "I'll go to Zurich and get Naomi. You take a team and head off to Vienna."

"Luke can take point. I'm going with you."

"Are you crazy?" she asked.

"I won't risk losing you."

"What's the risk? I'm a hybrid, remember? She can't

hurt me. You, however, she can kill. So forgive me if I'd rather have you shuffle off to Austria."

She watched his face. He wasn't happy, but it was clear that he knew she was right.

"It's Lihter," she said, just to push him that last bit over the edge. "Think of what he's done. Think of what he's planning. You have to be the one to take him down." She cupped his cheek. "Do that, and you know you'll be elected chairman. It'll be a landslide."

"I'll pull a weren team from the PEC and Alliance security," he said.

"One, that would take too long. You specifically requested no weren working this case, and there's no time to get them up to speed. Two, I can help the girl. I get what she's going through. And three, if after everything we've been through together you think I'm going to walk away from a fight just because you're a little bit nervous . . ." She poked him in the chest with her fingertip. "Think again, buster."

To her relief, he smiled. "You're right. A warrior needs a battle."

"She does," Caris said. "She really does."

And that wasn't even an exaggeration. Fear for the girl and fury at Lihter had welled up inside her so much that Caris was afraid she'd explode if she couldn't release some of it. Since Tiberius was heading off to capture the bad guy, more sex wasn't an option. And that left fighting.

A perfectly serviceable option, in Caris's opinion, though significantly less fun than getting naked.

"I'm still sending a team. Two snipers. Vamps, but in hazmat suits."

She rolled her eyes. "I think you're overprotective."

"I probably am."

She pressed a kiss to his lips. "That's okay. I love you anyway."

"You'll be careful?" he asked.

"Always. You?"

"I'll do what I must to come back to you," he said, and since she couldn't argue with that, she melted into his arms and gave him the kind of kiss that proved just how much she wanted him to come back to her safe and sound.

◆

Richard Erasmus Orion III fiddled with the button on his pristine white lab coat. "So, uh, you guys are from Division 12? Isn't that a pretty long way from here?"

"We don't mind," Gabriel said, his eyes on Orion's nervous fingers. "I figure the more frequent-flier miles the better."

"Right. Right." Orion managed a false laugh, then went back to playing with the button. He was either guilty of something, knew someone who was guilty of something, or he was the most nervous civilian that Gabriel had ever met. "So, uh, what can I do for you?"

On the way to Los Angeles, Gabriel had considered how to handle Orion. He'd planned to be subtle. To pull information out in a slow, delicate process.

Now that he saw how squirmy and nervous Orion was, Gabriel was thinking that a good cop/bad cop routine would work well. Actually, plain old bad cop should do just fine.

"You're related to the vampire known as Caris?"

Plink! A button on Orion's lab coat popped off and went flying across the room. "Uh, yeah. She's my . . . something. It gets complicated after so many generations. But, yeah. We're related."

"You two pretty close?" He'd already pulled Orion's cellphone records and seen dozens of calls to Caris.

"Oh. Well. You know."

"Actually, I don't. That's why I'm asking you."

"Right." Another nervous laugh. "Sorry. I'm pretty much a lab rat. Talking to cops makes me nervous."

"Really? Why? Have you done something wrong?"

"What? No!"

"Has Caris?" Everil asked, apparently deciding that he wanted to play bad cop, too.

"Wrong? What could she have done that's wrong?"

"Oh, I don't know," Gabriel said. "Forgot to pay a parking ticket. Returned her library books late. Stalked dozens of werewolfs all around the world. Killed one in Zermatt. You know. The usual stuff."

He kept his eyes on Orion as he spoke, and he saw the way the color drained from the human's face. The way his Adam's apple bobbed as he swallowed. The way five beads of sweat popped out on his upper lip.

"I don't know what you're talking about," Orion said.

"Really?" Gabriel stroked his chin. "You said you two were close?"

"Yeah. I mean—yeah. If Caris was involved in something strange, I'd know. And she's not. Involved in anything strange. Strange or bad."

"You're sure?"

Orion nodded vigorously. "Hell, yeah." He reached

out and grabbed a candy jar in the shape of a hand. "Tootsie Roll?"

Gabriel took one, then stood, cocking his head so that Everil would do the same. "This has been very helpful. It's always good to be able to put a theory to bed."

"Right," Orion said. "Sure. That makes sense. Glad I could help."

"If we think of anything else, we'll be in touch."

"You do that." He tapped the phone on his desk. "Just feel free to call. No need to come all this way."

But there had been a need. Gabriel needed to see Orion's face. Because it had told him everything.

◆

"This is excellent progress," Koller said, as Gabriel and Everil sat across from him.

They'd gotten one of the Division 6 staff para-daemons to open a wormhole, and while it wasn't the most pleasant ride back to Switzerland, it had the benefit of being fast.

"Opportunity, access. Planning. You have her in town looking for a man. We can require your PI friend to turn over his records." Koller shut the file folder. "Gentlemen, I'm impressed."

"Thank you, sir," Gabriel said. "Obviously we still have work to do. I particularly want to nail down motive."

"Of course. Of course. But all that can come after we issue the arrest warrant."

Gabriel frowned. "I don't think—"

"What?" Koller leaned forward, the crease above his nose deepening as it always did when he was annoyed.

"I think we're better off waiting until we have the case. Like you said."

"We *do* have the case. Motive isn't an element of the crime. We have more than enough evidence to arrest, and probably enough to convict. I'll have the warrant issued today. If we don't move on this, the task force might. And I don't want a task force stepping in to claim credit for solving a crime in my jurisdiction. Understood?"

"Yes, sir," Gabriel said.

"Absolutely, Mr. Koller, sir," Everil chirped.

"Good. Now you two track our suspect down. I want her in custody within forty-eight hours."

"How are we—" Everil began, but Gabriel caught his eye and shook his head. He cast a quick glance toward his boss. "Don't worry. I've already figured that one out."

He'd taken the initiative of putting a trace on her phone already. His intent hadn't been to use her phone as a tracking device to locate her—he'd been hoping to gather more evidence—but at least they were prepared. In fact, the information would come in contemporaneously to his own PDA and show her GPS coordinates whenever she made a call. Handy stuff, technology. And the shadow world always got the best gadgets first.

She hadn't made many calls, though. In fact, the only one he'd recorded timed perfectly with one initiated by Orion. But what was especially interesting about that call was the fact that it originated in London—at the exact GPS coordinates of Tiberius's mansion.

Gabriel wasn't sure what that meant, but he was absolutely certain that it did mean something. Sooner or later, he'd figure out the details.

They might be arresting her now, but he wasn't letting up on the investigation. Before this case went to trial, he was determined to know everything there was to know about Caris.

He'd arrest her now because his boss ordered him to. But he wasn't going to have another Jillian on his hands.

He wouldn't be able to stand it.

CHAPTER 21

♦ "Has there been any additional chatter?" Tiberius asked, speaking into the headpiece he wore to communicate with his team, a human invention that the shadowers had adopted. Centuries before, they'd used telepathic shadowers to relay information among various members of an assault team. This method was a lot less cumbersome. "Any indication that Lihter knows we've got an interception plan?"

Static crackled in his ear. "Nothing," Slater said. "We're moving ahead on schedule."

According to their intelligence sources, Lihter was scheduled to depart the private Viennese airfield at 7 A.M. Tiberius and his team had been in position for two hours, arriving well before dawn. Now the lookouts were positioned in dark corners inside the hangar. Tiberius and Luke were in the jet itself, having already compelled the human pilot and copilot to cooperate.

The intel suggested that Lihter had chartered a human-operated jet so he could move about without attracting the notice of shadowers. Few shadowers flew on commercial planes. Instead, they chartered private planes operated by other shadowers, ensuring that their unique needs would be satisfied on the flight.

Unfortunately, there had been no word about how many staff would be traveling with Lihter. Tiberius assumed there would be four—front, back, side, side. Presumably one guard would enter the jet first to check it out. He'd examine the cockpit, find the pilots happy and smiling, then examine the rest of the jet. That would check out fine, too, because Luke and Tiberius would be hiding in the plane's ventilation system as mist.

There was a risk, of course, that the bodyguards would inject some sort of atomized hematite into the body of the jet, but both Tiberius and Luke considered the risk minimal, particularly since Lihter had discussed his travel plans over an encrypted line that, as far as the weren knew, remained secure.

When the front man had approved the in-jet situation, he'd signal for Lihter to enter. And that was Tiberius's and Luke's cue. They'd materialize, moving in immediately for an attack on the front man and Lihter. They were going for a capture, not a kill, and Tiberius anticipated that the assault would be accomplished quickly and cleanly.

Meanwhile, the team in the hangar would move in as well, capturing the backup staff and providing additional support.

Then they'd all celebrate a job well done.

So far, however, things weren't moving along as planned.

"He should be here by now," Tiberius said.

"Roger that," Slater said. "There's still time to get him on board and in the air by his scheduled departure time. Maybe he's just stuck in traffic. Wait—hold on. We've got a visual."

"Is it our guy?"

"Looks like it. SUV. Tinted windows. Hired car, so I can't run the plates."

"His approach?"

"Straight for the hangar," Slater said. "Gotta be our guy."

"Steady. Signal when the team is approaching the jet."

"Roger."

Tiberius glanced at Luke, and the two remained silent, waiting for the sound of footfalls on the pull-down staircase—their signal to transform into mist. But there were none.

"Tiberius. We've got a problem," Slater said. "I think you should break cover and get down here."

"What is it?"

"Hard to say. But it's not Lihter, that's for damn sure."

No, Tiberius had to agree, it certainly wasn't. The only occupant of the black SUV was a Mr. Alfred Delaney, the very human, very confused CEO of a chain of fast-food restaurants.

Caris.

He ripped out his cellphone and dialed fast, but he didn't get an answer. He dialed the two snipers he'd sent with her. No answer there, either.

Trap. They'd walked into a goddamned trap.

"I'm taking the jet," he said to Slater, willing himself not to let fear drive him. That was the way of mistakes. Methodical. Calculating.

That's what would get Caris back.

And his first calculation was to get to Zurich as fast as he possibly could.

"It's daylight," Slater said. "That jet's windows aren't treated."

"I'll keep the shades down," Tiberius said. "But I'm going. Get a car with tinted glass to meet me in Zurich. Have the tower radio the hangar number."

"Will do," Slater said. "And Tiberius? Good luck."

♦

The parking garage was right in the middle of Zurich, filled with cars and humans and so much motion that Caris could see why they'd picked it to make the switch of a kidnapped girl.

She had the two snipers, Jeph and Carr, crouched one level up, looking through the railing at the parking space below where a small Audi had just pulled in.

They'd come in an SUV designed with specially treated glass to keep out the harmful sunlight. The parking garage was mostly enclosed, so although it was day, they were safe.

The snipers were both in hazmat suits, white and bulky. Hopefully they wouldn't get caught on the human security camera. Because if they were, Caris was sure someone would call in some sort of terrorist threat.

Caris bent down, trying to get a better angle as the Audi parked. "That's it," she said. "One fuzzy die, one little green monster hanging off the mirror." That had been the signal, at least according to the encrypted conversation Tiberius's men had decoded. "Driver's going to get out, drop the key behind the back tire, and get the hell out of there."

The girl was in the trunk, presumably drugged, because why else would she be so quiet?

As she'd expected, the driver's-side door opened, and a tattooed werewolf got out. He walked behind the car, then tossed a key down onto the ground. It landed with a *clang* that echoed through the garage.

"I'm going in," Caris said. "Cover me."

She moved quickly toward the car, then bent down to

snatch the key. She glanced around, saw nobody, then carefully put the key into the lock.

She turned to Jeph and Carr, now behind her in the shadows, saw the subtle nod of their heads. They were rock-solid in position. If anything jumped out of that trunk to attack her, they'd hopefully be there to take it out. Assuming she couldn't handle it first.

Slowly, she turned the key. Slowly, she lifted the trunk.

She saw a blanket, and she peeled it back. She saw Naomi's hair first, and she said a soft word, intent on soothing.

The word died on her lips, though, as she pulled the blanket the rest of the way. Because the girl in the trunk was dead, her head having been sliced from her body, a silver dagger jammed through her heart.

Caris whipped around, not wanting to see. Not wanting to know that they'd failed this poor girl.

As she did, her phone started ringing. She reached for it, but at the same time she heard the distinctive *thwap, thwap* of a tranquilizer gun.

She hit the ground, her eyes looking toward Jeph and Carr. They were on the ground, both sprawled out. Either tranqed or dead.

Tiberius. Oh, God. What was happening with Tiberius?

Lihter's plan had to have been a trap, too.

She needed to warn him, but she had to get out of there first. She couldn't go out into the sun, but she could hide in the building, and they'd have one hell of a time finding her as mist.

Except it didn't work.

She couldn't transform.

And as she turned her head, trying to figure out why,

she realized that all three of the cars beside her were painted the same odd blue color.

The cars had been redone in hematite, and its proximity was messing with her abilities.

It was clever, she had to admit.

But that was the last thing she thought. Because the next tranq dart got her, and she fell face-first against the asphalt.

♦

"What the hell do you mean, she's gone?" Tiberius yelled into the phone. He'd ordered a Division 12 team to the parking garage right away, and now it was overflowing with jinns and para-daemons and other creatures that had no problem working during the daylight hours.

Tiberius himself was still in the plane, and the fact that he was so goddamned impotent at the moment was driving him crazy. He finished listening to the useless spiel about how the PEC was doing everything it could. Then he slammed the phone shut and turned to Luke.

"They got her."

"I'm so sorry."

"The girl was in the trunk. She was dead."

Luke nodded. "I gathered that much from your side of the conversation. Tiberius, we'll get her back. And the good news is that we don't have to worry about the larger threat. We can focus all our resources on Caris."

"The larger threat?"

"The hybrid," Luke clarified. "She's dead. Lihter's biological weapon is no more."

Tiberius closed his eyes. Because he was going to have

to do now what he probably should have done before. "The threat isn't over, Luke. In fact I'm guessing the threat is worse than ever."

Luke eyed him through narrowed lids. "What do you mean?"

"Caris is a hybrid. Reinholt changed her almost twenty years ago. I banished her, and she went to live with Gunnolf. Hide in plain sight, like they say."

"Oh." His friend nodded slowly, diplomatically. "Well, that explains a lot of things. And you're right. We need to find her. And soon. The full moon rises tonight at ten, and if we can't find Caris by then I think it's a fair guess that the Black Plague is going to spread through Europe again."

"It won't," Tiberius said. "We're going to stop it."

They had to. Because stopping it meant saving Caris, and there was no way Tiberius was going to fail to do that.

"I'm all for stopping it," Luke said. "But we've been searching for Lihter for days. The guy hasn't left a trace."

"He has now," Tiberius said. "He has Caris."

Luke's brow furrowed, and then he smiled with understanding. "Blood. You had her drink your blood."

"I did indeed," Tiberius said. And then he closed his eyes, leaned back, and tried to feel Caris burning inside him.

CHAPTER 22

The metal door burst open, ushering in a shaft of moonlight that rent the darkness of the cell and illuminated Caris, still bound to the wall. She turned her head to the side, the brightness painful after the prolonged darkness.

She forced herself to look. A creature stood there, his hulking form silhouetted against the rising orb of the full moon. Werewolf.

It happened in an instant—the recognition of what was in the doorway, and then the realization that it was no longer at the door, but at her side, claws ripping through her clothes, teeth sinking into the flesh at her shoulder. In her mind, she fought. Raged against the beast and ripped it apart with her bare hands. In reality, she was trapped—chained to a wall, her body so weak from lack of blood and the infusion of hematite that even the daemon howling within seemed weak and sluggish.

The smell of her own blood washed over her, and as her vision faded, she saw it stain the floor. Saw it sink into the stone. Gone. Empty.

She'd been drained to nothing more than a shell. Not dead, though. She'd died a long time ago. Now, like this, she would welcome true death, but her vampire nature clung to existence, and so she hung there, flesh hanging off bone, body hanging from the stone wall. A corpse, emaciated and raw and alone.

Once again time had no meaning. She floated, her mind her only refuge. Hours, days, years. Perhaps only minutes. She had no concept, no marker by which she could measure time. It meant even less than it had when she'd walked the earth as an immortal. It simply was, unlike her, who was not.

And then the blood came. Sweet and warm and metallic, it dripped over her lips, then down her throat, and from somewhere in the vast tunnels and caverns of her mind, the being that was Caris tasted it. Absorbed it. Became it.

Blood.

More came. Not all at once, but in fits and starts. Enough, though, that she slowly came back to herself. The earth began to turn again for her, and time began to have meaning. The wait between blood visits was painfully interminable. But then he would come—the one who had ripped her apart. The one who was now saving her. He would come and he would tilt the smallest of vials into her mouth.

Sweet, sweet blood.

One day, she realized that she could speak. "Why?" she asked, the blood still lingering on her lips. The word came out as a croak, but she could tell he understood her. She still wasn't able to open her eyes, but she could hear him. Sense him. And he hadn't left. He was standing in front of her. Standing and breathing.

"Do you know what happens when a vampire is bitten by a werewolf?"

Obviously she knew. If the vampire was weak, the werewolf ripped her to shreds and left her a shriveled corpse on the ground. If the vampire was strong, she ripped the fuckwad's head off and went about her merry way. Too bad her encounter had happened when she was weak.

"No," she said. "I'm not sure that I do."

"Assuming the attack is during a full moon, the vampire becomes infected with the weren virus."

She swallowed, thinking of herself. Thinking of Tiberius.

She opened her eyes, squinting against the candlelight. "You're saying I'm going to change."

"The vampire will continue to live his—or her—life," *he said, continuing as if he hadn't even heard her.* "Days will pass. Weeks. And throughout all that time the earth rotates on its axis and moves in orbit around the sun."

"I'm not interested in an astronomy lesson."

"Another full moon comes—it is inevitable. And when it does, the vampire dies."

He looked at her, and despite the mask he still wore, she saw his brow lift, as if he was silently daring her to be sarcastic now.

She stayed silent.

"The vampire's basic nature stems from death, a werewolf's from life. Perhaps you know the mythology? Two brothers, the fathers of our races, cursed by the third brother whom they murdered for his power? It's more than a bedtime story, you know. Vampires and werewolves are cursed enemies, and their flesh shall not be joined. Try to mingle the two, and you've distorted nature itself. The natural result is annihilation."

Her chest had constricted with his words. Whether they were true or not, she could hear in his voice that he believed them.

"*You did all this just so you could kill me? Why the hell didn't you just drive a stake through my heart?*"

His laugh was low and without humor. "*Kill you? I did all this to save you. And not just you. I did it for love. Because I must get it right.*"

"*But—*" She thought over everything he'd just said. Then realized there was only one possible explanation. "*No,*" she said, with a firm shake of her head. "*You can't do that. It's impossible. Everything you've just told me proves it's impossible.*"

His masked face tilted up, his dark eyes meeting hers. "*Soon, you'll either be more than you were before, or you'll be dead.*"

He left then, his words still echoing in her cell.

Hybrid. Dear God, he was trying to make her a hybrid.

She couldn't survive that. There were no more hybrids. Were there?

She closed her eyes, forced herself to remain calm. Supposition didn't matter. She'd know the truth soon enough. He'd promised that when the moon rose, she'd be either changed or dead. No matter what else she thought of him, about that, she was certain he spoke the truth.

Daily, he brought her more blood.

Daily, her strength grew.

And daily, she feared the glowing orb of the moon ripening in the small window of her cell.

◆

Static crackled above her, and Caris realized it was coming from speakers embedded in the ceiling. After a mo-

ment, the crackling stopped, and she heard an overly
cheerful, sanctimonious voice. "Caris, Caris, such a
pleasure."

"If you want to be civilized," she said, "you might
consider unstrapping me." She was bound all over.
Arms, chest, waist. Really not good. The gurney itself
was made of hematite, which prevented her from shifting into mist.

"We're so excited to have you as a member of our little family. Seriously. It's a stupendous honor, and we're
going to celebrate by scheduling your first performance
tonight at the rise of the moon. Of course, I was recently
a tad put out by another hybrid's failure to live up to my
expectation of toxicity. So I'm sure you'll understand if
I put you through a little test."

She forced herself to stay stoically silent. She had no
idea where she was, and she knew that neither did
Tiberius or the others. She could only hope they'd found
some clue in the parking structure that would lead them
here, but, honestly, she was a little doubtful.

Of course, there was the blood.

She perked up a bit at the thought, remembering the
taste of Tiberius's blood on her tongue. The excitement
of feeling his desire cross her lips. She wished he was
there now. She wanted to see Lihter die. She wanted
Tiberius to lock his arms around her.

But wishes and wanting weren't how things worked.
She knew that one well enough.

And the only way to survive was to take care of yourself.

She could do that.

"Caris? You're being extremely rude. I said you were
going to have a little pop quiz first."

She continued to ignore him as she scanned the room. She saw some sort of rail on the floor, and it seemed to be a track for her gurney. She could see her reflection in the glass. Herself, the gurney, the space beneath. Below her, just like in a hospital, was a white bag filled, presumably, with her clothes. How bizarrely quaint.

She'd hoped for a weapon, but didn't see one. Though considering how strapped down she was, it wouldn't have been much use.

Then again, she *was* a weapon.

"Now don't you worry," Lihter was saying. "I'm sure you'll pass. But it's best to check these things ahead of time, don't you think?"

Once again she didn't answer; she was too busy wriggling her wrist to see if there was a way she could maneuver it so the strap cut into her skin. All she needed was a little bit of blood. After that, the acid would do the trick.

She started wriggling, then froze as she realized that the gurney itself had started to move, and she realized it was following electronic tracks out of the cell. The gurney moved through a series of air locks and into another cell, this one empty. But in the cell next to it, she could see three humans—a man, a woman, and a child.

"Let's just see what we see, shall we?" Lihter said, his voice once again coming tinny through speakers.

And then the gurney seemed to ignite—electricity burning through her, the pain so intense she couldn't bear it, the heat rising around her until she couldn't think, couldn't move, couldn't do anything but scream and scream for it to stop.

But it didn't stop. It never stopped.

It went on and on and on.

And then the wolf was there—bursting out, her daemon fighting to keep it down. But the moon was too close to full and the pain was too great, and her body was changing, becoming the wolf, and Lihter was winning and the wolf was winning—

—and then with one final, violent rip the wolf emerged, and Caris lost herself in the haze of the wild.

◊

Lihter watched as the wolf in the cell thrashed about on the gurney, managing to knock it over on its side, but not managing to free itself from the straps.

"Beautiful." He turned to Behar, who stood beside him, operating the controls on the console. "Didn't I tell you I'd find another hybrid? A life lesson for you," he said, then pointed across the room at Rico. "Set reasonable goals and you can accomplish them. Now," he said, turning back to Behar. "Let's make sure we really are right about this one."

"Turning on the air corridor now."

In the cell, a vent opened, connecting Caris's cell to the one occupied by the humans that Rico had delivered earlier that day. A family pacing and terrified, with the father banging on the walls as the mother comforted the child.

A family that drifted off the autobahn in search of a gas station and found death instead. Poor them. But their sacrifice supported such a noble cause.

"Now," Lihter said, and as Rico came up behind for a better look, Behar turned on the suction feature, drawing air out of Caris's cell and into the humans' chamber. At first, nothing happened, and Lihter clenched his fists at his side, fearful that this was another false start. That he was cursed to never find a toxic hybrid.

"It spreads more easily by contact," Behar said. "And humans tend to harbor the infection longer than shadowers before showing symptoms. But don't worry—yes." He pointed to a digital display. "Some of the virus is transferring into the humans' cell."

The cell was small, but it still seemed to take forever. Lihter paced, watching.

The clock clicked to noon. Then 2:05—2:10.

"*Dammit*. Is this going to work or isn't it?"

And then the little girl sneezed.

She released her mother's hand long enough to wipe her mouth, then clutched her mother again. Mom picked her up. Kissed her.

And then Mom sneezed.

The little girl's eyes turned red. Snot started to drip out of her nose.

Concerned, the father came to look at her. He pressed his hands to her face, felt her forehead. Then he looked up at the ceiling, at the air vent. The father knew, Lihter realized.

He knew that death was upon him.

Lihter watched the show a bit longer—the screaming, the ranting. And then the comforting.

But he already knew what happened in the third act.

They died.

Lihter didn't bother to watch. He had plans to finalize.

By 5:15, the show was over, and there was nothing left in the cell but the shells of dead humans.

It was an exceptional test run.

Tonight they'd have more humans to infect and then release back into the world—crowded airports, train stations, shopping malls. Tonight they'd open the vents. Tonight they'd release hell on earth, and after it had burned its way over the globe, only the werens would be left standing.

Hallelujah.

CHAPTER 23

Tiberius had come as far as he could with blood.

She was here, somewhere deep in these mountains in Liechtenstein. He knew they were in the general vicinity—he could feel it.

More than that, he could feel her fear, and it was just about killing him that he couldn't find the way to her.

"What else can we do?" he asked Luke. All around them, the team had fanned out, and for the last hour had been doing a physical search of the small section of mountainside that called to him in his blood. "Heat signatures?"

"Not through the stone. Not if they're deep."

"Cellphone?"

Luke lifted his brow. "You think she has it? You think it's on? If *I'd* taken her, I would have tossed it out a window."

"But you didn't," Tiberius said, grateful for the small bit of hope that her abductor's potential sloppiness had left him with.

"She had it with her," he continued. "Jeph heard it ring before she was taken. Whether it made it to the mountain, we don't know. It's probably not on her anymore. But even if it's in a storage closet, if it's on we can get close."

"On it," Luke said, then left to issue orders to the tech guys.

Meanwhile, Tiberius and the rest of the team fanned out across the area like ants, searching for caves, hidden doorways. Anything that would answer the question of how Tiberius could feel Caris's presence in a big old hunk of stone.

Luke returned. "Her phone's not on. Someone might turn it on, so we're locked in. But I'm not holding my breath."

"Fuck."

That was the hope he was clinging to. That they could lock on to the phone and narrow their search. And now that hope had died, but he'd be damned if he'd give up. He signaled to one of the agents, who hurried to his side.

"Bring me the map of the search grid."

The agent complied, and Tiberius studied the map, noting marked-off areas, including those that had been explored visually only, and those that had been examined with metal detectors. "Get the metal detector over here," he said, pointing to a rocky area.

"Sir, we searched there. It wouldn't be feasible to—"

"Do it."

He watched as the team fell into action, hoping he wasn't wasting precious time. The agent was right, of course. Access to a hidden chamber would likely be in a more accessible place. But if he'd been designing a secret chamber—

"Sir!"

He hurried over. The metal detector was held over a huge boulder emitting a high-pitched whine.

He looked at Luke, who nodded, and the team swooped in to examine the rock.

Except it wasn't a boulder.

Instead, it was a doorway, and they used acid to quietly burn away the lock. They pulled the door open and peered into a labyrinth of twisting corridors.

"Split up," he said to the men. "Go fast but quietly. Keep your systems set for Caris's signal. It's unlikely, but maybe we'll get a hit off her phone."

One of the jinns on the team poked his head inside, looked around, and said, "I damn well hope so. 'Cause without a map, there's no way we're finding any fucking thing in that maze."

"You're wrong," Tiberius said. "We'll find them. We'll find them because we have to."

Silently, though, he feared that the jinn was right.

◆

They hadn't bothered to right her gurney, and now Caris lay on her side, her sanity coming back to her, the wolf departing. At least for a few more hours.

Moonrise was close, and the wolf wasn't going far.

Frankly, that was pissing off her daemon.

Good. She wanted it mad. Wanted it hard and furious and deadly. Caris was so used to fighting her daemon back that she had to force herself to let go. Because right then she didn't *want* to fight it. She wanted it to rage. She wanted it to kill.

So much power inside her, and she'd never been able to call on it. Not the daemon that would take over, sending her to a dark, horrible place. Not the wolf she despised, whose very presence was deadly.

But Lihter was using her now, and that wasn't something Caris took kindly to.

Lihter wanted her to be his goddamned little weapon?

Let him fucking try.

The cell next to hers was jammed full of humans. Lihter had been shoving them in there all day. Poor, lost humans that he intended to infect and send out into the world, using her curse—using *her*—for his own political gain. He was a bastard and a coward, and somehow she was going to bring him down.

Unfortunately, she was still a little hazy on the how part, but she was certain that killing him was going to come into play somehow.

That part, she was looking forward to.

Once again she surveyed her surroundings. The new cell was one in a long line; the wall to her right was metal while the one on her left was translucent. The wall behind her was concrete and in front of her the wall appeared to be made out of Plexiglas. It had an air lock and filtration system so a person could simply walk in through a system of filters and fans without having to touch—and presumably contaminate—a door.

Her perspective was a little odd. The gurney had fallen on its side, but because she was strapped so tightly, she was at a right angle to the floor. The bag from under the gurney was in front of her, and she saw a hint of black and silver peeking out of the bag.

Her phone.

Like a dream her words to Tiberius came back to her—*you can just trace my cellphone.*

She'd been half teasing, but the truth was that he could. For that matter, it might be the only way he could, since they still didn't know if the machinations that Reinholt had put her through when he changed her had made the blood bond impossible to form.

Except that she was on a gurney, and it was at least an arm's length away.

And she had no arm. Or she did, but it was useless to her, seeing as it was bound to her side and attached to a gurney.

But still she had the acid.

She'd tried before, without success, but she'd been interrupted. More, she'd been at a different angle. Now her weight was on her wrist, making the strap cut even more into her skin.

If she just wriggled. Just wriggled a little bit more.

And then she smelled it—burning cloth. Melting metal.

Not a lot of acid, but it was there, on the strap, and if she tugged harder maybe she could—

She did it!

Her arm was free, and she stretched out, reaching, her fingers not quite there. She drew in a breath, trying to gather all her strength, then jerked her body in an effort to make the gurney move.

It did. Less than one lousy inch.

But maybe it was enough.

Outside, she heard the cold, efficient footfalls of Lihter.

Come on, come on . . .

Her fingers brushed. Missed.

Another try . . . and *yes!* She got it.

She scooted it toward her and pressed the power button even as she heard Lihter screaming instructions to one of his flunkies.

The phone came on, and she jammed the speed dial button. At the same time, the idiot called Rico kicked the phone out of her hand, grabbed it, then powered it off.

"Tsk-tsk," Lihter said. "But it's nice to know you have spunk. That's an admirable quality."

"Screw you," she said, which was really lame, but she was thinking more about whether the call had time to connect than how best to insult her insane captor.

"Well, I'd love to chat all night, but look at the time." He tapped the face of his wristwatch. "Ten o'clock. Moonrise. Your wolf comes out a bit later, I understand? Not to worry. We'll help it along." He cocked his head, then smiled at her. "Are you rested my dear? I'll grant you that the sideways gurney is less than comfortable, but considering this is our big day, we didn't want to take any chances."

He moved toward the console, then spoke into a microphone, calling his team. When they were all in place, Lihter smiled again. "Well. Let's get started, shall we?"

She opened her mouth to curse him, but what came out instead was a scream. He'd said he was going to speed up the process, and he'd cranked up the voltage on her little table. She'd gone from nothing to searing, jolting, horrific pain in the blink of an eye.

Once again, the wolf rose, and once again she fought, but she knew she was going to lose. Goddamn it all, she *couldn't* lose. But her daemon was no match for the force of the wolf. It gathered up inside her. Gathered and growled and burst forth.

And as the wolf overcame her, she saw something that finally, for the first time, gave her hope.

She saw Tiberius storming into the room.

♦

Tiberius saw her across the room—strapped to a gurney behind a wall of glass, the change coming on her.

He saw the wolf emerging—limbs elongating, fur erupting. But she wasn't a werewolf to him. She was Caris. She was *his*. And the bastard who had done this to her was a dead man.

Around him, the team had already fanned out, going one-on-one with Lihter's men in front of glass cells filled with innocent humans. Luke was leading that team— a wild thing, a fighting machine.

Other agents swarmed into the lab, heading for the console, going hand to hand in hazmat suits as Lihter's weren soldiers forced them back.

Tiberius ignored it all.

He marched straight down the middle as if he were walking across the goddamned Red Sea.

Straight across the room toward *him*.

Faro Lihter.

The weren saw him coming—and he had the gall to smile.

One of his idiot flunkies decided to move in on intercept mode, grabbing a chair as he did and slamming it against the floor. The chair shattered, and the flunky rushed at Tiberius, a stake in hand, the wolf emerging as he burst forward.

Perfect.

With all the speed that more than two millennia can bring, Tiberius grabbed the guy's arm, wrenched the stake out of his hand and purposefully thrust it into his own belt, and casually ripped the weren's head off.

Then he returned Lihter's grin and kept on walking.

To Lihter's credit, the weren was beginning to look a little nervous.

So nervous, in fact, that he turned around and raced for the air lock. Also perfect.

Tiberius followed, and as he did, Luke fought his way across the lab, heading toward the console so he could shut down the airway between Caris and the uninfected humans.

Tiberius paid no attention to them—he knew Luke would get it done. He was only interested in Lihter. Lihter, who thought he was so clever to hide in there with the virus.

Not good enough. Not nearly good enough.

Tiberius smiled. So far, Lihter was acting completely predictably. Hopefully, he'd keep it that way.

Tiberius followed the weren in, felt the air whooshing around him, heard Lihter's laughter, calling him a fool.

And then he saw awareness in Caris's eyes. He saw *her* under the wolf. Saw Caris and her daemon fighting to bring the wolf back despite being deep in the throes of it. Despite the full moon.

Could she do it?

He saw the determination in her eyes, and right then, his money was on the woman, not the wolf.

More than that, though, he saw fear in her eyes. *For him.*

He didn't have time to reassure her. He was too focused on his quarry. More than that, he wasn't entirely sure he'd survive this. But he had to try. For Caris. For the world.

In front of him, Lihter wasn't doing the one thing that might give him a fighting chance. He wasn't bothering to bring out his own wolf. To do that would mean he couldn't speak. And Tiberius could tell that Lihter—predictably—had a few things he wanted to say.

"Go ahead, then," Tiberius said.

"What?"

"Something you want to tell me?" He was circling Lihter, his legs starting to feel a bit weak. The virus was strong. She was strong.

Yeah. Maybe his brilliant plan wasn't so brilliant after all . . .

"You're dead, Tiberius. You think you're clever, but the second you walked through that air lock, you died. She's toxic. And now you're infected."

"You may be right," Tiberius said. "But I think I can live long enough to watch her kill you."

He rushed forward then, getting to Caris's side before Lihter even had time to turn.

She'd managed to burn through a strap, and he began to work on the remaining buckles and straps on the gurney. Her wolven scent enveloped him, making his daemon rise. Anger for what Reinholt had done to her. For what Lihter was doing right now.

It was time to pay the price.

"What . . . doing?" She was fighting, forcing the words out as he worked on the buckles near her feet. "Daemon . . . strong . . . I . . . can . . . fight . . . Don't be . . . Stu . . . pid."

"I'm sincerely hoping I'm not," he said, then whipped around as she let loose a horrible keening sound—a howl of fury mixed with pure terror.

Lihter was there, grabbing for the stake Tiberius had put at his belt—and then plunging it straight into Tiberius's heart.

He fell, the stake bringing him down, Caris's scream echoing in his ear.

And the last thing he saw before the world went black was the wolf that was Caris leaping off the table and knocking Lihter to the ground.

♦

"No!"

Caris's scream came out as a howl, because the wolf was running the show. But the horror of seeing Tiberius fall like that ripped right to the core of her and she grabbed on to it—grabbed control, grabbed the daemon, grabbed all of the strength that came with being a hybrid.

She hauled herself up through the darkness of the wolf. Higher and higher, until she was controlling it, rather than it controlling her.

It felt strange—her body elongated, her muscles tighter—but it felt powerful, too. And right then she was all about the power.

On the ground, Lihter shifted. Tiberius had grabbed the weren when he'd fallen, and they'd both tumbled to the ground. Tiberius lay as still as death, but Lihter was moving, clawing his way back to his feet.

Outside the cell, two of his men raced toward the air lock.

"No!" Lihter called. "Stay out!"

They ignored him and rushed in, and she took the opportunity to explore the creature she now was. The strength and speed and skill she had—but had never been able to use.

She used it now, and she was at their sides in the blink of an eye. With one slice of her claws, she ripped into the soft flesh of their bellies. Then she grabbed them, one in each hand, and swung them like a child's toy. Then she let them fly.

They slammed against the concrete wall, both out cold.

They were weren, so they weren't going to get infected. Too bad. But she'd deal with them later in some equally satisfying way.

She turned her attention to Lihter, letting go a little bit more with the daemon. She hadn't managed to completely pull back the wolf. It was still there, still showing on her body, still filling up her blood.

But she'd backed it off considerably, and there was serious power in the balance she'd found. She wondered if she called on her vampire side during a full moon, could she prevent the change entirely?

She looked hard at Lihter. "I guess I owe you thanks," she said. Her voice was rough, but she had one. The vampire part of her was holding on, balancing the wolf. Making her *more*. She was truly badass now for the first time—for the only time, because she could never let go like this on purpose. Not with the plague.

But with Lihter around? Well, that wasn't really a problem. And she was going to get the most out of it. She was going to destroy him.

"I've got some mad skills here," she continued. "Wouldn't have had the chance to explore them if you hadn't tried to fuck me over."

"You'll never get out of here," Lihter said. "All of them, they know what you are now. Do you think they'll let you survive?"

"I don't know," she said. "But I know that I'm not going to let *you* survive."

She moved—and was at his side.

She lowered her voice, got in close to his face. "I'll give you a choice. Turn yourself in to the PEC. Or count to three and I'll rip your heart out."

The expression on his face was nothing short of revulsion.

"No? Well then, I'll decide for you." She reached back, ready to thrust her arm forward.

He squealed. "No! No! I'll turn myself in!"

"Good boy," she said. "You made the right choice."

She waited a beat, savoring the thought of him in a PEC cell, but it just wasn't enough. Not for the wolf. Not for the daemon.

"Sorry," she said, as she punched through his rib cage. "But I really want you dead."

♦

With Tiberius's head cradled in her lap, Caris looked out through the glass wall of her cell, watching as Luke examined the knobs and dials on the huge console.

"Now," he said. "The air's clean."

Thank God.

She'd been in until moonset, holding him, her chest tight with fear that she was wrong—that he'd been wrong.

Her hands trembled as she reached for the stake still embedded in his chest.

"Please," she whispered as she pulled the stake free.

It was silly, she knew. He was still there—not ash, not

gone—so the stake couldn't have completely penetrated his heart. And yet he had been dead—if not, the plague would have taken him.

What if death kept him?

"Tiberius." She pressed a kiss to his forehead. "Tiberius, please. Please wake up."

He didn't stir.

She looked up at Luke, frantic. "Could it be the virus? Did it infect him after all?"

"I don't know," Luke said.

"Then get Orion on the phone!" she snapped, and immediately regretted it. "I'm sorry," she said. "I'm just so—"

He stirred.

"Tiberius!"

He shifted in her arms, and she blinked back tears of relief. "Damn you," she said. "Do you have any idea how scared I was? Don't ever do something like that again. If it had gone wrong, I'd—" She trembled. "You could have been wrong. The vampire in Orion's story died *while human.* What if that had been the crucial difference?"

"I know," he admitted. "But I had to take the risk."

"Why?"

"For you," Tiberius said. He looked sideways at the now-empty cell. "You couldn't have handled it if you'd infected the others. If you'd infected the world."

A wave of love overwhelmed her. "It wouldn't have been my fault," she whispered. "It would have been Lihter's." And that was true, and she knew it was true. But at the same time, Tiberius was right. She couldn't have handled any more. The burden she had was hard enough to carry. At least she didn't have to carry it alone.

She clutched his hands tight in hers. "Thank you."

His smile was all the answer she needed.

"Is it clean? Can we leave?"

From outside the cell, Luke nodded. "You're good. Come on out."

They stood, then started to walk to the air lock. She froze, though, when she saw the laboratory door open and two men walk in. One short, with the gangly gait of a fairy. The other tall and handsome with a dark complexion and intelligent eyes. Two uniformed officers walked by their side, their faces terse and unreadable.

She glanced up at Tiberius and saw that he'd clenched his jaw. Apparently he didn't like this development any more than she did.

The tall man stepped forward, then pulled out a badge and flashed it. "I'm Agent Gabriel Casavetes, and by the power vested in me by Division 12, I'm here to arrest you, Caris de Soranzo, for violation of the Fifth International Covenant by and through the murder of Cyrus Reinholt. Do you understand?"

She glanced at Tiberius, who looked downright murderous himself. "The murder of Cyrus Reinholt is an Alliance matter," he said. "I thought I made it very clear that a task force had been appointed."

"And we're happy to share our evidence," Casavetes said. "But as I'm sure you know, where murder is involved, dual jurisdiction can be claimed."

Beside her, Tiberius tensed, and Caris could sense an explosion. She reached for his hand and held it tight.

She'd known when she shot Reinholt that it could come to this, and while she wasn't particularly keen on the thought of being executed—of leaving this world and Tiberius forever—she'd done what she had to do. She'd killed the man who'd destroyed her.

And no matter how dire the price she now had to pay, she wouldn't take it back even if she could.

CHAPTER 24

❧ "I don't give a fuck if he's on the goddamned moon," Tiberius shouted into the phone. "Find Nicholas Montegue and get him back here now."

He was in a conference room at Division 12's headquarters in Zurich, pacing while Everil watched him. The fae's partner, Gabriel, was there, too, but he hadn't said a word. Just hung his head as if he didn't have a goddamned thing to do with any of the bullshit that was going down in that room.

"*Goddammit!*" Tiberius howled, and then smacked the table so hard he cracked the wood.

Not one of his better days or one of his more diplomatic moments.

He didn't care. All he cared about right then was Caris. Nicholas was his advocate, his legal council, and Tiberius needed him there right then. But even with Nick on the case, it wasn't enough. Dammit, she shouldn't have been arrested in the first place.

"How the fuck could you do this?" he asked Everil, getting right in his face, letting the daemon play out as far as he dared.

The fairy took a step back, but when he spoke, his words were strong and measured. "She murdered a man. She killed him in cold blood."

"Cold blood?"

"She hunted him down. Met him in a dark forest. Put

a bullet through his head." The fairy nodded vigorously. "We have the evidence. It all adds up."

"The evidence," Tiberius repeated. "To prove she did it, right?"

"Yes, sir."

"How about the evidence that proves why?"

The fairy's eyes cut toward Gabriel, but the hellhound didn't look up. "We—we don't need evidence of motive. It's not an element of the crime. She killed. She pays. That's the way it works. That's the foundation of the entire system!"

"Is there a brain in your head, or just a tape recorder? Don't spout platitudes at me or theories or lines from the detective handbook. This is a real woman you arrested. A woman with a past. A woman with motives. Are you really telling me you didn't even examine those motives before tossing her into a cell?"

"We intend to explore that question further during the interview," Everil said. "That's a perfectly appropriate method for further interrogation." He swallowed loudly. "But our investigation suggests that it ties back to her status as a hybrid—"

Tiberius kicked a chair over—this time because the fairy's speech reminded him that word about Caris's hybrid status had already leaked outside of the PEC. It had spread like wildfire, and there was no way to contain it. No way he could save her from it. From what people were going to think about her.

But if he couldn't save her from that, he could still save her from a trial. And he would. Even if he had to make sure these two lost their fucking jobs in the process.

"Ah," Everil said, eyeing the chair.

Tiberius turned to him calmly. "Go on."

"Right. Well, we believe that further investigation will prove that Reinholt intended to expose Caris as a hybrid. Caris obviously was not pleased with that idea."

"You guys worked that out all by yourselves?"

Everil pursed his lips. Gabriel continued to stare at the tabletop.

"You're both idiots," Tiberius said. "Reinholt's the one who *made* her a hybrid." He let the announcement hang there for a moment. "He captured her. He tortured her. All so that he could figure out how to make a hybrid. Do you have any idea what she went through? In case you forgot, a werewolf bite usually kills a vampire. What must he have done to her in order to weaken her daemon so much that she survived?"

Everil stood openmouthed, contemplating this new truth. Gabriel, on the other hand, lifted his head. His skin had gone completely pale, and Tiberius was certain the hellhound was about to throw up. The door opened and Luke stepped in.

"It's over," Luke said.

A stranglehold of fear clutched at Tiberius. "Caris?"

"No, no, the election." He looked up, and for the first time Tiberius could see his expression—confused, but also elated. "In light of Lihter's death, the Alliance convened an emergency meeting. They held the election early."

"Dammit," Tiberius said. "I wasn't told."

Luke went on, ignoring him. "Congratulations, Mr. Chairman. You won."

Tiberius let the words seep in, expecting a deep flush of pleasure. But it didn't come—how could it when all he could think about was his fear for Caris?

"But—but—" Everil's mouth continued to move even though he stopped making sound.

"What?" Luke demanded.

"Those are just excuses. She did the crime." He looked from Gabriel to Tiberius. "She killed him. She has to pay. That's the way it works."

Across the room, Gabriel rose to his feet. "Pardon her."

"What?" Everil asked, voicing the very question on Tiberius's tongue.

Gabriel stood up straighter and tried again. "You're right," he said. "She doesn't deserve to be tried for this. She doesn't deserve to be executed for it. Not after he took her. Not after he tortured her."

"Perhaps you should have thought of that before you arrested her," Tiberius said coldly. "It's a Division 12 matter. That's not my jurisdiction. It's out of my hands."

"No," Gabriel said, "It's not. The Alliance chairman can issue a pardon. Tiberius—*Mr. Chairman*—you can set her free."

◆

The battle of the century raged inside of Caris. Fear, anxiety, guilt. Love and nobility. Even loneliness. All bits and pieces rattling around inside of her.

All making her daemon crazy. Making the wolf snap and rise.

She wouldn't lose control.

Her cell was small and glass, and beyond those walls she could hear her cellmates. Their taunts and jeers. *Die, hybrid! Filthy, stinking half-breed! Death-bringer!*

She could hear them, but she couldn't see them. Her

eyes were closed, looking inward. She had the wolf leashed, the daemon, too, and she was using all her concentration to pull them apart. To keep them from snapping and biting and tormenting each other.

Let one get loose, and that would be the end of it. She'd lose control. She'd change.

And even though they all now knew—even though the cell was sealed and no toxin could escape—she wasn't about to give them the satisfaction of actually witnessing what she was. She wasn't about to let Lihter or Reinholt win. *She* controlled the change, dammit. She did, and she had for years.

Today, though . . .

Today, all her fears were pushing up against her. Sliding against her skin, taunting and teasing. *There's no escape,* the fear whispered. *You've delayed it, but you can't escape it. The day he changed you, he ended you. You knew it. Tiberius knew it. And you were just too stupid to accept it.*

No.

Yes.

The daemon kept prodding her. The wolf kept kicking her. They were strong. They were determined.

She was losing the battle . . .

And then he was there. His scent, his touch.

Tiberius took her hands, squeezing them lightly. She squeezed back, taking the power he was giving her, sharing the strength that he offered. With him, she battled back the wolf. No way in hell was she going to change now. No way in hell was the wolf coming out.

Slowly, slowly, a calmness settled over her. Even more slowly, she opened her eyes.

He was smiling at her. And despite the horror of the

circumstances, she couldn't help but smile back. "Thank you."

He reached out and stroked her cheek. "It's been hard?"

She considered lying, but this was Tiberius. She didn't need to lie to him. "It's been horrible. They all know," she said, nodding vaguely toward the guards and the other prisoners.

"They're fools," he said. "Ignorant fools."

She shook her head. "You're sweet, but you're wrong. We once thought the same about hybrids."

"Then we were ignorant as well."

"We watched Marseilles die."

"We watched a hybrid that'd gone mad destroy it. You are not mad."

She managed a half smile. "No. Though sometimes I get a little pissed off."

He laughed, then pulled her to her feet. His arms closed around her, warm and protecting. "Mmmm," she murmured. "Let's just stay this way forever."

"Okay," he said.

She tilted her head back so she could see his eyes. "Easy for you to agree, seeing as my forever will be over in just a day or two."

He pressed a finger to her lips. "You shouldn't joke about such things."

"I have to. If I let it get to me . . ." She trailed off with a shrug. "Well, you saw what I was doing when you came in."

"Even so. And besides, your forever is considerably longer." He paused long enough for a smile to reach his eyes. "You're not going to be executed."

Her brows lifted. "Your faith in Nicholas Montegue's

legal skills is admirable. But I actually did kill the man. It's going to be hard to wriggle out of this one."

"Fair enough. You don't think Nick's good enough to get you off. How about me?"

"You?" She leaned forward, tugged at his collar, and peered down his shirt. "You got a legal career hiding in there I don't know about?" When he didn't answer, she leaned back. "Seriously, it's okay." Not the exact truth, but close enough. "I'm prepared for this. I knew it was a possibility when I went after him. I've always known, but it was worth it."

"I agree," he said. "He deserved to die. Slower, and a lot more painfully than you managed, in fact. But you're still not going to be executed."

She squinted at him, trying to figure him out. "Life in prison?"

"Nope."

She frowned as she looked harder at his face. Was this a pep talk? Was there a punch line? But no. It was more than that. "Tiberius, what's going on?"

"You've been pardoned."

"What? By who?"

"By me."

"Great. As soon as you get me transferred from Division 12 to Division 6, I'm a free woman. Actually, that's not a bad idea. Maybe Nick could—"

"The Alliance chairman can pardon in any division."

"Well, sure, but—" And then she got it. Without warning, she threw herself into his arms, knocking them both backward. "You're in? But how?"

"Early election," he said.

She cupped his face with her hand, a wave of pride surging through her. This was what he'd wanted. What *they'd* wanted, for so long. More than that, it was what the shadow world needed. A man like Tiberius holding the reins.

"I'm so proud of you." She kissed him, long and hard. Then pushed back, just so she could look at him again. "Chairman. Wow."

"Caris." His voice was serious, and she leaned back a bit.

"What is it?"

He took her hands, and she held them tight. Afraid for bad news. Afraid for—well, just afraid.

"I want you at my side," he said, and the fear started to melt away. "We lost almost twenty years. I don't want to lose even one more."

She swallowed, her throat filled with tears, her heart tight in her chest.

"Tiberius—"

"The world now knows that you are a hybrid. The secret is out, and there is no reason to continue to pretend that you went to Gunnolf as a traitor. We can make the truth public, and you can sit at my side." His words squeezed her heart. "You can be with me as you were always meant to."

She blinked, and a single tear crept down her cheek. "I want that, too. So much."

"Good—"

"But I don't want that life." She had to push the words out, for fear that if she didn't, they wouldn't come. "The public life. I can't do that. Not now. Not anymore. Not with people knowing what I am."

"It will get better," he said. "People will forget. And Orion is so close to finding an antidote, maybe even a vaccine. Those things make what you are less scary.

That and the fact that you've been walking around for almost twenty years without the world dying."

"People aren't like that, Tiberius." She squeezed his hands. "But the fact that you believe it explains why you're such a good leader. You have faith. I don't. I think people will look at me and see a giant target on my back. And the more I'm at your side the more I'm rubbing it in their faces."

"Caris, I—"

"Please don't misunderstand. I love you. And I'm so proud of you. But I can't stand beside you. I'm thinking an island off the coast of New Zealand is more my speed these days. Lots of beach, you know?"

"I don't want to lose you again."

Her smile was bittersweet. "You haven't lost me. But I can't be by your side." She pressed her palms to his cheeks and looked into his eyes. "You're a born leader. This is your chance. Hell, this is your dream." She held his eyes for a second, terrified that the tears would come soon, and that he'd see. She pulled him close, taking strength from him, because she knew it had to be this way. She couldn't be in the public eye. And she could never, ever ask him to step down.

"Caris," he said, his voice low and desperate. He said nothing else, just pulled her into a long, slow kiss. When he finally pushed away, there was regret in his eyes. But also determination.

"I've already submitted the pardon. You'll be released tonight at sundown. I'll have a car waiting. Have the driver take you wherever you want to go."

She nodded. She wanted to make him promise to come see her, but that wasn't fair to either of them. They needed to make this break. And this time, she was leaving because of love.

He opened his mouth to speak, but she pressed a kiss to his mouth. "Please. Don't say anything. And thank you. For the pardon, I mean."

She got up and moved across the cell, the blanket wrapped tightly around her and her back to him. She stayed there, perfectly still, until she heard the cell door close behind him and his footsteps disappear down the corridor of the detention block.

Only then did she sit on the edge of her cot and let that single tear turn into a deluge.

CHAPTER 25

🜄 "The speeches are open to the public," Luke was saying, "but we can expect that most attendees work at the various divisions. I thought we could start in Paris, then essentially circle the globe. Europe, the United States, Asia, and on."

He paused, but Tiberius barely noticed. Morag Crill had offered them the use of the governor's apartment atop the Division 12 headquarters so they could go over the various details necessary for Tiberius's smooth transition into power. Important stuff, but even so, Tiberius's head wasn't in the game. Instead, he was standing at the shuttered window, counting the seconds until the sun sank below the horizon and the shutters lifted to let in the night.

Her car would already be in the parking lot. The guards would be processing her paperwork.

And any minute she'd be escorted down to the parking level.

After that . . . after that she'd be gone.

"Tiberius?"

He shook it off. "Sorry. Yes. We'll go country to country. That's fine."

"Great. And the speech? We have the theater reserved for midnight. There's time to fix it if there's anything you want to tweak."

Tiberius took the papers Luke handed him and glanced

down. As far as he was concerned it was written in Greek. Not actually a problem since he both spoke and read Greek, but—

"She refused," he said, his voice barely a whisper.

"I'm sorry?" Luke asked. "What?"

Tiberius tossed the papers onto the nearby desk, then lifted his eyes to meet Luke's. "I asked her to sit at my side. To join me again. To step back into the role she once had."

"She refused?"

Tiberius nodded. "She did."

Luke's expression remained unchanged, the diplomatic skills he'd acquired over the years showing themselves. "Do you blame her? She is—well, she would stand out a bit, wouldn't she?"

"I presume you mean because she's a hybrid, and not because she's exceptionally beautiful?"

Luke grinned. "Yeah. Because she's a hybrid."

"She doesn't want the spotlight that goes along with public office."

"Considering the fear that surrounds hybrids, that's probably smart."

Tiberius nodded, letting the words sink in. Then he looked at his friend again. "Tell me honestly, do you fear her?"

Luke hesitated only slightly, then shook his head. "No. Caris is a lot of things, and we've had our differences. But you say that she's learned to control the change, and I believe it. But what I believe and what you believe doesn't matter. It can't matter. Not when you're stepping up to be a leader. What matters is what your public believes."

"Spoken like a true politician."

Luke bowed his head ever so slightly. "I've picked up a few things over the years."

"And what if it was Sara we were talking about?"

"What do you mean?"

"If Sara wanted to walk away from the shadow world. If she believed that the only way she could be happy was to move to Fiji and live in a hut."

"A hut?"

"A comfortable hut," Tiberius conceded.

"She is fond of the ocean."

"Would you go with her?"

"I would," Luke said without hesitation. He cocked his head, his eyes widening as he watched Tiberius. "You aren't saying that you—"

"I must."

"But you can't. Tiberius, you've just been elected chairman. You've been working toward this goal for how long? Thousands of years?"

"I have," he admitted. "And do you know why?"

"You've told me hundreds of times. To help the people. To keep the shadowers in control, the species cooperating. To make sure the humans aren't abused. To prevent another Dark Ages. Tiberius, you wanted this job so you could be the first line of defense against men like Lihter."

"Everything you say is true. I'll even go further to say that I would do a good job of it."

"Of course you would."

"And why not? I was born to it. Told I was meant to lead. Told that it was in my blood." He glanced out the window, wondering when her car would appear. "It is in my blood, Luke. But so is Caris."

"What are you saying?"

"Another man can lead them. Perhaps I could do better, perhaps not. But another can take the job. Another man cannot take my place beside Caris—I would not have it. Nor, I think, would she. And I know that no other woman can fill her place in my heart."

Luke watched him, his silence speaking volumes.

"I'm immortal, aren't I?" Tiberius said, as he considered the notion that had been brewing in his mind. "Who's to say I can't return to power next week, next year, next century? One day Caris will be cured. Either that or the world will accept her. Do you believe she'll wish to live an eternity on a beach?"

"Caris?" Luke said. "No. Eventually she'll get restless. I'd be willing to bet on that one."

"And I want to be at her side when she does," he said, realizing then that his mind was made up.

"But the election—"

Tiberius lifted a hand, cutting him off. "Leave that to me."

"How?"

"Easy," Tiberius said. "All I need from you is one very small favor . . ."

♦

"You come." The guard, an ogre, unlocked the cell and held the door open as Caris stepped out. She'd hoped that Tiberius would come by one last time to say good-bye, but he hadn't, and she told herself that was for the best.

Good-byes were the hardest. But maybe with some time the pain would ease and she could see him again. Maybe he'd even come to her little beach somewhere.

She pictured it, a small cabin near the water. Time to read, to think, to relax.

Once upon a time it would have sounded like heaven. Now it just sounded lonely.

With the ogre at her side, she walked the long corridor, trying to ignore the jeers and catcalls. The curses. The shouts that she was a freak, that she was toxic, that she'd be the ruination of the world.

Then again, maybe alone is good.

When they reached the exit to the parking garage, a blue-haired receptionist looked up from her computer screen. "Your car is waiting," she said in slow, heavily accented English. She indicated the opaque glass doors. "Right through there."

"Thanks." Caris headed out, pausing just outside the doors.

Free. She was really free.

She drew in a deep breath, then climbed into the back of the limo. "Airfield," she said, then told the driver the hangar number of the jet she'd chartered. She was going to Scotland first. She wanted to say good-bye to Gunnolf. And then she'd head to New Zealand and her new, exciting life.

Too bad she wasn't particularly excited about it. How could she be, without Tiberius at her side?

As the limo started to spiral up toward the exit, she realized it didn't much matter. If she was by herself, one beach was as good as another. *Dammit, Tiberius.* She wanted to scream curses at him, but she couldn't. He'd been aiming for the chairmanship his entire life. She could be sad, she could feel sorry for herself, but she also couldn't be anything but proud.

The limo straightened as it reached the last stretch of

the parking structure before the street. A pause as the driver waited for the gate, and then they were moving again.

And then, with a hard jerk, they weren't.

"Watch it!" she called. She'd almost slid off the seat, he'd stopped so fast.

He didn't answer, and she was about to open the glass barrier and tell him ever so politely to watch his damn driving, but then the side door opened.

And there was Tiberius.

Her hand flew to her mouth, her chest swelling at the sight of him again.

He slid into the limo without another word, then tapped the barrier. The car started moving again.

"What are you doing here?" she asked as he sat next to her. Too close to her, actually, because he was only going to make it harder. "A last-minute good-bye? Because it's a nice thought, but I'm not sure I can stand it."

"Not a good-bye," he said. "I'm not ever saying good-bye again."

"I don't understand."

"I resigned."

"What?" He wasn't making sense.

"I resigned. I appointed Luke as the interim chairman. There will be an election in six months. He might run, he might not."

"I don't understand," she repeated. Everything was fuzzy, as if she was listening to a dream, and she'd wake up and find that nothing was real. Please, please don't let it be a dream.

"You don't want to be at my side when I'm chairman. Fine. I get that. I can't convince you otherwise, and I wouldn't try. But I'm not living without you, Caris. And if that means I won't be chairman, then I won't be chairman."

"But—but it's everything you've ever wanted."

"I thought so, yes. Once. Now I know better. You're everything I've ever wanted."

She blinked, tears welling. "You did that for me?"

"No," he said, pulling her into the kind of kiss that proved just how much he meant it. "I did it for us."

He hooked his arm around her and she snuggled close. "It's been years since I've been to New Zealand," he said.

She tilted her head to look at him. "I'm making a stop first. I hope it's okay." She licked her lips. "I want to go see Gunnolf."

She watched his face, looking for some sign that seeing the weren—his old enemy, his rival—disturbed him. But she saw nothing except his smile.

"Good," he said. "I need to thank him properly."

"Thank him?"

"For you," he said. "For taking care of you."

She blinked, then realized that her eyes had filled with tears. "That's not all you have to do," she said, deliberately adding a tease to her voice. "It seems to me there's something you owe him. We stopped Lihter, after all."

"The Highlands," Tiberius said. "Right. It's certainly doable. I gave up the chairmanship, but have done nothing about the various governorships yet. Of course, we should probably alter the terms of that agreement. Just slightly."

"Oh?"

He reached for the control that operated the privacy screen, then watched as the barrier rose to block them from the driver's view.

"If I give up the Highlands, I think I deserve something in return."

"Do you?" she said, easing into his welcoming arms. "Well, I think that can most definitely be arranged."

And as she lost herself in the depths of his kiss, her one regret was that the airport was only ten minutes away.

But that was okay. The flight, at least, was longer.

Can't get enough
of J. K. Beck's sexy Shadow Keepers?

Get ready to sink your teeth into
When Darkness Hungers,
coming soon from Bantam Books.

WHEN DARKNESS HUNGERS

Turn the page to take a peek inside.

CHAPTER 1

The two vampires moved with steady purpose, the low fog curling around their ankles as if the oily darkness of the moonless night was caressing them. *And why wouldn't it?* Sergius wondered. Hadn't he often embraced the darkness, drawing it close like a lover, letting it wrap around him, smothering him even as it soothed him with its warm familiarity?

And yet he yearned to be free of it—unbound from the pinch of the dark. That was why he'd come tonight, because he'd heard rumors about this witch. About her extraordinary powers. How she could heal. How she could make people whole.

People, perhaps. But what about vampires?

Her gifts might not extend to his kind. More than that, she might refuse to help him. He shoved the possibility aside, burying it beneath a blanket of false optimism. No matter how poor the odds, he had to try. The burning inside him had become so violent—so *raw*—that he had no other options. Because if he couldn't ratchet back the darkness, it would certainly consume him. And once that happened, Sergius would be gone forever, lost inside an inky black void filled with only the scent and taste of blood.

"There," Derrick said, grabbing Serge's arm and tugging him to a halt. He tilted his head back, his nostrils flaring. "Can you smell it?"

Sergius glanced sideways at his companion, noting the harsh gleam in his eyes and the hardness of his jaw. He forced his thoughts aside, afraid that Derrick might somehow discern his true purpose merely by glancing at his face. With a sigh, he closed his eyes and let the night wash over him. The magnolia trees were in full bloom and the cloying perfume of their blossoms battled with the more woody cologne of the cypress and pine trees that dotted this stretch of land upriver from the *Vieux Carre*. He caught the scent of the Mississippi River, the coolness of the water coupled with the fetid tang of decay. And beneath it all, the pungent, heady smell of death.

"War," Derrick said. "It's as if the stars have aligned for our pleasure, bringing death and chaos along with the approaching Union fleet." He sighed. "I haven't dined so blissfully well since the British blundered into the colonies. Although, no. We feasted well in 1812. Do you recall?"

"How could I not?" Serge replied, the memory bringing a fresh wave of decadent hunger. They'd spilled much blood those nights. Had practically bathed in the sweet, metallic liquid. At the time, Sergius's daemon had roared in ecstasy, powerful enough to battle down Serge's petty protests and hesitations. Strong enough to take over until Serge lost himself in the warm, glorious wonder of fresh blood, only to claw his way back to the surface days later, heavy with self-loathing and furious with his inability to suppress the daemon as so many of his kind had managed do.

The daemon lived in all vampires—a bone-deep malevolence that emerged from the human soul when the change was brought on. But some vampires were able to successfully fight it, to regularly battle it back down until their human will took precedence. Serge did not count himself among that fortunate group. His daemon ran high and wild. Pushing. Craving. Battling Serge's will with such persistence over the centuries that he inevitably succumbed, sliding into a bloodlust that caressed him as sweetly as madness.

How he envied those of his kind who had learned to either tame that vileness, or at least conjure the strength to suppress it. He longed for the mental clarity that accompanied being in charge of one's own body and mind. Of not being a slave to the bloodlust.

He'd been fighting his daemon for almost two millennia now, and its power still humbled him. Even now, his daemon was rising at the mere thought of blood.

Beside him, Derrick threw his head back and laughed, undoubtedly anticipating the glory of the kill. He shared none of Serge's hesitations and experienced none of Serge's guilt. They had traveled together on and off for years, and Serge knew that it was almost time for them to part ways. Being with Derrick only stoked the hunger that burned deep within him. Tonight, though, Serge had his own purpose for joining Derrick. *The witch.* But that was not a purpose he intended to share. He knew only too well that Derrick would neither understand nor approve. Like Serge, the younger vampire's daemon clung close to the surface. Unlike Serge, Derrick was more than happy to fan the flames of its appetite.

"How far?" Serge asked.

"Just down that lane." Derrick thrust his hand out toward the left, indicating an overgrown dirt road. There was no moon, but with his preternatural vision, Serge could clearly see the once white plantation house, now gray and in disrepair. And not because of the war thrumming around them and threatening to subsume this gentile property, but because of neglect, pure and simple. The occupants of Dumont House had priorities other than the upkeep of their family's homestead. The Dumonts were vampire hunters.

"They may not all have gone on the hunt," Serge said. According to Derrick's sources, the Dumont men had ridden earlier, intent on their goal of attacking a vampire nest hidden within the tombs of the St. Louis Cemetery that bordered the *Vieux Carre*.

"I hope they didn't," Derrick said. "Nothing would please me more than to drain them dry and leave them to rot in the cotton fields. Nothing, that is, except doing the same to their women."

An unwelcome trill of pleasure shot up Serge's spine, brought on by the inescapable truth of Derrick's words. There was pleasure in pain. Pleasure in the release of blood. In letting the daemon rage free and surrendering to the power of its foul appetite. Pleasure, yes. But torment, too.

"You're quiet tonight," Derrick said.

"I'm savoring the feed." The lie came smoothly to his lips, and he knew that Derrick would not doubt him.

Derrick laughed, low and hearty. "Ah, my friend. So am I. Look—one of the slaves making rounds." Across the clearing, a dark figure moved. An elderly male carried a single candle, the flame protected by a bowl of glass. He walked swiftly, his head turning to and fro, and Serge couldn't help but wonder if the slave had sensed their presence. But surely not. The inky night was impenetrable to human eyes. Undoubtedly he feared for the safety of the menfolk in the city, and was ill at ease with his obligation to protect the women in the big house.

Beside him, Derrick stood as still as a statue. "You hesitate?" Serge asked. "That old man would have made a tasty appetizer."

"Let him live and suffer from the knowledge that he had no way to protect the females." He turned to Serge, eyes dancing with mirth. "Besides, I prefer the flavor of blood that's not quite as aged. Come on."

They strode boldly to the house, then rapped hard at the heavy front door. At first, there was no sound from within, then Serge heard the light tread of footsteps. A woman. He imagined her in a loose gown, breasts full and unbound by a corset, her lithe limbs naked beneath the thin material. Immediately, his body tightened and the daemon twisted within, ready to take and taste. And oh, by the gods, wasn't that so very tempting. . . .

The footsteps stopped on the other side of the door, and for a moment there was only the tremulous sound of a woman's breath. Then the stern clearing of her throat, as if she was bolstering her courage. "It's late. Who's there?"

"We come to warn your men," Derrick said, thickening his accent. "The Yankees approach, and they mean to occupy this property. Is your husband home?"

"Who are you? I don't recognize your voice."

"The brothers Wilcox, ma'am," he lied smoothly. "We've ridden hard from Metairie Ridge to warn your pa. Please, this plantation can't fall. Not with its proximity to the river, the train and the main road. Let me speak to your menfolk."

Serge caught the scent of her hesitation. The rumors of the Union's impending arrival were as thick as the famous New Orleans fog, so Derrick's story was wickedly credible. More than that, he'd used the Wilcox name, referencing the two brothers who were known to be well-placed Confederate supporters. A risky proposition if the woman knew the men personally, but brilliant if she believed.

"Please, ma'am," Serge said, as he saw Derrick shift forward, as if losing patience. With one solid blow, Derrick could break down the door, and that was a result Serge didn't want. The noise would draw the rest of the house's occupants, and he needed to face his quarry alone. "We must speak to your father. Open the door and call him down. We realize the impropriety of the hour, but war ignores all social graces."

For a moment, he feared that the woman would brush off his plea. But then he heard the thunk of the lock turning. A moment later, the door swung inward, revealing a young woman of about twenty. Derrick and Serge bowed deep, removing their hats in a broad, gallant motion.

"My husband is gone this night," the woman said. Behind her, a burly black man stood, his expression fierce. Clearly, he was there to make sure no harm came to the mistress of the house.

"Your father, then."

"Dead these many years. Please, tell me what news, and I can inform my husband upon his return, or Sampson can ride to him now if it is urgent."

"Oh, it's most urgent," Derrick said, hooking an arm around the woman's waist and moving so fast to Sampson's side that he surprised even Serge. In mere seconds, the man was on the ground, his neck snapped neatly in two. For a moment, the room was completely silent, as if time hadn't yet caught up with the horror. Then the dam broke and the woman's scream filled the night, only to be cut off a second later when Derrick sank his fangs into her pretty, pretty neck.

He drank deeply, then pulled away, his mouth bloody as he looked at Serge and shifted the woman as if in invitation. "Care for a nibble, my friend?"

By the gods, yes . . .

The scent of her blood enveloped him and her soft moans teased his daemon, urging it to come out. To play and to feast. He could practically taste the coppery warmth of her blood flowing over his lips, could feel the softness of her skin beneath his fingers and the featherlight beat of her fluttering, fading pulse at his lips. The pleasures of blood rivaled even the pleasure of the flesh, and right then the daemon wanted both. Wanted to get lost in the hedonism of sweetly spilled blood.

No.

No, goddammit, no.

His body tightened as he dredged up the remnants of his own will to force the daemon back down. *He* was in charge. Serge. Not the daemon. Not here, goddammit. Not now, when he'd come so far and with such an urgent mission. "Only a nibble?" Serge said in reply, forcing amusement into his voice. "I'm looking for a feast. Not a wench with the honeyed taste of fear already drained from her."

Derrick chuckled. "The first bite is indeed the sweetest, though the struggle that follows adds spice." He gave the woman a shake and she writhed in his arms, the pungent scent of her fear reaching out to Serge and making his hunger rise. He took a step toward her, then halted.

"Enjoy," he said. "I crave the hunt as much as the kill." He didn't wait for Derrick to answer, afraid that if he stayed he would succumb. Instead he turned and moved swiftly away from the woman's moans and the seductive scent of her pain.

The kitchen was only a few yards from the big house, and he found the witch there. She stood behind a large wooden cutting block, a hatchet that had undoubtedly beheaded many chickens lodged in the wood in front of her. A single candle illuminated the room, and the flickering orange reflected in the woman's dark eyes. In her hand, she held a stake, and the absence of any scent of fear told Serge that she knew how to use it.

"You are a fool to come here, vampire," she said.

"Help me, and you will survive the night."

A single brow arched, making her beautiful face even more exquisite. Her *cafe au lait* skin glowed in the candlelight, her striking cheekbones and aquiline jaw giving her the appearance of the lady of the manor rather than a slave. "You're a cocky beast. I assure you, I'll survive. You will not be so lucky." She twisted her hand, just enough to bring the stake into the light, making the wood glow warm.

For an instant, the lure of sweet oblivion washed over him, and Serge lost himself in the temptation to draw her wrath and accept the stake. To allow death, that most elusive of companions, to finally take him. He couldn't do it, though. There was no fear—he'd lost himself too many times to the unknown darkness that was the daemon to ever fear the relative calm of death. But there was stubbornness. And, yes, there was the passion of his will. The small pleasures of the flesh and of the earth. He had once craved immortality with all his soul—so much so that he had compromised that very soul. He had made himself what he was, and he would remedy that error. Somehow, someway, he would make himself whole. And then, once he had lived life without the pain and horror of the daemon's madness, perhaps he would welcome death. But that day had not yet arrived.

"I can make him stop. The vampire I came with. He's in the main house right now, and I doubt that your mistresses will survive the night without my intervention."

Her thin smile was as cold as any he'd ever seen. "You're a fool if you think they matter to me. I'm nothing but chattel to them."

"And your own life? Do you value it so little? You put on a pretty show of bravery, but you know what I am. You know what I can do. And I'm not alone. Are you truly so foolish as to believe that whatever claim you have over the dark arts will protect you from one who has lived within that darkness for centuries? That you can protect your child? Your lover?"

He watched her face carefully as he spoke, noted the way her eyes flattened and the line of her mouth thinned. She meant to give nothing away, and yet she'd failed. His words had hit the mark, and he knew that the information for which he'd paid such a steep price had been true. Evangeline truly was the daughter of voodoo queen Marie Laveau. She had taken a lover—a Dumont house slave named Tomas. Most important of all, she had a child, a five-year-old girl who lived on the Dumont estate and was the product of a liaison between Evangeline and Carlton Dumont, the master of the house.

Serge didn't want to kill the child, but if that was what it took to get what he came for, then the little girl would die. Not because he would will it so, but because the daemon was pushing too hard. He could feel its cold edges pressing against his mind, against his will. Sharp, like a knife edge, and so very demanding. He'd come here to turn that knife back on the daemon itself, to lock it deep inside and give him that control. She could give him his life. And by doing so, she would save her own.

But if Evangeline refused him, he knew that he couldn't hold it in. The daemon would explode . . . and no one near him would be safe.

"Tomas is not here," she said with an arrogant lift of her chin. "Nor is my sweet Lorena."

He could smell the lie upon her. "Do you doubt that I would do it?" he snarled, taking a step toward her. He needed her scared. Needed her willing to do what he asked. "Do you doubt that I would leave your child drained upon this very floor? That I would sink my teeth into your lover's neck?"

Her jaw tightened. "Why should I help the likes of you? A vile creature that kills for gain and pleasure?"

A surge of anger rushed up within him, and he wanted to attack. To lash out and cut the insult out of her. But he battled it down, forcing the daemon into submission, drawing on what little strength he had in order to keep his fingers clenched tight around the fraying strands of his control. "I do not wish to be that creature."

She snorted. "Liar."

He took a step toward her, and her eyes went wide with victory. As if she knew that he was weak and unde-serving.

No, goddammit, no!

"Do not condemn me to remain this way." The words felt ripped from his throat, and he clutched the side of the butcher block, his nails cutting gouges into the hard wood.

"Condemn you? You're already condemned. Killer," she spat. "Destroyer."

His fingers sought the blade that was sunk deeply into the block. They curled around the handle and he pulled it free. She didn't even flinch, but her eyes never left him.

"A killer I am," he admitted. "But so are you. Do you think I have not heard the stories? That all the people in Jefferson Parish are ignorant of your methods and those of your mother? You draw blood for power. You kill to satisfy your own whims and plans. You may not have fangs, Evangeline, but you do have claws, and you are not so different from me."

"Persuasion is an art, vampire. And one in which you lack skill. You should woo me, not insult me."

"With false niceties? We both know what we are. But beyond that, I know what I want to be."

"I am not interested in your desires." But he could see in her eyes that she was lying. He'd piqued her curiosity, and he pushed forward, taking advantage of that small victory.

"Hear me now, witch," he said, then hurled the hatchet across the room. It sailed past her ear, then landed with a thunk in the wall, the blade buried to the hilt. "I want the daemon cut out of me. I want it gone."

Her expression never changed, but he thought he saw respect in her eyes. "That is not possible. Even for one of my skill, I cannot remove that which is a part of you."

"Yet you *are* skilled—if the rumors are true, you're even more skilled than your mother." He glanced at her face and saw that the flattery was working. "Surely you could do something." He took another step forward.

"There is blood on my hands, Evangeline. Blood that I did not wish to shed. I will take responsibility for my own actions, but these deaths are not mine to claim, and yet they haunt me. They torment me."

"And you wish me to believe that even with the daemon locked up deep inside that you would not kill? That the hunger would not drive you to drink of the vein? My master has killed many vampires, sir. I know well that not all of those kills were made when the daemon was high. Some of your kind simply enjoy the hunt and feed on the pain."

She was right, of course. Derrick was just such a vampire.

"How do I know that you do not count yourself among them?"

"You don't," he said simply. "But I don't know either. I crave the chance to find out."

"And if you also crave the blood?"

"I will," he said, because to lie to this woman would get him nowhere. "What matters is whether I can control it."

She remained still, her eyes piercing him, and he knew that he had surprised her. The question was, had he intrigued her, too? He waited, standing still with the kind of patience he'd not displayed for many a year. But for this moment, he would humble himself. He needed her help, his self-respect be damned.

"There is no guarantee. And you must trust me fully. There may be pain. There will most surely be blood. And if you attack—if I fear for my life—I will not hesitate to stake you."

"Can you do it tonight?"

"Keep your word, and it will be done."

Derrick. He turned to go. To find and stop his friend from killing the humans in the big house.

"Tomas," she said. "Find him first. Protect him."

"And your daughter?"

"She is my worry, not yours."

He nodded, then continued toward the door, but he hadn't gone two steps when it burst open wide. Derrick stood there, his linen shirt stained red. He held a man in his arms, the scent of death already clinging to him. With aplomb, he tossed the body onto the floor of the kitchen, then turned a grinning visage to Serge. "So. You found her."

Serge felt his body turn cold. "Her?"

"The Dumonts have themselves a witch." He took a step forward, his foot landing on the man's ribs. The sick crunch of breaking bone filled the cook house, matched only by the wounded, keening wail of Evangeline herself.

"Tomas!" she cried, then turned to snarl at Serge. "Never! Never will I—"

But she didn't get the words out. He couldn't let Derrick know that he'd asked the witch for help. He had to silence her, and he rushed forward, knocking her to the ground. He had no intention of hurting her. No plan to permanently silence her. But fear and fury were driving him forward. Fear that he'd lost his chance for a cure. Fury that Derrick had interrupted. And, of course, there was the hunger. And she was warm in his arms, her own fear tugging at the daemon. Teasing it. Taunting it. Until it overcame all strength and burst out in a bloodred rage.

The daemon took over, and in a hungered frenzy, he

sank his teeth into the witch's neck and drank deeply, drawing in her fear, her anger, her wretched power.

The part of him that remained Sergius faded deep inside, curling up with self-loathing. But the last thing he saw before the daemon subsumed him was the stern silhouette of the four Dumont men, their crossbows aimed at Derrick and himself.

And the last thing he thought was that if nothing else, the sharp sting of death would finally rip him free of the daemon.

Do you want more Caris and Tiberius?

Read on for an exclusive short story
about how these fated lovers
fell in love at first bite. . . .

Get ready for

SHADOW KEEPERS: MIDNIGHT

CHAPTER 1

◊ "Do it, then," the werewolf taunted. "You think you can kill me? You think your powers are greater? That you have well and truly defeated me?"

The vampire held the beast against the wall, his arm as strong and sure as stone pressed against the wolven bastard's neck. He should have broken it already. Should have ripped the weren in two. "Where?" he growled, his face so close to his prey that the foul scent of the weren filled the space between them, turning his stomach. "Where is the *conte*'s son?"

"You see? You cannot kill me." Baloch's voice was smug, his expression more so, and Tiberius pressed in harder, cutting off the weren's air, making his mouth open and his eyes water as he gasped for breath. But the beast was right. The one thing Tiberius couldn't do was kill him. He needed the wolf alive—at least until he found the boy.

With one violent motion he pushed back, releasing the pressure of his arm against the werewolf's throat, replacing it with the tip of the knife he pulled from the sheath at his thigh. There was no full moon tonight, and Baloch had not called upon the change. He stood before Tiberius now as a man. But all Tiberius saw was the monster.

"Do you think the point of a knife scares me more than the death you can bring at your hand? It doesn't,"

Baloch said, and the bastard had the temerity to smile. "Perhaps it is true," he continued, stepping closer so that the point of the knife cut into his leathery flesh. "Perhaps I cannot best you as an equal. Perhaps your strength is greater than mine. Perhaps if it were only the two of us in this room, with no baggage or obligation between us, then I would be dead by now."

"You damn well would," Tiberius said, unable to resist the temptation to speak.

"How ironic that it is the boy himself who protects me."

"Irony?" Tiberius retorted. "You hide behind the life of a child. It is not irony that guides your hand today, but cowardice."

Anger flashed in those deep gray eyes. "I am no coward, vampire. The boy is *mine*. A debt rightfully paid, and I will not bow to you or to any man who claims otherwise." He lifted his hands, then placed them flat on either side of Tiberius's blade. Tiberius could feel the pressure of the weren's touch and knew that he could fight it. That he could match the wolf's power. That he could subsume it. One quick thrust and the knife would slide through those hands and slice open that neck. The coppery scent of warm blood would fill this small, dank room, and Tiberius would watch the coward fall, his lifeblood staining the stone floor as much as his blood-thirsty depravity now stained his heart.

"Kill me now," Baloch taunted. "I see the desire in your eyes. *Do it*. Do it, and then feed. Lay me out and suck me dry. Do your worst, vampire. But know that once you have, you will never find the boy."

The muscles in Tiberius's arm quivered with the desire to kill. And not just because this arrogant bastard had taken an innocent human, but because of what he was—a werewolf. A filthy, stinking, common werewolf. Within Tiberius, his daemon growled, a familiar rage fueling the hunger—the urge to rip and rend and kill. *To get revenge.* Against this werewolf, and those like him that had once maimed and tortured a boy who had been not much older than the *conte*'s son himself.

No.

Memory closed around him, a red, pulsing wall, but he fought it back, fought back the daemon and the desire, and focused only on where he was and what he was doing. He'd conquered his past. And now he would preserve the boy's future.

With one flick of his wrist the knife jerked upward, leaving a clean, thin slice on Baloch's jaw. The weren howled as the blood flowed. Sweet, tempting blood. But it raised no desire in the vampire. Never would Tiberius lower himself to feed off weren blood. He would rather starve than stoop so low.

The weren's lip curled up, but he held himself still with visible effort. "You're going to regret that."

"I sincerely doubt it," Tiberius said, even as a war cry burst from Baloch's mouth. Suddenly the cramped room filled with the echo of pounding feet. A dozen weren burst through the dark passages leading to the stone chamber, their knives drawn and their faces held tight. It was three days until the moon was full, and the wolf was high in Baloch's men. None had fully called forth the beast, but Tiberius could see the wildness in their eyes and he could smell the animal on their skin.

Tiberius pulled away, his knife held ready, as Baloch caught a dagger tossed by one of his underlings and grinned a black-toothed grin.

"Looks like I win," Baloch said.

Tiberius said nothing, cursing his own miscalculation. He'd been watching the werewolf, but obviously not long enough. The beast was cagey. It was clear now that he'd known all along that Tiberius had spotted him in the densely packed Roman alleys and that the beast had led him into a trap. Tiberius had seen the werewolf only as the vilest and most base of creatures; he had forgotten how clever the wretched could be. He'd underestimated Baloch, and now he would pay the price. He only hoped that payment wouldn't be taken out of the boy's flesh.

He looked around the crumbling room, so dank and dark, and knew that for every werewolf he saw snarling at him, at least two more were hidden in the shadows. "You win nothing," he said, his eyes burning into Baloch's. He moved toward the alpha, and that was all it took. Baloch gave a tight jerk of his head, and the room came to life, like vermin scattering from a flame.

They were on him in a second, and as Tiberius thrust out, blocking the sword of a stalwart beast with pock-marked face, he felt the euphoria of the fight rise within him. But there was danger, and he needed to keep the boy at the forefront of his thoughts. He needed to leave and regroup.

He would go—yes. But before he did, he couldn't resist taking a few of the vile creatures down.

The sword withdrew before being thrust out again, its wielder holding a stake in his shield hand. Tiberius moved with speed born of almost two millennia upon this earth, and in the blink of an eye, he stood with his knife bloodied and the werewolf's sword arm lying useless on the dirt floor. The creature's howl of pain echoed in the chamber, but it was nothing to Baloch's sharp cry of *"Enough."*

The fighting ceased. Even Tiberius, who held another weren's back to his chest, with his blade pressed up against the foul creature's neck, froze in the motion of decapitating the creature.

Baloch approached him, fury rising off him like steam as he passed the wounded man, who now lay whimpering and bleeding beside his detached limb. "Harm another of my men, and even if you do find the boy, you shall not find him whole."

"Touch even a hair on that boy's head, and you shall find that you suffer the same injury tenfold. You," he said, drawing the knife slowly across his captive's neck so that it raised only the finest line of blood, "and those you hold dear."

He didn't wait for Baloch's reaction—he'd been reckless to remain after the weren soldiers had arrived, and he would be a fool to stay now that they were angered and injured. He thrust his captive forward, sending him toppling into Baloch, and then Tiberius was gone, a black raven soaring high above the weren, to perch atop the stone walls where the decaying roof had collapsed years earlier. He transformed back, and stood now as a man, looking down at the weren who stared up at him, hate shining in their eyes.

"This is far from over, Baloch," Tiberius said, speaking only to the leader. "You should have left the boy alone, and you could have lived out your days in peace. Now there is only fear to fill them, and the knowledge that I will return; and when I do, you will come to a bloody, painful end."

"You are a fool, Tiberius," Baloch said. "And you

316 of J. K. Beck

spin a clever tale. But there is no fear in my heart. I am the victor here, and you are the one who is retreating."

And so he was, Tiberius thought. But as he lifted his arms and transformed into the sentient mist that would carry him to the *conte*'s nearby palazzo, he saw fear crease Baloch's stalwart features, and right then, that was enough.

CHAPTER 2

Carissa de Soranzo tightened her knees and gave Valiant a light kick, urging the horse faster and faster. She wanted to fly across the field. To flee her father's house, to race from Velletri, from Rome, from her very life. She wanted to soar as far as the horse would carry her. By the Virgin, she wanted to race all the way to the sea and never stop until she lost herself in some far-off land where she could throw off the mantle of her life and hide from her family—and from her fears.

Antonio.

She tugged at the reins, pulling her horse to a stop, then bent over and pressed her face against the beast's neck, already damp with exertion and now doubly so with her tears. She was living in a world gone mad, and her father forbade her to even speak of it. Her brother— the baby of the family—kidnapped. Her father gathering his men, not to rescue his own flesh and blood, but to join the papal forces fighting against the Spanish encroachment. Her famous anger rose hot within her, and she heard the echo of her nurse's voice telling her to calm herself. That such fits of temper were not becoming a lady of her station. The books she read, the rapiers she secretly trained with, even the horses she rode astride the way her two older brothers had taught her. None reflected the woman she was supposed to be, and most of the time she bowed her head in modest agreement and retired to her needlework. Not this time. This time she wanted the anger to boil over. The anger and the fear.

It was the fear that fueled her. That made her spur her horse and turn it around. It was the fear that made her race, not away from her home, but toward it. Toward home and toward her father. And toward the slim, faint hope that he wouldn't abandon Antonio to fate. Or, worse, to the whim of Baloch de Fioro, a terrifying nobleman about whom nobody spoke outright but everyone whispered. Dark words, spoken in shadows. About how Baloch called upon demons. About how he spilled blood not just in battle but for pleasure and for nourishment. About how he placed the heads of his enemies on pikes, how he communed with demons, and how he called upon the power of dark forces to keep the walls surrounding his palazzo impenetrable. She knew not which whispers were rumors and which were true, but she didn't care. He'd taken her brother—and that was sufficient to fuel her hate, and her fear.

She paid little attention as her stallion carried her toward home. She'd been so lost in her worries that she hadn't realized just how far she had traveled—and that alone was enough to incur the wrath of her father. Night was falling as she approached the western gate of Velletri, and she sat up straighter, pushing her worries aside as she took stock of her surroundings, one hand resting on the hilt of the dagger she had hidden within the folds of her skirt. She'd stitched the garment herself, the folds carefully designed to allow sufficient room to permit her to sit astride her beast, and with enough pockets and pouches to hide any number of weapons. She might have ventured farther outside the gates than was wise, but in the main she was no fool. And despite her father's disapproval, she knew how to protect herself.

"Child!" Agnes cried as Carissa dismounted, then tossed the reins to a stable boy.

"I'm not a child," Carissa retorted automatically.

"As to that, you are much mistaken," her nurse said, her expression formidable.

"I am three-and-twenty, twice betrothed, twice widowed before my wedding day, and I'll not be treated as if I were still a babe in the nursery." She neglected to mention that she was once again betrothed, this time to an elderly Roman nobleman who walked with a stick and smelled of dead fish. That was a fact that she tried to think upon as little as possible. But with two fiancés dead, young men would no longer vie for her, and her father had arranged the marriage despite her objections. Giancarlo, he'd said, was the only man for a hundred miles who didn't believe that betrothal to her was a heinous curse.

"Riding off outside the city gates and telling no one where you've gone! I've been frantic, fearing you were taken just the same as your brother."

Carissa closed her eyes. "Forgive me," she said with genuine regret. "I never meant for you to worry."

"You never mean it, girl. And yet I worry anyway."

The weight of guilt settled upon her, and she crossed to Agnes's side, then pressed her head against the older woman's shoulder. "I am truly sorry," she said. "I understand now the fear that must plague you whenever I do something foolhardy." The tears threatened again, and she squeezed her eyes shut.

"Courage. You will see your brother again."

She pulled away enough to peer into Agnes's face. "Do you truly believe that?"

"Of course I do," Agnes said, but Carissa saw the lie in her nurse's eyes.

She swallowed, then forced a smile. "I must speak to Father."

Something close to fear flashed across Agnes's face. "You mustn't disturb your father. Does he not have enough worry with the Pope demanding more men, and his youngest-born taken?"

Carissa lifted her chin high, her most innocent expression painted on her face. "You think his only daughter cannot bring him comfort? I shall not disturb him. I only wish to bid him good night."

"You think me a fool, child," Agnes said, her stern expression ruined slightly by the small twitch at the corner of her mouth. "Go if you must, but be wary. A guest has just arrived and speaks to your father in the salon. Pray you don't interrupt their counsel."

A guest? Carissa tilted her head in acknowledgment, then hurried from the room, her curiosity speeding her pace. Had he taken her pleas to heart? Had he engaged a mercenary to find Antonio—and to bring him back?

She crossed the courtyard, her mind whirling, and as she climbed the stairs to her father's apartments, her heart was beating so loudly it drowned out the sound of her own thoughts. All she could feel was hope. All she wanted was for her father to hold her in his arms and tell her that everything was not lost. That her fourteen-year-old brother—the light of the family—would soon be restored. *A mercenary.* That had to be it. His own troops were committed to fighting on behalf of the pa-

pacy, but he had taken matters into his own hands. He wouldn't sacrifice Antonio to fate, and she felt ashamed that she had ever feared as much.

"You will do no such thing!" Her father's voice boomed from behind the solid oak door. Carissa froze, then edged along the wall until she stood just beside it. The door hung slightly open, and she eased closer, afraid of being caught while her father was in a temper, and yet too wound up by her own hopes to back away and wait for the morrow.

"I ask only for your assistance in that endeavor. Baloch's walls are well-fortified, particularly against my kind. Let me leave here with ten able men, and your son will soon be returned to you."

Carissa's heart swelled—he *was* a mercenary. And he was going to rescue Antonio!

But her joy dried up at her father's sharp "Never."

"You are a fool, Albertus." The voice was low and steady and full of assured authority. Carissa's jaw dropped in wonder. In all her years she had never heard her father spoken to thus.

"You dare," her father snarled. "You dare to walk into my home and insult me?"

"I dare much, sir, but today I speak only the truth. I have come to you on my own, with no ulterior motive, bearing an offer to bring your child home."

"No ulterior motive? Your kind?"

"I go in payment of a debt, sir, not out of any affection I feel toward you."

"You owe me no debt," Albertus growled. Carissa frowned, confused. This man was offering to help; why the devil was her father insulting him?

"It is an obligation owed to your family," the stranger

continued, still in that calm, forceful voice. "And I will fulfill my bond. If not for you, then for the boy."

"And in doing so, you will incur Baloch's wrath. I will never be safe. My family will never be safe."

"You think that I will let him live?"

"I think that you are as much a devil as he is. We don't need your help—" And here her father's voice trembled, not with the shame of abandoning his son, but with fear. "I'll have nothing to do with the likes of your kind."

"You know what Baloch intends when the moon is full. You would stand here now and condemn your son to such a horror?"

"And you offer something better?"

"I offer life. I offer to return him to you."

"You think I trust you—you who are as vile as the creature that stole my son?"

There was a scuffle, and then a thud accompanied by her father's muffled cry, so filled with terror that Carissa couldn't help herself. She pressed herself against the door and peered around its edge, only to clap her hand tightly over her mouth to stifle her own startled cry. Her father was flat against the wall, his eyes wide with terror, his feet dangling inches above the wooden floor. He was held there by the stranger's hand at his throat, and Carissa could see her father's face in the candlelight, glowing even more red as he tried to catch his breath.

"I should kill you now for comparing me to a beast such as that." The stranger whispered the words, his broad, cloak-covered back to Carissa. She had no trouble hearing, though. The words fell hot and heavy, carried by the force of the speaker's anger and disgust.

"I meant no disrespect," her father croaked, yet even from across the room, she could see by his face that it was a lie. He feared the stranger, but he hated him more, and Carissa didn't understand why. The man was offering to rescue Antonio! Was he an occultist? As dark as Baloch himself? Was that what her father meant when he called the man a devil? And even if he was, did such heresy matter when balanced against the life of her brother?

"I should kill you right now," the stranger repeated, his voice low and rough and full of honest disgust. "But we are bound, you and I, and I respect that even if you don't." He released his hold, and her father dropped like a sack of grain to the floor. Carissa gasped, but his fall muffled the sound. Even so, the stranger cocked his head. Only slightly, but she couldn't shake the feeling that he knew she was there.

"I free you from your obligation." Her father's voice came out raspy, and he gasped in deep lungfuls of air as he spoke. His words were bold now that he knew he wouldn't perish at the stranger's hand, and when he angled his head up to look at the man, Carissa saw the familiar fire of authority burn in his eyes. "Begone, fiend."

"Nothing would give me greater pleasure than to extricate myself from your service. There are those in your line I respect, and I hope that fate will bring more in the future. With you, however, I have neither sympathy nor patience, and nothing would give me greater pleasure than to break your neck and leave you to rot on this floor, worth nothing more than food for the rats. Be glad that my obligation is not yours to withdraw or my face would be the last you ever gazed upon."

Albertus cringed back against the wall, and Carissa realized that what she was seeing was fear. Even though this stranger had sworn not to hurt him, still her father cowered. "Go," he said, his voice trembling.

The stranger looked down at the old man on the floor, and even from her perspective behind him, Carissa knew that his expression was colored by disgust. "You are not worthy of the bond once made on your behalf."

He turned then, and Carissa saw his face, bold and ferociously beautiful in the firelight. It was a warrior's face. A politician's face. This was a man who not only could move mountains, but build them.

This was a man who could rescue her brother, and yet her father had cast him away.

She melted into the shadows as he passed, his long strides taking him away from her down the hall. She watched him go in wonder. Had her father gone mad? It made no sense, and though she knew he would be furious to learn that she'd been eavesdropping, she had to understand.

Before she could talk herself out of it, she burst into the room, then stopped cold when she saw the fury flash across her father's face. He masked it quickly, though, shifting his features into the familiar smile, the cheerful facade he always wore in her presence. Never mind that she was twice as capable of understanding politics and strategy as her brother Malvolio. Never mind that other noble-born women were taken into their father's or husband's counsel. For Albertus that was no life for a woman, and no daughter of his would have her head filled with the trappings of a man's world, any more than her hand would hold a man's weapon.

She loved her father greatly, but about that she thought him a rare fool indeed.

"The hour is late," he said, his voice full of more weariness than she could remember hearing. "You shouldn't be here."

"I heard, Father." She said nothing else for fear that if she spoke more her words would consist only of sharp accusations and hurtful barbs.

Her silence didn't matter, though. Her father looked at her, and he understood. "You think I have done wrong, but you don't understand the kind of man he is."

"I don't care," she said, the words out before she could think better of them. "He has offered to bring our Antonio back to us. Father, how can you turn him away?"

"I'll not have help from his kind—"

"But—" She stopped herself, realizing she didn't know what to ask or how to ask it. "Even a cadre of ten soldiers could make the difference between rescue and—" She stopped, refusing to allow herself to think what would happen to Antonio should he not come home. She'd heard so many stories of Baloch's cruelty. Of how even the Pope avoided him, sending no demand that Baloch's men fight at his side. She didn't know if the stories were true or not, but she couldn't bear the thought that such a fate might befall her brother.

"My men are engaged," Albertus said. "But even if they were not, I'd not condemn even one of my soldiers to follow that . . . that *man.*"

"But it's Antonio." Tears welled in her eyes, and she held them wide, determined not to cry. Such feminine weakness would do nothing to sway her father.

For a moment, he only looked at her, and she thought she saw compassion in his eyes. Then the candle flickered and there was nothing but harsh reality there. "I wish the boy no harm," he said. "But the moon will rise full in three days, and when it does, he will no longer be a son of mine."

His words made no sense to her, but she couldn't question him. Her hope had died too painfully—as if a fist had reached out and squeezed all the breath from her body. She thrust her hand out, grasping for purchase on the wall before her knees gave out.

"Go to sleep now," he said gently. "I would not expect a woman to understand the heart of these matters. But my words will look less harsh by the light of day."

He stroked her cheek as he passed, the way he used to when she was a child, as if a father's touch could soothe her. It didn't. It infuriated her.

She stood, frozen to the spot, as his footsteps receded down the hall. Only when she could no longer hear her father did she turn and leave the room herself. She walked slowly, pushing through the fog of her thoughts and regrets.

Antonio.

She closed her eyes, took a deep breath, and then walked faster.

Somehow she would get her brother back.

CHAPTER 3

Tiberius had come by horse, intending to lead a small cadre of soldiers away from this place and toward Baloch's stronghold. He had expected Albertus to thank him—hell, he'd expected the doughy old fool to fall to his knees and praise Tiberius as a god—and it infuriated him that not only had Albertus refused his help, but he'd impugned the bond that had existed between Tiberius and the De Soranzo family for more than a millennium. In the end, though, it didn't matter. Tiberius had vowed to protect the family, and by the gods, he would honor that vow, no matter how hard the puerile prick of a father fought against him.

Beside him, Nightshade lifted her head and snuffled. He stroked her soft nose, then pulled an apple from his saddlebag and fed it to her. "He is a fool, old friend," Tiberius whispered.

"He is."

The timid voice came from behind him, and it was a measure of Tiberius's distraction that he hadn't heard the human approach. He breathed in deeply now, catching the scent of fear mingled with perfume. *A woman.*

He turned, his irritation at being interrupted fading when he saw her. She was exceptional: dark hair that fell in loose curls around her face, lips so bloodred they seemed to beg him to feed, and skin so pale she could have been carved from the finest marble. She was by far the most beautiful woman he had seen in centuries, and yet it wasn't only her beauty that held his attention but the way she carried herself, tall and proud and determined.

Beside him, Nightshade whinnied—a demand for another apple—but the sound seemed to break a spell, and Tiberius strode forward even as the girl clutched the edge of the stable's door and refused to retreat, her feet planted with obvious effort.

Tiberius simply watched her, letting the silence between them grow heavy.

She shifted her weight from foot to foot, but her eyes never left his. She had mettle, this female. He remained silent, more interested in watching her than in hearing what she had to say. But as the seconds ticked by, his perception changed. Not many women could stand silent and strong in front of him. Most babbled or dropped their eyes, intimidated by his very presence. That she could bear the weight of the silence even while holding his gaze intrigued him, and he found himself reluctantly fascinated by a female for the first time in a very long while.

"Speak, then," he finally said, sacrificing a victory at the hand of curiosity. "Who are you that comes to see me off?"

"Someone who hopes that you will ignore my father's words and hold tight to your quest."

"Your father has abandoned the boy to the hand of fate."

"I thought we had already determined that my father is a fool."

She spoke with such seriousness that he had to force himself not to laugh. "You speak the truth."

"I can offer you no men to help you in this quest, but I am as capable as any man." She bowed, low and serious. "I offer myself as your aide."

"Do you, now?" By all rights, he should be either irritated or amused. He was neither, his thoughts traveling in a much more base direction. Slowly he looked her up and down, noting the soft curves where her breasts rose behind the fine silk, the slim waist that he could easily fit both hands around. She would undoubtedly break in battle as easily as she would in bed.

Her cheeks flushed, and though no human could have seen the color rising beneath the dark of the night, he saw the blush clearly.

"I'm stronger than I look," she said.

"You would have to be," he said, and this time he did laugh when her glare hit him as solid as a punch. "Forgive me," he said. "Your father irritated me like a burr beneath a saddle. I cannot help being relieved to find his daughter much more appealing company."

"I'm not interested in being appealing. I'm interested in rescuing my brother."

"I see that. But it is no quest for a woman."

He saw her lift her head to argue, then subtly drop it again. She had pride, this girl, but she also knew that he spoke the truth.

"Perhaps not. But you could do it. You could bring Antonio home to me."

"I am flattered you think so highly of my skills," he said.

"Please. He is so young, and must be so frightened."

Anguish lined her face, and he was overcome with the urge to pull her into his arms and comfort her. It was an urge that both disturbed and delighted him—she was not a woman he should have, and yet it had been far too long since a woman had moved him.

"What is your name?"

"Carissa," she said impatiently. Her brow furrowed in thought. "You told my father you needed troops. I cannot assign his men, but I know where my father keeps his purse. I can give you money to hire mercenaries. The taverns are full of them—men who will do any job for a price."

"Are they, now? And how would you know such things?"

"I may be a woman, but I am not a fool. People talk. I listen."

"There are men who would happily take your coin—and who would then take the profit and run at the first hint of danger."

"I see." She pressed her lips together as she thought. "And have you no men of your own to call upon? You do not have the look of a man without means."

"Don't I? Tell me, then. What do I look like?"

He heard her breath hitch. "You look—you look like a man who can get things done. You look like a leader of men."

Not men, but he was a leader. And he did have resources upon which he could draw. Allies that she would neither understand nor believe. Followers that would terrify her.

But he could not call upon his friends for this task. The obligation to protect this human family was his and his alone, and this particular mission was more dangerous than Carissa knew. Baloch's palazzo was reinforced with hematite, the one substance that vexed a vampire, that chipped away at his strength and destroyed his ability to transform. And since Baloch had likely hidden the boy deep within the palazzo's cellars, Tiberius would be putting his own life in jeopardy by breaching the fortress. He could not in good conscience ask his friends to join this quest.

He'd intended to use Albertus's troops to assist the rescue. Now he would go in alone, with stealth as his most precious ally. He would feed before, in the hopes of retaining as much strength as he could despite the proximity of hematite. But if he was attacked as he'd been in the Roman crypt, he would be unable to escape the way he had when Baloch's men had converged on him.

Then again, he feared that by going to the palazzo he was walking into Baloch's arms. He'd cornered the cagey werewolf in Rome with the hope of discovering with certainty where the boy was held. The palazzo made the most sense—but it also made a perfect trap.

Still, he had no choice now. Having failed to extract the truth from Baloch, Tiberius had no option but to start looking for the boy in the belly of the beast. If the boy was not there, Tiberius had no qualms about torturing one or more of Baloch's guards to find the boy's true location.

She was watching him, her green eyes intense, and he saw on her face the moment she made her decision. "Please," she said, moving toward him for the first time, her face blazing and determined. "I'll give you whatever help you need. I'll do anything you ask. But please, please help my brother."

Something dangerous roused within him—and not his daemon. No, this beast was desire, and it was alive and hungry. "There is no help you can offer me," he said.

She moved closer, until only the thinnest veil of air separated them, and he breathed in the scent of her, lavender and anise mingled with the musky scent of desire. He felt himself harden even as his tenuous hold on chivalry weakened, leaving him with only the basest, purest knowledge: He wanted her. He would have her.

She swallowed, the movement of her throat the only indication of her nerves. "Not help, then. But perhaps motivation?" Her breath was shallow and fast, and the tempo of her heartbeat filled her ears, her blood pulsing like a demand. "Please," she whispered again, and as she did, she rose up on her tiptoes and slid her arms around his neck. "I'll do anything."

Skin brushed skin, and he thought for a moment that he would explode from the intensity of the pleasure coursing through him. Richer than wine, more satisfying than blood. Her touch alone could fill him, but even so, it wasn't enough. Where Carissa was concerned he was greedy and unabashed. He wanted her, and right then, nothing else mattered.

Right or wrong, he would have her.

◆

"Anything?" His voice, rough with passion, ripped through her, awakening senses that she didn't even realize existed within her. She wasn't a stranger to a man's touch—she'd been betrothed twice, and though neither man had bedded her, they had asked for and received kisses that felt as chaste and flat as those she bestowed upon her brothers.

Now, though . . .

Now her body tingled. Her clothes felt heavy. And an

unfamiliar warmth glowed between her legs. She shifted, pressing her thighs together beneath the folds of her skirt, but that only made the heat grow and she knew— she just *knew*—that she wouldn't be satisfied until she felt his hand upon her there. His hand, yes, but also the whole of him.

"Carissa," he whispered.

She told herself she was thinking only of Antonio. Of doing whatever she could to help her brother. But that was a lie. She wanted this—this feeling, this sensation. She was betrothed to an irritable old man, her future spread out before her like a desert. This man was an oasis, dark and strong and virile. A man who could make her feel all the things she'd dreamed of feeling. A man who could give her sweet memories to cling to through the long, hard days to come.

He was a man who could help her, and in more ways than one.

"Yes," she said, tilting her head up to look at him. "Anything." And then, before she could talk herself out of it, she pressed her lips to his.

His mouth opened against hers, his breath hot upon her. He clutched her tight, one hand around her waist pulling her close, the other holding the back of her head, his fingers curled in her hair. Their bodies melded together, their tongues finding, tasting, devouring. Her head spun with new sensations, and she felt as if she were falling and climbing all at the same time. She wanted to consume him and be consumed by him, and she lifted her own hands to his head, her fingers twining in the silk of his hair, trying to pull him even closer.

His mouth tugged and teased her lips, and she moaned as he trailed kisses across her cheek to her temple, her ear. "You are certain?" he whispered, the words so low she almost imagined she hadn't heard them.

"Yes," she breathed, and then, to prove to him she meant it, she took his hand and placed it on her breast, hoping his touch would quell some of the fire that was burning through her. It didn't. It only made the flame burn hotter.

"Please." It was the only word she could manage, but it was enough. His hands were upon her, his mouth at her neck, hot and wild as her pulse beat against the pressure of his lips. His fingers were quick and nimble and had the laces of her bodice unfastened in an instant. He pushed her back until she was pressed against the side of the stable. Then his head dipped down, his mouth closing over her breast and his tongue teasing her nipple. He pulled away, and she sighed at the sweet sensation of the gentle breeze caressing her now-damp skin.

"Lift your skirts," he said, and as she did, he knelt before her, his breath hot upon her thighs. Her sex tightened and quivered, and she shifted her hips, longing for something she'd never had but instinctively knew that she wanted.

Soon his fingers touched the skin that his breath had tickled, and she had to bite her lip to keep from crying out. She clutched her skirt tighter, and he slid his hands down, cupping her at the waist as his tongue traced kisses up her legs to the apex of her thighs. He laved her, the tip of his tongue touching her in the most intimate of places. It was a naughty, erotic sensation, and one that she wanted never to end. This was the feeling she'd longed for, the pleasure she knew would never be hers, and dear Lord she wanted it now—all of it, everything he was willing to give her, and more.

She shifted her hands, using only one to hold her skirt and the other to cling to him, to clutch tightly to his shoulder as the power of his intimate kisses ripped through her. He was driving her mad with pleasure, the sweetness almost unbearable, and she feared that if he didn't stop she would explode, and yet if he did stop she would weep.

Something built inside her, like the heavens coursing through her, spinning faster, glowing hotter, until she could do nothing—*nothing*—except cry out and tremble as her body was ripped apart from within.

He caught her as her knees gave out, his arms tight around her waist, holding her upright. His lips on hers, letting her taste the sweetness of her sex. "More," she whispered, her hands already working to push off the cloak he wore and to unfasten the laces on his white linen shirt. She wanted to speak, to tell him what his touch meant to her, how it swelled within her, but she couldn't find the words. So instead she told him with her fingers. Exploring and caressing, touching and discovering.

Tentatively, she pressed her lips to his chest, breathing in the musky scent of him. He tasted of earth and desire, and when she tilted her head back to look at him, the expression on his face—on that warrior's face, now soft with need and desire—almost made her come undone.

"I must have you," he said, his voice a low growl.

She tried to answer but had forgotten how to speak. Instead she merely nodded, then took his hand in her own and cupped his palm roughly between her legs. He made a rough noise in his throat and pulled her closer, and suddenly his breeches were down and she felt the hard length of him pressed against her. "My cloak," he whispered, nodding toward where it lay now on the ground. "Not as soft as a bed, but—"

"I don't care. I only want you."

She lay down, tugging him down with her, not wanting to lose the contact between them. "I cannot wait," he said, and she almost laughed, her relief was so great. She wanted him right then, that moment, that instant, filling her up and taking her higher.

She spread her legs, drawing him down. With fingers eager to know every inch of him, she reached out, stroking the velvet steel that was the length of him. She saw him tremble at her touch, and understood her power as a woman. "Now," she whispered. "Please, please, now."

He was both gentle and demanding, thrusting slowly at first until she could bear it no longer and grabbed his hips, forcing him harder and deeper. It hurt—dear Lord, it hurt, but only for a moment. Then the pain shifted, erased by a pleasure like no other she'd known. It ripped through her, so sweet and yet so tumultuous, and she never wanted it to end, and when he collapsed, spent, beside her, she sighed with the deepest of pleasure and curled up next to him, soft and satisfied.

They lay like that as time ticked past them, her fingers tracing idle designs on his skin, her body reveling in the joy that he had given her.

Then he shifted so that he was facing her, and he pressed a kiss to her lips so gentle it was like a whisper. "I will get your brother back, Carissa," he murmured. "About that, I give you my word."

CHAPTER 4

❧ "Someone comes," he said.

Carissa sat up abruptly, her head cocked. "I hear no one."

His face was firm; the softness she'd seen after he'd brought her to the brink of heaven had vanished. "Trust me." His eyes met hers. "I must go."

She nodded, straightening her clothes as she climbed to her feet. She was adjusting her laces when his hand took hers, and he tugged her to him. "Goodbye, Carissa." His kiss was hard, and needful, and full of things unspoken.

"Wait," she said after he released her. He'd stepped away from her with such speed that he was already all the way across the stable, his horse untied. How had he moved so fast?

He stopped, then looked at her in silence.

"I don't even know your name," she said, suddenly overwhelmed with an inexplicable sadness. He'd delighted her with a sensual feast, but now she understood fully what she would never again have with a man. She would be married and well cared for, true. But this moment—this feeling—was gone forever.

"Tiberius," he said. Then he leapt upon the horse's back, kicked the beast's flanks, and was gone.

Carissa stood, staring into the suddenly empty darkness.

She heard the swift crunch of feet upon the ground. "Carissa?" Agnes's voice echoed through the yard. "Are you out here?"

"Here," she called back, as Agnes shuffled into the structure, huffing under the effort of moving her ample form.

"Whatever have you been doing, girl? I've been looking everywhere for you, and—" She cut herself off quickly, those perceptive eyes narrowing as she peered hard at Carissa's face, then dragged her eyes down to Carissa's chest.

Carissa forced herself to keep her chin upright, but she feared she knew exactly what Agnes was seeing— bits of straw in her hair and décolletage. Whether or not she could see any evidence of Tiberius's lips upon her neck and breasts, Carissa didn't know. Certainly she still held the memory of him there, and it took all her willpower not to lift her hand and stroke the spot where last he'd kissed her.

"What have you been doing, child?" Agnes repeated, only this time her words held a much sterner tone.

"Nothing that need concern you," Carissa said, adjusting her skirt as she prepared to hurry past Agnes and back to her own quiet apartment in the palazzo.

Agnes's firm hand stopped her.

"Nurse!"

"Don't 'Nurse' me. Do you think you are too old for my switch?" She plucked a piece of straw from Carissa's cleavage and wagged it in her face. "You are not!"

"I have done nothing for which I must be ashamed."

"Then you *have* done something?"

Carissa said nothing. With Agnes, it was often better to hold one's tongue.

"Nay, girl. I'll not get the silent treatment from the likes of you. Speak to me now, or we'll go inside and you can speak to your father."

Carissa scowled. "Very well, then. I've set the matter straight."

"What matter?"

"The stranger came here intending to rescue Antonio, but Father flatly refused him."

"No!"

"Yes," Carissa said, spurred on by the vehemence of Agnes's response.

"But why?" Agnes asked.

"I don't know." Carissa frowned, remembering the invectives her father had fired at Tiberius, calling him a devil and suggesting that he would never trust a man such as him. "It makes no sense."

"Well, go on, girl. What happened?" She crossed her arms over her breasts. "Or shall I guess?"

Carissa lifted her chin. "I persuaded him to ignore Father's directive. He will rescue Antonio. He gave me his word."

"Hmmph." Agnes looked her up and down, her scowl growing deeper by the moment. "Persuaded him, did you? I can tell by looking at you how you managed that."

Carissa wanted to shrink from the reprobation in her nurse's voice, but she held her ground. "Think what you will, but I'll not apologize for my actions. Antonio's life is at stake. There is no sacrifice too great."

Agnes snorted. "Sacrifice! By the Blessed Virgin, I saw the lad when he came into the palazzo. You made no sacrifice there, girl!"

"Agnes!"

"Come now, don't be coy. We're both women." Her tone darkened. "But I know the way of things a sight better than you, I think."

Carissa frowned, her amusement fading in light of the change in Agnes's tone. "What are you talking about?"

"So he said he would help you? Said he would go out into the world and bring your brother back to you?"

"Yes."

"And all he needed was a good, solid send-off. A woman's warmth before he rode off, risking his life on our behalf."

Carissa shook her head slowly. "It wasn't like that. I—"

"You think it was your idea? That your feminine wiles persuaded him?"

"He swore," she said, though her words sounded hollow.

"I do not doubt that he did. A man who would use a woman thus would have no moral code that would keep him from breaking his word."

Carissa stood rigid, her mind in turmoil. He had sworn, true, but Agnes was right—she had no way of knowing if his word was good. Her father didn't trust him, and yet she'd given him her body in exchange for a promise.

Flames of anger rose up within her, but the anger was directed as much against herself as it was against him. She'd wanted what he could offer so badly that she'd accepted his word without question, then reveled in her own satisfaction. But this wasn't about her—it was about Antonio—and hot shame burned her cheeks as she realized how little thought she'd paid her brother under the guise of acting only for him.

"He only wanted in your skirts, girl."

Carissa closed her eyes. Perhaps Agnes spoke the truth. Perhaps she did not. But the truth was that she had no way of knowing if Tiberius had been truly sincere. She'd lain with him for her own pleasure, and yet Antonio could very well still be in danger.

Agnes went to her, drawing Carissa into her arms the way she had when she was a child. "Do you truly think a stranger to our house would risk his own life against your father's wishes, and with no men to battle at his side?" Agnes spoke kindly, but her words were firm and full of certainty. "No, dear girl. The man you lay with was many things, but he was not sincere."

She wanted to believe Tiberius—every instinct within her told her that Agnes was mistaken. Carissa had felt the truth of his words and seen the integrity of his heart. But there was no denying that she could be wrong, and if she waited to find out the truth of it, her brother could well be dead.

"I am a fool," Carissa said.

"You're not the first woman to have succumbed to a man's treachery."

Carissa frowned, shoving Agnes's words to the side. None of that mattered now. All that mattered was finding Antonio. "If Tiberius won't go after Antonio, I must find someone else. Someone I am certain will accomplish the task."

"Have you not heard what I've said? Your father's men are engaged, your brothers several weeks' ride from this place. Even if you could find the coin to hire a mercenary—"

"They'd only run at the first sign of trouble." Carissa sighed. "I know." She pressed her fingers to the bridge of her nose. There had to be a way—some way in which she could bring her brother home. It wasn't as if Baloch could be reasoned with. For that matter, even approaching him would be a challenge. Any man who presented himself at his gate would surely be turned away and—

She stopped pacing.

"What?" Agnes said. "You've thought of something?"

"Some*one*," Carissa said. "Someone who can infiltrate Baloch's palazzo." She met Agnes's confused eyes. "The mission is more than simply breaking Antonio out, you see. If we do that, Baloch will certainly seek retribution."

"Of course."

"So Baloch must be killed."

Agnes said nothing. She just looked at Carissa in the same intent way that Carissa remembered from when she was a child.

"*I* will kill him," Carissa said, before she could talk herself out of it. "I will kill Baloch, and I will bring my brother home."

◆

She left immediately, dressed in Antonio's old clothes, her long hair hidden under a cap. She smeared ash from the grate on her face, hoping to disguise the fact that she had no beard, and planned to ride hard, fast, and meet as few people as possible.

Her plan was simple. She would ride as fast as she could the twenty miles to Baloch's palazzo outside Lariano. It would be hard—on her body and on the horse—but she was cognizant of time ticking away. She'd heard her father and Tiberius speak of the full moon, and she knew the stories about Baloch and the occult. She could only assume that he intended to do something horrible to Antonio when the moon hung full in the sky. She planned to have her brother free and long gone before that happened.

She'd never ridden to Baloch's palazzo, of course, but from the stories her brothers had told her, she expected to arrive close to dawn, and she planned to take a room at a nearby inn. She'd bathe and rest and when she woke, she'd dress in the silken garments she'd rolled up and shoved into her saddlebag. She'd adorn herself with the jewels she'd sewn into the lining of Antonio's cloak. And she would scent herself with the oils that Agnes had packed for her, however reluctantly.

Even now, as she stopped at a stream so that Valiant could get his fill of water, she could picture with perfect clarity the expression on Agnes's face as Carissa rode away from the gates of Velletri. "I understand why you must go," she'd said before they parted. "But still my fear overwhelms me."

"Pray for me, Agnes," Carissa had implored. "You pray for me and I shall pray for Antonio, and together we will bring him home."

She hoped Agnes was praying hard, because her nerves were raw. While on horseback, her attention had been occupied with the rough terrain, staying off the main road, and her increasingly sore rear end. Now that she'd dismounted and was walking to loosen her battered muscles, her mind had time to wander—and to wonder.

Could she succeed? Was she only condemning herself along with her brother?

Since she couldn't bear to think of it any longer, she remounted Valiant the moment the beast finished drinking. "Sorry, old friend. But we still have a long way to go."

This time, unfortunately, her body had become used to the motion of the horse, and her mind wandered despite her best efforts to control her thoughts—and it was that very motion that guided the direction of her thoughts. She could remember the way his hands had stroked her. The way he'd traced her lips. The way he'd murmured in her ear, so soft his voice was nothing more than a whisper upon the wind.

She wanted to believe that she would find him on the road to Lariano, but she'd seen no evidence of another traveler, and she feared that Agnes was right—he'd taken what she had to offer and gone his own way. A burst of anger at his treachery ripped through her, followed in short order by the familiar frustration with her own foolishness.

But still, she could not deny that given the chance she would do it again. She'd wanted to be in his arms, and it was not even his treachery that frustrated her so much as the fact that she would never see him again.

By the Virgin, her thoughts were in a dither, and her overwhelming exhaustion was not helping matters. By the time she reached the small inn on the hill overlooking Baloch's palazzo, she was in a ripe fury. She was also exhausted. The sun would rise in only a few hours. She needed sleep and a bath and food, and she left Valiant in the inn's stable and then hurried to the door, expecting that she would have to wake the owner in order to gain admittance. She didn't.

The place was not the quiet little inn she'd imagined, with darkened tables in the tavern and guests snug in their blankets upstairs. No, this place was loud and raucous and hot from the blazing fire. The air was thick with the smell of sweat and ale and unbathed bodies, and as she stepped over the threshold, all faces turned toward her. Harsh, battle-scarred faces, puffy and pale from too much ale.

Without thinking about it, she took a step backward, then immediately recognized her mistake. She wasn't a woman in this room, she was a young man. A young man who'd just shown fear. And to these men, that made her a target.

She strode forward, forcing her back to stay straight and her head to stay high. She didn't want to, but she looked at each of the men at the tables as she swung her gaze across the room searching for the innkeeper. There seemed to be no one, however, who fit that role.

"He looks too young to have a sword," one of the men said, staring directly at her crotch. "Not a hard one, anyway."

He cackled, almost falling out of his chair with mirth as his fellows joined in the laughter, albeit more subdued.

"What you doing here, boy?"

"I'm a traveler," she said, trying to force her voice lower but not doing a good job of it. "I came for food and shelter."

"He's a traveler," a particularly foul man said to his companion. "Does he look like a traveler to you?"

His companion looked her up and down, squinting in a way that made the scar across one eye bulge. "Doesn't look like a traveler. Looks like a thief to me." Scar stood, his hand on his dagger. "Turn out your purse, boy. Let's see what you've stole from your betters."

"I have no money." It was true—taking coin from her

father would have taken too much time and been far too risky. She had only the jewels she had hastily stitched into her clothing.

"He lies," the first man said.

"We don't like liars," Scar said. He moved around the table from the left as the first man moved from the right. Behind them, another stood. Carissa swallowed, her fingers closing around the hilt of Antonio's sword. She had his dagger as well, still sheathed at her waist, and the weight of it comforted her.

"Little boy wants to fight," Scar said.

"I—no." She backed up a step, praying she could reach the door, but Scar wasn't having any of that. He rushed forward and got right in her face, his breath so foul she almost passed out.

"I said, show us your money." He pulled his dagger, but she was faster, and her own sword was out and flying in an instant, the tip of it slicing a new scar on the brute's already marred face.

He howled with pain and took a step back while his friends stepped forward, all eyes on her. "You're going to regret that," the man who'd first spoken to her said. In truth, she didn't doubt it. She had real skill with a blade, even her brothers said as much. But she was one woman, and these were four armed men.

Scar lashed out with his own rapier, and she parried skillfully, her attention no longer on the men but on the battle. She held her own, her feminine grace a help more than a hindrance as she leapt upon the table, positioning herself best for attack. And attack she did—this was not a defensive game, and she knew damn well she was fighting for her life. When one of the men approached from her left, she shifted her sword hand and pulled her dagger with her right. Doubly armed, she fought like a wildcat, with all the passion and skill her brothers had taught her.

They would be proud, yes, but even the hours of practice they had endured at her behest were not sufficient against the strength of these grown men. One managed to hook the tip of his sword in the quillon of hers and send her sword flying across the room. She lifted her dagger in defense, but the odds were against her. As another man came at her from the front, Scar grabbed her from behind, tossing her to the ground in one swift, hard motion. The dagger flew from her hand, skittering across the floor to rest beneath a table.

"Down and disarmed," Scar said. He pressed his hand to her chest to hold her down, his eyes going wide as he did so. "What ho! Look what we have here!" Scar ripped off her brother's cloak, then tugged at her doublet and shirt, until they ripped open and she was struggling in his arms wearing only Antonio's riding breeches and the bit of linen she'd wrapped around her chest to bind her breasts. Scar slid a finger between the linen and her flesh. "Soft little thing. Let's see what we've got here, shall we."

Around him, the men snickered and chortled and begged Scar to hurry so they could have their turn.

He spit on his hand, then rubbed her face. "Soft skin under all that ash. She'll do for a poke, I think. And she's got enough fire to last the night for all of us."

"Keep your filthy hands off me."

He slapped her without warning, and she cringed at the raw, animal lust she saw in his eyes. Fear flooded her, and with uncommon clarity she saw the future laid out before her. She was going to be raped tonight—ripped apart by all these men. Battered and broken, and quite possibly killed.

No.

Perhaps she couldn't win against all of them, but she could damn well take a few of them out. At the very least, she was going to die trying.

"Give us a kiss, girl," Scar said.

"Let me go if I do?" She tried to sound terrified. It wasn't hard.

"Aye, of course. I'm a gentleman. Aren't I, boys?"

A murmur of laughter mingled with vague agreement.

"All right, then," she said, trying not to gag as his lips came closer and closer to hers. And then, at the moment his lips brushed hers, she reached down and snatched his dagger from his hip. She thrust upward, aiming for the fleshy part under his neck, but suddenly he was no longer on top of her. Instead he was flying across the room, landing atop a table that collapsed beneath the weight of him.

She stayed on her back, breathing hard, clutching the blade—and looking up at the tall, dark man in front of her, his face painted with a fury more intense than any she'd ever seen. *Tiberius.*

Relief mingled with hope coursed through her. One of the other men rushed him, but Tiberius swatted him away as easily as if he were a fly. The man tumbled through the air, smashed into the side of the tavern, and collapsed like a rag doll.

Around him, the other men shifted nervously.

"Leave this place," Tiberius said. "Now."

They hesitated only a moment, then scurried out into the fading night.

Tiberius held out his hand to her. She stayed where she was.

"Come," he said. "You need a drink and a bath."

"Why are you here?"

His brow lifted ever so slightly. "Where else would I be, with Baloch's palazzo so close and your brother hidden deep in its bowels?"

She smiled, all her worries evaporating.

"Come," he said again, and this time when he held out his hand, she took it, then let him pull her up and into his arms. She clung to him, letting him draw out her fear—for herself, for Antonio. Letting him hold and comfort her.

And when he kissed her, her heart soared.

Tiberius was with her now, and everything would be okay.

"Did you believe I would fail? Or that my word was not my bond?" They were in the room he'd taken, a place to rest during the daylight hours. A place to plan and plot and think.

He'd been thinking about her.

Carissa. The warmth of her body. The gentle caress of her touch. The way her scent had driven him almost to madness.

He'd thought—and then she'd appeared.

Now she frowned, her eyes refusing to meet his as she used a dampened cloth to wipe the ash from her face. "I doubted you. I'm sorry."

"You thought I wanted only to bed you," he said, coming to her side and taking the cloth from her hand. "You thought I would leave your brother to linger in the dungeon of that son of a whore."

She looked at him then, her eyes imploring. "I told myself that couldn't be true, but I allowed my conviction to be swayed by the beliefs of others." She reached up, cupping his hand against her face. "In the end, I knew that the only way to be certain that Antonio was set free was to rescue him myself."

"By whose counsel did you abide?"

"My nurse's. She said you wanted only in my skirts. She said that no one was reckless enough to not only defy my father but to cross Baloch."

He drew his hand away and stood, though the break in contact with her bordered on painful. A single thin blanket lay on the bed, and he picked it up and draped it over her shoulders, hiding her soft, tempting skin as well as the treasure he knew was hidden beneath those ridiculous linen wrappings.

"Do you wish me to leave?"

He answered her with a kiss, the intensity of his need for her surprising him. He *should* be angry. Not because she had failed to trust him—under the circumstances, she'd perhaps been wise not to do so—but because she'd put herself in such bitter danger.

But there was no anger. There was only relief—that she was safe, that she was with him, and that even now she was opening her mouth to his, pressing her body against his, touching him with the same desperate intensity that filled his heart.

He didn't hesitate or think. He merely pulled her close, hearing the blood burning hot in her veins. *Desire*, oh yes. But not for her blood. For *her*. The taste of her, the touch of her, and he kissed her with a passion long dormant. Kissed her as if there would be no tomorrow for him instead of a thousand upon a thousand. Kissed her as if she were the only woman he had ever had or would ever have. The only woman he had ever needed or would ever need.

He had never felt this way before, and the intensity of emotions vexed him, but he knew that they were true. He'd met his match in her, and he wanted her more than he could remember ever wanting anything or anyone.

He kissed her, but he didn't have his fill of her. How could he, even being immortal, ever spend enough time with this woman to satisfy his cravings?

In his arms, she moaned as she opened herself to him. Her lips, her tongue. He tasted her, consumed her, craved the touch of her skin against his. "Carissa," he murmured, his hands slipping beneath the blanket to brush the linen that covered her breasts, delighting when he felt her breath quicken, the scent of her desire enveloping them both.

"Please," she whispered.

He needed no further encouragement. He slid his hands over her soft skin, pushing the blanket to the floor and leaving her standing in only those ridiculous breeches and the linen binding. He caught the edge of it and began to unwind, delighted when she laughed and spun for him, helping the process along. And then there she was, her breasts naked in front of him, her nipples hard and alert and so very tempting. "Ah, Carissa," he breathed as his hand cupped the weight of her breast, "I fear the danger you placed yourself in, but I must admit I'm glad you're in my arms."

"I will never doubt you again," she said.

"Never again," he whispered, and his lips closed over hers. She tasted sweet, like a ripe berry, and he wanted to indulge until he'd had his fill. He slid his hands over her soft skin, then down between her thighs, his body hardening even more when he felt how slick and ready she was for him. "Come," he whispered, then led her to the bed. He didn't want to wait, wasn't sure he could wait; he leaned over her, taking his weight on his arms, and then thrust inside.

She was tight and warm, and her body closed around his, pulling him in, milking him, taking him to the edge and back again. Her soft moans urged him on, and when her hands clutched his back and she demanded that his thrusts be harder, deeper, he knew that he would deny her nothing. She was his, for then and forever, and he would have her completely.

Over and over he claimed her; deeper and deeper he took her, watching her face with each thrust, seeing her lips part and her eyelids twitch as her passion grew, and then—when he was on the brink himself—she arched up, taking them both over at once until finally, sated, he collapsed on top of her and could do nothing more than breathe in her scent and thank the gods that fate had brought her to his arms.

"I feel alive," she whispered after they'd lain together in silence for an eternity.

"As do I," he said.

She rolled over to face him, her expression remarkably serious. "I must tell you," she said, stroking his cheek with the palm of her hand. "I'm betrothed."

Her words were like a knife to his heart. "To whom?"

"An old man," she said. "I don't love him, and I know—I know I will never have this again." Her teeth grazed her lower lip. "That was why . . . in the stable . . . I wanted you to save Antonio, of course. But I also wanted to know how it felt. How it felt to be loved by a man."

"And now?" he asked.

Her smile bloomed. "Now I know. And now I want only you."

She spooned against him, and he stroked her hair, thinking of her words, and wondering at the depth of pleasure they brought him. Idly, he ran his hand over the curve of her breast and the rise of her hip.

"A boy," he scoffed. "As if it were possible for you to pass as a boy."

She smiled up at him. "It was a sound plan—at least until I was discovered."

"And attacked. And almost violated."

"Indeed," she agreed. "That part did not go as I had planned it." She pressed her head against him, and he reveled in the joy of having her near—he who had spent centuries as a warrior and a leader now brought to his knees by the touch of a woman, and willingly, too.

"I could have killed him," she said, shifting in his arms to face him. Her green eyes were blazing, and there was no mistaking the sincerity of her words. "I would have sliced his throat without a moment's hesitation. He was foul. He took liberties he had no business taking, and I would neither mourn his passing nor fear for the safety of my soul when he fell dead at my feet."

By the gods, he loved her.

The realization shot through him, so simple, so true, and so utterly inconvenient. He could not have her, of course. Not forever. She deserved life and the sun, and those were two things he could not offer her. But the truth of the word weighed on him nonetheless and could not be avoided. *Love.*

"I shall call you Caris," he said after a moment, then put his hand over her heart. "Be Carissa to all others, but let me see the warrior within, for hers is a heart that understands my own."

♦

Caris.

She liked the way it sounded. Most especially, she liked the fact that it was a name he'd given her. As intimate as a kiss, more precious than a rose. She wanted to curl up in it, in him, and never leave this bed. Here was safety.

Here was the fantasy. The belief that everything would be okay. That Tiberius would never leave. That Antonio would be saved. That her marriage to Giancarlo would never come to pass.

And that Baloch would never be heard from again.

The mere thought of his name sent fear coursing through her, and she shifted in Tiberius's arms, covering herself with the blanket as she sat up to look at him. "Why did you come? Why are you willing to face Baloch?"

Something dark flashed in his eyes, and she saw for a moment the man her father had so feared. "I come because I must. Facing Baloch—that, my darling Caris, is a happy bonus."

The way he spoke Baloch's name sent a shudder through her. So much loathing, so much hatred. There was more here than Baloch's horrific reputation, and until she understood it, she knew she would never fully understand the man who lay beside her. She pressed her hand to his chest, stroking the taut skin that she had so recently claimed as her own. "What is Baloch to you?"

A shadow seemed to cross his face, and she worried that he wouldn't answer. But then he sat up, pausing only briefly before rising and going to the single tiny window. He'd insisted that the curtains be drawn tight, and now he pressed his hand against the wall beside the drapes but did not push them aside. "The question isn't what is Baloch to me, but what is Baloch."

"All right," she said. "What is he?"

He turned to face her. "Do you know why your brother was taken?"

"Of course. Baloch—" She closed her mouth, frowning. She'd intended to say that Baloch sought to smite her family, but that did nothing to address the greater question. The question of *why*. "My father says that he is a monster. That he commands dark forces. That he is no friend to the Pope. That he is no ally to any man."

"Everything your father says is true," Tiberius said. "And yet it doesn't explain anything."

"Do you know why he took Antonio?"

"I do."

She swallowed, something in his voice sending a wave of dread through her. She didn't want to ask the question, and yet she couldn't sit there and stay silent. "Tell me."

"Your father killed his son," Tiberius said, his voice far too matter-of-fact for the words. "And he has taken Antonio as a replacement. An heir."

"No." Caris realized she was shaking her head. "No, that can't possibly be right. I would have heard. The authorities. Surely they would have come. Would have talked to my father." She stood, the blanket wrapped around her, and began to pace the room. "He didn't kill anybody."

"He didn't kill a man," Tiberius said.

"But you said Baloch's son—"

"How were you intending to secure your brother's release?"

"By killing Baloch."

"A worthy goal. How?"

She nodded toward the saddlebag he'd brought to the room for her. "There are garments in there. Finery. Oils. Perfume. I intended to speak to the man himself. To tell him I had come to negotiate for my brother's release."

"He would never agree."

"And I would not expect him to. But I am a woman, and I know that I am desirable. And Baloch is a man. He would see me."

"He would. And then?"

"I may not prevail against four men, but I can take down one man with my dagger." She looked at him hard, examining his face for any hint of doubt. There was none.

"I saw you fight. I don't deny your skill."

She nodded. "I would kill him. And then I would find my brother."

He nodded thoughtfully. "Your plan is not without merit," he said. "There are some weaknesses—Baloch's men, for one. But stealth and cleverness could see you safely over that hurdle."

She smiled, pleased with his praise.

"Even so, you would fail."

Her pleasure faded. "You cannot know that for certain."

"On the contrary, I can." He moved across the room, and the certainty in his gait that had so impressed and attracted her before was now slightly irritating.

"And, pray, what flaw do you see? Baloch lies dead on the floor. I locate and free my brother. I grant you it is not a perfect scenario, but failure is by no means certain."

"You would not kill him," Tiberius said as he bent down to pick up her dagger.

"I would. You think that because I am a woman I would lose my nerve? That I do not have the strength to thrust a blade through flesh? You are wrong, sir."

"I do not doubt your ability. But this dagger will not kill Baloch."

Confused, she looked at the curve of the steel blade, the jewel-encrusted handle. Her eldest brother had used that very same dagger in battle, and it had saved his life. She knew it would kill, and do the job well.

"To kill Baloch, you need a blade made of silver."

"I don't understand."

"Baloch is not human. And neither was his son."

She drew in a sharp breath. "Not human?"

"On the night of the last full moon, your father was out riding. He shot a wolf. That wolf was Baloch's son." His words were calm. Measured. But his eyes—his eyes were heated, passionate. And they were full of conviction.

Caris crossed herself, her heart beating rapidly. She knew of Baloch's dark nature, of course. It was no secret that demons walked in dark places, and that the church gathered its forces to fight against such heresy. But she had never once believed that she would live to see these things up close. The thought that her brother—sweet, innocent Antonio—was at the mercy of a creature spawned from the heart of hell . . .

"No," she whispered. It was the only word she could push past her lips, but there was no force behind it. She could see too clearly that Tiberius spoke the truth. However impossible, however horrible, what he said was true.

"Baloch took Antonio, and he will make him a werewolf. He will make him his heir."

She didn't realize she was falling until Tiberius was at her side, gripping her around the waist and leading her to the bed. Her knees had turned to water, but how he'd come to her so quickly she didn't know. Right then, she couldn't wrap her thoughts around anything. Nothing was real, and the world was a nightmare come alive.

"And you," she finally asked. "You . . . hunt were-wolves?"

He hesitated for only an instant before nodding.

"Why?"

"They are vile creatures," he said, his expression raw. "An abomination. Even as men, you cannot trust them."

There was more to tell—she could see that much in his eyes. But she saw pain there, too. Perhaps he once had a brother like hers. Perhaps he had a family debt to pay.

The thought triggered something in her memory. "What did you mean?" she asked. "When you were speaking with my father you said you were bound to our family, and he said that he honored no such bond."

"It is a long story," he said, moving to her side and drawing her against him. She pressed her head against his bare chest and sighed. Just the touch of him felt like coming home. "Suffice it to say that I will always protect you."

"And my brother."

"Even your father," he agreed, "though it pains me somewhat to do it." He pressed a kiss to her forehead. "The sun has set. We must go."

"We?"

He nodded. "I wish it weren't so, but I cannot leave you here. Those men will return."

"I can take care of myself," she said, then immediately regretted the words. Even if it were true—and if several men came, it undoubtedly was not—she still wanted to remain at Tiberius's side, especially since he would be taking her straight to Antonio.

He smiled with understanding. "Perhaps you can. But my bond requires me to see to you as well. And that is a job I can best undertake with you at my side. More than that, though, I wish you to be near me."

"Oh." Her heart fluttered, a small bird beating its wings.

"Take this," he said, then pressed the hilt of a dagger into her hand. "It is silver. If the need arises, do not hesitate to use it."

"I won't."

A flicker of a smile touched his lips.

"My Caris," he said, and then he reached for her hand.

CHAPTER 6

They left the inn on foot, not willing to risk that Baloch's guard would hear approaching horses. Tiberius would have preferred to leave Caris out of this—the thought that he was putting her in harm's way weighed heavily on him. He'd meant what he'd told her about the scoundrels in the inn; they would undoubtedly come back, and if they found her alone, they would surely break her. Just the thought of their using her so brutally made the daemon rise within him, and even now he regretted not ripping their throats open when he'd had the chance. He'd held back only because Caris was present, and he had not wanted her to witness the eruption if he allowed the daemon even the slightest bit of room to emerge.

For so many centuries he'd toiled in solitude, fighting to tame the daemon that lived inside him, that had emerged, as in every vampire, at the time of the change. For the most part, he had succeeded, his daemon buried so deep now that it preened and snarled only when faced with the chance to confront a werewolf.

At least that was the way it had been before.

Tonight his daemon begged for release, screaming with rage and crying out to destroy the men who would harm Caris. And it was that surge of fury as much as the swell of contentment that convinced him that he loved her.

He considered taking her only part of the way on this quest. The forest and hillside were rife with small caves where she could find shelter and wait for him, away from the lascivious treachery of men who would do her harm. But even then he feared for her. Animals roamed the dark—and worse. This close to a full moon, there was no doubt that Baloch's men would bring the wolf out, if for no other reason than the pleasure of running fast and free over the leaf-covered ground. Baloch himself most likely roamed the forest this night, and that was why he and Caris were moving slowly now, with Tiberius evaluating their surroundings at each step.

All those reasons underscored his decision to keep her at his side, and yet in the end it was pure selfishness that swayed him. He simply wanted her with him.

No. That wasn't entirely true. As much as it pained him to admit it, he needed her. Or, rather, he could use her. He knew well that the walls of Baloch's palazzo were infused with hematite, and while Tiberius's age gave him superior strength, even he could not completely overcome the effect of that vile mineral.

Moreover, he had to admit that her plan for infiltrating Baloch's lair was a good one. And it wasn't as if she was a typical female who didn't know which end of a knife was the dangerous one.

He turned to look at her as they walked, no longer surprised by how the mere sight of her seemed to lift him up. She was his muse, his gift, and if it were possible, he would walk to the ends of the earth with her and never look back.

"What?" she asked, though her smile suggested that she knew the direction of his thoughts.

"I was merely thinking that even the glow of the stars and the moon dims in comparison to your beauty."

She quirked a brow. "A nice sentiment, but I am more likely to believe that you were thinking of how best to infiltrate the palazzo."

"As clever as she is beautiful," he said, then silenced her burst of laughter with a long, sensual kiss. "We are close," he said when he finally pushed her gently away, his gaze firm on her rapturous face. "Are you ready?"

"I am."

She wore the gown she'd traveled with, a deep emerald green that brought out the color in her feline-shaped eyes. It was cut low and cinched at the waist, so it accentuated the ample curve of her breast. Her skin, already pale and smooth, glowed as luminescent as mother-of-pearl in the moonlight. It was one of the inherent ironies of nature that the moon could provide such beauty and at the same time bring forth a monster such as Baloch and his kind.

As they approached the treeline, he took her arm, tugging her back into the shadows. He stroked her cheek, then looked deep into her eyes. "You will not be alone."

She swallowed and nodded, and though he could smell the fear upon her, she didn't hesitate. She pinched her cheeks to give them color, then smoothed her skirts. She kept her right hand in the fold of her skirt where he knew she had stowed her dagger. Another was strapped to her leg, hidden beneath the thick folds of material. And then, without further talk, she stepped away from the trees and walked toward the crushed stone path that led to the palazzo's gate.

He transformed immediately, shifting into the black

raven he favored. She looked back, and he could see the surprise on her face at finding him gone, but she didn't slow her step, and soon he was flying in lazy circles above the gate, watching with avian intensity as she approached the first of their prey.

From his position up high, he watched as she drew near the two guards at the gate. Her shawl fell slightly, revealing her soft shoulder. She said something, laughed when one guard replied, then idly trailed her finger over her collarbone, drawing his attention to her breast.

Tiberius swooped, transforming back into himself behind the second man—and using the man's own dagger to slice his throat even as Caris turned and saw him, her eyes going wide.

"Where did you—"

But she didn't finish the question, her words catching in her throat as he grabbed the other guard's neck and twisted, his pleasure at watching the weren fall profound.

"My dagger?" he asked.

She lifted her skirt and released the hair ribbons she'd used to bind it, then handed it to him. "I don't understand."

"I know," he said. She didn't understand how he'd arrived so quickly. She didn't understand why she had to carry his blade. She didn't need to understand, though. She only needed to recognize that everything they were doing worked toward the goal of saving her brother.

He took the silver knife, then stabbed each of the guards in the heart in turn, ensuring that they were truly dead. He looked back at her then, afraid he'd gone too far in her presence, but she merely lifted her skirt away from the pooling blood and stepped over them.

He held out his hand to assist and couldn't hide a thin, pleased smile. She truly was a most remarkable woman.

"You say that Baloch is in the forest, but what if he returns?" she whispered as they passed through the gate and into the open-air courtyard. They kept to the shadows as Tiberius examined the area, his vampiric eyes probing deep into the dark, his keen hearing and smell searching for any hint that they were not alone in the atrium.

"I hope he does," Tiberius said, once he was confident no one was watching them. They'd spoken earlier of his belief that Baloch would be out in the wild tonight, as was his habit. Unfortunate, Tiberius thought. He would very much like the opportunity to plunge a dagger into the bastard's heart. But within these walls he was weakened, and he could already feel the nearby hematite sapping his strength. Better to get Caris and Antonio out safely, and then return to fight Baloch on another day. A day when he could savor the pleasure of watching Baloch's life bleed away.

In front of him loomed the main apartments of the palazzo, a low, sprawling building, with the exception of one tower that rose up as if to kiss the sky. The courtyard surrounded the palazzo, a lush garden that wound around the building with flower beds and crushed-stone walking paths. Quietly he led her through the flowers, following one of the paths until they reached the back of the palazzo and the entranceway to the lower chambers and the dungeon that his sources told him faced the south wall.

As they moved in silence, Caris's question—*Why?*—seemed to echo in his mind, and he shivered, a profound cold that ran through his bones. Century upon century had passed, and yet he could still see himself, battered, abused, beaten. Ripped open and left to die while the sun beat down upon him so hard that the desperate thirst was even more excruciating than the pain that had radiated through every inch of his body.

And then he had seen those eyes—Caris's eyes. Even after so many generations, Horatius's eyes still lived in the family line. The old man had dismounted from his horse and tended to Tiberius himself, his servants only fetching water, wine, and cloth. And when it had become clear that Tiberius was surely doomed, Horatius had listened to Tiberius's whispered tale about what had happened, the hatred he felt, and the dreams of revenge—dreams that had kept him clinging to life well beyond another man's breaking point.

Horatius's wrinkled face had tilted back toward the sun, and he'd closed his eyes, deep in thought. Then without a word, he had lifted Tiberius himself, placed him gently into his cart, and risked his own life to take Tiberius to the one person who could give him a chance to make that dream of revenge come true.

A vampire.

He'd sworn an oath that night to protect Horatius's family even above his own, for it was that family that had saved him, that had kept his dreams of revenge as alive as the body that still survived to this day.

He looked now at Caris, and he wanted to share his past with her. But even more, he wanted her to know that although he'd come to rescue Antonio out of a familial obligation, that obligation was no longer the driving force. *She was.* She'd opened up a world to him. Made long-dormant feelings stir. He wanted her with him forever, and yet he could say nothing. He was, at the end of the day, a coward. He'd seen the disgust on her face when he'd revealed the truth about Baloch. And while he certainly felt the same way toward the weren, he also understood that her reaction wasn't aimed only at that one vile group but at all Shadowers.

Tiberius had endured many things in his long years upon the earth, but the one thing he could never bear was to see the same look of disgust and fear on Caris's face that he had seen on her father's.

"Tiberius?"

They'd arrived, and he tugged her to a halt. "Keep your dagger ready."

She nodded, her face set, her grip firm.

The lock was solid, but the wooden door broke easily with a single kick. Even with the presence of hematite, he hadn't faded too far, his many years upon this earth coming to his aid. But they were still outdoors, the impact of the mineral weakened. Soon they would go down narrow passageways and would be surrounded by walls, floor, and roof mortared with the dreaded infusion. He would weaken more; that was certain. The only question was how much.

"Stay close," he said as he began down the stairs, his senses acute. He had expected more guards, more trouble; the fact that penetrating Baloch's lair was so simple reeked of a trap. But what kind of trap?

"There," Caris whispered, pointing to a passage that led off to the left. It seemed to descend further into the bowels of the earth, and he nodded. If Antonio was being held here, his cell would likely be deep inside the fortress.

They turned—and as they did, Tiberius heard a sharp *clang* and a contemporaneous *snap, snap, snap* even as he felt the sharp sting of something fast and hard embedding itself in his thigh. He didn't think, he only reacted. The *snap* was still echoing in the air when he grabbed Caris and tossed her in front of him, then leapt forward himself, just out of harm's way.

"Caris!" She lay on the ground, a wooden stake gouged into her right shoulder, another in her left thigh.

"Go," she said, her voice weak and her face pale as she sat up, her features contorted with pain. "Go and find Antonio."

He ripped the stake from his own thigh. The pain was intense, making his leg tingle and his muscles cramp, and he realized that Baloch had coated the tip with hematite. A clever booby trap for encroaching vampires. "I will not leave you here," he said, turning his attention to the stakes still embedded in her body.

"I can't walk," she said. "And you must hurry. Baloch will be back soon."

"No," Tiberius repeated. "If there are any weren in the dungeons, they'll surely smell your blood. They'll come. They'll kill you." He pushed away the memories that threatened, forced down the rising daemon. Now was not the time. He knelt in front of her and gripped her hands tightly. "They'll do worse than kill you."

"No, Tiberius. Dammit, *no*." She shifted, then winced from the pain of her wounds. "Please, if you care anything for me, go get my brother."

His heart twisted—he could not willingly sacrifice the boy any more than he could sacrifice her, but his choices were untenable. Leave her, and she would die. Carry her to safety, and the boy likely would. There was only one solution that made sense, and it was the solution he most dreaded. There was no alternative, though; he reached out and gently tilted her chin so that she had no choice but to meet his eyes. "I care everything for you. And I can heal you. Do you trust me?"

A flicker of astonishment crossed her face, but she didn't flinch, didn't blink. She simply nodded, slowly and firmly. "I trust you."

"Very well."

He shifted his position, then closed his eyes, thinking of blood until he felt his fangs grow and sharpen. He didn't look at Caris—he didn't want to see her reaction. Instead he bit his own wrist until the blood flowed freely. "I'm going to pull the stakes out," he said. "It will hurt—and for that I'm sorry. But once I do, you must drink." He lifted his wrist as if in explanation. "Drink," he said, "and you will heal."

◆

Drink?

The word was still echoing in her head as Tiberius pulled the stakes from her body. She screamed, the pain almost unbearable. And then before she had time to think, Tiberius had one arm around her neck and his wrist in front of her lips, and he was begging her again to drink, and by the Blessed Virgin, she knew then what had been tickling at the back of her mind. His strength. His swiftness. And most of all her father's fear.

He was a vampire.

Dear Lord, she'd fallen in love with a vampire.

Love. She turned the word over in her head, but there was no uncertainty. Her heart didn't lie. She loved him. And when she lifted her head up and looked into his eyes, she was certain that he loved her, too.

"Drink," he repeated. "My blood can heal you. It can strengthen you."

"Will I—"

"—change? No. The effect is only temporary. Please, Caris. Loathe me if you will, but do not deny me now. Every moment we waste, the danger grows."

"Loathe? No, I—"

"Please." His voice held such anguish that she couldn't argue. She closed her mouth over his wrist and drank deeply, surprised by the intense, coppery taste, but even more surprised by the intimacy of the act. This was the man who'd kissed her and stroked her, who'd touched and filled her in ways that no man ever had. When she pressed her lips to his wound and drank, she could feel his strength coursing through her like the warm glow of good wine. Her shoulder and thigh itched and burned, and she realized with mild surprise that her skin was knitting, the wound vanishing in an instant.

"That's it," he whispered, his voice low and powerful. "Just a bit more. There, there now."

She pulled away, afraid that if she kept going she would never stop. She wanted this too much, wanted him too much. And the power of her need terrified her.

"Antonio," she whispered. It was the only word she could manage.

"Come." He reached for her and as she took his hand and climbed to her feet, she saw the movement behind him.

"Tiberius!" she cried, flinging the dagger even as she called out the warning. He whipped around and did the same, his blade landing hard and true in the heart of one and killing it instantly, hers missing the heart only by inches, but still buried to the hilt.

Tiberius leapt up, then knocked the living weren back against the wall. It landed with a thud, then bounced back, rushing Tiberius, who ripped the blade from the creature's chest and used it to slice the weren's throat. Blood spurted, and the creature fell to the ground, his life pumping out of him.

"Thank you," he said, turning to her. "Your placement of the blade was most convenient."

Despite the horror of the attack and her wounds and the situation as a whole, she couldn't help but smile. "I—" she began, looking wide-eyed at Tiberius. "Did you see that?" She'd thrown the blade with a power she'd never known before—and while she may have missed the target, she'd come close, and hit deep.

"You have uncommon skill," he said, a smile in his voice.

"I think it is more fair to say that *you* have uncommon skill."

"Which I am happy to share. Hurry, there will undoubtedly be others."

After a few more twists and turns in the dim, dank corridors, she was beginning to think he was wrong about that. True, they'd encountered—and handily avoided—a few more traps, but for the most part their path was clear.

"Wait," Tiberius said. "Hold still."

She froze, watching intently as he turned in a circle, breathing deeply and peering into the musty shadows.

"There," he said, pointing to a heavy, rust-covered door.

"Antonio?" Eager, she rushed toward it, only to be stopped by his arm, firm against her chest.

"Watch."

He turned slowly, scouring the ancient tunnels. "Here," he finally said as he tugged down a brass candleholder. He stepped on the metal, holding one end firmly in his hand as he straightened it, until finally he had a two-foot length of brass. "Stand back," he said, then rammed the lock with the end of the makeshift pole. Immediately a flurry of stakes flew from hidden springs within the doorway and a spray of dust exploded from above. Tiberius turned away, his hand covering his nose and mouth. Caris did the same, uncertain why, but not willing to breathe anything that Tiberius wouldn't.

When the dust settled, she clutched his hand. "You would have been killed if you'd approached the lock."

"That was Baloch's plan. And if I wasn't killed, the additional hematite would have weakened me sufficiently that he could have easily subdued me."

"Hematite?"

"The dust. It is a metal—a mineral—and a bane to vampires. And while I do not have to breathe to exist, it is a habit I enjoy. Had I caught a lungful of that stuff, I would be so weak now I could barely stand."

She tensed, the thought of Tiberius reduced in such a way troubling her deeply. She touched his shoulder, wanting to comfort, but he was already moving toward the open door—and the cell beyond.

She followed, terrified of what she might find there. Her brother, alive or dead? Another prisoner? Or perhaps nothing at all.

She stepped carefully over the threshold, walking where Tiberius walked in case there were other traps, then gasped when she saw the muslin-covered heap in the corner. It didn't move—for all she knew, it wasn't even a person, but then Tiberius nodded gently. "It is him," he said, and she didn't doubt. She ran toward him and pulled the cloth down, then cried out in joy and anguish when she saw the boy who lay beneath. A mere shell of himself, curled up and fetid, barely breathing, so thin he might be a skeleton. But he opened his eyes, and she saw the recognition flicker in them. His lips parted, and she shook her head, her tears falling onto his papery cheeks. "No, don't speak," she whispered, her heart overflowing with relief that he was alive, and fear that he wouldn't survive the night. "There will be time enough to talk."

The effort of opening his eyes seemed to have exhausted him, and he faded back into stillness. Panicked, she turned to Tiberius, who stood beside her now, a calm port for her terror. "He lives," Tiberius said. "I'll carry him."

She caught his sleeve. "Heal him."

He exhaled, and she watched the conflict play out on his face. Finally he shook his head, and she thought her muscles would go slack with disappointment.

"Why not?"

"This entire fortress is imbued with hematite, not only the dust we encountered. Just being here has greatly reduced my strength. I cannot transform into an animal," he said, the implication of his words shocking her, but she didn't question him. "I cannot transform into mist. I am, right now, not much stronger than a mortal man, and he is so far gone. With the hematite and the blood I gave to you, I don't have the strength within me to pull him back from the brink, and you do not have the strength to carry two of us out."

She had to concede the point—and hope that their

path getting out of the palazzo was as clear as the one going in.

Naturally, it wasn't.

The first thing they saw as they stepped out into the night was Baloch himself—heading straight toward them.

At least two dozen men flanked Baloch—and they were spreading out, filling the courtyard and destroying Tiberius's planned line of retreat.

"Come," he said, tugging her back down into the dungeon. He hated the thought of retreating but hated more the possibility of losing Caris. Or Antonio, for that matter.

With the boy flung over his shoulder, he raced through the tunnels, Caris's hand tight in his. She was keeping up, but her strength would fade soon. They needed to get out, to get away from the palazzo. Away from the hematite and to a place where he could fight Baloch and not be at a disadvantage.

With luck, he knew just the place.

The trouble was, he needed more than luck. He needed blood.

If what he planned had even the slightest chance of working, he needed to feed; he needed strength. He could not feed on the boy without killing him, and he would not feed on Caris. If anything should happen to him, she would need all her strength to survive. He could not tap what he'd given her.

Which left him only one option, a despicable one. And even that relied on chance.

"Where are we going?" Caris asked.

"Up," he said. He pointed to the right, to a small passageway he'd noticed as they came in. He'd caught the scent of it—yeast and meat and sour milk—and if he was right the passage led to a kitchen that was either part of the palazzo itself or separated only by a small atrium. The palazzo was his goal, specifically the tower. It might work—it might be suicide. But if he didn't try, they would all three undoubtedly die this night.

"You're taking us *inside*?" Fear and shock colored her voice as they burst into the kitchens. A thin weren woman stared at him but made no move to attack, and as much as he despised her, he could not bring himself to kill her. Not when she stood with a child at her hip and a spoon in her hand.

Instead he tugged harder at Caris's hand and yanked her through the room and into the comparatively fresh air of the courtyard. Behind them, a warning bell clanged—the werewoman sounding the alarm. He would pay for his moment of charity.

"There," he said, racing toward the wooden door on the far side of the atrium. Unless he missed his guess, it led up and up to the looming tower that was the hallmark of Baloch's palazzo. It was a gamble he had to take—there was no time to try other doors, not with Baloch's men surely circling the palazzo even now.

He burst through it, then froze when Caris screamed. A huge, hulking weren male stood in front of them. He'd called upon the change but hadn't finished the transformation, and now he stood as a man, with the elongated features of a wolf.

"You will not pass," he growled, then leapt upon Tiberius, knocking him and Antonio to the ground.

"No!" Caris cried, and hurled herself at his back, her

knife sliding into his flesh so that the creature threw back his head and howled.

It was all the advantage Tiberius needed. He took his own knife and thrust it deep into the creature's jugular. What he did next, though, he did only for Caris. Because he needed to see her away from this place alive. Because he needed the strength to save the brother she loved.

He pressed his mouth to the foul creature's throat, and he drank, the weren male's blood filling him, fueling him. The blood couldn't completely overcome the effect of the hematite, but it would replenish what he'd lost healing Caris, and it would give him additional strength as well. For her, it was worth the horror of drinking from that which he despised.

The only question remaining: Would it be enough?

"Fiend!" Baloch's voice echoed through the atrium. "You dare drink from one of my men?"

Tiberius rose, taking the weren's body with him. Then he hurled it through the doorway. It hit Baloch's approaching men, making them tumble backward. As they stumbled to regroup, Tiberius retrieved Antonio and turned back toward the stairs. "Go," he shouted to Caris. "And do not stop until you reach the top."

"He is mine!" Baloch cried behind him. "He dies at my hand, and mine alone."

Those odds were fine with Tiberius, but not here, not now. He turned and raced up the stairs, taking Caris's hand as he did and pulling her along with him.

It was treacherous going. The stones were slick with age and the steps were narrow and uneven. The moon might be close to full, but the tower had only the smallest of slits for windows, and only a few shafts of pale moonlight filtered through. They pushed forward, though, and eventually emerged onto the roof of the tower, a low stone wall the only thing separating them from a long fall to the hard ground.

"You cannot transform," Baloch said, emerging behind them. "Even now, you stand upon hematite."

Tiberius took a step to the side, so that Caris was behind him, then a step backward, so that they were at the edge of the tower.

"I don't need to transform to kill you," Tiberius said, and right then he was certain it was true. The weren's blood was powerful, ripe as it was from the waxing fullness of the moon. He might not be able to transform, not with his feet planted on hematite-infused stones, but he was stronger than Baloch knew, and the element of surprise could be a powerful ally.

His fingers twitched with the desire to go for his knife, now back in the sheath at his hip. He wanted it, wanted so desperately to thrust the blade deep into this vile weren creature who thought nothing of torturing and starving and abusing an innocent boy.

He wanted—but he couldn't. The risk was too great, because if he lost, Caris and Antonio were surely dead.

"Attack, then," Baloch said. "You want to hurt me? To kill me? Try your best, vampire. Try now, because you are not leaving this tower unless I am dead upon it."

"I wish that were so," Tiberius said. "But I think that in this regard you are mistaken."

And while Baloch's face shifted comically into confusion, Tiberius tightened his grip on Antonio with his left hand, then clutched Caris around the waist with his right.

"What are we—" she began, but she didn't finish the question. By then he had begun the leap off the tower, and her question had turned to a scream.

"No!" Baloch said, and as Tiberius sprang away, he felt a tug on his leg and realized that Baloch had leapt, too, catching him in midair as they cleared the tower.

As they hurtled toward the ground, Tiberius shook his leg, but it was no use, and as he was about to give up, Caris reached over, yanked out Tiberius's dagger, and thrust it hard and fast through Baloch's eye.

The werewolf howled and let go—and began to tumble alone to the hard ground below.

Tiberius didn't see him fall. They were free of the hematite walls now, and as the ground rose up fast beneath them, he held tight to Caris and Antonio, then transformed into the sentient mist that would carry them away, safe at last.

He took them only a few miles, his strength still diminished by the hematite and now strained by the burden of transforming not only himself but two humans. Beside him, Caris sat wide-eyed, her hands exploring her body, her lips parted in wonder. "Tend to your brother," Tiberius said. "It will have been roughest on him, I fear."

Something like pain flashed through her eyes, and he thought that she would linger, but then she hurried to Antonio. Tiberius lay there, content to watch her care for her brother and struck by the dichotomy between the loving young woman and the budding warrior. When she came back, her manner was subdued as she sat down next to him. "He's ill, but I believe he'll live. You saved him."

"I did not do it alone."

Her smile was both timid and proud. "Did I kill him? Is he truly dead?"

"A silver dagger through the eye and into the brain? Yes, I think we can safely say that Baloch is now dead."

"Good," she said, and he agreed wholeheartedly with the sentiment. "It had worn off," she said softly. "I didn't feel stronger when I thrust the blade. Not stronger in that way, at least. I just wanted to destroy him, and that gave me the strength to thrust the blade in true."

"You have plenty of strength of your own," he said. "You never needed to borrow mine."

He watched her face as he spoke and saw with a twinge of sadness that she did not meet his eyes. They hadn't talked about what he had revealed to her in the tunnels—there had been no time. But now the truth was settling down around them, and there was no denying what he was any more than there was denying his fear that by revealing what he was to save her, he had lost her as well.

"Tiberius . . ."

He could hear the hesitation in her voice, and he closed his eyes against the words he knew were coming. Words of regret, if not fear. For whatever he hoped could exist between them, he had been of this world for too long not to know the way of things.

"I'm to be married soon."

His heart twisted; this was more difficult than he could have imagined. "I know."

"You have told me that you're sworn to protect my family."

"I am," he said. "You, your husband. Your children." He clenched his fist around a nearby stone, crushing it to dust. Just the thought that she could lie with another man . . .

"Please don't think that I'm asking you to rescue me from that. What I say now has nothing to do with Giancarlo. But, Tiberius, please. I don't love him." He watched as she drew in a trembling breath, hope sprouting within him again. "I love you."

It was as if the heavens opened up and sang. "What I am, it doesn't scare you?"

"The only thing that scares me is being away from you."

He couldn't speak. Her words, her love, they filled him, and all he could do was pull her close.

She melted against him, and he sighed with pleasure. *This* was where she belonged, at his side, in his heart. "Will you turn me?" she whispered.

Her lips were pressed to his chest as she spoke so that the question reverberated through him, bringing equal parts pleasure and pain. He wanted to be strong and tell her no; he feared he would tell her yes.

Now he only kissed her hair and told her that he loved her.

She lifted herself up onto her elbows and peered into his eyes, the question so clear it didn't need to be spoken.

"I fight the evil inside myself every day. There is pain. There is anguish and rage and blind fury. And, Caris, my love, there is an overwhelming urge for blood. To feed. To kill. I hate to think of you consumed by that."

"You bear it," she said.

"I have no choice."

"I love you," she said, pressing her lips to his. "So I have no choice, either."

◊

Caris jerked awake, then realized with horror what had yanked her so rudely away from the pleasure of sleeping in Tiberius's arms—the sound of her father.

"You get away from him, you filthy little trollop," he roared, his face mottled with anger. "Did I raise a whore?"

Tiberius was on his feet now, and she clung to his side, her eyes darting from her father to Antonio, who had awakened and was struggling to sit up.

"I suggest you watch your tongue, sir," Tiberius said.

Albertus snarled. "You vile creature. I knew I couldn't trust you."

"Father," Antonio said, his voice little more than a croak. "Father, no."

But Albertus's attention was only on Tiberius. "Do you think I don't know what passed between you and my daughter in the stable? Do you think I don't know how you have despoiled her?"

"Father, please." Caris stepped toward him, her hands out, imploring. She saw him pause, then turn and look at her. The harshness left his face then, replaced by the soft features of the father who'd cuddled her upon his knee as a child. "Father," she whispered, then ran to him when he held out his hand, realizing too late that she was a fool to trust him.

He grabbed her wrist and tugged her to him, his knife at her throat.

Two guards flanked him, crossbows now raised, wooden stakes loaded and pointed at Tiberius. "We will walk out of here," Albertus said. "And you will walk away from my family and my daughter. You are both fortunate Giancarlo will still have her. You will marry at dawn," he said to Caris, "and I will be well rid of you."

Her body went cold and rigid. She tried to speak, but there were no words. She told herself it didn't matter—Tiberius wouldn't let this happen to her. He wouldn't let the marriage happen, wouldn't let her father speak to her thus.

And when Tiberius spoke, it was as if every hope inside her had swelled, and she clung to his words like the last leaf of autumn clinging fast to a tree.

"You are taking her nowhere," he said.

"Dead or married," Albertus said. "Do you think that at this moment I care how my daughter leaves you? But she *will* leave you."

"Kill her, and I will kill you."

"You won't," Albertus said. "There is a bond between us."

"No," Tiberius said. "There isn't."

For a moment, Caris saw fear flicker on her father's face, but it passed. "Kill me, then. But the girl will already be dead, and you possibly along with her," he added, nodding at the marksmen beside him. "Let us leave, and she lives. And so do you."

Caris held her breath as Tiberius turned to look at her. "I would rather be dead than away from you," she said.

"And I cannot bear the thought of you lying cold in a grave."

"Then it is settled," her father said. "We go."

He started to turn away, the matter resolved, then lifted his hand as if gesturing for his men to follow.

They moved in unison, firing their crossbows at Tiberius as a scream of abject horror echoed through the cave.

It was her own, of course, and as Tiberius fell, one of the stakes having flown straight and true to his heart, so did she, prostrate on the ground as the man she loved died, and the horror of her life to be bloomed red and fetid in front of her.

CHAPTER 8

Caris sat at Antonio's bedside, watching his sleeping face. A tear trickled down her cheek, and she bent over and kissed his forehead. "I shall miss you, little brother."

She closed her eyes and breathed deep, her body numb, her mind fuzzy. She was sleepwalking now, so unlike the flurry she'd been in when they'd first returned, ignoring her pain and her tears as she rushed through the palazzo to the healer's apartments. She'd tugged the old man out of bed and had stood in his chamber while he thrust his arms into a dressing gown, all the while urging him to hurry, hurry, her brother needed his tending.

Now she knew that Antonio would be all right. It would take time, but he would survive. The knowledge soothed her. At least it had not all been for nothing.

Her heart was about to burst in her chest, so full was it of more unshed tears. She'd been unable to cry in front of her father. She'd been forced to sit under his watchful eye and listen to his talk of Giancarlo as she watched in her mind, over and over again, the way the man she loved had fallen, the stake going straight into his heart.

She gasped, her breath a raspy shudder. "Tiberius," she whispered, wishing that his name could conjure him. It couldn't, of course. Her dreams of him had died with him.

She squeezed her eyes, and another tear fell, this one leaving a dull, wet stain on the wedding gown she wore.

Less than an hour now, and her father would come for her. Less than an hour, and her life would be over.

She stood and went to the window. It faced north, toward the cave, and she thought of Tiberius. Longed for him, craved him, but couldn't have him. She'd found the one man in all the world she truly wanted, and fate—and her father—had destroyed him.

It was horribly unfair.

There was a soft tap at the door, and then Agnes entered, carrying the goblet of wine Caris had requested. "This is good," Agnes said. "It will calm your nerves."

"I loved him," Caris said, taking the wine and crossing to her dressing table. "I don't wish to live without him."

Agnes sat on the bed, her face buried in her hands. "I should never have told your father, but he knew—or he had an idea—and I cannot lose my position."

"I know." Caris's back was to the nurse, and now she opened her jewel box, removing the small paper envelope she'd taken from the healer's chamber. "I'm not angry with you. I am merely sad beyond belief." She dropped the powder into the wine and stirred. "I have nothing left now. Nothing to look forward to except a loveless marriage to an old man who does not care for me."

"You mustn't think that way," Agnes said, standing up. "Things will be better on the morrow."

"Things can never be better. Not without him." She stood up and took her nurse's hand. Then she lifted the glass to her lips with no hesitation. "I am truly sorry, darling Agnes," she said before drinking. "Give my love to Antonio."

The poison worked fast, and she saw Agnes's mouth open—heard her startled cry as Caris fell to the ground.

She smiled as the world began to fade around her. "Now," she whispered. "Now I go to my love."

◆

In a cave outside Velletri, the vampire stirred.

His daemon, angered at the attack, roared awake, writhing and fighting, urging the man to sit up, to stretch, to come alive once more.

He did.

With a start, Tiberius opened his eyes, gasping and jerking upright. He looked down and saw the stake protruding from his chest. It had penetrated his heart, but unlike in a younger vampire, penetration alone was not enough to kill. To destroy one as old as Tiberius, the stake must both enter the heart and exit through it.

Albertus's men missed their mark. He smiled, thin and dangerous at the thought, but the smile faded in the wake of a more pressing concern—*Caris.*

He was on his feet in an instant. By the gods, that idiot Albertus intended her to marry at dawn, and although he knew not what time it was, it was already well into the night when they'd arrived at the cave. Dawn couldn't be more than an hour away.

He had no time to waste.

The thought was still in his head when he transformed, this time into a raven, and took to the skies toward Velletri. The faintest hint of orange glowed at the horizon when he swooped into the courtyard, intending to peck the eyes out of the groom if need be. But there were no wedding preparations. No revelers, no musicians.

Instead there were only a handful of servants, and they moved through the garden with shell-shocked expressions.

Caris.

Dear God, what had happened to Caris?

Without concern for the consequences should Albertus find him there, he transformed back into himself and strode across the courtyard toward the main door. He didn't know where her apartments were, but he tilted his head back, sniffing the air. Her scent was everywhere, filling the palazzo, making him crazy with longing—and with fear.

He followed her trail toward the stairs, then climbed quickly, desperate to find her. As he turned the corner into the northern wing, he heard a sharp, startled "Oh!" and found himself confronting a round-faced woman with tear-stained cheeks. "You," she said, her voice filled with both awe and terror. "But my lady said that you were dead."

He was at her side in an instant. "Caris?"

"Yes. She told me her father—she told me he killed you."

"He did," Tiberius said. "Take me to her."

At that, the woman collapsed, falling to the ground in a fit of hysterical sobbing.

"Woman," he cried, gripping her arm tight and lifting her. "What is it?" he demanded, though he was already dreading the answer. "What has happened?"

"She's dead!" she cried, her words filled with a torment rivaling his own. "You were dead and she was to be married and she—she—" The woman could manage no more.

He stood there, frozen with shock, unable to believe it was true. He could still feel her. He could reach out in his mind and follow the connection of the blood they'd shared. So how could she be dead?

"Tell me," he demanded, shaking the woman. "Tell me how she died."

"P-p-poison."

"Take me to her." His voice was harsh, firm. He would not hope. He couldn't afford to open his heart to hope—not yet.

They hurried to her chamber, and he found Caris laid out on the bed, her arms crossed over her chest, her face soft in repose. "Get out." His voice was low, so low he feared the nurse would not hear him, but she backed away toward the door as he moved with terrible purpose toward Caris. "Let no one enter."

The door clicked shut, and he fell to her bedside, thrust to his knees by the weight of his anguish. He would destroy Albertus—if she was truly dead, he would destroy the man with his bare hands.

"Caris," he said, taking her hands as he pressed his ear to her chest. "Carissa, my love." He caught the scent of her immediately, lavender and anise, along with the harsh smell of death. He listened, blocking out all other noise but the sound of her, hoping to hear the beating of her heart, but there was nothing. No blood moved in her veins. No air flowed through her lungs. Her heart sat silent and useless, and he wanted to rage about the room, to cry out with anguish. To kill the man who had done this to her.

And then . . .

A noise. So soft it could be mistaken, so fragile it could be broken. But it was there, a hint of vibrancy. A flicker of hope. And then, *yes,* a slow, weak beat of her heart.

She lived. Death stood in this room waiting for her, and Tiberius knew there was no fighting it. She was too far gone, the scent of death overpowering that of life.

But he could cheat death. By the gods he could cheat the smug bastard right out of his prize.

He didn't hesitate, didn't debate. He knew the torment he would wreak upon her, knew all the reasons that he should let her slip softly into death's arms. But he also knew that he couldn't live without her—and that she did not wish to live without him.

Without further hesitation, he bent over, sank his fangs deep into her neck, and drew the last bit of life out of the woman he loved.

EPILOGUE

A full moon hung over Velletri as the two vampires stood hand in hand on the hillside overlooking the De Soranzo palazzo.

Old age had long taken Albertus, and now the De Soranzo family was presided over by Antonio, a fair-haired boy who'd grown into a strong, handsome man.

Tonight his children played in the courtyard, the girl and the boy passing a ball between them.

Caris smiled, enjoying their laughter. "Come," she said, tugging at Tiberius's hand. They moved swiftly together, and when they entered the courtyard, the children looked up.

"Auntie!" said the boy, dropping the ball and running fast to her. She picked him up and kissed him, looking at the face that so resembled the face of her brother Mercutio, now lost in battle. "Wherever have you been? It has been years and years."

"Egypt," she said, and pressed a gift into his hand—a clay tablet covered with picture writing. He looked at it with awe, then turned to show his sister, who still hung back. "It's okay, silly. She's our auntie."

"I've been away," Caris said. "Five long years. You were only two when I left. You've grown up."

"I have," the seven-year-old nodded. "Daddy says I'm his big girl, and I look just like his sister." She cocked her head. "I look like you."

"Indeed you do," Tiberius said. "You are a most beautiful young woman."

"Children!" Antonio's voice rang out, and then the man himself appeared. He hesitated only a moment, then ran to his sister's arms, whole and strong and fully grown.

"Fatherhood shows on you," she said, teasing as she stroked the gray in his hair.

"Not all of us can be immortal," he said, laughing as he held his hand out to Tiberius, then shook it heartily. "I was beginning to fear for you. It has been so long. Will you stay awhile? Theodora will be most vexed if you do not stay and tell us of your adventures."

She looked at Tiberius, who nodded, his warrior face now soft. "We will," she said. "We have many stories to tell." Even after twenty years, the world she now lived in felt fresh and new. "Battles and adventures," she added. "You will be most entertained. Your big sister has become quite the warrior."

"She always was," Tiberius said, his hand pressed against her back.

"And where next?" Antonio asked. "For I know that you will not stay long in my house."

"The Far East," Caris said. "There are alliances that we wish to make. Men of our kind look to Tiberius to lead them, and a leader must have allies."

"And after that?"

"The new world," Tiberius said, "but that may not be for many years."

"We're not in a hurry," Caris added, leaning against the man she loved and feeling his arms close tight around her.

And why should they hurry? They had all the time in the world. . . .